BITCHES IN FRONT! BITCHES BEHIND! BITCHES AT THE SIDE!

They were everywhere, firing and ducking and taking out the NVA as if each man had been assigned a particular enemy soldier to dispose of. Clockwork and precision seemed to be the order of the day, or so Sergeant Jackson thought.

"You Bitches don't do too bad!" he said when the air had cleared and the dust settled.

As they humped it out of there, Jackson looked back at the enemy bodies sprawled on the road, as if carelessly flung there, and knew they would make it as a team. There was a big difference now since their search and destroy patrols out of Camp Rascal. He didn't know how it had happened. Maybe it was because they knew they were on their own, miles from help. Or maybe it was because they all felt they had something to prove.

Whatever it was, it was working!

BLOCKBUSTER FICTION FROM PINNACLE BOOKS!

THE FINAL VOYAGE OF THE S.S.N. SKATE   (17-157, $3.95)
by Stephen Cassell
The "leper" of the U.S. Pacific Fleet, SSN 578 nuclear attack sub SKATE, has one final mission to perform—an impossible act of piracy that will pit the underwater deathtrap and its inexperienced crew against the combined might of the Soviet Navy's finest!

QUEENS GATE RECKONING   (17-164, $3.95)
by Lewis Purdue
Only a wounded CIA operative and a defecting Soviet ballerina stand in the way of a vast consortium of treason that speeds toward the hour of mankind's ultimate reckoning! From the bestselling author of THE LINZ TESTAMENT.

FAREWELL TO RUSSIA   (17-165, $4.50)
by Richard Hugo
A KGB agent must race against time to infiltrate the confines of U.S. nuclear technology after a terrifying accident threatens to unleash unmitigated devastation!

THE NICODEMUS CODE   (17-133, $3.95)
by Graham N. Smith and Donna Smith
A two-thousand-year-old parchment has been unearthed, unleashing a terrifying conspiracy unlike any the world has previously known, one that threatens the life of the Pope himself, and the ultimate destruction of Christianity!

Available wherever paperbacks are sold, or order direct from the Publisher. Send cover price plus 50¢ per copy for mailing and handling to Pinnacle Books, Dept.17-216, 475 Park Avenue South, New York, N.Y. 10016. Residents of New York, New Jersey and Pennsylvania must include sales tax. DO NOT SEND CASH.

BLACK BITCHES
DANCING WITH CHARLIE

CHUCK
BIANCHI

PINNACLE BOOKS
WINDSOR PUBLISHING CORP.

PINNACLE BOOKS

are published by

Windsor Publishing Corp.
475 Park Avenue South
New York, NY 10016

Second printing: October, 1989

Printed in the United States of America

Dedicated to

My wife, Virginia Brown Bianchi, without whose help and encouragement I would never have finished this project. And to all the brave and unsung heroes who fought in the Vietnam war.

Acknowledgments

The author would like to thank Senator Clayton P. Elam, Senior for his "behind the scenes insight" into this novel, and also his son, Paul "the Bug" Elam, for his technical advice. I would also like to thank the United States Marine Corps representative of First CAG (Combined Action Group) Chu Lai, and Sergeant William B. Walls for his insight, cooperation, and information.

AUTHOR'S NOTE

Sitting in a darkened control room, Robert Jackson reached over and flicked the toggle switch on the complex equipment board in front of him. His voice carried through the microphone to the weary musicians and recording artist grouped inside the soundproof booth several feet away.

"Try it again, Davy. That was a little bit better."

Chair springs squeaked as Jackson sat back and ran his thumb and forefinger across the recording console again. A yellow handball glove adorned his right hand as he began flipping switches while his assistant engineer stopped and rewound the thirty-two track digital tape. The sign outside the door of Studio C read: "Davy Jones (Monkees) Recording Session."

As the musicians paused to discuss their arrangement with the lead singer, Davy Jones, the engineer turned to Jackson again. His face was frankly skeptical as he said, "Come on. You ate monkey meat, man? That's hard to believe!"

Grinning, Jackson pushed his Vietnam vet baseball cap to the back of his head. "It didn't taste too bad, either."

"I've known you for years," the engineer said. "This is the first I've ever heard you talk about Vietnam."

Shrugging, Robert Jackson—known as T.D. because somewhere down the line his brother Raymond had hung the name on him for his ability to lay down tracks on tape better than most recording engineers (track dog)—rocked back in his cushioned chair and stared at the darkened studio glass. Pipe smoke wreathed his head as he thought for a minute.

"Well, it's not always something I want to remember. Hell, that was over twenty years ago. It's over and done with. Nobody cared that we went over, and nobody really cares now."

"That's not true," the engineer argued. "There's a lot of people who care what happened over there, T.D. It's just that it's an embarrassment to some people, because none of you were allowed to come home from war like all our other wars. If I hadn't been too young, I might have gone, too. I've thought about that a lot."

Jackson's eyes shifted to stare at the engineer. It was early morning, the normal time most recording engineers were working on late-night sessions, and he was tired. The memories of Vietnam and the Bitches began to flood back, and he didn't know if he wanted to remember them. Maybe the engineer was right. Maybe he should be proud of it, but it had been a long time and not many people had wanted to listen. His brother Raymond had listened, but only because he had been there, too. And after a while, a man learned to stop talking about it when people said cruel things or turned away.

"Tell me some more," the engineer was urging, and Jackson shrugged.

"Ah, you don't want to hear it."

"Sure I do. You guys are unsung heroes, and I think it's time people started listening. You should write a damn book, T.D.!"

Laughing, Jackson reached forward and flicked another toggle switch. "Hell, man. I can't write no book about it. You're the writer, Chuck. You write one for me."

After a brief moment of thought, the engineer nodded decisively. "All right, T.D., I will!"

And I did.

I have taken certain license with the story of Robert L. Jackson, altering names and places to avoid embarrassment to those who do not wish to be recognized.

C.B.
Memphis, Tennessee
1988

CHAPTER 1

Tokyo, Japan, 1966

"GRID COORDINATES . . . 696969 . . . Ready guns." Smitty paused to hiccough. "Elevation—forty-five degrees."

"Roger," came a deep voice. The weapon slid slightly downward, steadied, and quivered in readiness. "Windage?" the navigator growled.

"Negative. No wind."

"Countdown!"

"Ten, nine, eight, seven, six, five, four, three, two, one . . ."

"Fire, Corporal Jackson!" was the hiccoughing command.

There was a popping explosion, followed by a spurt of foam, and the cork from the champagne bottle flew in a graceful arc through the smoky air to score a direct hit. The cork smacked the beautiful young Japanese singer directly between her scantily clad breasts. Her singing stopped abruptly, and she glared at the Marines.

A wild chorus of whoops, yells, and burps then rose from the large table where the drunken Marines were seated.

"Direct hit!" screamed PFC George Crawford, usually called "Crawdad."

"I heard of hitting on a broad before, Jack, but if you expect to make any time with her now, you'd be better off buying her a Timex," Smitty smirked, using his best imitation-Groucho voice.

Lifting the sticky champagne bottle to his lips, Corporal Robert L. Jackson just snickered as he guzzled the remainder of its contents. The young black corporal lowered it finally and burped in satisfaction as he eyed the furious songstress. Stamping her foot in rage, she was chanting a furious Japanese litany that was occasionally punctuated by an American swear word. This quickly degenerated into a high-pitched shriek denouncing American Marines.

Jackson turned to his companions with a bleary smile. "If that chick can't sing no better than that, she deserves to be hit with a little heavy artillery."

There was general agreement as the other members of the newly formed First Squad seated at the table began to follow suit. New coordinates for their "champagne cork artillery" burst were called. James Mudders, better known as Mudboy, got a direct hit on the bass drum with his cork. George Crawford—Crawdad—got lucky and blew out one of the red stage lights swaying over the shabby bandstand. But it was PFC Paul "the Bug" Clayton's shot that really started the whole place "rockin'." His misguided cork, by means of ricocheting off one of the speaker cabinets, found its way into the eye of an Army

14

private who was in the act of making out with a slinky-garbed prostitute at the edge of the bar.

In only a matter of minutes, the table of drunken Marines was totally surrounded by a wall of none-too-happy Air Cav guys. While the private stood there glaring with his one good eye while his injured eye streamed tears, the Marines began to realize just what was ahead. Coming from behind the rickety bar stretching along one entire wall were a couple of Japanese bouncers who, Jackson would later comment, resembled what would look like the offspring of a grizzly bear and a sumo wrestler.

Corporal Jackson then deemed it necessary to proceed with the action. Rising to the full height of his six foot stocky frame, Jackson coolly said, "Bitches, it's time to rock and roll. . . ." Then an empty champagne bottle seemed to magically sprout from his right hand before finding a home against the forehead of one of the sumo wrestlers.

The table immediately followed, shoved forward as the Marines clambered over in best obstacle-course fashion. The rigorous training that every Marine endured in boot camp was now serving them well. Jackson vaulted over the bar and began to toss "grenades" of fresh pineapple and oranges. He was joined by PFC David Baroni, who grinned widely as he lobbed a few of the grenades at the Air Cav guys with unerring accuracy.

Band members abandoned their instruments and scattered, some sliding under tables and crawling on hands and knees to reach the exit. The Japanese singer, wisely deciding to cease berating the Marines, had leaped through the tacky red curtain made of

15

shimmery foil and disappeared.

One of the Air Cav officers aimed a flying leap at Smitty, missed, and scored a perfect hit on the huge bass drum in the center of the stage. He landed with a resounding thunk and the tinny clang of cymbals crashing around his head. It looked like it was Marines 2, Army 0.

PFC Carrigan, a huge coal miner from Butte, Montana and an aspiring professional wrestler, heaved a struggling Air Cav man into the air. He twirled him like a pinwheel as the unhappy Air Cav man beat wildly at the air with fists and feet. Carrigan paused for a moment, then he spotted the corporal. A wide grin split his craggy features as Carrigan hollered to Jackson, "Here, Corporal—catch!"

Jackson grinned back, ducking a wild swing then lashing out with a fist to catch the hanging Air Cav man on the jaw. Carrigan absorbed some of the shock of the blow as the Army private sagged limply, then he tossed him behind the bar on top of Baroni and Jackson and went in search of another victim.

Witnessing Carrigan's feat, one of the Army pilots snuck up behind the massive Marine and crashed an empty champagne bottle against his skull. Carrigan paused, turned to face the pilot, and asked mildly, "Now, what did you have to go and do that for?"

Stunned, the Army pilot gave a weak shrug and a halfhearted grin, and began backing away. It was too late. PFC Carrigan's meaty fist flashed out to catch him on the jaw, knocking the pilot unconscious. Dusting off his hands, Carrigan resumed his search.

Bug's elbow found the groin of one of the Army guys, while Mudders slung a dish of rice and fish in

16

the face of another. Crawford, ducking the shower of rice and fish, was busily trying out his judo techniques on the ribs of an Army officer. For the next ten minutes, a flurry of fists and feet was all that could be seen. Beer bottles, brown rice, and broken chairs flew through the air as if an Oklahoma twister had been unleashed inside the confines of this Japanese-American nightclub.

There was a mad scramble of people either entering the fray or leaving the bar. Most of the civilians evacuated the bar after the first punch, leaving only fifteen or so Air Cavalry guys, the two bouncers, the Japanese owners, and Corporal Robert Jackson and his newly formed First Squad, popularly—or unpopularly, depending upon your rank and point of view— known as "The Bitches."

By the time the whistle-blowing Military Police got there, all that was left was a heap of Air Cav men whimpering and holding their bloodied heads, broken ribs, and aching privates. Corporal Jackson and the other eleven members of First Squad had resumed their seats at the table and were calmly ordering more drinks and complaining about the fact that the band had stopped playing and the service was slow.

Heads began to pop up from behind overturned tables and the littered bar as the Japanese owners registered protest in loud singsong voices. As the MPs surveyed the wreckage, the Japanese jabbered shrilly, pointing their fingers and waving their arms in agitation.

Loud laughter rose from the table of Marines, and the ten burly MPs exchanged glances. Then they advanced on the Marines. Final score: Marines 0,

The sound of metal food trays hitting the cold concrete floor of the prison cell might as well have been an artillery round going off in Corporal Jackson's head. He squinted painfully, rolling his head from side to side. The sound persisted, and he opened a bruised eye to survey his new surroundings.

Bars. A bare cot. No pillow. No blanket. Cold, hard concrete. *What the hell?*

A vaguely familiar voice came from somewhere nearby, and Jackson's head rotated in the general direction. He squinted around the pounding pain in his skull, trying to recognize the blurry face that floated somewhere just beyond the field of his vision. Success. It was Mudders.

"Hey, Jack! You get that number?"

"Uh, what? What number?"

"The license number . . ." Mudders drawled seriously.

"What license number are you talking about, for God's sake, Mudboy?" Jackson demanded, groaning when the effort to speak caused knifelike pains to shoot up his spine and radiate through the back of his skull.

"The license number of the friggin' Mac truck that ran over our heads last night! That's what number I'm talkin' about. . . ."

Fuzzy chuckles came from most of the members of First Squad, immediately followed by groans.

"We musta done ourselves in," Jackson guessed, his narrowed gaze shifting from Mudders to the others. They were all in the brig. Every last one of them. "MPs?" he guessed again, and there were concerted nods. "Yeah, I think I 'member a few guys wearin' some kinda white armbands. Only, I thought they were nurses. . . ."

"Nurses!" someone bellowed. "Man, you must be crazy? Those guys were *bad* with a big *B*, Corporal. . . ."

"Yeahh," Jackson agreed, wincing at the pain behind his eyes. "They were bad, all right, but not as bad as we are."

"Then somebody tell me why we're behind bars and they ain't," Crawford put in dolefully.

" 'Cause *they* were wearing the armbands," Mudders said.

"That's all we need—armbands?"

"No, we need a way outa here, man," Jackson shot back, realizing that the situation was not good. Here they were, the entire First Squad, stuck in the brig while there was a war going on. And they hadn't even made it to the battlefield yet. No, they were still in Japan and still awaiting their orders. Hell, they might not make it to that tiny country called Vietnam before the war ended! It was 1966, and pretty soon the good ole US of A was going to kick the shit outa that country, and the First Squad wouldn't even get their boots muddy. That wouldn't do. No, it wouldn't do at all. . . . They were ready to fight. Six weeks of jungle training in the Philippines followed by two more weeks on Mount Fuji in Japan for a more advanced preparation, had them more than primed to go to war in Vietnam.

The longer the young black corporal lay there meditating about the grim situation, the more it worried him. The gunner, Chief Warrant Officer Benson, wasn't going to like it. No, he sure wasn't. It had only been three weeks before that he'd had to get Jackson and the "Bitches" out of the brig in Okinawa for the same thing—fighting.

"Yeah," Jackson mused. "The ole man ain't gonna like this one damn bit. Hell, we'll probably be dodging sharks in the South China Sea all the way to Vietnam if he can arrange it. . . ."

There was the rattle of a tin cup on the bars, dragging Jackson's attention to PFC Wendell Grover. "Hey, Jack, what's gonna happen to us?"

Wincing at the noise, Jackson grunted. "I dunno, but it don't look good, Grover."

A blond head rose from a bare cot, and bleary eyes gazed expansively at the disheveled group. PFC Paul Clayton drawled, "Well, the best I can recall, the charges for public drunkenness and disorderly conduct warrants fifteen days in the brig, bread, and water. But for striking a superior officer and destruction of public property, well, the last I heard, it was five years and a dishonorable discharge."

"Thanks for them heartenin' words, Bug!" Jackson snapped.

Clayton. He was the analytical one with all the answers, and the thing that always got most of the guys—whether they wanted to admit it or not—was that he was usually right. Consequently, he had earned the nickname of "the Bug." It wasn't just because of his annoying habit, but because he was an engineering genius who, at the mere age of seventeen, had successfully employed a wire tap on the political opponent running on the ticket opposite his father. It was bad enough that he had successfully managed to bug the candidate's telephone line in a local commissioner's race in order to get the poop on suspected extramarital endeavors. That he'd been caught was a major embarrassment.

"Tell me again about the time you blew up that bridge, Bug," Smitty said dreamily, gazing at the cracked concrete ceiling and smoking a cigarette. "I sure do like that story."

"Aw hell!" Baroni snarled. "I've heard it so many times I could repeat it in my sleep, Smitty. Don't you ever get tired of hearing it?"

"Naw. I can just see some little kid out blowing up an old wooden bridge in Bloomington, Indiana! I bet that was some sight. . . ."

"That's why I'm in the Marines, Smitty," Bug said. "They like guys who know something about pyrotechnics."

"I thought it was because the judge gave you a choice between five years in the pen or enlisting," Jackson countered, slanting him an assessing glance.

"Yeah, that too" was Clayton's answer.

"Reckon it had anything to do with his old man being an ex-CIA agent?" Smitty asked. "Like they say, 'The Marines are lookin' for just a few good men.' "

"Well, my daddy did teach me everything he knew," Paul said modestly. "He was real proud when the President gave me that award for being the youngest licensed HAM radio operator. I was the first seven-year-old to get one." After a thoughtful pause, he added, "I don't think our careers in the service are going to get off the ground, guys. We are in *big* trouble."

Despair etched their faces as the Bitches of First Squad sat there listening to the Bug. They knew he was right. They were in a helluva lot of trouble, but somehow they knew that Corporal Jackson would figure some way out of this situation. Jackson was the main man, the uncontested leader of the group, the one who held things together when they began to unravel. He wouldn't fail them.

But Corporal Robert Jackson wasn't as sure of his prowess as they were. He lay on the bare, cold cot and stared at the ceiling, wondering for what must have been the ten thousandth time just how he'd managed to land himself in the Marine Corps. Hell, one day he'd been just an eighteen-year-old kid enjoying the good life in Memphis, Tennessee, and the next— slam! Reality had hit with an iron fist. What other choice could he have made? It was the Marine Corps and freedom of a sort, or the inexorable, slow grinding-down he would receive at home. Home. That was another world now, another life, another Robert L. Jackson. Here, he was Corporal, or Jack. And he was responsible for getting these guys out of—or into, at times—trouble. So what did he do now?

Time ticked slowly past while the men listened to the constant drip of water down one wall. A fly buzzed somewhere, annoyingly just out of range but close enough to make them swat at it occasionally.

Jackson's fist shot into the air suddenly, startling Smitty into dropping his cigarette. "I got it! . . . I think," Jackson added as he lifted his pounding head to a ninety-degree angle.

"What—the fly?" Smitty asked, and Jackson gave him a sour glance.

"No, Smitty—the solution! When Gunner gets here I'll just—"

A massive steel door clanged open, banging against the bars and leaving the First Squad's heads vibrating. The sound of the Gunner's voice may as well have been a dozen 105 howitzers going off in twelve aching heads.

"Corporal Robert L. Jackson, on your feet, you poor excuse for a shitbird of a Marine in this man's Corps. Do you call yourselves *Marines*?"

Jackson and eleven other men rose to their feet, some steady and some wavering, but all attempting to appear at attention. Licking dry lips, Jackson winced at the pounding pain in his head as he answered.

"Sir, yessir! We are Marines. You have trained us to fight and defend. . . ." Jackson began.

"Fight? Did I hear you say *fight*?" Gunner scowled, drawing his bushy black brows into such a thunderous frown that his eyes almost disappeared. His stocky frame drew itself into a tight knot of fury as he ground out, "I believe I did hear you say *fight*?"

"Sir, yessir!"

Gunner shook his head wearily, as if he knew what was coming. "Explain to me, if you will, how you managed to temporarily disable these ill-fated GIs!"

"Sir, yessir!" Jackson took a deep breath and said, "Well, it seems that the GIs in question came to our table and started to complain about our way of appreciating the beautiful Japanese singer by toasting her with champagne. It was then that the officers started referring to our branch of the Armed Forces as 'morons.' Morons, yes, I believe that was the word he used. Is that correct, PFC Smith?"

Picking up quickly, Smitty nodded. "Yes that is correct. I also remember a vague reference to Marines partaking in sexual intercourse with their mothers, sir."

"Enough said, Corporal, I get the picture. The fact remains that you are still in a whole helluva lotta trouble." Gunner's leathery face crumpled into a scowl. "Listen up! The owners of that bar filed a claim of two thousand dollars for damages and personal inconvenience charges against you. The Army officer you thumped hasn't recovered consciousness, or we haven't heard from the brass on that yet."

While Jackson and the others began to sweat, slowly realizing the seriousness of the charges against them, Gunner paced the concrete floor of the cell, his hands behind his back. Finally, he stopped in front of Jackson and leaned so close that the corporal could count the whiskers on his chin.

"Jackson," Gunner rasped in his thick, whiskey voice. "You could lose your rank and end up bustin' rocks in some prison for the duration. And that goes for all of you. But I don't want that. No, I'm a pretty nice guy, Jackson, and I have something else in mind for you gentlemen." His smile was not reassuring as he locked eyes with the sweating corporal. "Are you anxious to hear it?"

"Sir, yessir!" Jackson lied.

"Well, it seems that you boys like to fight. I'm glad to hear that. Let me inform you shit-for-brains that you bitches are gonna get your little chance to do

24

some fighting. That's what Marines are trained to do, right? Are you Marines? I can't he-e-e-ar you!"

"Sir, yessir!" twelve men bellowed as loudly as aching heads and dry throats would allow. That wasn't enough for Gunner. He intended to push them, to punish them. He sneered at them, demanding a louder response.

It came again, echoing through the concrete block stockade. Gunner shook his head. He secretly liked the young Marines, mainly because they had more spirit than any of the other squads that had been in training the past few weeks. And, had it not been for a previous date with a nurse, he would have been with them. So being somewhat of a "shitbird" himself, the chief warrant officer didn't mind a bit that twelve of his Marines had kicked fourteen Screamin' Eagle asses, not to mention denting the heads of some ten or eleven MPs. But they lacked discipline and self-control, and that was inexcusable in his eyes. "What? I can't he-e-e-ar you!" he intoned again.

The concrete walls reverberated with the sound of twelve men screaming at the tops of their lungs, and finally Gunner was satisfied.

"Good. Well, this is your lucky day, boys. It seems that I have friends in high places. I can reduce your sentences, possibly even get 'em to drop all the charges if you're *real* lucky. But the fact remains that the taxpayers don't like footing the bill for torn-up Japanese bars, so you're gonna have to scrape up all the cash you can to keep 'em happy for now until I can talk to the brass and get your paychecks garnished.

He let this soak in for a moment while he paced the

25

floor in front of the straggling lineup of hung-over Marines, piercing them with a granite stare. As Gunner passed Mudders, he heard an indistinct mumble.

"Garnished? Like with parsley or somethin', man?"

Gunner whirled, his narrowed gaze shriveling the budding comedian. "Do you find this amusing, Mudders?"

"Sir, no sir!" Mudders made a valiant attempt at remaining erect, his unfocused eyes straining to fix upon the chief warrant officer.

"Then I suggest you shut up and listen up!" Gunner's gaze shifted to the others. "You will ship out at 0600 hours in the morning, whereupon you gentlemen will be introduced to some *real* fighting." After a short pause, he added softly, "And if your luck holds, no one will find out what I'm doing and keep your assess in here where you belong for last night's escapade. If your luck should run out, gentlemen, I will not lift another finger to help."

The steel doors clanged shut behind him, and the men of First Squad exchanged glances and began their usual ritual of what prompted their nickname— "bitchin'."

"I wanna fight, but I don't wanna end up sitting in some muddy hole sweating and shooting at the air," one of them said.

"Yeah, I want to haul ass and kick shit," came another voice. "I bet we end up filling sandbags and humping packs into the mountains. . . ."

Jackson just shrugged, glad they were going into action at last. But he had this inescapable feeling that they were about to embark on something for which he wasn't ready. All his training had made him bad—*real* bad—but how bad would he be once he got into it?

"Man," Smitty was saying. "I thought maybe we could sit this one out in Tokyo or something!"

Jackson laughed aloud at that and flexed a muscled arm. "And waste all our training?"

"Oh, I don't know. Getting dropped in the middle of a war to kill or be killed sounds fair to me," Bug said at last, his voice rising above the others. There was a sudden silence, when nothing could be heard but the dripping of water from a leaky pipe. Eleven pairs of eyes slowly turned to glare at him.

CHAPTER 2

"Move it, move it, move it!" came the voice of CWO Charles Benson as he orchestrated the squads from the windy deck of the aircraft carrier USS Enterprise into the waiting choppers. Corporal Jackson stood at the doorway of one of the UH-1 Huey slicks while herding his squad inside. As the last man ducked inside, he jumped hastily aboard himself and swung into a steel seat. Next to him was David Baroni, the Italian-American from San Francisco.

"Hey, Jack!" Baroni shouted over the whoop-whoop of chopper blades. "What's this I hear about some wounded Marines coming in?"

Jackson shook his head, pulling his helmet lower over his forehead. "I don't know, man. All I know is that it's gonna be *hot*, real hot! We're the second assault wave of some operation. I think I heard the Gunner talkin' to the captain and callin' it something like Operation Deckhouse or deck-something. We're goin' in to some place called Song Cau right now and headin' right for the hot spot. I don't know. But I do know there's a helluva lot of Marines that are on this

28

ship, and about a third of 'em flew in only a couple of hours ago."

A worried frown creased Jackson's face as he looked past Baroni and out the open door of the chopper. Hot metal decks of the Enterprise stretched in shimmering waves, crisscrossed with painted yellow lines and littered with wooden chocks. The South China Sea glittered blue and hot in the sunshine, and there wasn't a sign of a cooling breeze.

"Assault wave, huh? Yeah, well if that's true, they sure ain't wasting no time finding Charlie and making some contact," Baroni observed.

Jackson turned his head to answer but there was a sudden lurch, then the huge chopper bumped into the air, catching the two Marines off balance. Grabbing hold of a dangling strap to keep from falling out onto the deck, Jackson muttered, "Yeah, no time at all, Baroni, no time at all."

It seemed like only a matter of minutes before the beautiful South Vietnamese coastline was in sight. Picture postcard white sand beaches and palm trees were all that could be seen. The members of the squad were not too concerned about the beauty of the place, however, as the helicopter skimmed the shoreline and the sound of the door gunner's machine gun began spraying the area.

Jackson's gaze was drawn to the expression on the face of the gunner as he let the bullets fly in hundred-round bursts at a time, totally defying what he had learned in boot camp. Jackson's MOS being the same, he remembered the first time he had used the gun. His instructor had told him that "anything over a hundred round burst at a time will melt the barrel in a matter of minutes, and anything over a twenty round burst if you were in the bush would give the enemy plenty of time to get your position in his sights." Those instructions sure didn't matter now. And the gunner seemed to be enjoying the hell out of his work.

Gripping the strap over his head more tightly, Jackson thought he heard a few *plinks* on the side of the chopper as it started to descend. He took a quick check of his part of the fifty-caliber machine gun he was carrying. He had the burden of the receiver. It was weighing on him heavier than the bulky Korean-era flak-jacket, two bandoliers, four grenades, three canteens, a .45 handgun, and his forty-five-pound pack and the M-14 he refused to relinquish, even though he'd been warned against carrying that much weight. It looked as though he was destined to hump this weight for at least a while—providing he made it through the next few minutes.

Huey gunships escorted their slicks in to the LZ. The choppers hovered a good four to five feet above the sandy scrub brush as the men of First Squad began to jump out of open doorways, some falling belly-first in the sand, others with an even-footed thud, covering their eyes from the biting sandstorm the blades of two slicks were churning.

Jackson ran crouched over like the others, his breath coming in harsh, labored gasps. He felt like some sort of clumsy sea turtle, weighted down with all his gear and scuttling across the hot sand in a lumbering gait. But he didn't falter, following the ragged line of Marines as they ran inland and sought cover behind the nearest trees they could find. Another wave of Marines ran toward the empty chopper, carrying what looked to be blood-and-sand-covered rain ponchos with wounded, screaming men.

The makeshift litters that served as stretchers cradled men with parts of their faces blown away, men with no legs, and a man whose intestines were barely held in by swathes of white gauze. Jackson stumbled when he saw that one, and his broad face creased into gray lines. This was real. This was no fake blood like on the movie screen, like his kid brother would play with on Halloween. This was the real thing, and he was running right into it.

Terror had never entered Jackson's mind until now. Just a few short days ago the total view of the Vietnam conflict had been a dream, a John Wayne movie, someplace where he was gonna go and do his time, then leave. Now, the reality of it struck him like a thunderbolt. Looking at those wounded, bloodied Marines stunned him, and he couldn't take another step. His life flashed before him like a speeded-up film clip, only he could remember every detail and every emotion. Every good thing that he had ever done as well as every bad thing he wished he could forget was staring him right in the face. They were all there. The first time his mother had kissed him after he had made her a Christmas card, the first time his father had kicked his butt for taking the car without permission, the first time his brother had shaken his hand after boot camp, the first time he'd made love to his wife . . .

A hard slap on the back shook him out of the dream world into reality. "Hey, Jack! Snap outa it. You look like you seen a ghost or something," Baroni

31

muttered as he fell behind the lagging corporal. "I guess they weren't kidding when they said this place was hot, huh? Hey, are you as scared as I am?"

"Huh? Yeah, right," Jackson replied dazedly. "Where's the other slicks? Where's the Gunner? What the hell are we supposed to do?"

Baroni didn't answer as he crouched in the sand, looking over his shoulder every few seconds as if he expected to see a fully armed VC descend on him from out of nowhere. There wasn't anything to say, no answers for the corporal's rhetorical questions. They all had questions that wouldn't get answers.

F-4C Phantoms snarled through the air, clawing at the blazing blue sky in sixty-ton metal streaks. They were painted green and light brown, twenty tons of bomb carriers flying low over the white sand and green trees of enemy lines.

The rattling sound of M-14's mixed with the return fire of AK-47's, shattering the air. M-79's sounded with their peculiarly empty *whoomp* that delivered a grenade to the target. Then the sound of gunships riding shotgun on more slicks zooming in for a landing on the beach drowned out any other distraction. The two other metal birds descended and dropped their passengers so fast it was like dropping leaflets or supplies instead of men. Jackson stared through the hot beat of the sunlight and wavering sheets of heat wafting up off the sand, wondering how the hell he had gotten himself into this mess. . . .

He could see the Gunner some twenty-five meters south of him, with his RTO crouching under cover behind a palm tree. The firing suddenly ceased, and Jackson drew in a deep breath of relief. Then Gunner

32

signaled for him and his respite was at an end.

Jackson groaned, then turned to the men beside him. "Ya'll hang tight here. I'm gonna go find out what's going on. Here, Baroni, hang onto this."

After tossing his fifty-caliber receiver to the sand next to Baroni, Jackson threw himself down, too. He felt like a sand crab, scuttling along in perfect boot camp fashion for a few meters. Only when he realized that he wasn't taking any fire did he rise to a half crouch, feeling faintly foolish and definitely "cherry." He zigzagged in Gunner's general direction, arriving in a shower of sand and sweat as the gunner pulled out his map.

Gunner didn't say anything for a minute; he just sat studying his map and squinting his eyes. Then he looked up at Jackson's sweat-shiny face. "OK, Jack . . ." Gunner chewed his bottom lip reflectively, glancing back at the map, then saying, "Looks like Second Platoon took care of this pretty well. They got five confirmed dead Vietcong and one wounded, probably more. They seem to think the rest of 'em have already bugged out. But they're gonna head this way and continue the cleanup. You see this village, Song Cau?" He pointed to the map. "It's about three klicks north of here. We're gonna go check it out. I want you and First Squad to take the lead. You walk point. Baroni's the slackman. I'll be right behind you with Second and Third Squad. If there's any sign of trouble, I want you to open up on that fifty-caliber like all hell a'breakin' loose. You understand?"

Jackson nodded, his breath coming in short, rasping gasps for air. "Yeah, Gunner. But what about when we get to the village?"

33

"The captain wants us to search every hut and round 'em all up. The old ones, the young ones—all of 'em. Seems some S-2 Intelligence guys want to ask these people a few questions." Gunner's lips curled in a sneer, and he shook his head. "Any more questions, Jack?"

"No, sir."

"OK, then. Let's move it!"

Only a matter of minutes had passed before Jackson was picking up his machine gun receiver and gear and repeating the same orders to his squad. They moved out. Walking in a direction parallel to the shoreline, the men of First Squad moved in tense silence. Jackson walked point, wondering why in the hell a man who knew absolutely nothing about what was going on had been assigned to such a dangerous position. He might not know anything about this kind of fighting yet, but he knew enough to know that walking point wasn't exactly the safest place to be. And Gunner knew it, too. Maybe he was testing him, but shit! This was a hell of a way to do it!

White sand beaches stretched to their right and dense green jungle loomed on their left, resembling a tropical vacation spot like Hawaii or Florida. Only the drone of whirring choppers in the distance and the chatter of automatic weapon fire reminded Jackson that this was no vacation paradise.

The young Marines walked cautiously in a column formation until the jungle foliage gave way to an open expanse of terrain. Jackson and Baroni both halted at the same time, and Jackson signaled the rest of the squad to get down. Off to the west was an open area of rice fields and paddy dikes, but to their immediate

34

front was a small village, with some twenty-five to thirty thatched-roof dwellings. They were mostly rude one-roomed huts, with straggling fences and rice mats hung up to ward off the sun.

Turning to Jackson, Baroni scooped off his helmet, raked a hand through his thick, dark hair, and muttered, "Well, what d'ya think?"

"I don't know. We better get the Gunner up here and see what he says." Jackson kept his eyes fixed in the general direction of the small hamlet. "Pass the word down the line."

Only minutes had passed before Gunner and Zoot, his RTO (radio-telephone operator), were next to Jackson. Gunner surveyed the area with his vintage WWII field glasses. They were huge binoculars, with thick plastic lenses and casing that reflected sunlight in glittering bursts.

"OK, Jack. Looks pretty good. I want you and First Squad to head on into the village through that main gate and start searching the huts and rounding up all the people in the center." Pointing his finger and speaking in a low tone, the Gunner continued, "I'll stay here with Second Squad and will send Third in after you make it through the first few huts. There's supposed to be an ARVN platoon flanking you to the west." He paused to spit on the ground. "Our allies—the Army of the Republic of Vietnam— ain't much, Jackson. Those poor excuses for soldiers are about as useless as tits on a boar hog, but brass says we gotta use 'em. I do, but I don't trust 'em. You might want to make note of that. As far as we know, this is a village of "friendlies," but there's been a lot of Vietcong activity near here, especially west of here on Highway 1. We think some might just be living in this place in their little hidey-holes, so take caution and search the place good. I mean real good! You got it, Jack?"

"Got it!" came Jackson's reply, and he and First Squad were off. Moving through the open fields of grass that lay between them and the village, Jackson slapped at the razor-edged blades of chest-high elephant grass to keep it from slicing his skin. Two curious water buffalo lifted their heads to gaze at them, chewing their cuds and cutting the young Marines curious glances, but other than that—nothing. Jackson recalled all he'd heard about land mines, and how they were stitched into all the rice paddies and fields for the unwary Marine to step on and get blown to hell. He stumbled over something once and froze in place, sweat streaming down from under his helmet as he waited for the roaring explosion that would take off his legs or blow him apart. It was nothing but a rock and he pushed on, hoping no one else had seen him falter. The sharp grasses tore at his unprotected arms, leaving tiny crisscrosses of cuts that immediately attracted swarms of minute, worrisome insects. Jackson swore softly, and slapped at them when he could. It was useless. They only returned to buzz around the scent of blood.

As he and the other members of First Squad neared the perimeter of the village, he could see the smoke of small cook fires and smell the foul scent of rotten fish. His mind flashed back to childhood memories of fishing with his father on the banks of the mighty Mississippi River in Memphis, Tennessee. Man, he'd loved to fish, and even more than that, eat

36

fish. Catfish, fat catfish breaded in cornmeal and deep-fried to a golden brown was his favorite.

But memories of catfish and hush puppies faded as fast as they came when the high-pitched chatter of people from the village attracted his attention. As he cautiously swung open the leaning gate of the rickety fence that surrounded the hamlet, first checking for telltale wires that indicated booby-traps, Vietnamese children stopped talking and just stared at him in round-eyed fear or amazement. He wasn't sure which it was. Maybe it was because they had never seen American Marines, especially a black American Marine. Whatever it was, the kids kept their distance and didn't say a word.

Ignoring them—and feeling conspicuous because of their intent stares—Jackson gave terse orders to Mudders and Crawford to search the row of huts to their west. Turning to Smitty and Bug, he snapped an order for them to search the others. Carrigan and Grover began herding the older "Mamasans" and "Papasans" standing outside their huts into the middle of the village.

It was then that Jackson caught a flicker of movement out of the corner of his eye. Swinging around, he saw what looked like a young boy clad in black pajamas running out of the first hootch. PFC Sanchez, a short, stocky Mexican in Jackson's squad, gave chase, running and wildly firing his M-14 at the young Vietnamese. Leaping the fence, Sanchez followed the fugitive into the dense jungle that backed up to one side of the village.

"Dammit!" Jackson swore softly. "What the hell does he think he's doing?"

"I dunno," Smitty paused to say. "Mebbe he thinks he's *Juan* Wayne."

Shaking his head in disgust, Jackson cupped his hands around his mouth and yelled at the top of his voice, "Sanchez! Hey, what's the matter with you? Get your dumb ass back here!"

When Sanchez skidded to a regretful halt and made his way back to Jackson, he began to sputter excuses, but Jackson wasn't buying any. He cut across the man's rapid stream of chatter with a snarl.

"Man, don't go running off in the damn jungle like some kind of fool. You can get yerself killed that way! I don't think you're playin' with a full deck, Sanchez. Let the little sucker go. Gunner or the other squads will catch up with him. You got it?"

"Chit, man. I wanted to get the little asshole. . . ." Sanchez began saying, but Jackson interrupted again.

"Just shut up and get back here and listen up. Get over to the other end of those hootches and start searching 'em—now! And I don't want any firing unless you're fired upon. This ain't the Alamo! These people are supposed to be 'friendlies,' and until we find out different, we're just supposed to round 'em up and search the area. Now, have you got that?"

There was no response. The arrogant Marine just glared at Jackson without answering. Jackson felt the blood rush to his head, and his mouth tightened. Who the hell did this guy think he was? Santa Anna? Stepping closer, Jackson eyed the much-shorter Mexican coldly. This time his voice was even louder. "I said, have you got that, Sanchez?"

"Yeah, I got it," Sanchez said sullenly.

Only slightly satisfied, Jackson pivoted on his heel and stalked away to cool off. Baroni joined him, wisely keeping his mouth shut and his eyes open as they approached the leaning line of huts. Jackson slung Baroni a quizzical glance, then shrugged, grinned, and swung his M-14 up to the ready as he stomped across the dirt and ducked into the low doorway.

Blinking his eyes to adjust to the dim, hazy light inside the thatched hut, Jackson blinked again. His stomach lurched and he took a step back, bumping into Baroni, who was only two paces behind.

"What the hell?" Jackson muttered sickly. "Man, what is goin' on?" Hell, he was thinking, nothing at home had prepared him for something like this! This—this was more than he had bargained for, more than the DI had drilled into him at Camp Pendleton.

He could feel Baroni beside him, both of them staring and frowning in confusion. They stood in the doorway, staring at a young girl squatting in the middle of the hut. Her face was flushed red, her long black hair damp with sweat and hanging down her back in snarls. A thin cotton skirt was pulled up past her waist, and she was hugging her knees and hovering over a reed mat. She looked rather young and her face was contorted with pain, but not the tiniest whimper came from her lips. A small bloodied mass seemed to be dangling from between her legs, but she was so absorbed in what was happening to her that she didn't even notice the huge Marines darkening the flimsy doorway.

Shaking his head, Jackson pulled off his helmet and wiped his forehead with his sleeve. A wave of nausea made him slightly dizzy, and he lowered his rifle muzzle as he grabbed the doorjamb for support. Then the girl sighed with relief and lay back on the mat. Reaching down, she lifted the slimy mass of newborn onto her stomach. The young Marines stood in stunned amazement for what seemed like a half hour but was in actuality probably only a few minutes. Then, as reality sunk in, Jackson literally shook himself like a wet dog would. He pulled his helmet back over his forehead and stepped out of the hootch.

"Hey, Doc, better get over here. We got a customer for ya!"

Still feeling slightly sick, Baroni and Jackson promptly entered the next in line of hootches to be searched. The first few were clean. But they hit pay dirt on the fourth one. Baroni went in first, ducking into the hut and holding his rifle at ready, with Jackson bringing up the rear.

"Lai day! Lai day!" Baroni shouted in Vietnamese, telling them to come out. No one moved.

"Hey, man, looka what we got here," Baroni breathed softly, and Jackson stepped closer to peer over his shoulder. Instead of old men and women or little kids, they had found a young Vietnamese man whom they immediately suspected of being a VC. And with him was a young woman of exceptional Asian beauty. They were both huddled in a corner of the shabby hut, frantically stuffing items into a small spider hole beside a woven basket. They whirled around when they heard Baroni, and the young man's hand dipped to his side, going for what looked like a pistol.

Without stopping to think, Baroni reacted. A loud

40

explosion tore the air as he fired his rifle, hitting the man in the shoulder. There was a sharp cry and the young man lurched sideways, gripping his arm. Blood trickled from between his brown fingers and dripped to the dirt floor.

Jackson lowered his weapon and gestured with it, motioning the two stunned Vietnamese toward the door. "Baroni!" he yelled. "Get them out of here and tie 'em up with these rags." He snatched up several old tattered cloths from a straw basket by the door and flung them to Baroni. "I'll search the place."

Baroni was shaking, and he kept sucking in huge gulps of air. Finally, he looked up at Jackson and muttered, "Hell, Jack, I haven't ever shot anybody before!"

"I know, man," Jackson said. "Neither have I. But this is war, Baroni, and he didn't give you any choice."

"Yeah, that's right. That's right. . . ." Baroni nodded and gave the injured Vietnamese a push toward the door. "I guess I didn't have a choice."

Jackson watched as they left the hut, and he was wondering how he would feel when he had to shoot someone. It was inevitable, of course, but when the time came, would he be glad? Would he be so hyped-up that he wouldn't care? Or maybe it'd be one of those "kill before you get killed" things. But now he couldn't worry about that. Now he had a job to do.

Left alone in the dimly lit hut, Jackson turned over baskets, rice mats, wooden plates, bowls, and stone crockery in his search. It took several minutes of searching, while the sweat dripped down his face and neck and drenched his clothes, but he found something. In a large hole dug into one corner and hidden by a small cook stove and several large pots, he found what the two prisoners were trying to conceal: an NVA field pack, an NVA uniform, one AK-47, several rounds of ammunition, three potato masher grenades, a couple of land mines, and a bag filled with medical supplies.

Grinning, Jackson sang out, "Whooa! Papa's got a brand-new bag!"

Standing outside, Baroni stuck his head in the door and said, "You say somethin', Jack?"

"Naw, but looka here!" Jackson triumphantly held up his prizes, grinning from ear to ear. "Not bad, huh?"

"No, that sure isn't! Look at that pack, man! Hell, it's a lot better than ours. Look at those wide, soft straps, and it's a lot bigger. . . ."

"Forget it, Baroni. The pack's mine," Jackson said in a cheerful tone. He held out the rifle. "You can have this."

Now Baroni grinned. "Fine with me, Jack, fine with me. But what about the pistol that almost killed me? Who gets that?"

"You deserve that, man. Besides, I already got too much weight I'm packing as it is."

"Yeah, I know." After a pause, Baroni continued, "Well, Jack, what now?"

Jackson shrugged as he continued to empty his heavily laden pack and stuff items into his new NVA pack. "Well, let's keep searching these hootches and herdin' up the folks. Oh, and Baroni, better get Doc to look at the guy's wound when he gets finished with the chick who had the baby."

Only a matter of minutes passed before the young black corporal was re-saddled and out the door. It was hot, stinking hot, with buzzing insects and the press of air almost suffocating him. How did the Vietnamese stand it all the time? It was hotter than July in Memphis, and he'd always thought that had to be the worst weather he would ever experience. Sweat streamed from under his helmet and made his shirt stick to his back in huge wet patches. One of the old-timers had said this weather was "peachy" compared to the monsoons that hit Vietnam. Then the rain would come down so thick a man could drown standing up outside. Ditches and potholes in the road would fill up, making the terrain slick and impassable. But that was later. Right now, he was hot and miserable and wishing for rain.

Squinting against the bright sunlight that bounced off metal helmets and guns, Jackson marched down the middle of the village. He paused when he noticed the Vietnamese men in uniform. They were peering over the villagers that were grouped in a circle and under guard by men of First Squad. It was Jackson's first glimpse of any ARVN (Army of the Republic of Vietnam) soldiers. They were almost comical in appearance, because of their unfitting uniforms and wobbling helmets that were much too large for them. Most of them looked so young they could have passed for a Boy Scout troop from Chinatown. All but one, that is. As he drew closer, Jackson saw that the leader was a little taller and much older than the rest of his men.

His gaze flicked over them, then moved sideways as he noticed the Gunner's squad entering the village to the south. They marched in his direction. Jackson moved on, passing by the hootch where Doc was still attending to the young mother. He heard the sound of a baby's whimper and stuck his head inside the door and asked, "How goes it, Doc? A boy or girl?"

"A boy, a beautiful baby boy," Doc Weathers answered as he carefully lifted the infant and continued wiping the residue of birth off him.

Beauty is in the eye of the beholder, Jackson thought as he stared dubiously at the infant. Did all babies look like that? All red and wrinkled like a wizened monkey? But who was he to argue?

"That's great, man, just great. But I tell ya, Doc, that has to be the grossest thing I've ever seen! Man, I've never seen one born. When my wife has our kid I sure don't wanna be around in the operating room." There was a short pause, then Jackson thought to ask, "How's the mom?"

Glancing up at him, Doc's bright blue eyes were wet and shiny as he said, "Fine, she's gonna be just fine. I tell ya, Jack, no matter how many births I've seen, it never ceases to amaze me. I mean, it's a miracle," the sensitive Navy corpsman added. "The miracle of life." Holding the infant cradled in his arms like a father would, the Doc seemed momentarily lost in thought. Then he looked up at Jackson again and grinned. "This is the last thing I expected when I got assigned to Marine Raider unit. The very last thing."

"Yeah, well, me too! But you do have another customer waitin' outside with Baroni. A wounded NVA. Take your time, though, 'cause I don't care if he bleeds to death or not. He almost got me and

Baroni."

The Doc was surprised as he replied, "No, man! Is that the shot I heard a little while ago?"

"Yeah, but like I said, take your time. This kid is more important right now," Jackson growled before stepping back outside the hootch.

Gunner and two other squads had entered the village, and the burly chief warrant officer was talking to the ARVN officer. As Jackson walked up to them, he saw Gunner struggling to try and understand the ARVN officer's broken English. Gunner turned to Jackson in disgust and said, "Jack, what's going on here? I can't get nothing understandable outa this guy except his name. Captain Ngo Dai."

"No die?" Jackson repeated, then shook his head and grinned. "That's an appropriate enough name, I guess."

After hearing a brief report on the roundup, the Gunner nodded in satisfaction. "Well, Jack, get the wounded NVA and the young girl over here right now. We'll let 'old silver tongue' here question 'em." He jabbed a thumb in the direction of the irritating officer, who just kept chattering in Vietnamese and broken English.

Bug and Baroni forced their way through the herded villagers with the two prisoners in tow. When they jerked to a halt in front of Gunner, Jackson noticed a strange expression flickered on Captain Dai's features.

Jackson noted the reaction with a frown, the look of shock and fear that jolted the ARVN officer as he stared at the faces of the prisoners like he knew them. Then Captain Dai was on his field phone jabbering in his shrill, annoying voice.

"What's he doin'?" Jackson muttered, and Bug shrugged in reply.

"I dunno—calling for a chopper, I think."

The two prisoners hung their heads and stared at their feet, obviously scared to death. The girl was shaking, and the suspected VC looked as if he might fall down in a faint. Jackson watched the scene curiously, wondering how the ARVN felt about their countrymen. Did it bother them that they had to interrogate their own kind? That they fought them in the fields in a brutal civil war? Maybe. But maybe not, he decided a minute later when the ARVN officer finished his call on the field phone and turned to the prisoners.

Turning in a smooth motion that caught Jackson by surprise, Captain Dai flicked up the butt of his handgun and struck the suspected VC full strength across his jaw. Blood gushed, and a couple of teeth flew from his mouth as the slight figure fell sideways in the dust. The young Vietnamese girl fell to her knees beside him in an effort to avoid the same fate. It didn't help.

Looking up at the ARVN officer towering over her, the girl began yelling at the top of her lungs in rapid-fire Vietnamese. Standing by Jackson and watching, Bug muttered a faint, "Oh, so that's what it is."

"You understand that, Bug?" Jackson asked, and he nodded.

"Only a little . . . hey!"

Jackson swung his eyes back just in time to see Captain Dai do the same thing to the girl as he had to the NVA. Only this time he used his foot, his boot

46

heel smashing across her face just under her nose.

Anger and disgust creased the facial features of the Gunner as well as the three other young Marines standing close beside him. Jackson, Baroni, and Bug surged forward, but Gunner signaled for them to halt.

"Don't interfere," he said tersely.

Only Bug seemed to understand what was going on, and Jackson leaned close and quizzed, "What are they saying, man?"

Bug edged closer to Jackson and said, "Well, I didn't catch everything they were talking about, but it seems they know each other or are related. The girl was calling the ARVN captain a traitor or something to that effect when he kicked her down. I don't know, Jack. This whole deal is confusing to me."

"Yeah, me too, Bug. Me too! But I tell ya I don't like it. I don't like it one damn bit!" Jackson said.

"One thing's for sure. At least those two aren't gonna be doing much talking now. I get the feeling the officer wanted it that way, too."

Gunner's face was getting redder by the minute, and when Captain Dai lifted his handgun as if to swipe it across the girl's face, Gunner stopped his arm in mid-swing. Startled, Dai turned to Gunner. His fearful gaze turned to a grin as he said, "It OK! It OK, Marine. He North! He North VC. You no understand. We make talk. We make talk."

"Make talk, my ass," the Gunner growled in a deep voice. "They won't be talking much more if you keep sluggin' 'em like that, you little asshole!"

Captain Dai continued to talk and repeat his actions to no avail with the Gunner. Rounding on the

47

Marines, Gunner finally snapped, "Hell, don't anybody here speak Vietnamese? Shit! I can't understand a damn word he's saying."

Bug stepped forward and said, "I do a little, Gun. Very little. Maybe just enough to get me in some deep shit!"

"Go ahead and ask him what the hell is going on!"

Bug turned to the ARVN officer and began to slowly search his limited vocabulary for the proper words. The officer concentrated his attention on the Marine's lips in an effort to understand. This exercise in frustration continued for several minutes before the sound of an approaching chopper filled the air.

It was an old Korean-era helicopter that had been so graciously donated to popular forces of the Republic of South Vietnam. It landed not far outside the fence surrounding the small village. When the dust storm it kicked up subsided slightly, the ARVN officer and two of his squad members yanked the prisoners to their feet and shoved them toward the chopper.

Turning to Gunner, Bug said, "Captain Dai here said he was gonna ask them some more questions. All I could understand was that the guy was a North Vietnamese Army officer and the girl was his wife, and that she was also an NVA nurse. I also got the distinct impression that these two guys knew each other. I dunno, Gun. Seems pretty fishy to me."

"Yeah, Bug. Me too. But what the hell! Let the ARVNs fool with the prisoners. They can probably get more out of 'em than we can. Besides, at least they understand each other's lingo." Turning to Jackson and Baroni, Gunner continued, "You guys find

48

anything else in the way of documents in the prisoners' pack?"

"No, sir, just personals and a wallet with some pictures and letters and stuff," Jackson said. "Here it is." He fished the wallet from his pack and handed it to the Gunner. "Oh, and we also got his AK and pistol. . . ." Jackson tried to continue but Gunner interrupted him.

"Yeah, yeah, yeah, I know. I can see the nice new pack on your back, Jack. That's great. You're gonna need it with a load like you're humping. Anyway, the S-2 guys can have these letters when they get here. But until they do, I want you and your squad to keep searching the rest of the hootches."

"Yessir," Jackson said, and motioned for Baroni to join him. The stocky Italian fell right in beside him, grinning like an idiot and shrugging his shoulders.

"Some life, huh, Jack?"

"Yeah, it's great. Glad I joined the party," Jackson shot back, unable to help grinning, too. "You're crazy, man."

As Jackson gave the orders for First Squad to fall out and resume the search, the rattling sound of the ARVN chopper lifting off snared his attention. Shading his eyes with one hand, he watched as it took off and rose straight up about two hundred fifty feet, then hovered.

"Look at that," Baroni said. "Man, it's just hovering there . . . I wonder why."

Jackson shrugged. "I dunno, man."

They stood and watched as the droning chopper hovered lazily above the small village of Song Cau. Five minutes or more passed while all of the villagers

49

and most of the Marines just stood there watching the craft.

"Think they got engine trouble?" Baroni finally guessed, but Jackson shook his head.

"No. If they did, they'd land, wouldn't they?"

"Yeah, I guess they would." Another lengthy pause, then, "But why are they just hovering there?"

As the young corporal stood gazing at the helicopter, his blood froze in spite of the sweltering sun. There was something falling, a dark speck against the hot blue sky. Squinting, he tried to see what it was. Part of the old chopper, maybe? Then he heard a faint wailing cry and knew what it was.

"Sweet Jesus," someone said behind him.

Time slowed as the form cartwheeled through space, long hair whipping in the hot wind and arms and legs flailing frantically. It was the young Vietnamese nurse.

"Bastards!" Jackson growled as the silhouette of her body plummeted out of sight behind the row of hootches to the west of the village.

Then Jackson and Baroni were running in the direction of where the young nurse had fallen, with Bug and the Doc hard on their heels. Heavy ammunition belts jiggled with metallic sounds as the men ran across the dust and skirted the edge of the rice paddy beyond the village. Jackson saw her first, crumpled in a formless heap on a hump of muddy dike. She was indented into the soft ground like a giant hand had pushed her there, and she was still breathing. Barely. Blood trickled from the corners of her mouth and out her nose, gouty clods mixed with mud as she struggled for air. Doc knelt down beside her and clawed away the muddy debris that was clogging her air passage, being careful not to move her neck. But it was too late to do anything for her. Her eyes rolled back in her head as she gave a last gasp, then there was a faint rattle deep in her throat.

Stunned, the Marines stood staring and for one split second almost felt and saw the spirit of the young girl leave her body. A shivering, a cold shivering spiked Jackson as he stood in utter horror. He had never seen anyone die, had never thought it would be so . . . personal when he did. You aimed your rifle, squeezed the trigger, and somewhere out in the bush an anonymous man died. It was that simple. Or you dropped bombs, or fired your fifty-caliber from the open doorway of a chopper, spraying tiny figures on the ground that you couldn't see and didn't know.

But this—this death was useless. She was a woman, for the love of God, and a nurse. The thought flashed through his mind that she was an *enemy* nurse, but the horror of the situation still lingered. It would be listed on the records as a kill. Though in this instance the word *murder* was more accurate. Jackson was stunned, horrified, and infuriated all at the same time as he gazed down at the young woman's broken body. She couldn't have been more than sixteen or seventeen, though it was hard to tell with the ageless Vietnamese.

Doc broke the silence. "Oh, Lord Jesus, take her soul." He mumbled some other kind of prayer so low the others couldn't really hear, then asked for help getting her body out of the mud to be brought back to the village for her own to bury her.

As the four Marines carried the lifeless body back to her people, the chopper from which she had fallen was coming down for a landing near the edge of the village. Jackson glared angrily at it as he watched the blur of blades slow, then stop. When he witnessed the ARVN officer kick the wounded young man out onto the ground, it was too much for him. Leaving Baroni, Bug, and Doc to carry the body, Jackson sprinted to the LZ where the ARVNs were standing. Pushing his way through the middle of the herded villagers, the angry black corporal looked like a charging bull as he neared Captain Dai, who stood over the prisoner.

Before anybody could stop him or even see what he intended, Jackson grabbed the officer by his helmet with both hands and brought his head swiftly down to meet his upcoming knee. The surprised ARVN grunted with pain, then fell backward and hit the dirt like a bag of potatoes. Jackson planted his right foot squarely into the ARVN's ribs with all the power of a professional football field goal kicker. As the officer yelled, two of the little soldiers of the captain's goon squad jumped on Jackson's back in a frantic attempt to stop the raging Marine.

Sensing danger, Gunner leveled his M-14 on the remaining men in the ARVN platoon, yelling at the top of his raspy voice, "First Platoon, lock and load!"

It wasn't really necessary for him to have given that command because most of the Marines had already seen what was going down. By keeping the ARVNs at bay, Gunner gave good leeway for the rest of the Marines to watch the fight.

Jackson threw off the two little ARVNs as if he

52

were swatting flies, aiming the majority of his short, chopping blows in the direction of the officer still lying in the dust. Finally having done enough to let off some of the steam that had been building up since they'd landed, Jackson stopped, breathing hard and staring down at the officer sprawled on the ground.

As reason and sanity slowly returned, Jackson slanted a glance at Gunner. His face gave away nothing. He just motioned with his rifle for Jackson to step back. Baroni and Bug stepped closer to the corporal as the ARVN kept murmuring incoherently in Vietnamese.

Bug shook his head and said, "If you hadn't hit him, I would have, Jack."

The ARVN officer was still jabbering in that sing-song high-pitched voice that was so irritating. Jackson scowled. "What's he saying, Bug?"

"Hard to tell. Something about black. Something about bad. He keeps repeating it like if he says it enough times, he'll make us understand. Hell, I dunno."

Pushing to his knees, the officer swayed slightly. The Marines just watched, still holding the ARVNs at bay. Slanted eyes narrowed even more, looking like tiny slits in his round, bruised face as the ARVN mimicked Bug, repeating in English, "You one bad black, you one bad black." He glared at Jackson with hatred burning in his eyes.

When he finally had enough energy to stand and walk, Captain Dai staggered to the wounded prisoner kneeling in the dust. Gunner shook his head when Jackson would have stopped him, and they let him go. Still half dazed and stumbling, the officer muttered, "You bad? Show you bad. . . ." Lifting his pistol in a quick movement that took them all by surprise, the ARVN officer pointed it at the head of the kneeling prisoner. Boom! The young NVA fell dead as the officer kept murmuring.

Jackson stared down at the lifeless body of the boy, feeling slightly sick. The North Vietnamese prisoner was lying with his head at a crooked angle, one side of his skull gone. Flies were already starting to swarm. The angry black corporal looked up at the smirking ARVN officer's bruised face. So this was Vietnam . . .

CHAPTER 3

The slick roared through the saddle of a thirty-five-hundred-foot mountain, and Jackson peered out at trees so thickly packed they looked like a wedge of broccoli. Mountains jutted into the sky in every shade of green, from pale to dark, at times fading into blue and brown where the foliage was stripped. He could see the remains of a footbridge dangling into a river and now useless. Coconut palms and banana groves dotted the ground around a ruined village.

They were headed north, to "see some action" Gunner had said. Jackson shrugged. He was still bothered by the ARVN officer and what he'd done, and wondered about man's inhumanity to man. Did it matter what race these people were? They were people and, as such, were supposed to be equal if he believed in the doctrine of his Christian upbringing. Wasn't that a big deal now in the States? Black versus white and everybody hating the other? Even the popular songs of the day sang about it. There was a big movement going on, a movement that was supposed to bring equality between the races. He hadn't thought that much about it until now. It was just something that had always been, though he had friends who hated whites.

Shaking his head, Jackson looked back down at the land below. Tanks were fanning out on roads that looked like brown wiggles, looking for land mines. They were twenty miles south of Da Nang, near the Thu Bon River. A rattle from a fifty-caliber below forced the pilot to pull the slick up to twenty-two hundred feet. VC. They were waiting down there, hoping for more American mistakes.

At night, the VC worked the rice fields in small clearings and moved supplies along trails tucked into almost inaccessible areas. There were infiltration routes snaking down from Laos, where they moved their supplies by bicycle, elephant, or on their backs.

The slick rocked heavily in a burst of air current, and Jackson saw a thin column of black smoke mushroom from the ground. A Phantom out on an air strike had dropped D-3's—two-hundred-fifty-pound bombs—on suspected VC. It looked like heavy damage had been inflicted.

Jackson held onto the canvas strap as the slick banked left in a curving arc and descended not far from that column of smoke.

"Great," he muttered, and somehow Baroni heard him over the *whump* of the chopper blades.

"What, Jack?" he shouted.

"We're being set down in a hot area, Baroni!"

Grinning like an idiot, Baroni nodded. "Great!"

"You're crazy, Baroni," Jackson observed without rancor, and the Italian nodded again.

* * *

"All right, Bitches," Jackson said to his men as they hunched over a dinner of C-rats that evening. "This is the plan. . . ."

"You mean we got a plan?" Carrigan asked in amazement. He was wielding his P-38 in a valiant effort to open his C-rats and was losing the battle.

"Gunner does, anyway," Jackson said shortly. "Lissen up. We've got night patrol. We wear cammo on our faces and soft issue. Got that?"

"No helmets? What if we get hit?" Smitty wanted to know.

"There's less chance of being hit if they don't hear you coming from a mile away," Jackson snapped back. "Those helmets bang around in the jungle. Wear soft issue . . . your boonie hats. Got that?"

They got it. First Squad moved out at 1900 hours, in the faded light and darkness of the thick trees. A quarter moon gave pale light as they filtered through the trees. They humped for hours, drifting along the edges of villages and sweeping through peanut fields and scrub forest in a wide arc on their patrol. The dark was unnerving. It seemed to haunt them with unidentifiable noises, and Jackson had to keep telling his men to space out.

"Don't bunch up!" he snarled at one point. "We're too easy-pickin's that way!" Jackson realized how inefficient and "cherry" First Squad was, and he wished Gunner had given him at least one old-timer to smooth out the rough edges. It would have given the men in First Squad more confidence, too. How could they have much confidence in a corporal who was just as much an FNG—fucking new guy—as

57

they were?

Jackson was walking point. He pushed aside a branch hanging in front of him and caught a sudden whiff of something that smelled like a long-dead fish. He froze and made a "get-down" motion with his hands. Baroni was slackman—walking behind the point man—and he caught the motion and passed it on to the rest. First Squad hunkered down on the trail and waited.

Jackson contemplated his actions. On the one hand, he could bring in the squad and take a chance on blowing away whoever it was waiting off the trail ahead; on the other hand, he could take an even bigger risk, do it himself, and instill confidence in his men that their leader had leadership ability. *If I don't get killed doing it!*

His heart pounded so loudly that he wondered why no one else could hear it, and his mouth was bone-dry. What the hell was he doing here, anyway? He should have stayed at home and not been so damned stupid. But he *was* here, and there were guys behind him who counted on him. Shit. There wasn't much else he could do.

Having sunk to one knee on the trail, Jackson brought up his M-14 and slid his K-bar out of its sheath. The long bladed knife gleamed silently in the moonlight, giving him a bit more courage. He waited, praying his quarry wouldn't see him before he could see them. After another minute slide past, he inched forward as quietly as possible.

Two shadows sat just off the trail, half hidden in a clump of bushes and reeking of *nuoc mam*, the Vietnamese sauce they poured over their rice dishes. It had a distinctive strong odor and had given away the position of the two VC squatting just a yard away from him. Jackson inched closer and rose to the balls of his feet.

Leaping up and throwing himself forward, he landed on the two men and knocked them sideways. His K-bar sliced into the side of one man's neck and he snapped it out the front with a quick motion, effectively slashing his throat. Still stunned by the unexpected charge, the other VC was fumbling with his AK-47, trying to snap it up to shoot. Jackson took him out with his M-14 in a quick burst. The impact of the bullets flung the VC backward.

Adrenaline pumped through him as Jackson stared at the two dead VC and realized what he'd done. It had all happened so quick. Without stopping to think about what he was going to do, he had just acted. He sucked in a deep breath and inhaled the strong odor of *nuoc mam* and blood.

Baroni crashed through the bushes behind him, arriving as Jackson turned and brought up his M-14, in a smooth reflex action.

"Hey! It's me, Jack!"

"Well, how about announcing yourself the next time?" Jackson lowered his rifle as Baroni stared down at the dead VC.

"Holy shee-it, Jack! How'd you know they were there?"

Without a single flicker of an eyelash, Jackson said, "Because I'm *bad*, Baroni. Remember?"

Jackson's bravado earned him the complete confidence of First Squad that night. They might not have agreed with him at times, but they had confidence that he knew what he was doing and would do his best to keep them alive. Only Robert Jackson had his doubts about his ability, and he kept that to himself. Why spoil their fun?

Three months in-country, three months and twenty-something firefights, and some one hundred forty VC were confirmed dead. A good body count for the brass, Jackson reflected. And here they were three months later, humping heavy packs through thick jungle, broiling sun, and now rain. It had been one hell of an education.

The big things were easy to learn. It was the little things that could get a man killed. Simple things, like dogtags rattling if a man didn't take them off the chain. Dogtags were ID, so to keep up with them, the First Squad tied them to their bootlaces. And they learned to smear them with boot polish or cammo to keep them from reflecting the sunlight or moonlight.

When the rains hit and they had to wade though chest-high streams, they learned to keep their perishables in plastic and stuff them between their helmets and helmet liners. And they found out the need for bending the pins on their grenades when they humped the bush, bending them back so the rings wouldn't catch on sticks or branches, pull out the pin, and blow them all to hell.

And a few of the men learned the hard way about putting Halazone tablets in each canteen of water. Dysentery struck with the first gulp of untreated water. In a hundred and twenty degrees of sweltering humid heat, they drank a lot of water. Then there were the malaria pills and salt tablets. Forget a salt tab and a man was likely to pass out from heat exhaustion.

Corporal Jackson discovered the need for removing his helmet in the scorching heat. He had his brain almost literally fried by leaving it on and had been disoriented for a day and a half.

There were all sorts of practical lessons to be learned now, lessons that weren't in any book. M-14 rifles had to be oiled every single day to prevent jamming at crucial times. Machine guns had the same requirements, and during the monsoons the weapons rusted within the space of a few hours. Lighting up a cigarette at night was suicide, because if the enemy didn't kill you, another Marine might. And leeches had become commonplace. The invertebrates had to be burned off with a match or lighter to keep the head from remaining embedded in the skin, and trouser cuffs were tied tightly to keep some of them out.

Important lessons for the newbys, and they learned quickly. First Squad was with the First Marine Division, the FNGs who caught the brunt of every dirty job.

Jackson swung his machete across the thick grass barring the path to the stream ahead, hacking away foliage and juggling his rifle at the same time, cursing the rain, Vietnam, and the Marines. It was the First Squad's job to cut the path for the rest of them, to make it easy for the others. And it gave him a lot of time to think—too much time to think.

The First Marine Division. Jackson had always wondered why they were called the First Division. He pondered the thought that it might have been they were the First because they were the best. No, he thought, that ain't why. This platoon was the misfits, the ones who couldn't hold a Private First Class stripe past sunset. The First because they were the first troops into a battle, then? No, again. It was the Ninth Marines who were first into this so-called *conflict*. . . . Well, he concluded at last, it must be because they were the first Marines to "Ask not what your country can do for you, but rather what you can do for your country. . . ."

The words of John F. Kennedy flickered through his mind as he pushed on. He could remember when the local Memphis TV station WHBQ had broken from its regular programming to a special news announcement to show the chaotic scene of a Dallas, Texas street parade where the President had been assassinated. Jackson could remember vividly where he had been and what he'd been doing. He'd been half dozing on the large secondhand sofa his dad had bought with money won in a poker game in the back room of a bar on Beale Street. His mother had been in the kitchen making lunch, and had suddenly stopped and begun crying, coming to kneel before the TV set. Tears had thickened her voice as she'd prayed, pleading with God to "Have mercy." His truck-driving dad had sworn long and soft under his breath.

Patriotism had never been something he'd thought much about until now. He wondered why. It was taken for granted, maybe, like hot and cold running water and toilets that flushed and soft mattresses at night. He'd always taken those for granted, too.

Home-cooked meals instead of food eaten from little tin C-ration cans. Shingle roofs to keep out the rain. Those images weren't much consolation to Jackson now. The heavy rains of summer drenched his aching body as he sloshed through the ever-increasing torrents of water that filled his nose and blurred his vision. A man could drown in this shit!

Home was far away, seeming like a faded dream as he gripped his weapon across his chest, military pressing a hundred-pound barbell in a parallel line above the stream he had to ford. The dream dissolved in reality when he pushed through the water ahead of his men. Leeches attached themselves to his body, and he swore softly under his breath.

Robert L. Jackson, Memphis-born and grown, three thousand miles away from everything he knew and loved. What the hell had happened? What had made him join the Marine Corps in the first place? He hadn't been drafted. He was married and had a kid on the way. He could have copped out, stayed home and fought his own kind of war, but he hadn't. Of course, it was the home front that had kinda spurred his decision to join. Joining the Marines and getting shipped out to shoot at a bunch of anonymous faces had seemed a hell of a lot easier than staying in Memphis and sorting out his tangled life. Three women wanting him, and all he could marry was one. Jesus, what a mess! He'd done the best he could, done what he thought was right, but it had still left a lot of hard feelings. Maybe this was the coward's way out, but if it was, he was beginning to think it was a lot harder than the other way.

What was it his daddy used to say? Something

about worrying being useless? Well, he was right. It was useless, just plain useless.

Some other words of his daddy echoed in his head now. Words to a tune, a blues song that he'd heard his daddy sing whenever things seemed hopeless, when the rent was due and money was tight. "Worry don't climb no hills, worry don't pay no bills. . . ." Well, that was right enough. It sure didn't! All his paychecks were going to pay for the damages inflicted on that bar in Tokyo!

The tune faded from his memory as Jackson reached the opposite banks of the muddy stream and slushed out. He took out his cigarette lighter to burn off the leeches clinging to his arms, his neck, anywhere they could find to put their greedy mouths. What a country! Insects as big as some birds, snakes as big as a man's arm, prowling tigers, monkeys, elephants—and the Vietcong, the most dangerous of all. The beauty of the land was deceptive. It hid dark, slithering death in the dense jungle foliage and blinding slash of rain.

The distant sound of choppers and some mortar fire could be heard as the corporal burned off another leech from his forearm. A few hundred meters further up the stream, Jackson could barely make out the vague, blurred outline of the makeshift command post of India and K Companies. Rain pounded dirt, grass, and Marines with unrelenting fury, and he squinted through the steamy air as he trudged forward with his men behind him, heading for the compound.

First Platoon entered the security of the CP with a feeling of relief to be out of the jungle. Some Marines moved slowly through the compound while others lounged in their shallow bunkers. As Jackson's eyes adjusted to the dim light diffused by rain and the fog of his own breath, he saw a familiar figure loom ahead. He blinked, hardly able to believe his eyes. It was Willie Joe Clemens, an old high school buddy, and he was sloshing his way through mud and rain up the hill just ahead of Jackson.

"Willie Joe!" Jackson yelled. "Willie Joe Clemens!" He could feel the big grin on his face and felt slightly foolish to be so happy to see a guy he'd not thought of in a long while. Maybe it was just the idea of seeing somebody he'd grown up with that got to him. Someone from *home* . . .

The tall, lanky Marine turned and gave a start of surprise. "Jack, that you? Man!"

Jackson reached him in two long strides, and the two embraced briefly, both wearing big, foolish grins and babbling out questions and answers in a rapid-fire exchange of words. Jackson's squad bunched behind him as he and Willie Joe waltzed down Memory Lane for a few minutes, recalling mutual friends and their football days in Memphis.

"Where you guys going, Willie?" Jackson ended finally, pushing back his helmet to let the rain drip directly on his face.

"Got orders to go up the hill."

Jackson turned to look back. "Up this hill, huh?"

"Yeah, we got orders to go up this hill and make contact—and don't come back till we do."

"Damn! Sounds kinda hairy, Willie Joe."

Clemens shook his head. "Yeah, I know! But fuck it, Jack. We gotta do something to get outa this shit.

65

This ain't Charlie up here. We got more respect for these gooks. We call 'em Mister Charles 'cause they ain't no hit and run chicken-shits like the local VC. These guys are the 22nd North Vietnamese Army regulars, a whole fuckin' battalion, and they are fuckin' crazy. I mean, I seen 'em still running straight for ya with one of their legs blown clean off, firing like there was no tomorrow. Shit, they gotta be the bravest little sonsabitches I ever seen or doing some damn good dope!" Willie warned.

"Well, Willie, I guess we'll be following you and bringing up the rear. I don't know yet. I haven't heard from Gunner, but I know we can't get no further north. This is the DMZ, 17th parallel, the end of the line. I heard him talking on the horn about this being a major operation, so we're probably in for some deep shit," Jackson said slowly. His broad face was creased in a frown, and some of his foreboding must have transferred to Clemens, because there was a long pause in the conversation.

Willie Joe squished through the ankle-deep mud, shifting from one foot to the other. He swallowed, and Jackson could see his prominent Adam's apple bob like a fishing cork in his skinny neck. "Yeah. Well, see ya at the top, Jack" was all Willie Joe said then.

"Yeah. Later, brother." Jackson gave a "thumbs-up" for luck, then signaled to his men to follow.

A couple of hours later found First Squad happily chowing down on fresh C-rats and reading and re-reading letters from home. They had regrouped and gone for resupply, then had dug into their bunkers for the night. Now it was time to kick back and rest for a while, to do whatever it was Marines could do in this godforsaken country being chewed by artillery and mortar fire.

Mortars were the evening's serenade as Jackson found the driest spot available and settled down with canned ham and lima beans—the closest thing to disgusting that he had yet encountered in a tin can—and dug out his letter from his pack. He hadn't had a chance to read it yet, preferring privacy to the public tearing open of envelopes from home. It was like a prize. First you get this done, then that, and then you can sit back and read about The World. If the letter was from his mother, it would be long and newsy. She would ask, as she always did, if he had seen his brother Raymond, who was also stationed in Vietnam. And then she would write about home, and he could close his eyes and think about ice cold beer, hamburgers sizzling on the grill, and his mama's home-cooking. He could smell the scrubbed-clean air after a summer rain instead of this rotting jungle vegetation, hear lawnmowers instead of mortars, see the girl next door hanging out a load of fresh-washed sheets instead of stacked sandbags and mud bunkers. Yeah, a man needed privacy for letter reading!

Jackson leaned back against a sandbag, put his feet up and crossed them at the ankles, and carefully pried open the letter from home. It felt light and flimsy in his big hand, too thin to be bringing him memories from across the miles.

His smile slowly faded as he scanned the ink-scrawled lines running in irregular dashes and pauses across the paper. *Divorce*. Divorce? Divorce!

The paper crumpled in his fist, and he stared blankly at the opposite wall of sandbags. Divorce.

She wanted a divorce, had gotten tired of waiting and decided that one of his friends would make a better husband. Jackson's mouth was dry, and he felt like a lead weight sat in his stomach.

PFC Sanchez, sauntering past the stone-faced corporal at the time, misread Jackson's expression. Or maybe he read it too well, if a bit unwisely. "What's the matter, Corp?" he asked breezily. "Jody got your girl?"

Jody, meaning bastard who takes your girl while you're gone . . .

Surging upward in a red haze of pain and anger, Jackson never uttered a word as he punched Sanchez in the mouth with his fist. There was a pent-up fury in him, a bottled-up anger that had needed the outlet Sanchez unwittingly provided with his careless remark. But it wasn't enough. He couldn't take out his frustration and private agony on his men and he knew it. He would have to work this out alone.

After Jackson wordlessly stormed away from their bunker and into the steady drizzle, B-gunner Baroni gave a warning shake of his head to the angrily sputtering Sanchez.

"Let it rest man. You said the wrong thing at the wrong time." He gazed after Jackson. "And I'm sure as hell glad Jack's on our side in this crazy war. I've never seen a look like that on a man's face. . . ."

Mean. Mean and reckless were the only words to describe the young black corporal during the next few days of fighting. The months of humping through the boonies, combined with the physical exertion, then the mental stress delivered in a wallop with the mail call, had made Jackson a walking time bomb. He had no smile for jokes, which often lightened the load for everyone in the platoon. And he certainly had no tolerance for the squad's "bitchin'."

The men of First Squad could bitch better than any Jackson had ever heard. If it was raining, they'd bitch that they preferred sunshine. If the sun was shining, they preferred rain. And if it wasn't one thing, it was another, all the time.

Finally fed up with listening to it, Jackson growled, "Listen up, shitbirds! I've had enough of your damn bitchin'. We got our orders from Gunner. First platoon is gonna be TAD—Temporary Assigned Duty— with India Company on this operation, an operation code named Hastings."

Smitty waggled his eyebrows and an imaginary cigar at Jackson, imitating Groucho's voice as he said, "Hey, Jack, don't get Hasty with us! Remember, Hasty makes Waste-y."

Jackson didn't laugh. He just stared at Smitty for a moment with the stone face they weren't accustomed to seeing, with no humor or tolerance in his eyes. "You got a real flare for comedy, don't ya, Smitboy?" he said after a moment of uncomfortable silence. "I swear, you guys would bitch if you were hung with a new rope, wouldn't ya?" Jackson shook his head and looked back down at the map he held. "Never mind. I ain't in no mood for jokes or anything else right now. Just shut up and listen."

First Squad listened. Jackson spelled out the plan in precise detail, interrupted occasionally by a nervous joke from Mudboy or Smitty. Jackson knew the men used humor as an outlet for the fear they felt. He'd done the same—before.

Sparing a brief regret for the lost comradery with his men, Jackson reflected on the the time that had passed since he'd received that "Dear John" letter. It had been hell for him. War was hell anyway, everyone knew that. But without the thought of someone at home waiting on him, a someone he cared about and could dream about at night, carrying her memory with her picture next to his heart, what was it all for? What was the use in living through it? He might as well take as many of the enemy as he could with him. And he fully intended to do so.

Jackson straightened his shoulders, feeling the eyes on him as he tried to concentrate on the map. Maybe he should try harder to get back his former rapport with his men. He'd hate to lose their respect.

He needn't have worried. The men of First Squad had a lot of respect for Corporal Robert Jackson. They liked him as a man and respected him as a leader. The past months had proven Jackson to be a more than competent leader. Not only was his physique impressive, but so was his sixth sense about separating the bullshit SOP—Standard Operating Procedure—from actual field experience. He'd proven it time and again during the past months in the bush. Hadn't he walked point more than his share of the time? Jackson's coolness under fire was impressive, and he seemed able to smell out a trip wire, booby trap, or land mine before anyone else.

"Uncanny," Baroni said.

"Pure luck," Sanchez countered.

But the results were the same: undiluted admiration from the members of First Squad. Jackson looked out for them and they knew it. It was a great motivator. The only thing was, now that he'd gotten that letter, would he be too reckless? Too ready to die? Word of his "Dear John" letter had traveled fast, and the men were wary of him.

The old Jack that they had known just a few days before had disappeared and been replaced by an angry, "more than willing to die" zealot who was about to unleash his animosity on an entire battalion of NVAs that were waiting for them on top of the hill. This could spell trouble with a capital *T*.

Paul "the Bug" Clayton commented on Jackson's new attitude with a laconical, "Well, like my daddy always said, 'The proof's in the puddin'."

So now the big question loomed ahead of them: What would happen tomorrow on the hill?

CHAPTER 4

Talk had circulated through the squad about Jackson's letter from home, so most of the men steered clear of the corporal. It was widely hoped that his depression and anger would soon pass, though it seemed as if it grew worse with each step up the hill. The weight of his M-14 and fifty-caliber machine gun receiver was the physical complement to the emptiness and rage that warred in his heart.

Marine Recon had located four main trails and numerous footpaths the NVA were using near the 17th parallel. Daily, they were filtering troops and tons of equipment and supplies across the DMZ into South Vietnam, through what was most commonly referred to as the Ho Chi Minh Trail. This trail was not one particular trail as some might think, but rather a maze of foot trails and bulldozed roads, and even underground tunnel networks the enemy used to their advantage.

India, K, and Charlie Companies' mission was to take Hill 682. Corporal Jackson and First Platoon were attached to India Company as a provisional rifle squad on this operation. Jackson's men—Crawford, Mudders, Doc Weathers, Smitty, Carrigan, "Bug" Clayton, Baroni, Sanchez, Grover, Delisi, and Gagliano—were in First Squad.

There were two hundred seventy-three men in India Company and they were to ascend the hill first, with K and Charlie Companies to flank them on either side.

As the men began to slowly toil up the hill, they came across what appeared to be one of the main trails. One by one they paused to listen as they received the hand signals that passed down the line of sweating Marines. Time passed in a trickle of minutes, dragging by as they waited tensely for the next signal to move. When Jackson—alert and wary and noticing that there was a total absence of sound—gave the signal, the Marines inched forward. No birdcalls sounded in the thick underbrush; no monkeys chattered in the trees. Total silence, a silence so pervasive and thick it could almost be felt.

Most of India Company had only made it a little more than halfway up the hill when mortar rounds hit the front ranks in a rattle of thundering fire. It hit the front line first, then tore into the ranks behind Jackson and his squad. Blistering hailstorms of AK-47 bullets ripped through the first few platoons of India Company, leaving most of them dead or wounded and screaming for medics.

India Company cowered down in the sparse underbrush, with no real shelter and no way to get to any. As he fumbled with the fifty-caliber, Jackson shouted an order to his squad to fall back, hoping there was somewhere to fall back to. Then Jackson and Baroni leaped backward into one of the craters the mortars had made and frantically began to assemble the tripod, receiver, and barrel of the fifty-caliber. Within only a matter of seconds, the gun was on the tripod and Jackson began spraying in the direction from which he saw the enemy's automatic fire coming.

It occurred to him as he manned the gun that someone had once commented on the life expectancy of a machine gunner in a firefight. The average was around eight seconds. Not a very good average for a young man.

Kneeling in the dirt chewed up by a frenzy of bullets, Jackson kept his fifty-caliber rattling in a bone-jarring shower of death. All around him men were falling, dead or dying or just screaming. Splinters of steel fragments from exploding mortar shells spit death into the air at random, and Jackson kept firing.

There was no time to think about what was happening around him, no time to wonder if he would make it or what if he didn't. There was only time to load and fire, for Baroni to feed the hot metal belt through the fifty-caliber, then to take out as many of Charlie as he could with his M-14.

Jungle foliage was being shredded like lettuce around him by the withering blast of bullets, stripping trees bare. As it fell away almost as if by magic, it revealed some well-camouflaged bunkers.

"Bull's-eye!" Jackson breathed softly, whipping his machine gun around and pouring it on.

Small khaki-clad men darted for cover, their red scarves fluttering in the hot wind, AK-47's chattering back. A grim smile curled his mouth as Jackson

74

worked the machine gun toward them in a sweeping motion. The heavy gun thudded against his chest as he kept firing, and he saw bodies lifted into the air by the force of the bullets. NVA heads exploded in a curious shower of crimson froth as the devastating fifty-caliber slugs tore through them, and arms and legs whirled in grisly imitations of miniature pinwheels as they were parted from their bodies.

In the dim light made even more hazy by the thick cloud of smoke, Jackson could barely see his burned, blistered hands. To prevent meltdown, Baroni would use gloves to remove the barrel from the fifty-caliber every hundred rounds or so, then would screw in another one. Once or twice the used barrel was so hot it set the ground on fire around it. It was during the lull while Baroni replaced the barrel that Jackson spared a moment to be glad he'd ignored everyone's warnings about lugging around that heavy fifty-caliber. It had sure come in handy in spite of the dire predictions!

Self-congratulations abruptly gave way to self-preservation as an incoming mortar whined down to explode some ten meters away on Jackson's left flank. Ducking quickly, he grabbed Baroni and dove back into the crater. A metallic clang sounded loudly against the side of his helmet as he hit the dirt, and Jackson gave a dazed shake of his head. Ears rang like church bells, and he could barely hear. Gunfire sounded muffled and distant, a low accompaniment to the ringing in his ears. Gingerly feeling the side of his helmet, Jackson discovered an indentation one quarter of an inch thick. Loose shrapnel had decorated his metal helmet with a vengeance!

Only minutes earlier he had been complaining to Baroni of his helmet being too hot and had almost taken it off. The only thing that had stopped him was an indefinable feeling, a premonition maybe, that had made him keep that hot sweatbox on his even hotter head. Sweat poured down the sides of his face. This was too close for comfort. Maybe he should pay more attention to his instincts instead of orders, he decided then, and right now instinct told him to move—and fast.

"Come on, Baroni!" Jackson yelled as he snatched up the hot gun and began to shift from their crater to another one just made by a mortar hitting on their right. First the left, then the right. The next mortar would be right on the money, Jackson thought as he scuttled across the torn earth between the craters. Baroni was hard on his heels.

He was right. The next one hit minutes later in the spot where they'd been, and he stared at the smoking hole with detached interest. If they'd still been there . . .

It was as if it were happening on a big movie screen, Jackson thought once. Only the sickly sweet smell of death and the hot breath of bullets kept him aware of the reality of war. Everything he did was automatic, his reflexes taking over when his instincts might have urged him to run. Maybe it was a dream, a nightmare, and he wasn't really firing bullets from a fifty-caliber, watching men explode into nothing recognizable, hearing men he'd eaten with, talked with, fought with, die with agonized screams and that peculiar gurgling sound. And knowing that maybe he'd be the next one launched into the air by an exploding

76

rocket or grenade didn't make it seem any more real to him.

Reality would come later, long after night fell in a thick, pressing cloak of darkness, hiding the enemy as well as themselves. The Marines couldn't move forward, couldn't move back. But neither could the NVA.

India Company called frantically for air and artillery strikes, Gunner ducking bullets as he hugged the mike. The RTO lay sprawled on the ground, sightless eyes staring into space, his radio still attached to his back as Gunner begged for help that wouldn't come. They were too close to the enemy. Choppers couldn't angle into the area because of the withering fire of the NVAs. Charlie and K Companies were having the same bad luck; they were pinned down in position.

Dead and wounded littered the battle area with little hope of getting them out any time soon. When possible, Jackson, Baroni, Delisi, Mudders, or one of the others would leap from behind cover and drag a wounded man back to the comparative safety of their shelter. But those opportunities were few and far between. Most of the time they had to listen to the cries of the wounded growing weaker and weaker, some finally fading away entirely. It was at those times that Jackson felt most helpless, most infuriated. Would it never end?

The next twenty-eight days—the time between July 7 and August 3—would be the longest weeks of Jackson's life. Day after day, the Marines of India Company were whittled down by the 324th Battalion, North Vietnamese Army. And the nights were the worst.

When dark settled down over the jungle and fire-blasted fields, Charlie could crawl so close to the Marines that their faces would no longer be anonymous blurs under the bright flare of rifle fire. Flares arced continuously in the black sky, making it light one minute, dark the next. At these times, Marines would go down to the bottom of the hill to resupply, taking wounded with them and bringing back up ammo, water, and food.

Jackson lay back on the hard ground, his muscles too tense to allow him to relax, his mind refusing to cooperate with his efforts not to remember *the letter.* It didn't matter that the dark was frequently split with orange bursts of rifle fire and an occasional "Fuck you, GI!" in a Vietnamese accent. Grenades usually accompanied this sentiment a split second later, followed by an agonized howl and scream of "Corpsman!" This, in turn, precipitated another volley of shots from both sides.

During a moment of unexpected quiet from both sides, Jackson stared up at the smoke-blurred night sky while he thought about nothing. It was a struggle to think about nothing, he learned. How hard could it be to empty your mind of anything but the moment? But it was, and he turned over on his side and gave Baroni a swift nudge in his ribs.

"Hey, Baroni. What'cha thinkin' about, man?"

Turning his dirt-smeared face toward Jackson, Baroni gave him a wide-eyed stare before answering. Then, with an embarrassed grin, he confessed, "Home. Hot dogs, cold beer, CYO dances with all those wild Italian Catholic chicks." Another pause, then, "Ya ever think what you'd be doin' if you

78

weren't here, Jack? I mean, I used to think this place was just temporary, kinda like a dream. But now—now I think I've woken up and this place ain't no damn dream at all. This is forever. . . ."

Jackson couldn't say anything for a minute, then he summoned up the less-than-comforting reply, "That's a hell of a thought, Baroni! But for right now, the only dancing we're gonna be doing is dancing with Charlie, and we better learn how to dance pretty damn good, too!"

"Yeah. That bothers me. And you know what else bothers me, Jackson?"

"No, what?"

"Everything I eat turns to shit. . . ."

There was a brief instant of dumbfounded silence, then Jackson burst into laughter. Punching Baroni in his shoulder with a bunched fist, Jackson said, "Get outa here, man!"

The next day was no better than the last, or the day before that or the day before that. The hours melded into one another with little to differentiate them. Different faces, maybe, different assault waves, but other than that, it was a continuous line of the same. Load, aim, fire, load, aim, fire, over and over and over again. Maybe move ten meters up, ten meters sideways. Slowly but surely, the Marines were making their way up that damn hill. It was their job, and by damn, they were gonna do it.

Those endless nights were always the same. Every morning at about 0300 hours the firing stopped for at least a couple of hours or so. It was always a welcome relief, and it took several nights for Jackson to notice something odd about that quiet. In spite of his somewhat impaired hearing capabilities, he could detect a strange rumble that seemed to drift up from the belly of the earth. That set him to wondering. . . .

It was during one of those lulls, when Jackson was feeling the faint rumbles and wondering about them, that Bug crawled up and fell into the hole with Jackson and Baroni. His round face was creased into a frown as he said softly, "Hey, Jack."

"Bugman, shhh." Jackson motioned with his finger to be quiet. "Listen. You hear that?"

"Yeah, that's what I wanted to talk to you about, Jack. I think I know what's making that noise."

Jackson and Baroni both perked up as Bug scooted closer. "Over near my foxhole I noticed a small hole a couple a feet away from me, an' when that noise started up again, I got this crazy idea. I talked to some tunnel rats that worked the Iron Triangle area down south, you know, around Cu Chi. They told me how the VC got this elaborate tunnel system down there. Anyway, to make it short, they told me every hundred or so feet underground the VC have to have ventilation holes. Knowing this, I just crawled over there to the hole and lit a match by it. Damned if the smoke didn't suck right into that hole, Jack! I think they got a tunnel and we're sitting right on top of it!"

"But what about the noise?" Baroni asked. Jackson answered before anyone.

"I know! A damn gasoline-engine-type air pump to suck fresh air down into the tunnel!"

"Bingo!" Bug exclaimed.

"Bugman, you never cease to fuckin' amaze me."

Jackson grinned. "Go tell Gunner and see what you can do to remedy this situation."

Bug scrambled off on all fours and was gone as quickly as he'd come. Jackson turned to Baroni and said, "What a guy, that Bug!"

It was no time until Bug had talked to Gunner and had returned to the hole with a few CS gas grenades. He carefully tossed one of them into the small oblique ventilation hole, then worked swiftly to stuff the hole with mud and debris so the gas would not escape upward. Within a few minutes, members of First Squad saw numerous other places where the gas was escaping, other ventilation holes, maybe even entrances. They decided to wait and see what happened.

AK-47 fire started further up the hill. Moving back to position, Jackson opened up and walked his red tracers up the hill until he hit the area from where the muzzle flashes were coming. A flare lit the night suddenly, and red-scarfed NVA could be seen scuttling out of holes everywhere, retreating up the hill.

"Look at 'em!" Crawdad crowed, standing up to lob a grenade. "They look like ants coming outa those holes!"

He and Mudboy began tossing grenades as fast as they could. Grover, the only other black guy in the squad and the grenadier, got off a couple as quick as he could, firing his M-79, while Smitty, Carrigan, Delisi, and Gagliano opened up with their M-14's. The firing ceased, and for the rest of the night all was quiet.

A little before dawn, Gunner found Jackson and told him to get his squad up the hill and get as many

Killed In Action and Wounded In Action as they could off the hill because they were gonna call in the 105's, 107's, and 155's as soon as possible.

"It seems that Mr. Charles retreated just far enough away for us to get a little artillery support," Gunner remarked in a relieved tone, then added, "We can't leave our boys up there. They're Marines, and damn brave ones."

Jackson and eleven other men of his squad, along with a couple of other Marines from Third Squad, began silently making their way through devastated landscape in search of dead. The fire-blasted terrain smoked where it had been bombed. Yellowish craters pockmarked the land ahead where thousand-pound bombs had been dropped by B-52's.

A Marine from Third Squad by the name of Kennard walked beside Jackson. As they struggled with the lifeless, mangled body of one of their fallen comrades, the NVA suddenly opened fire again. Bullets whirled past them in a buzzing fury. Jackson dropped for cover next to Kennard, with the taste of dirt and grass in his mouth as well as the less palatable bite of fear. He lay there with his arms crossed over his head, trying to make himself invisible, hoping it would pass soon. Peering over his arm to check on his comrade, Jackson sucked in a deep breath. Kennard was sprawled out on his back. The first blast of bullets had come so fast he'd had no time to react, and it looked as if he'd caught a round in the stomach.

A groan escaped Jackson as he inched forward and leaned over to take a look at Kennard. Bullets continued to fly past his head as he stuck out a hand to check the Marine.

"Jack!" Baroni was screaming, "Get down here!" Mortar rounds began to burst haphazardly around Jackson as he gave himself a push and rolled in an erratic line over the grass and rocks on the hill, over and over, head over heels, hoping like hell no stray bullet or mortar would find him.

By means of rolls, twists, and a sort of crawling slither, Jackson finally made it back to his foxhole. Baroni was manning the fifty-caliber. He looked up when Jackson tumbled into the crater beside him.

"Jack, they're all over the fuckin' place!" Baroni yelled over the noises of the chattering gun and shattering explosions.

Jackson didn't bother to acknowledge the obvious. Automatically, without even pausing to think about it, he began pulling pins on grenades and tossing them where he saw the enemy and even where he didn't. Every time one hit it would catapult three or four NVA into the air like a trampoline. Following Jackson's lead, Crawdad and Mudboy tossed their remaining grenades into the steady stream of enemy running down the hill. Carrigan and Bug were plowing their side of the hill with magazine after magazine of M-14 rounds on full automatic.

Crazy as it seemed, some of the NVA would still be advancing after they had been hit countless times in the chest and head. Blood would be streaming over them and they'd still be advancing, stumbling forward like something out of a bad horror movie.

One crazed NVA even made it all the way to Carrigan's foxhole after the Marine had emptied almost a full clip into the man's belly. Straining backward, Carrigan and Bug swung their barrels around and

83

simultaneously pulled the triggers. Nothing! Both Marines were out of ammo at the same time.

Bug began to feverishly reload, but it was too much for Carrigan. Rising to his full height, he towered above his foxhole as the NVA charged him. Taking one step backward for balance, Carrigan lifted his M-14 like it was a wooden baseball bat, positioning it on his shoulder in the best Babe Ruth stance, and swung like he was going for a home run in Yankee Stadium. The gook's face exploded in a shower of blood and bone as the rifle stock connected with a resounding thwack. The NVA dropped to the ground.

Carrigan shook his head as he wiped the rifle butt clean on the enemy's clothes. "Damn, that's got to be one of the bravest little son of a bitches I ever did see!" he muttered as he searched for a full ammo clip to reload.

"No," Bug said as he continued to spray the area. "I think these gooks are primed with some damn good kinda dope! Did you see his eyes, man? Glassy. They must shoot these guys up with somethin', then send them out to kill and be killed. They don't even know when to stop . . . like those guys! Look," he ended, pointing with his rifle barrel.

Carrigan turned to look at the NVA soldiers stumbling across the hill and craters, some with missing arms that couldn't even hold a rifle and some with chests full of lead, their eyes glassy as they kept going.

"It's like the fuckin' zombie movie, *Night of the Living Dead*," he breathed, staring with detached fascination as the enemy kept coming in erratic waves.

"Yeah, only this ain't no damn movie, and these guys are out to kill us," Bug shot back, squinting along his rifle and squeezing the trigger. An NVA went down as the bullet tore into his leg, knocking it from under him. "And maybe that's the way to slow them down—make 'em crawl."

When the assault wave began to slow, Carrigan reloaded. His adrenaline was pumping as he surged up out of his foxhole and brandished his M-14 over his head. Letting out a whoop like Tarzan of the jungle, Carrigan yelled, "Come on, you bunch a little doped-up gooks! I got something for ya. Come on! Come on and get some!" The Tarzan yell rose over the noise of battle, accompanied by the rhythmic spraying of automatic fire.

Bug reached up and snagged Carrigan's belt, giving a hard yank to bring him back down into the hole. "Get down here! I swear, I think you've knocked your head against the roof of one too many coal mine tunnels."

Jackson added his order for the hulking Montana boy to cease fire. "Shut up, Carrigan, and quit wasting ammo," he yelled across the ground. "We're gonna need all we can, so save it, man, just save it."

Stress had them all tense and ready to crack as First Squad tried to fire in all directions at once. It was more than enough; the maximum of sheer panic and surge of adrenaline one moment, then the nerve-racking waiting in silence the next, was beginning to take a toll on all of the men.

Then the assault receded, and it was quiet. No mortars fell and no rifle fire sounded except for an occasional random shot. For the moment the attack had ceased, and this was an opportunity for the men of First Squad to continue the search for wounded and dead.

Jackson was the first to climb out of his safe crater and return to the search. Leaving Baroni with the fifty-caliber to cover him in case of some ambitious NVA, Jackson edged his way back to where Kennard's body was sprawled in a pool of blood.

Crawling low to the ground, Jackson inched his way to a downed tree. He peered over the rough, bullet-chewed bark, and what he saw made him sick and furious at the same time. Two NVA soldiers were standing over dead Marines, ripping at them in a sideways motion with the points of their bayonets, gutting them like animals.

Something hit Jackson as he watched, a cold fury that blotted out common sense and self-preservation. Maybe it was the methodical manner of the NVAs as they plunged, ripped, and slashed, or maybe it was their expressions of satisfaction that got him, but whatever it was, Jackson felt a raging hatred that totally engulfed him.

Leaping up with reckless abandon, Jackson didn't care that he was in full view of the two enemy soldiers. Running in a half crouch, he opened up on full automatic, firing at them like a crazed lunatic. Luck was with him. The NVA were so engrossed in their butchery that they didn't hear or see him coming until it was too late. The first spray of bullets caught them totally by surprise, and they tried to swing their weapons up to fire. Jackson's bullets smacked into them with satisfying thumps, and he kept running as their bodies jerked rhythmically with each hit. A few feet before the NVA finally fell, his clip was emptied.

Reaching them, Jackson didn't pause. In the same smooth motion the NVA had used, he plunged his own bayonet into the already-dead enemy soldiers, then slashed them like they had slashed his comrades.

The short, undeclared truce was over. Spurred by Jackson's vengeance, other Marines had leaped from their craters and were hard on his heels. Carrigan, Bug, Smitty, Mudboy, and Crawdad followed his example, and rifle fire racketed in the air again as they were fired upon by NVAs on both flanks.

None would have considered themselves as heroes, only as friends looking out for their buddies. That was what it was, pure and simple. No more. No less. The result: some ten or eleven more dead NVA.

After surrendering to his frenzy of vengeance by decapitating the dead NVA and smashing their heads, Jackson stumbled over to where Kennard still lay. He dropped to his knees beside the Marine's body.

Kennard had been ripped open with a bayonet, and a length of his intestines lay looped in grayish pink curls on the ground. Fighting nausea, Jackson began to methodically stuff the fat loops back into Kennard's torn abdomen. He did his best to button the shirt over them, hoping to keep them inside Kennard's body. It seemed obscene, somehow, that a man's guts should be dragging in the dirt, and he felt a compulsion to keep Kennard together.

Then, dragging Kennard's body back down the hill as the sun colored the east with faint light, Jackson saw the extent of the devastation wrought during the night. Red was the color of the day. Blood was every-

87

where, drawing insets and smelling sickly sweet, already drying in the heat.

Shuddering, Jackson was reminded of pictures he'd seen in the *Memphis Press-Scimitar*, photos taken by a satellite sent into space. The ground around him looked like a cratered moonscape, hacked and dented by meteorites, maybe, and decorated with the charred remains of a forest fire. And he thought suddenly of Cates Butcher Shop down on Third Street, where his mother used to send him for fresh meat. All those red, raw sides of beef hanging in the back, and the hogs strung up on huge meat hooks had had the same kind of stunned, surprised look on long-dead faces. Death must look the same for every living thing, Jackson thought as he reached the bottom of the hill with Kennard.

Marine bodies as well as NVA ones lay in bloody, jellied pools across tree stumps and half in and half out of mortar holes. Parts of the human anatomy—hands, legs, heads, even feet still wearing barely scuffed regulation boots—cropped up everywhere. The odor was nauseating, making a man almost lose his breath as the sun rose and began to ripen the quickly rotting flesh.

But the worst was over. For the remainder of the day it was mostly quiet, with only an occasional burst of fire from stragglers of the beaten 324B NVAs. Time was spent hauling the dead and wounded down the hill to a secured LZ near the river. Body bags were stacked in the LZ like cordwood as choppers arrived, loaded them, then took off as fast as they'd landed.

It fell to Jackson and Baroni to help load body bags on board the choppers. While they were hurrying toward a waiting chopper with one of the slick, anonymous bags between them, Baroni stumbled and dropped his end. It landed with a solid thunk that made Jackson wince, and he bent quickly to help pick it back up.

Sweat poured from his head, spattering on the bag as he bent close. Jackson had just helped lift it again when he heard a muffled cough come from inside the bag. Startled, he almost dropped the bag in his haste to tear it open.

It was Kennard. A chill shot through Jackson when he saw that the man was still alive. His eyes were open, and he was coughing up phlegm.

"Medic!" Jackson yelled as loudly as he could. "Medic!"

"That—that's Kennard," Baroni said as he helped Jackson rip away the rest of the body bag from the Marine's face.

"Yeah, man, I know," Jackson choked out. His hands were shaking, and he could hardly believe Kennard was alive. The medic had arrived and was pushing them aside, all professional and expert as he began to shove needles into Kennard's arm.

"I'm sorry man, I'm sorry!" Jackson said to Kennard. "I thought you were dead, man. . . ."

Kennard's voice was a hoarse whisper as he mumbled, "I did, too."

Jackson's lips twitched. "Don't worry, man. Doc's here."

"What happened here, Jack?" Doc asked as he shot Kennard up with some antibiotic.

Shaking his head, Jackson said he didn't really know. "We dropped him, Doc, and when we went to pick him back up . . . I mean, it was just an accident! We're both dead tired and I guess . . ." He ended with a helpless shrug.

Doc Weather shot him a smile. "Well, you might have just saved his life. Apparently, that fall knocked the wind back into him. A few more minutes, and he'd have been on that chopper with no air and no hope. . . . This is one lucky soldier!"

Dazed and unbelieving, Jackson kept mumbling over and over, "Sorry, man. I'm sorry I dropped you. . . ."

Weathers gave him a nudge. "Hey! Don't worry about it, Jack. I'm telling you, he's probably alive because of you! It's not your fault he was in this body bag. I was the one who looked at him and pronounced him dead, remember? Now shut up and help get the rest of the wounded on those medevacs."

Nodding, Jackson complied, but he and Baroni would occasionally pause and look at one another with a sort of stunned disbelief. The incident with Kennard left the rest of the day with a surrealistic aura, as if nothing else could happen that would shake their composure. It didn't matter how many mangled men they had to load. The one incident had left in them a feeling of hope for the future, the thought that maybe, just maybe, Someone was up there watching.

It was around sunset when Gunner gave the orders for them to move out. Jackson was sitting with Baroni, eating C-rats and gazing into space, not really thinking of anything special, just letting time drift past.

Standing straddle-legged, Gunner bellowed, "Jackson! Get your men and saddle up. We gotta *di-di* outa here pronto. We got air and arty strikes coming soon."

Jackson groaned. "What? You mean we gotta hump outa here? Why can't we ride on the slicks?"

Gunner shook his head. "Too many of you for one slick, Jackson. Besides, Corporal, we got our orders. Don't ask me. I ain't in no better mood than you about this shit. I guess they want us to recon our way back to Highway 9, then maybe we can hitch a ride with some deuces back to Quang Tri."

"Fuck, if it ain't one thing, it's another!" Heaving a sigh, Jackson scooped out the last of his corned beef hash and spread it on a stale cracker. He shoved it into his mouth and chewed slowly, wondering just how in the hell they expected what was left of India Company to do much of anything.

The two hundred sixty-three men in India Company when the battle started had been diminished to just sixty-nine men. The consolation was that some eight hundred eighty-two North Vietnamese regulars had been killed, with the hope of a lot more than that being wounded. Maybe the little bastards would be out of commission for a long time, Jackson reflected as he tossed away his empty C-rat can.

Orders were orders, and India Company prepared to obey. As the weary Marines fell in and began to march south, they splashed through Ben Hai River and toward Highway 9. The frigid mountain water was a relief from the scorching heat, and Jackson knew he could deal with this kind of wet a lot better than the constant monsoons. Even the leeches were better than rain up a man's nose that filled his lungs with hot, moist air.

"Hell," Jackson muttered to Delisi. "Don't this damned country have any compromises in the weather? It's either hot enough to fry your brains or wet enough to boil 'em!"

Delisi, a short, dark Italian who looked more like the Frito Bandito than a Roman, gave a weary shake of his head and said, in a tortured New Jersey accent, "Hey, man! It beats being shipped out in a body bag."

"Occasionally," Jackson admitted. "Occasionally."

A dull roar filled the air, and they looked up to see jets winging across the sky in metallic streaks of light. Tilting back his head, Jackson watched them slice past, then saw a blinding flare of napalm light up the top of the hill they'd just left. The ground shook like an earthquake had hit, and the entire horizon was ablaze in seconds. A second blast immediately followed, then another. Artillery rounds thundered against the mountain in relentless fervor.

"If anything was left on top of that hill, it is now definitely 'toast,' " Jackson mused aloud. Finally, he was able to joke again in the midst of horror, and it was a release.

"Yeah, toast of tortellinis!" Delisi joked as he clambered up the riverbanks and wiped his rifle dry. The ground was still trembling, a faint vibration that made the river water shimmer and the high grasses dance. Jackson looked around him. If he didn't look up to see the black clouds in the sky but kept his eyes on the peaceful water and soft, waving grasses, he could almost think he was home, and right up that country road would be a white frame house with a wraparound front porch and apple cider in a cool

92

stone jug. But he wasn't. And in the air was the smell of napalm, Vietnam perfume. . . .

CHAPTER 5

The hump was slow and tedious. The memory of Hastings lingered in the minds of First Squad as they trudged toward the highway. When they finally made it through chest-high elephant grass that slashed at unprotected arms, faces, and necks, arriving at Highway 9 cursing the grass and the worrisome insects attracted by the bloody scratches, several five-ton trucks were squatting in the road, blessedly awaiting the weary Marines. Transportation! Relief from the boiling sun and tall grasses! Sitting instead of walking!

No one minded the cramped quarters inside the trucks, or that a collective body of men stuffed inside the back of a truck had a certain fragrance that could be compared to a garbage dump. It didn't matter that much to the weary Marines. And it sure beat walking. Two hundred klicks and ten sweat-soaked Winston cigarettes later, Jackson and the others arrived at the outskirts of Chu Lai.

The five tonners rumbled to a stop on the sandy beaches of a peninsula. A few shabby huts, wrinkle-eyed old women, young Vietnamese kids, and leaky fishing boats were framed in the view from inside the trucks. Gunner's voice reverberated louder than the truck engines as he bellowed, "All right, men! This is the end of the line. Fall out and fall in!"

As the sweaty Marines tumbled out of the trucks, Gunner watched them assemble in ragged lines before he continued. "Take off your packs and rest awhile. We gotta wait a couple of hours until the ferry gets here to take us over to Chu Lai. And listen up! Word from intelligence is that we are not—I repeat *not*—to buy anything from these villagers. Got that? No candy, Cokes—anything." Gunner walked along the lines, his hands behind his back, his eyes hard. "Although the villagers have been ordered not to sell Americans anything, they have a tendency to do it anyway, so the final solution rests with you. Two Marines are dead from poisoning, and it is believed that the VC are buying goods on the black market, poisoning them, and selling the shit back to us. Just another nice way Charlie employs to welcome us to Vietnam." Gunner's brow lifted as he scanned the line, and he gave the order to "Dismiss!"

Hot and sweaty, the Marines were only half listening to Gunner as they sucked in fresh salt air and felt cool wind blow on their faces. Poisoned Coke and candy didn't seem nearly as bad as being crammed in the back of a truck and being banged over two hundred klicks of rocky roads. And the lure of the waves on the beach made more of an impression than anything else right now.

Gunner was barely out of earshot before the lines of men had dumped weapons and packs on the sand

95

and stripped down to their skivvies. It was a race to see who got to the water first.

Jackson shrugged out of his heavy pack and let it fall to the sand. Then he dropped down in front of it, leaned back, crossed his arms behind his head, and just watched his men run into the sea like school kids at recess.

Bug and Baroni imitated Jackson, preferring to remain onshore for the moment, a natural wariness holding them back from acting on impulse. For Jackson, it was a trait newly learned, this waiting and watching, this unnatural caution that kept him from plunging into the breakers beside his men. There was no obvious danger, yet he could not bring himself to throw aside his caution.

Looking at the beach, it was easy to imagine a tropical paradise, a vacation spot, but the memories of his wife's letter and the past few months of battle would not fade. They intruded with sharp-edged clarity. Relaxation was difficult for Jackson, but he could appreciate the fact that it was less hard for his men.

Seeing the men's tension evaporate as they splashed in the ocean, wrestling and playing piggyback like carefree kids, was of some consolation to him. They deserved a break. Maybe Gunner was right and they were a bunch of misfits, but they were also some of the bravest men he'd ever known. His gaze drifted over them, from the mountainous Carrigan to small, dark Delisi. . . . They were the best damned team in the Marines as far as Jackson was concerned. And they were his family now, his only family.

Damn, he loved them like brothers. Their color didn't matter, nor their race. The luck of the draw had brought them together, and comradery and danger kept them tight. One man could depend upon the other. These men were all he had to live for, to fight for.

Stretching, Jackson's gaze shifted to Baroni. The hot-tempered Italian had covered his ass more than once in the bush and probably would again. Baroni didn't ask for or expect thanks, and it was an unspoken understanding that Jackson would do the same for him. It was the same with all of them.

A clinking sound drew Jackson's attention to Bug, who was fiddling with a pair of needle-nosed pliers and an M-14 cartridge. A familiar Winston dangled from between his lips as Bug concentrated on the shiny shell cradled in his palm, and Jackson shook his head. Hell, that guy was something else. Never a wasted moment for him. Bug was always fooling around with his weapon or some new kind of gadget he was trying to invent.

Crawdad and Mudboy were engaged in a familiar ritual—argument. Crawdad was sitting in a lotus position, arguing that his old '57 Chevy could outrun Mudboy's brother's '63 Corvette any day of the week. It was a favorite argument. The only thing that they agreed upon was that they liked C-rations. That incomprehensible compromise baffled Jackson. He figured that any man who would confess to actually liking the metallic taste of what was unaffectionately referred to as "that shit" had to be a little off his rocker.

And Delisi and Gagliano, the stud brothers as Baroni called them, were engaged in their favorite activity bullshitting one another. Delisi was always bragging about all the women he'd had, and Gag would always come up with a more fantastic romantic interlude. Disgruntled, Delisi had once remarked, "Hell, I don't fuckin' understand it. A guy screws over a hundred or so chicks and gets called a womanizer. I don't understand it, I just don't understand it."

But Gagliano had topped him with, "Yeah, yeah, Delisi! I believe you screwed that many *girls*, not *women*. The hundred girls you banged—hell, their total ages probably don't add up to much more than that! You like little girls. I love women. I like women the way I like my wine. The longer you wait on it, the better it is when you pop the cork. I mean, I like older women. I like my meat 'well-done.' "

Delisi had sputtered and stammered but had not been able to think of a good comeback for Gag's boast, and Jackson knew he would try again.

Then there was always Smitty. Crazy Smitty, who couldn't say anything without impersonating a famous actor or a comedian. There were times Jackson was convinced that the spirit of Groucho Marx was now dwelling in the young Marine's body. Smitty couldn't talk without mimicking the famous comedian's eyebrow twitch and cigar smoking. But for a point man, Smitty was the best. He was quick, real quick. He had eagle eyes in the bush and more than once had saved them all by detecting booby traps in the jungle.

Carrigan, on the other hand, was slow but steady. Rock-of-Gibraltar-type chin and a slow wit. The guy couldn't catch a joke if handed a catcher's mitt. Yet when it came time to *dance with Charlie*, the Montana coal miner could do the watusi.

Doc Weathers was the most idealistic. He had a heart of gold. He'd joined the Navy as a medic, thinking he could save lives and do "something" worthwhile with his own life. The Peace Corps had appealed to him, but the Marine Corps had gotten him. Weathers had grown up around guns on a ranch in northern Idaho, where his father had run an outfitter and guide service for big game. At a young age, Doc had decided to become a veterinarian, but this war had started and pressure from the ole man to follow his footsteps in the service was too great. He'd enlisted.

PFC Wendell Grover had joined for another reason. He just loved to fight. A golden glove champ at the age of sixteen, the sight of blood aroused him. The street gangs had taught him the hard way. The "gloves" had given him the discipline to do something with his uncharted anger. Marines taught him the control.

Sanchez. Sullen Sanchez had a chip on his shoulder so big you could build a house on it. Why? Jackson couldn't figure it. The guy was an accident waiting to happen. He was a follower and blamed his situation on everybody else. Sanchez refused to accept responsibility for his own actions. He thought the world owed him a living. This attitude was reflected in everything he did, and the platoon recognized it. Some early attempts had been made to rid Sanchez of his attitude, but one by one the men had given up on him. Now he was tolerated, a loner, and largely avoided.

Jackson shifted on the hot sand, then decided to go

into the ocean and cool off like the others. Rising, he started toward the wet sand where white froth curled in enticing invitation. At least the sea winds felt good, were a lot cooler than anything he'd yet encountered in this sun-blasted country.

As Jackson waded through the hot sand, hopping slightly because it burned his feet, he happened to see Sanchez talking to a village kid of about fourteen or fifteen. The skinny kid in loose shorts and no shirt had a satchel slung over his shoulder and was gesturing animatedly while he spoke with Sanchez. Jackson paused to watch. He felt a surge of anger when he saw the kid pull a Coca-Cola bottle from his satchel and trade it to the Marine for American scrip.

"The dumb-ass sonofabitch!" Jackson swore. "Didn't he pay any attention to Gunner?" he asked aloud, knowing the answer. "What the fuck is wrong with him?"

Smitty glanced up from where he was sprawled on the sand, blinking in confusion, thinking Jackson was talking to him. "Huh? What'sa matter, Corp?"

But Jackson was too mad to reply, and he stormed across the beach toward Sanchez. He reached him just as Sanchez lifted the opened bottle to his lips. The side of Jackson's left hand connected with the bottle, slapping it away and into the sand, while his right fist bunched and came up under the hapless Marine's chin.

Sanchez collapsed in a heap on the broiling beach. "What the fuck is wrong with you, man!" Jackson snapped. "Do you have a fuckin' hearing problem or just some sort of death wish? You dumb-ass shitbird! Didn't you hear the Gunner explain that this shit

100

could be poisonous? Do you wanna die, Sanchez? You dumb-fuck . . ."

Levering himself up out of the sand with one arm, Sanchez glared at the quickly gathering crowd of Marines. "Chit, man. I was thirsty!" Sanchez spat out a broken tooth and reached up to touch his bruised jaw.

"Yeah? Thirsty enough to die? You dumb-ass! I swear, you're a fuckin' idiot!" Jackson shot back.

Rounding on the kid who had sold Sanchez the Coke, Jackson motioned for Carrigan to hold him. "If he's selling bad stuff, we need to know where he got it," he said, and Bug agreed.

"Hey, Jack," Bug said, drawing Jackson away from the others. "I got an idea. Maybe we ought to scare the beejesus out of that kid, give him something to remember if he's tempted to disobey American orders again. What'cha think?"

"What'cha got in mind?" Jackson countered.

Pulling an M-14 round from his top pocket, Bug handed it to the disbelieving Jackson. "This."

"On a kid?" Jackson demanded with a scowl. "That's a little radical, ain't it Bug?"

"Huh? Oh, it won't kill him," Bug explained quickly. "I fixed it. Look. This will scare the shit out of the little bastard, but that's all. I call it a Winston round. You take the bullet out, remove almost all the gunpowder, then put a cigarette in place of it. It won't kill him, but he won't know that for a minute or two. I've been toying with the idea of patenting it for military use in riot control. Definitely non-lethal, but it'll sting like hell!"

"Give it here," Jackson said as he pulled his magazine of ammo out. Stepping aside, he replaced it with the single round Bug had given him. Then, locked and loaded, Jackson swung around and scowled fiercely at the terrified young Vietnamese kid. He brought up his weapon in a smooth motion and leveled it at him. As the kid let loose with a shrill squeak, Jackson squeezed the trigger. Pop! The round left the chamber and hit the kid square in the chest.

Obviously thinking he was dead or dying, the kid dropped to the sand. He lay there for a moment, his mouth and eyes wide open as he began to slowly realize that he was not as seriously injured as he'd thought. One bony hand began to explore the slightly burned mark on his bare chest where the cotton filter and tobacco had barely penetrated his skin.

Realizing he'd been tricked, the indignant teenager sat up and glared at Jackson. "You bad!" he shouted in pidgin English. "You one bad black!"

Those men not close enough to know what was happening thought Jackson had shot the boy. They stared at Jackson in disbelief and awe.

Irritated, Jackson decided to be sure how much this kid knew. Grabbing one of the Coke bottles that had fallen from the kid's satchel, Jackson smashed open the top against a rock, then snatched the boy up from the sand. One hand forced open the boy's mouth by pinching his jaws, while his other hand held the broken Coke bottle. Deliberately Jackson poured the warm contents of the bottle into the boy's mouth.

Coca-Cola splashed over the kid's face, down his throat, and onto his chest, and he wriggled frantically in his efforts to avoid swallowing it. Jackson's grip tightened.

"You know!" he growled. "You little bastard . . ."

The Vietnamese kid was struggling against Jackson, gurgling and choking, sputtering half in Vietnamese, half in English, "No drink! No drink! Bad . . . bad . . . black . . ."

"Yell, you little bastard, and I'll show you bad medicine. You want to sell it to one of my men? Drink it yourself, boy, go on and drink it!" Jackson snarled.

Brownish liquid spilled all over the young peddler's face without trickling down his throat. Stunned Marines watched silently, some of them obviously wondering if Jackson were bucking for a Section Eight. He *looked* crazy, with glazed eyes and his lips drawn back in a feral snarl, the kid held tightly in his fist as he poured Coke all over him. Several men shifted uneasily from one foot to the other, exchanging concerned glances.

No one spoke as the frightened kid finally broke free of Jackson's grasp and he let him go. The kid ran like all the hounds of hell were behind him. His shrill voice floated back as he screamed, "Bad black! Bad black . . ."

It was Bug who broke the Marines' silence, his voice light and humorous as he observed, "I think we finally got you a new nickname, Jack! Every Vietnamese you tangle with seems to think you are one bad black, Corp. So . . ."

"Shut up, Bug." Jackson gave him a sour glance and turned around to stalk away. He dropped the nearly empty Coke bottle into the sand and stepped over it.

"Hey, I just think it's time for you to get your due reward, Corporal Bad Black."

Smitty took up the moniker, relishing a new target for his comedic talents. Imitating Groucho, he called after Jackson, "Corporal Bad Black, don't leave in a huff. Leave in a minute and a huff."

The results of the incident with the kid were not fully realized until the Marines had reached Chu Lai and the Coke bottle samples were tested for poison at the 91st EVAC hospital. Doc Weathers delivered the news.

"The test results are positive, Jack. That Coke was laced with cyanide. Lethal within seconds after consumption. If Sanchez would have . . ."

Jackson stopped him cold. "So go tell Sanchez, not me, Doc. I don't want to hear it, man. You guys think I'm nuts as it is. I want him to know I'm just looking out for his Mexican ass. I ain't got nothing against him, even though he ain't exactly wrapped too tight. He thinks I do. That ain't it, Doc. I had to 'thump' him for his own damn good and you know it. I want Sanchez to hear it from you! Go tell him." Jackson walked away, leaving Weathers staring after him.

CHAPTER 6

Corporal "Bad Black" and the "Bitches" of First Squad had received their orders. They were temporarily assigned to be Rough Riders based out of Chu Lai. The next weeks found Jackson and Baroni assigned a five-ton truck to haul ammo and supplies up and down the coast on Highway 1. Da Nang, Hue, Quang Tri, and all the scattered collection of huts in between—wherever a Marine CAP unit might need supplies—were their stops. Baroni was usually the driver, while Jackson perched atop the dusty cab and manned the fifty-caliber on the gun ring. Other squad members were also assigned trucks for the same kind of mission.

Now this wasn't too bad, they figured. This was a great change, riding in trucks instead of humping the boonies and dancing with Charlie—or so it seemed at first. The first few trips up north there was no action, only bumpy rides along rutted highways and through crude villages. Jackson even grew to appreciate the scenery, admiring the dense foliage and tropical blossoms that splashed through the countryside in bright colors. If he could manage to ignore the hostile stares from the people the Marines were supposed to be helping, he could occasionally pretend he was on vacation in Hawaii. But that wasn't often.

Here they were, risking life and limb to help people most Marines had never even known existed a year before, and instead of gratitude like in the old World War II movies—"Want a candy bar, Joe?"; "Want to meet my sister, Joe?"; that kind of thing—they got hostile gazes and Coke bottles laced with cyanide or strychnine. What the hell were they doing here? It wasn't like the politicians intended to annex the damn country or anything, or the USA was in danger of invasion by this land of farming people. Well, it was idealistic bullshit as far as Jackson was concerned, and he figured the only good thing about the war was that it generated home economy and was good business for the fat boys in Washington. Of course, they weren't the ones out in the bush getting mortars aimed at them, or bullets the size of soup cans, either. If just one of those complacent bastards spent an hour in-country, the war would probably fade away into ignominy. Meanwhile, he was just thanking whatever powers that be that he was riding a truck instead of humping long klicks through the jungle.

His gratitude was short-lived. It was while Jackson and the other guys in the convoy were making their way up to Da Nang that he realized nothing was "safe" in Vietnam. The trucks had scrunched to a halt and were idling in the middle of the road, and he peered over the top of the cab and mounted gun to see why. They were at a wide-open spot in the road, with a thick line of trees a few meters away on one side and a bridge just ahead. The problem was the bridge.

Vietnam had a wealth of bridges spanning tiny streams and wide rivers. This one cut over a deep brush-filled ravine and looked as if it had been there since the Ming dynasty. One side of the dilapidated structure had crumbled from neglect shortly before the truck convoy had rumbled down the road. The result was a wait, while an advance party of road engineers struggled to repair it. This suited Jackson just fine, because it tended to get hot on top of the truck and he needed a smoke, anyway. He climbed clumsily down, his leg muscles stiff from being cramped so long in one position.

Jackson had to yell to be heard over the noise of the idling truck engines. "Baroni, give me a smoke, man! I left mine back at the base!"

Baroni slid from behind the wheel and stood in the dusty road. He left the truck running and the brake on, as convoy etiquette demanded that the driver never turn off the engine. Grinning at Jackson, who was doing a series of deep knee-bends and jumping jacks to limber up his tightened muscles, Baroni leaned back into the cab and pulled out a pack of Winstons.

"You like riding on top, Jack?" he yelled over the noise of the truck.

Jackson was now running in place, his arms pumping up and down at his sides, his cheeks puffed out. "Not . . . too . . . bad . . ." he huffed between less-than-graceful thuds with his heavy boots. Baroni tossed him the Winstons and Jackson caught them, pausing at last. "It gets kinda cramped on top of that truck. The gun ring keeps my legs in one position too

107

long."

Baroni pushed his helmet back out of his eyes and looked around. "Think we'll have to wait here long?"

Sucking in a deep drag of his cigarette, Jackson handed Baroni back the red and white pack. "Naw, maybe an hour or so. You know how it is: hurry up and wait. Anyway, I don't mind. This gig is the life. I mean, it beats the hell outa humpin', don't it?" Jackson grinned as he swatted at a buzzing insect that whizzed past his left ear with an annoying hum.

"Sure does, Jack. Sure does," Baroni agreed as he lit a smoke and leaned up against the cab of the truck.

Jackson took another long drag off the cigarette and swatted again behind his ear. "Damn, what the hell is that? Has to be the biggest fly I've ever heard, even for Vietnam," he muttered in annoyance as the insect buzzed loudly past his head. "Where is the little bastard?" Swearing loudly, Jackson shook his head as he felt the hot whiz of another insect zip by in a whirring rush.

"Shit!" came Baroni's response, and Jackson looked at him in faint surprise.

Baroni had seen something from the corner of his eye. About five or six hundred meters past the grassy field on their left was the thick tree line. As Jackson had swatted at the "fly," Baroni had seen a puzzling thing—a dim single muzzle flash and a wisp of smoke drifting up from the top of one of the trees. But they'd heard nothing, no rifle report at all. Now it dawned on him: The noise of the truck engines had overpowered the sound of the shots.

"A sniper! Jack, sniper!" Yelling at Jackson to

108

take cover behind the truck, Baroni gave him a hard shove.

Jackson ducked automatically, not needing to be told a second time. "Where is he?" Jackson yelled over the noise of the truck.

Crouching beside him behind the heavy metal hood, Baroni lifted his right hand and pointed. "There, Jack. Right to the left of that larger palm tree but a little lower."

Baroni reached up and opened the cab door to the truck. "You think you can get him with the fifty?" Baroni asked as he grabbed for his M-14.

"I'll give it a damn good try. The little sucker was trying to take my head off!" Jackson growled as he climbed back up on the truck and grabbed the fifty-caliber. He whipped it around and pulled back on the trigger.

For the next few minutes the scorching sound of automatic fire power filled the air. Jackson took out the tops of trees like he was trimming shrubs with a chain saw. Carrigan, Crawdad, Gagliano, and Grover, who were manning the other cab-top weapons, opened up with automatic fire from the top of their trucks also. The sky was ablaze with bullets, and the air vibrated with a roar of sound.

When the firing ceased, Jackson gazed across the field at the chewed tree line. Baroni popped up over the cab to look at him, and Jackson grinned with satisfaction.

"Nothing could live through that. If there was anything alive within meters of that hailstorm of shit, I'd be surprised!"

"Yeah, me too," Baroni agreed. "We hit 'em with

109

one hell of a flyswatter, huh, Jack?"

Within a half hour, the bridge was repaired and the convoy was under way once again. They rumbled down the road without any more attacks, but Jackson's senses were finely tuned and alert as he scanned the area from atop the cab. Every shrub or tree line could hide the enemy. Every leaning hut could shield NVA. The earlier peace and beauty of the land was destroyed for him as he "saw" enemy behind every stone wall or shrub big enough to hide a man.

The convoy finally rolled to a halt in a small village where there was an Army artillery unit stationed. The trucks idled with a loud purring sound as Baroni leaned on the steering wheel and took advantage of the wait to catch some Z's. Jackson couldn't get that relaxed. He chose to sit atop the hood of the truck and check out a few good-looking Vietnamese girls that were standing outside the flimsy Army bar.

They didn't look too bad in their Americanized clothes, the short skirts and tight blouses that exhibited the fact they were ripe young women. And he was about to be unmarried, wasn't he? Not that it mattered so far away from home. . . .

Just as Jackson struck up a promising conversation with one of the young ladies, a young Vietnamese kid came bounding up. His high-pitched pidgin English was honed to a perfect begging whine as he tugged at the Marine's shirtsleeve.

"You got chocolate? GI, give me chocolate?"

Jackson gave the boy an annoyed glance. The kid reminded him of the boy who'd tried to poison Sanchez, with the same begging whine and act. He gave an angry shake of his head. He knew better than to

110

trust any of these kids. They weren't really kids anymore, not in this country. And they could kill a man just as quick. . . .

Jackson scowled. "Get the fuck outa here, kid. Can't you see I'm trying to make a little time?"

Even if the kid couldn't understand what he was saying, he could sure understand Jackson's scowl and the shove he gave him. But it didn't seem to matter. The persistent boy bounced right back like a yo-yo, begging for chocolate, money, or anything of value.

"Come on, GI. You got any gum? I know you got gum. Give gum to me."

Trying to remember that this was a kid of maybe ten or eleven years old, Jackson once more shook his head and glared at him, hoping the boy would get the message. But this particular kid was persistent to the point of being ridiculous. If Jackson gave in and handed him gum or money, it would only open the door for more and he knew it. So he continued to try to ignore the boy, deliberately turning his back to him as he talked to the giggling girls in short skirts.

Irritation boiled dangerously close to fury as the kid continued begging, tugging at Jackson's shirtsleeve and bouncing around him like a rubber ball. Finally, after the fifth time of telling the kid he had no gum or chocolate for him, the angry Marine turned to the boy and spat at his bare feet, missing them by an inch or so.

This worked a little too well. Insulted, the boy bent and scooped up several rocks, which he began to hurl in the general direction of Jackson, barely missing him. The rock throwing was accompanied by a rapid-fire chatter in broken English, "Fuck mother. Fuck mother, GI."

The pretty girls were now laughing wildly at the scene, and this embarrassed and infuriated Jackson. Hefting another rock, the kid tossed it and then another. One of the fist-sized rocks ricocheted from the truck's rearview mirror into the cab, striking the napping Baroni on the left side of his head. That did it for Jackson.

Jumping off the hood of the truck in a whirl of dust, he sidestepped to the driver's side to check on Baroni. Blood gushed from the side of his head but he was sitting up, still half asleep and wondering aloud what was going on.

"You all right, man?" Jackson asked.

"I dunno," Baroni answered dazedly. "I guess so. . . ."

Satisfied that his friend wasn't seriously injured, Jackson whipped around. His mouth was set in a grim line, and his eyes narrowed as he muttered, "I intend to get that little sucker."

There was a flicker of movement in the shadows of the hut, and Jackson saw the boy dart into the open doorway of the bar. Sprinting past the laughing prostitutes, Jackson burst through the door like a wild man.

Seated at the bar were two Army officers and a young Vietnamese prostitute, sipping on what was affectionately known as "tiger-piss beer." They seemed oblivious to the racket Jackson was making as he surged through the door.

"Where'd the little shit go?" Jackson demanded, pausing by their table. The large room looked empty except for some wide-eyed gooks and the Army offi-

112

cers.

They looked up at him with mild surprise. "I don't know. Why? What did he do?" was the reply.

Jackson didn't bother answering. There was a movement in the corner of the bar behind some old woven baskets, and he stormed over to investigate. Reaching down into one of the larger baskets, Jackson hauled up his catch. It was the persistent beggar-turned-one-man assault wave, and he was shaking all over and scared to death.

Though furious with the kid, Jackson didn't intend to really hurt him, just shake him up a little and maybe teach him a lesson about lobbing rocks at Marines. Throwing the kid back up against the wall and suddenly remembering the Coke bottle, he had the crazy thought that he should slash the little fucker's throat instead. Startled by this thought—shit, he was just a kid!—Jackson gave a shake of his head.

Man, he was civilized, wasn't he? What was he doing having thoughts like that about a little kid? But what were little kids doing going around and killing full-grown men? It was a crazy war, a topsy-turvy kind of place where nothing was as it seemed, where insects were bullets and kids were soldiers. . . .

Jackson took a step back, yanking out his .45 handgun and firing a few shots directly above and to the side of the kid. That should teach him a lesson, he thought with grim satisfaction.

But that was too much for the Army guys, who leaped up from their chairs at the table and protested. "Hey, man, he's just a kid. Leave him alone. Go tell his father."

113

Jackson gave them a disbelieving stare and almost laughed aloud. Tell his father? His father was probably VC! What the hell did these Army guys in their clean boots and fresh-shaven faces know about it? They looked like the worst action they'd seen was a cut from their safety razors. . . .

Shrugging, Jackson pivoted on his heel and reholstered his .45. "Yeah, tell his father shit! I ain't telling his father a goddammed thing! That kid just gave my partner a fuckin' concussion."

"What are you gonna do?" the Army lieutenant demanded when Jackson turned away.

"I *ought* to kill the little bastard." Reaching over, Jackson then grabbed the kid once more and bent him over his knee to paddle his butt.

"You can't do that!" the Army lieutenant raged.

Jackson never paused. He brought the flat of his hand down on the kid's thinly covered rump with a resounding smack. "I'll do as I damn well please, you assholes," he said without looking up. "And if you don't like it, get the fuck outa here!"

"Don't address me like that, soldier! You are talking to an officer! You shall address me as *sir*!" the lieutenant spat furiously.

That gave Jackson a moment's pause, and he finally looked up. He'd had enough. The nattily dressed Army officer with the clean face and shiny boots had probably never seen a moment's fighting. He'd probably never been any farther out than the compound and had never seen his men blown apart by kids like the one squirming across Jackson's legs. It was more than enough, and the recent close call had frayed Jackson's nerves to the breaking point.

His voice was calm but cold when he replied, "When I see someone that needs to be addressed as *sir*, I'll do it. But not until then! I've been in the jungle too damn long, and I've seen kids younger than this little asshole blow away some fuckin' damn good Marines! I tell ya I'm just fed up with this whole shit! If you want some of me, come and get it!"

Ignoring them, Jackson turned his attention back to the business of spanking the young Vietnamese kid.

The kid was screaming bloody murder as the two Army officers grabbed Jackson. That was their first mistake. The moment he felt their grip on his back, Jackson whirled and Jap-slapped them both so fast they didn't know what had hit them. They dropped to the floor like swatted flies, and Jackson calmly continued spanking the young beggar.

Finishing, he shoved the kid from his lap and stepped over the dazed officers on his way out the door. When Jackson reached the waiting truck, Baroni was just wiping off the remaining residue of blood from his head. Wincing, he applied pressure to the wound to deter further bleeding, then glanced up and looked at Jackson.

"What the hell happened, Jack?"

Still fuming, it took Jackson a moment to reply calmly, "Another little slant-eye trying to take us out. These damn people over here don't give a fuck about this war or us even being over here, Baroni." He bunched his fists and hit the side of the truck with frustration. "I swear, I don't know why we're here. To protect the likes of this? Kids who try to take us out and C-rat cans rigged up to land mines? Gates that blow you to hell when you open 'em and old women who lob grenades at you? Hell! This is too much."

There was nothing Baroni could say. There was nothing anybody could say. And it didn't matter, anyway. The brass would say it all when they heard about this incident. . . .

A few days later, the members of First Squad, Third Platoon sat quietly in their bunkhouse at Chu Lai headquarters. They were waiting for the final blow to fall, for the ceremonial sword to swing down and separate Jackson's head from his body. It was a grim and dismal group who lay on their bunks and stared at the tent ceiling, commiserating with their leader.

Baroni chose that moment to bound cheerfully in, a grin splitting his face as he surveyed the morose group.

"Hey, cheer up! Look what Santa brought you boys. . . ." He held up a cardboard box but got little reaction from the others. "Aw, come on! I went to a lot of trouble to get these requisitioned, and wait until you see what they substituted. I tell ya, somebody up there is thinking, yessir, they're thinking hard!"

At last gaining lackadaisical attention from the men, Baroni continued, "You guys remember those gloves I asked for? Nice heavy gloves so we wouldn't get calluses on our soft little hands from using machetes and machine guns and such distasteful things the Marine Corps insists we use? Well, looka what they sent us!"

Jackson sat up on his bunk and stared with wide-eyed disbelief as Baroni began distributing plastic packages of yellow handball gloves.

"Handball gloves, Baroni?"

"Oh, yes! Isn't the military wonderful? They know just what we need!" Grinning, Baroni tossed Jackson a plastic package. "Shall we repair to the courts, sir?"

"Repair that hole in your head, Baroni!" Jackson said with a laugh, throwing the gloves back at Baroni.

"Thanks for worrying. It feels a lot better now," Baroni said, gesturing to the long scratch on the side of his head. "For a while there, I thought my tongue wasn't gonna catch up with my brain. I mean, I was a little disoriented from everything."

Doc Weathers put in, "No wonder! You only had a concussion because of that little VC!"

"Maybe that's the reason we got these gloves instead of proper gear," Jackson quipped. He caught the package Baroni flipped back at him and tore it open. "Hey. What's this?"

Holding up the pair of yellow gloves, Jackson began laughing. Puzzled at first, Baroni investigated more closely, and Grover and Crawford and Carrigan began to howl with laughter. The package contained two right-handed handball gloves. They were all like that.

Groaning, Baroni observed, "Leave it to Supply to fuck up a wet dream, man." He threw the cardboard box to his bunk and flopped down beside it. "Oh, by the way, speaking of bad dreams, Gunner and the LT want to see you, Bad Boy." Baroni glanced up at Jackson

117

Jackson grimaced. "Yeah, yeah, I know. And by the way, if you see a *boy* around here, you give him a dollar."

Pushing up from his hard bunk, Jackson heaved a sigh as he trudged down the main aisle between the long line of racks lining the barracks. "Gunner probably wants to promote me or something," Baroni heard Jackson mutter as he reached the rickety door.

The screened door slammed behind Jackson as he stepped out into the hot sunlight. He knew he was in for some deep shit.

CHAPTER 7

Gunner sat quietly behind his desk, shuffling papers and looking grim as Jackson entered the tent. An officer introduced as Lieutenant Paul Springs from HQ stood behind him. The stone-faced lieutenant was looming like a vulture, Jackson thought as he paused just inside the door.

"Jackson, have a seat." Gunner was still gazing at the papers on his desk, signing them with a flourish, then ripping away the duplicates and separating them.

"No thanks. I better stand. Listen, Gunner, I know what this is all about. I want it to go on the record that I hereby formally apologize to the two LT's I thumped. I just lost my temp—" Jackson tried to continue but was stopped by the lieutenant.

Spring stepped forward. "Corporal Jackson, I didn't call you in here to talk about that. True, though, the two Army officers did file a formal complaint against you for getting their asses whapped. . . ." He turned back to Gunner. "Oh, I almost forgot. I better file them myself. Paperwork—

119

I love it. Let's see, here they are." The lieutenant shuffled through the papers, selected and quickly perused several of them, then calmly ripped them in half and threw them in the trash can across the room. Jackson's lower jaw dropped as Spring announced, "There. Complaints are now filed in the circular file cabinet." Then he turned to Jackson and continued, "Let me be the first to congratulate you, Sergeant Jackson."

The lieutenant held out his hand for Jackson to shake.

"What, sir? *Sergeant?* I don't understand. . . ." Jackson was stammering in disbelief.

Gunner too stood and shook his hand. "Congrats, Sarge! This calls for a drink."

"You mean I'm not gonna get in no trouble for thumpin' those two Army lieutenants?" Jackson's head buzzed, and he wondered if this were some kind of joke. Making sergeant instead of getting court-martialed? What was going on here?

Lieutenant Spring grinned and shrugged. "Hell no, Jack. You're a Marine, aren't you? That's what the hell we're over here for—to fight. Maybe not always with soldiers that are supposed to be on our side, but what the hell. Your record stands for itself in battle. One lone incident is not going to stand in the way of your promotion, and I know what you and your squad have accomplished. I don't need some sissy-ass Army officers messing up your record. Besides, from where I see it, they were in the wrong, not you," he confided.

The lieutenant then pulled a bottle of Scotch from Gunner's desk and poured three big glasses. Jackson, eyeing the amount of liquor being poured at such an early hour, protested, "Whoa, not that much, sir."

The lieutenant ignored Jackson's protest and kept pouring. "Sergeant, do you want to drink or don't you?" He gazed sternly at Jackson.

"Sir, yes sir. But . . ." Jackson stared at the glass.

Gunner and the lieutenant promptly guzzled their drinks and began pouring another while Jackson was only half finishing his first glass. Within a half hour and three more glasses, Jackson was thoroughly smashed.

When Jackson finally stumbled back to the barracks and reached the door, all eyes of First Squad were on him as he crashed through the entrance.

Seeing Jackson's condition, Baroni immediately thought the worst. "What's the news, Jack? Are you all right?"

"You want the good news first or the bad news first?" Jackson burped out with a stifled hiccough.

Propped up on one elbow in his shallow rack, Smitty did his Groucho imitation of a TV master of ceremonies. "Bad news! From Mr. Corporal Bad Black himself! Take it away, Jack!"

Leaning against a rack that seemed to veer away of its own accord, Jackson did his best to cooperate. "Well, the bad news is we're being transferred up to Da Nang Air Base. We got to provide some security for their perimeter or something like that. Hell, I can't remember." He sorted through his Scotch-fogged vocabulary for the right words that never came, squinting at the squad.

"What's the good news, Jack?" Grover screamed over the chorus of bitching from First Squad.

"The good news is . . ." Jackson paused, trying to remember it himself. "The good news issss . . . hiccough! I'm drunk and and . . ."

"We already know that, Jack," Smitty answered. "What else?"

"Anddd . . . da, I've been promoted to a sergeant!" Jackson managed to get out in a slurred voice.

A wild roar of whoops and yells filled the barracks. Pats on the back staggered him, and Jackson struggled against the overpowering urge to toss up all the Scotch he'd drank.

The trucks bounced along rutted Highway 1 on their way to Da Nang. Jackson, still a little hung over from the morning drinking bout, watched for VC behind every bush or tree as the trucks rumbled on. He was manning the machine gun on the third truck in the caravan, with an Amtrac in the lead. It was hard to think, hard to focus on what was going on around him as he fought waves of dizziness and nausea. No doubt, Gunner and Spring had thought it a great joke to get him so drunk then send him out, but he was not nearly as amused as they were.

Jackson sprawled on his stomach across the hot metal of the truck cab, balancing himself with difficulty and holding onto the gun to keep from falling off the truck. Damn the Marines, damn the Vietnamese, damn the war. And damn the ruts in the road that jounced him so painfully. He stifled a groan as the truck dipped sharply, then ground his teeth as he tried to focus on the truck ahead.

That was when it happened without warning. The truck right in front of his was hit with what had to be a command detonated land mine, because the Amtrac in the lead had made it past the spot without setting it off. The results were devastating. Newly made Sergeant Robert L. Jackson watched helplessly as the truck just ahead exploded.

The truck was carrying artillery duds, and Jackson gripped his gun and held on as the engine block disintegrated with all the fervor and fire of a small atomic blast. The shock wave was deafening as it seemed to almost suck his breath from him. It had to be an ambush. The men in Jackson's truck immediately leaped out and took cover where cover could be found.

Stuck on top, Jackson crouched down and waited for the first shots from the invisible enemy. None came. He waited with the heat pressing down and his heart in his throat, wondering from which direction they would hit again. He was vulnerable, out in the open like a sitting duck, and now he understood for the first time just how appropriate that phrase was. The minutes crawled past as he waited, and finally he dared dive down from the top to find refuge under a prickly bush at the side of the road. Still no gunfire, and the Marines began to emerge from safety to see the extent of the damage that had been done.

The decision: probably a lone VC or NVA regular who just wanted a little excitement on his own. The result: two Marines blown into unrecognizable bits of bone and flesh. One of them was Jackson's friend, PFC Wendell Grover, the only other black guy in First Squad. Jackson turned away.

It took a good two hours to clean the remains of the five-ton truck from the road so the convoy could continue, and the two dead Marines' body parts were then placed into body bags. When they finally reached the air base in Da Nang, Gunner called on Jackson to come to the air field's warehouse mortuary to officially identify Grover's mangled body parts.

Jackson's stomach heaved as he stood in the doorway and tried to collect his composure. The mortuary odor was overpowering. It was sickening. The sharp smell of embalming fluid mixed with the stench of death hung in the air in thick clouds. Finally, someone saw him standing there, his face grayish and his lips pulled back and asked what he wanted.

"I came to identify a man in my squad," Jackson mumbled as he was motioned toward a sheet-draped table.

Had it not been for the small cross tattooed on his left forearm—a souvenir from Tokyo while Grover and Jackson did a night on the town—he'd not have been able to identify Grover. Jackson flipped back the sheet and went to a corner. Sweat poured down him, drenching his shirt and dripping onto the floor as he struggled to hold onto his breakfast. He leaned against the wall and waited for the dizziness to pass.

Two guys wearing blood-smeared white coats stood off in a corner, casually assembling a man's body and putting it inside a casket. They did it as calmly and unemotionally as if they were packing Christmas presents. The huge room was filled with caskets ready to be sent back to The World and their families, while body bags holding other dead soldiers waited their turns to be identified, embalmed, and shipped out.

"How do you guys stand this?" Jackson finally asked one of them.

"You get used to it after a few months," the coroner said dryly and matter-of-factly. Jackson just stared at him.

Da Nang, the second largest city in South Vietnam, was a madhouse. The population was increasing with every new job the American "War Machine" created for the South Vietnamese people. The sound of jet fighters, enormous supply planes, small prop-type dive bombers, reconnaissance craft, and an assortment of helicopters was constantly in the air. On the ground there were fuel dumps, endless rows of ammunition dumps, bulldozers, tractors, jeeps, and every other kind of war tool needed.

Da Nang, elbowing into a bay of the South China Sea, was a perfect dumping-off spot for freight and military. The Da Nang River flowed through the old heart of the city, and was lined with docks and warehouses. In 1966 the population was nearly a quarter million South Vietnamese, ranking second only to Saigon. First Squad found that the city was detrimental to their hearing, vision, and lungs.

Landing fields thrummed with the thundering roar of jet fighters and dive bombers, artillery spotters and huge radar planes with humped domes. Reconnaissance craft circled the area and five different varieties of helicopters, and seven different varieties of transports blurred the air with a lot of noise. Jeeps, tanks, trucks, tractors, wreckers, bulldozers, earthmovers with seven-foot high wheels, and power shovels made

125

clouds of dust that hung in the air so thickly it was hard to see farther than a foot in front of a man's face at times. And it was hard to suck in a clean breath of air.

The US Naval Support Activity was stationed in Da Nang. Not many deep-water piers graced the port, and it was left to LCMs (Landing Craft, Medium) and LSTs (Landing Ship, Tank) to help the YWs (water barges) and YRs (repair vessels) meet the big freighters that churned into the bay.

In other times, Da Nang might not have been a bad place to visit. Flimsy little watercraft skimmed the waters like bugs, and the local fishermen hauled in huge catches in nets handed down for generations, patched and re-patched. And at night their fragile sampans were brilliant with tiny lights, looking like stars fallen from the sky and floating on the inky sea.

After a day or two of "Hurry up and wait" military-style, Jackson and Third Platoon, First Squad got their orders from Gunner. They were to hump some five klicks east of the air base and set up a watch on a hill overlooking Da Nang. This area was hot. NVA forces were getting stronger daily—hourly. Through the DMZ and Cambodia, small platoons carried weapons and equipment to the VC on the Ho Chi Minh Trail. But more than that, the scuttlebutt had it that General Westmoreland was beefing up the security at the air base at Da Nang because he knew something was going to happen. It could be a major offensive, and the Marines were ready.

They humped into the Marble Mountains six miles outside of Da Nang. It wasn't a bad hump, with the sea breeze cool enough as it blew off the coast. The road dipped down onto a wooded valley, with steep slopes rising high on each side, excellent hidey-holes for snipers, Jackson pointed out to his men. It was a point well taken. They all walked cautiously, looking around constantly, heads bobbing like they were on springs.

"Shit," Delisi muttered beneath his breath. "I hope like hell nobody's home around here!"

"And if they ain't?" Gagliano asked around the cigarette dangling from one corner of his mouth. "Who are we gonna find to play war games with, man?"

Jackson just half listened to the men behind him. His concentration was centered on the terrain. Every limb that moved in the wind was suspect. There were moments when he thought he must be paranoid, and others when he was certain the trees were alive with VC. It wasn't the best feeling to have, and it was obviously shared by the rest of the squad.

Moving into the dense jungle foliage was little better than being in the open, Jackson decided as they filtered single file in places along a narrow path. They humped for a while, whacking a path through the bushes where there was none, and finally came to a clearing that looked as if it had been carved into the wilderness by human hands.

"Hey, what's that?" Baroni asked from somewhere behind him, and Jackson paused to look up at the stone face of the mountain.

"I think it's a temple," Jackson answered after a moment.

"Hidden out here in the mountain?"

"Yeah. Wanna take a look-see?"

"Why not?" Baroni came back and motioned for the others to follow. They had to descend into the mountain, trekking into the cold air of the subterranean cave that was sacred to the Vietnamese.

It was a temple and it was guarded by one old man with a shaven head, white goatee, and the look of the ages written on his face.

"He's also the temple holy-man," Bug said after a quick question-and-answer session. "This is a shrine to Buddha."

The men let their gazes roam over the blue-gray stone of the mountain, staring at the figures carved into it, which looked as if they had been carved by time instead of man. Faded paint peeled in flecks from one of the statues carved in the shape of a fish, and there was another stone figure seated on the back of a fish and facing the front of the cave. There were temple walls and pillars, and a small stone courtyard with wide, shallow steps. Urns for incense and offerings were arranged in a half circle in front of the brightly painted figure perched on the fish.

"He says that this is a pagoda carved from living rock," Bug reported a minute later, "and that it is sacred to his people."

"Tell him we won't bother anything," Jackson said.

Grinning, Bug turned back to Jackson after another conversation and said, "He says we must be blessed with good fortune to have arrived at this spot undetected. Many have tried and been killed by snipers. See! Our luck is getting better!"

"Great," Jackson muttered. "I feel better already, Bug. Ask him if he can guarantee we'll get outa here alive. Come on, bitches! Let's hump on outa this

128

place. It gives me the creeps."

Buddha or some great force was smiling on them, Bug was to later say. Their luck held, and they escaped the hot area without seeing or hearing a single VC.

"I don't think it was Buddha," Delisi said seriously. "I think it was God, or the Virgin Mary. . . ."

"Naw, now come on, man!" Smitty argued. "If God was watching, do you think he'd let all this shit happen? I don't think He cares anymore!"

Jackson just listened, letting the men argue between themselves. There were times he had his doubts, too, but there was always something that happened to reinforce his faith in a Supreme Being, call Him God or Buddha. He wondered if maybe other nationalities just called God by a different name but were worshipping just like he did. If so, how would God manage not to take sides in a war? Or if He did take sides, what guarantee did he have that it was the side of the Americans? It wasn't something Jackson liked to think about, but there were times he couldn't help it. It was such a mixed-up war, with right and wrong blurring together sometimes. For reassurance, he patted the small Gideon New Testament that he always carried in his front pocket and walked on.

The rest of the hump went quickly and without incident. When arriving at the designated location on top of a hill, they found the view was breathtaking—or at least Jackson did.

"This place is something else!" Jackson mumbled to himself as he crouched down and watched in admiration as the bluish purple sun set over the northern ridge of mountains in South Vietnam. It was a sight the young Marine would never forget. It could almost pass for a spectacular view of the Smoky Mountains in Eastern Tennessee. He didn't realize he was thinking aloud as he murmured, "What in the hell are we doing here?"

Smitty must have been affected as well. His normal reaction to anything was humor, his way of combating the horror he witnessed. Scuttling closer to Jackson and overhearing his comment, his reply was serious instead of being a droll rebuttal.

"You know, Sarge, this place could be a paradise. Why are these people fighting? Why are we fighting? I just don't understand it, Jack. We take a hill. They take it back. They kill five of us, we kill five of them, we kill fifteen of them. It doesn't make any difference. Who gives a fuck about taking this rice paddy or that one? And the hardest thing for me to understand is our so-called allies. Back in Hastings they fought like Cub Scouts instead of men. They aren't even trying to win. Or they're the biggest fuckin' chicken-shits I've ever seen. Like that ARVN officer that kicked that prisoner out of the chopper back in Sung Cao." Smitty paused reflectively, and as Jackson remained silent and listening, he continued. "He was pretty fuckin' weird. I mean, he seemed to be playing both sides of the fence. Fuck, this is a civil war! Why don't we let them fight it out between themselves? We don't even know who our enemy is, for Chrissake!"

Jackson shrugged and shifted his gaze from the sunset to Smitty. "I don't know, Smitty. I just don't know anything anymore. The only reason I can think of right now for being here is to watch out for ya'll's asses. If we can make it back to the world in one piece, well, the rest of our lives will be just like gravy. You and the rest of the shitbirds are my only friends. You, the rest of the squad, and the platoon. If I didn't have something like that to keep me going, I'd go fuckin' crazy myself. As it is, I guess I want a little 'payback' from Charlie. That's why we are here." Jackson turned to stare back at the ever-changing hues of the sunset.

Smitty didn't answer, and they just sat there on the top of the hill and watched the sun disappear behind the distant horizon in a red ball of flame. Then, without speaking again, the two men rose and went back down the hill to help set up camp.

The evening sped by quickly as the Marines began to dig foxholes, set claymores, and basically set up camp for what the Gunner referred to as an "indefinite period of time."

Time is what was mostly on the platoon's mind now. Weeks had passed with no sign of enemy activity. Their only entertainment was the light show that "Puff the Magic Dragon" put on nightly. "Puffy," as Jackson referred to it, was an awesome sight to behold. The name came from the song performed by Peter, Paul and Mary.

It was an apt name for the beast. The reason they called it that was because at night the huge C-47 aircraft, with its numerous vulcan machine guns, would unleash its terror of fire power from open cargo doors. The sight was incredible. Red flames of tracers, flares, and bullets belched from the bowels of this American war machine. In minutes, it could kill anything within a perimeter the size of a football field. Thus evolved the metaphor of a dragon breathing fire on its victims from the air. And because Puff was positioned out of Da Nang, a seaport, it "lived by the sea."

Jackson had wondered more than once if the ending of the song would fit, the part where the boy no longer went to play and the dragon ceased to roar. The boy's name was little Jackie Paper, and Jackson couldn't help but make the connection. What if "Little Jackie" no longer went to play along the Cherry Lane? Would Puff cease his fearless roar? Would the war end? No. There would be another to take his place, and another, and another, until the United States was emptied of able-bodied men. He didn't make a damn bit of difference. He was an anonymous face in a war peopled by anonymous soldiers. No one would know or care. No one would notice if he were the one stuffed into a body bag piece by bloody piece. . . .

CHAPTER 8

Night hid the jungle in a dark blanket. If not for the pale flecks of light that filtered through in uneven patches on the floor, First Squad would have been totally blind and would have had to feel their way along.

"Another night patrol!" Sanchez grumbled. "Chit!"

"Lissen, man," Gagliano said. "If you're gonna cuss, do it right. "It's *sshhit*, not chit. You make it sound like a poker debt instead of something you don't wanna step in."

"You cuss your way, man, I'll cuss mine!" Sanchez shot back in irritation. "Besides, a poker debt is as bad as *sshhit*."

"He's got that right," Carrigan said gloomily. Due to a bad night with the cards, the hulking Montana boy now owed Jackson fifty bucks from his next pay envelope—which would leave him almost nothing. Like the rest of the squad, Carrigan was still being garnisheed for the bar in Tokyo. Only two more monthly deductions and it would finally be paid off.

Jackson's teeth flashed briefly in the dim light. "That depends on which side of the debt you're standing, Carrigan old boy!"

First Squad was patrolling the area just beyond Hieu Doc, where VC activity had recently been reported. They had a new man with them by the name of Myers. He was taking Grover's place. Jackson had him walking point for the first time, and Baroni was the slackman, just a few yards behind him. Myers was understandably nervous. He had joined the Marines right before getting his draft notice, figuring he'd rather be with the best. He was a short, pudgy young man of nineteen, and this was his second week in Vietnam.

Being a cherry, Jackson had gone easy on him, but now it was Myers's turn to be a part of the team. The kid wasn't bad, but he was so nervous he was making Jackson nervous. Walking point wasn't the best place to be on night patrol . . . or any patrol.

The jungle slapped insects and vines at First Squad, and Jackson could hear Myers's nasal asthmatic wheeze from his position four men back. Damn. If VC were around, they'd hear Myers coming a mile away.

Jackson was moving forward to tell Myers to breathe more softly, when he heard a sound. Later, he wondered how he had even heard it over Myers's rasping, but he had. It was a small sound, like a man's foot on a tree limb, and it wasn't coming from First Squad. It was coming from the thick bushes to the right of the trail. Leaves moved in a slight shimmy, and he knew they were waiting on the squad to pass before attacking. Myers and Baroni had almost passed their hiding place.

Slowing down, he fell back and motioned to those behind him to do the same. Myers, Baroni, and Bug were finally past the bushes. Those behind swung up their M-14's and Jackson bellowed, "Take cover ahead!" as he poured fire into the dense bushes.

Baroni, Bug, and Myers immediately hit the ground as First Squad laid some heavy-duty lead into the bushes. When the smoke cleared, Jackson ran ahead to check it out.

Four VC lay sprawled in their own blood in the bushes. One of them looked to be no more than fifteen and he was still alive, gagging on his own blood. Another VC tried to lift his head, and Sanchez whirled and kicked the AK-47 out of his grip. The force of the M-14 rounds had torn the man's abdomen to shreds.

Jackson looked up as Myers began vomiting his dinner all over the trail. "Damn, Myers! If you're gonna puke, at least have the decency to move over a bit!"

The pudgy Marine fell to his knees, emptying the contents of his stomach all over the trail. Baroni cursed and moved aside quickly.

"Dammit, Myers! Not on my boots!"

"I think Myers needs a good blooding, Sarge," Carrigan said.

"Blooding?"

"Yeah, like when you go deer hunting as a kid and get sick at the first kill? My dad rubbed blood on me to get me used to it."

"Sounds delightful, Carrigan."

"It might not work with Myers," Delisi pointed out

in disgust.

Jackson shook his head. "I don't think we need to go that far. He can get used to this way."

When Myers had straightened up and faced the squad with an embarrassed shrug, Jackson said, "Look, Myers. You need to get used to seein' this kind of shit. It happens, and you don't need to go to pieces in battle. If you're puking your guts out, you're vulnerable. I want you to help Sanchez clean up."

White-faced and trembling, Myers just stared at Jackson. "Clean up?" he echoed.

"Yeah. Go through their pockets and stuff."

Sanchez was already crouched by the VC and rifling their pockets. He had a small pile of personals on the ground. Looking up at Myers, he said, "You check the dead ones."

Myers obviously didn't want to, but he dragged his feet over to the two dead VC and knelt beside them. Gingerly, he reached out, gave a small cry when blood smeared on his hands, and began retching again. Sanchez just shook his head and kept working.

Jackson and the others tried to ignore Myers, standing back and letting him get accustomed to the dirty job. Some men had no trouble with this kind of thing. Others, like Myers, never got used to death and the gore that usually went with it.

When Myers finally got through stripping the dead VC of personals and weapons and stood up, Jackson gave him an encouraging smile and said, "Good job, Myers!"

Myers managed a weak smile and added the stuff he'd gathered to Sanchez's pile. Weathers was bent over the VC kid, checking him out to see if he'd live

136

long enough to be a POW. Brass had been clamoring for more prisoners and kills, and it looked like they were going to have a good night. Two kills, two prisoners. Not bad for a squad of misfits.

Looking down at the kid lying there with Weathers working on him, Myers gave a sorrowful shake of his head. His pudgy cheeks were pale and his eyes scrunched up into wet slits.

"He's just a baby!" Myers said.

Sanchez looked up. "Yeah? Well, don't you go believin' that chit, man! They don't grow no babies over here, only VC."

Myers gave the Mexican a sour look. "He can't help what side he's on. He probably doesn't even know any better."

"Chit!"

Ignoring Sanchez, Myers went over and knelt beside the moaning boy. The kid lay looking at the pudgy Marine with those fathomless eyes only the Orientals can have, eyes that have seen centuries of pain, sorrow, and death and know no other way of life. Weathers stood up, stepped to where Jackson stood, and said in a low voice, "This VC kid ain't gonna make it, Sarge."

Myers turned his head and looked up at Weathers, then back down at the dying boy. He gave a startled gasp, then a grunt, and his mouth slowly dropped open, his nasal wheeze even more pronounced than usual.

"Chit!" Sanchez yelled, leaping over to Myers, "The goddammed kid's stabbed Myers!"

The boy had obviously hidden a knife somewhere in the voluminous black pajamas he wore, and somehow Sanchez had missed it. The hilt of the knife now protruded from Myers's chest. Myers fumbled weakly, his fingers scrabbling at the hilt and his face wearing an expression of surprise.

While Weathers grabbed Myers and began working furiously on him, Sanchez snatched up his M-14 and emptied an entire magazine into the VC kid. Jackson never mentioned the waste of ammo.

When the noise faded, Sanchez walked over to where Myers lay on the ground. Dark shadows flitted across him, and the light from a fitful quarter moon played over his face for a moment. Sanchez could see a sad smile on Myers's mouth.

"You . . . were . . . right, Sanchez," he wheezed.

Sanchez shook his head. "Maybe. But you got the right idea, man. I—I'm sorry, Myers. I don't know how I missed that knife!"

Blood pumped from Myers's chest in furious spurts in spite of Doc's frantic efforts to stem it. Myers opened his mouth as if he were going to say something else, and more blood spouted so that he only gurgled.

Smitty was on the horn calling for a medevac when Doc told him not to bother telling them to hurry. "He's dead."

Sanchez stood up and looked down at Myers as Doc closed his eyes with a wave of one hand over the lids. His jaw was clenched, but other than that Sanchez displayed no emotion.

"The dumb-fuck," he said tonelessly. "He had no business bein' out here."

No one else said anything. They all felt Myers's death, but Sanchez felt responsible because he had committed the cardinal sin of not checking carefully enough.

"What'll we do with this other guy, Sarge?" Carrigan asked after a minute, pointing to the remaining live VC.

Jackson looked down at the man. It was a miracle he was still alive.

"After the medevac comes for Myers, we'll take him back to his village," he replied after a minute.

"What?"

Jackson nodded. "Yeah. He's probably from one of these little villages around here. His family might want to know what he's doin' late at night when he should be in bed." He paused a moment, then added, "In fact, we'll take all these VC motherfuckers home!"

"Uh, what you got in mind, Jack?" Baroni asked.

A grim smile lifted Jackson's lips as he said, "I got hanging these bodies on the compound gate as a warning in mind, Baroni. It might be kinda interestin' to hang around and see who comes to claim four VC, don't you think?"

Before noon of the following day, a conclave of villagers arrived at the main gate of the Marine compound. They were from Hieu Doc. More came from the south around Huong Lam. They stood out front and waited with grave dignity, clad in white robes and accusations. A Buddhist monk danced around like an organ grinder's monkey, his long yellow robes flowing around him as he banged on a primitive musical instrument and assaulted Marine ears with his nasal wail.

The dead bodies of the VC hung like rotten fruit from the gate, a gesture Jackson had suggested and Gunner had okayed. Myers's death had hit them all. Already in the noon heat the bodies had begun to swell and blacken, filling the air with a too-familiar stench.

As the crowd grew thin, cries could be heard, and the Marines marshaled around the perimeter with weapons primed in case things got out of hand. Gunner stood back and waited.

An hour after they had begun assembling, a small squad of ARVNs approached from the south and parted the crowd.

"Whose side are *they* on?" Jackson wanted to know, but Gunner couldn't tell him. They waited in silence, and as an officer separated from the rest of the squad and strode briskly forward, Jackson and Gunner chorused, "Shit!"

It was the same ARVN officer who had been at the village outside of Song Cau. Captain Ngo Dai stepped up to the compound perimeter and eyed Gunner, then flicked his gaze to Jackson. If possible, his eyes narrowed even more, looking like mere slits in his face.

"We meet again," he said politely, and Gunner nodded.

"Yes, Captain Dai. We do."

"You are in charge here?" Dai asked in the same precise tone.

"No, but I'll do for now," Gunner said. His stocky frame was braced as if for assault, and dislike was written all over his face as he stared back at Ngo Dai.

"Then perhaps you can tell me the meaning of this degradation?" the captain said, indicating the bodies on the gate with a wave of his arm. "I and my people find it most offensive."

"Not as offensive as First Squad found them," Gunner said calmly. "Those men were VC. They waited in ambush for the men of First Squad last night and managed to kill one of them. This *degradation* is a warning, Captain."

"Impossible!" Captain Dai slammed out. "These were simple farmers, peasants! One is just a boy!" His finger quivered in anger as he pointed to the boy who had killed Myers.

"That *boy* killed one of my men last night!" Jackson spat, unable to keep silent another moment. Hatred for the ARVN welled up in a torrent, almost choking him as he glared at the older Vietnamese officer. "And he killed him after our medic had tried to help him, and after the dumb fool sat down to comfort that *boy*. . . ."

"Enough, Sergeant Jackson," Gunner said quietly.

Captain Dai just looked at Jackson for a moment. "So, you are sergeant now. You must have been very successful in your few months here."

"Just a bit," Jackson ground out.

"It is a shame that your career in the Marines will come to such a brief end." Turning to Gunner, Captain Dai said, "I insist that these men be turned over to the villagers for trial. They have committed murder against innocent civilians and must be tried."

"No way in hell, Captain," Gunner said coolly. "If First Squad had not reacted so quickly, they would be dead now. These men were Vietcong. . . ." He jabbed a blunt finger in the direction of the bodies and said, "I intend to ask for a decoration for the service First Squad performed in ridding Vietnam of such vermin!"

Captain Dai's face flushed an angry red, and his hands curled into fists at his sides as he took a step closer. "You have no proof that these men were Vietcong! Even farmers in wartime must carry weapons to protect themselves from predators. . . ."

"Weapons like AK-47's, Captain Dai?" Gunner countered. "Those are Russian weapons carried by the VC. At 0200 hours this morning, First Squad was ambushed by the enemy and carried out orders to the letter: They killed them and confiscated the weapons."

Jackson motioned for Sanchez to bring up the confiscated AKs, which he did, flinging them at the feet of Captain Dai. The furious captain didn't move a muscle or even glance at the weapons.

"If it was so easy for you to take these weapons, do you not think farmers could have found them also?" Captain Dai asked. "Air strikes kill many. I believe you refer to them as KBAs, or Killed by Air. It is quite reasonable that those poor peasants found the weapons."

"Reasonable to an ARVN, maybe, but not to the United States Marines," Gunner said. A trace of contempt curled his lip as he gazed at the captain. "I'm beginning to wonder if you are as much of an ally as you pretend, Captain Dai. Your conduct today may come under question by my superiors once I send in my report. I would suggest that you prepare yourself for intense interrogation very soon."

Jackson wanted to applaud as he saw Captain Dai's face turn a deep purple. And he felt like cheering when Gunner continued in the same cool voice, "First Squad also apprehended certain documents that have been turned over to the S-2 Intelligence for translation. That should clinch any claims you may make to the contrary, Captain."

Stiffening, Captain Dai snarled, "I shall go over your head on this! I shall report this to your superiors and they shall demand that you surrender the men of First Squad to Vietnamese justice—especially their sergeant!"

"I doubt that," Gunner said to Captain Dai's back. The furious ARVN had pivoted and was stalking back toward the waiting villagers.

When several of the villagers moved toward the bodies hanging on the fence, the watching Marines brought up their rifles. Gunner gave a signal for the Marines to lower their weapons and let the villagers take the bodies.

"Now we know who they belong to," Jackson said quietly, and Gunner agreed.

"Yeah. Ain't we glad we got the ARVNs to help us win this war, Jackson?" Gunner turned toward Jackson with a grin. "And he especially seems to like *you*."

"The feeling," Jackson said, "is mutual!"

CHAPTER 9

Constant air traffic hummed in the clear, burning sky over the Da Nang air base. The zigzag of jet aircraft and Hueys stitched trailing patterns of exhaust in the air, and was one of the few reminders to the grounded Marines that they were in the middle of a war. They were waiting now, reduced to playing poker and tossing dice while they sat in shaded tents and sweated.

Day after boring day inched past the Marines of Third Platoon, dragging in an eternity of minutes as they waited for activity from "Mr. Charles" on the hill. But none ever came. All in all, they felt like they were living in the capitol city of the land of boredom. There was simply no action except an occasional light show from "Puff" at night. Waiting for action, waiting for orders to move out, and just plain *waiting* scraped already-excoriated nerves worse than the ever-present fear of dying in a heated battle. Although none of First Squad wanted to die, they longed for freedom from boredom. Even jungle patrol was better than the waiting and wondering, the not-knowing when or if *it* was going to happen. In the jungle, *it* was always there, pervasive and waiting, and a man knew it. And this wasn't like being back in The World. This was a putting-off of the inevitable, like going to the dentist or paying taxes. It was there, waiting just beyond the perimeter of the compound. The only question was *when*.

Desperate for distraction, most of the men spent this free time writing letters home, cleaning their weapons, telling stories, even drawing pen and ink sketches. Anything to keep them occupied during the monotonous guard duty had to be better than just thinking.

Crawdad, the platoon's striving young artist, took to drawing pictures of dragster cars or trying his hand at a portrait or two of the men in his squad. It was during one of those long, endless afternoons that Crawdad decided to do Sergeant Jackson's portrait.

"Hey, Sarge! Come over here. I got something I want you to see," Crawdad demanded in a lazy drawl.

Grinning—and expecting the worst—Jackson crossed the few feet between them and peered over Crawdad's shoulder. He blinked. "What's that supposed to be, Crawdad? Some kind of inkblot with a Marine helmet on top?" Jackson demanded sarcastically.

"Naw, Sarge. It's you. Don't you like it?" Crawdad asked, sounding hurt and surprised.

Squinting, Jackson leaned closer to look at the undistinguished dark blot on the paper. If one stretched his imagination, it *could* bear a slight resemblance to a man, though the imagination would have to be stretched to the limit. The dark inkblot was creased with a mouth that curved in a frowning grimace and pale eyes that looked like fish eggs glared from beneath the rim of a Marine helmet on the figure's head. Jackson shook his head and tried to think of a noncommittal answer.

"Well, Crawdad . . . uh . . . can't ya make my face a little more like Cassius Clay? You know, a little more handsome or something? I mean, I don't always have such a sour expression on my face, do I?"

"Well, Sarge, you are *Bad*, ya know, with a capital *B*. And, besides, I've never drawn a black guy before, so I thought I'd give it a try." Crawdad held it at arm's length, gazing at it in an assessing manner as if he were an art critic.

"Hell," Jackson continued. "The way I look in that picture, it could be a police mug shot, or even a wanted poster like the ones in the post office or something. I think I'm just a little bit better. . . ."

"That's it! That's it!" Crawdad cut in excitedly.

With a few more flicks of his pencil stub, the young artist sketched what appeared to be ten little white faces topped with Marine helmets. They were arrayed behind Jackson in a symmetrical group. Then he added at the top in bold letters "WANTED DEAD OR ALIVE," and at the bottom it read "BAD BLACK AND BAD BLACK'S BITCHES."

"There we have it. Your own personal wanted poster," Crawdad said proudly as he ripped the sheet of paper from his sketchbook and handed it to Jackson.

Jackson stared at it in stunned silence for a moment. This man was serious! It defied belief, but Crawdad really thought he'd created a masterpiece.

146

Shaking his head again, Jackson held up the large sheet of paper and began laughing.

"Thanks, man. It's something I've always wanted," he managed to say a moment later.

Bored by the lack of action and interested in Crawdad's antics, the other members of the squad couldn't resist stepping closer to see what the laughing was all about. In spite of sarcastic criticisms of his artwork, it was apparent that they all got a big chuckle out of Crawdad's portrayal of them. Baroni even went so far as to tack it to a tent wall, until Jackson walked by and removed it to stick on his helmet.

As time dragged slowly by and morale weakened, Jackson devised a plan to leaven the boredom with a dash of excitement. Besides, he was as bored as they were, and anything was better than sitting and waiting and enduring any more of Crawdad's artwork.

Late one night while stuffed into his foxhole and reduced to contemplating his navel, Jackson came up with the Perfect Plan. It was pitch dark, and the camp was asleep except for those standing watch. Spirals of concertina wire were rolled around the camp in several layers to give warning should enemies try that approach, and more men were stationed at various sandbagged bunkers staggered randomly around the perimeter. There had been no action for so long that a little fireworks couldn't hurt morale as badly as boredom was doing.

Shouldering his way closer in the dirt and nudging his drowsy companion, he laid it all out for Baroni.

"Okay, now at about 0200 hours, we are gonna open up with all we got with this fifty-caliber. We're gonna toss a few grenades and flares, maybe pop a few of the claymores at the perimeter. I intend to liven up this place with a little excitement."

"Why?" Baroni asked, dumbfounded.

" 'Cause it'll keep us on our toes and give the boys a little thrill, too. I know I could use a little excitement, can't you?"

Baroni gave a doubtful nod. "Yeah, but what will Gunner say when we do that and there ain't no one out there?"

"Ah, hell, he could probably use some action, too." Jackson laughed softly. "Don't ya think so, Baroni?"

Shrugging, Baroni muttered, "I guess we'll find out, Sarge."

It didn't take long for Jackson to get ready. He soon had their grenades laid out next to a couple of flares and the wire for the claymores.

It was one of those rare nights when nothing moved, when the sky was dark as pitch and the wind didn't even blow. The only sounds were far-off, seeming as if they might belong in the next dimension. The distant drone of a chopper or aircraft was a faint reminder that they weren't that far from the airbase.

Jackson huddled down in the foxhole and peered over the hard-packed dirt rim. It looked quiet. Nothing but the faint gleam of barbed wire spiraling around the compound showed in the occasional light of a flare. It would be all too brief. A flare, a shower of light, and the glitter of wire, then pitch-black again. Hours were marked by the burst of a flare and the silent tick of time. They were on fifty percent watch—one man sleeping while the other watched.

Giving Baroni a nudge to waken him, Jackson murmured, "You ready, man?"

"What? Huh?" Baroni mumbled as he wiped the sleep from his eyes.

"Get your shit together, Baroni-boy! We are fixin' to light up the night!" Jackson grinned, feeling like a little kid planning a Halloween prank.

Within moments, Jackson had begun to light up the hill with rounds of machine gun fire, reddish-orange bursts shattering the quiet and the night. Fully roused from his sleep, Baroni began tossing grenades into infinity while firing his M-14 down the empty hill. Both Marines screamed at the top of their lungs, "Gooks on the wire! Gooks on the wire!"

Reaction from the Marines was immediate. Seconds barely passed before the other Marines opened up also, firing at the invisible enemy, the tops of the trees, the dark night sky. The hill was ablaze with automatic fire, flares, and hand grenades. Somebody kept yelling, "They're all over the fuckin' hill, boys! Somebody call in 'Arty' for a spotter round!"

Gunner was calling in coordinates for the artillery rounds as the men of Third Platoon continued to fire down the hill.

After the spotter round was checked by Baroni and yelled back to Gunner for the okay to let 'em roll, the hill was one thundering concussion after another as the 108's from Da Nang gnawed at the outskirts of the perimeter. It showered the area for a good ten minutes of nonstop cratering, until the Gunner called a cease-fire.

Gunner made his way to Jackson and Baroni's foxhole in a sort of running waddle, his equipment banging against his side as he slid close. In the dim light afforded by flares and firing, Gunner eyed Jack-

149

son narrowly. His mouth was stretched in a grim line as he demanded, "Jackson, how many were down there when you opened fire?"

With all the solemn sincerity of a used car salesman, Jackson responded, "At least, aaaah, four or five."

Unfortunately, at that precise moment, Baroni also replied, "Forty or fifty."

Now thoroughly incensed, Gunner glared at the two men. Well, soldiers, which is it? Four or five, or forty or fifty?" He shifted position and glanced back over his shoulder at the absence of return fire before he turned back and snarled, "You men better make up your mind quick! 'Cause when morning comes, if I don't see a lot of dead gooks on this hill, your asses are grass and I'm the lawnmower! See, if I have to file an after-action report for HQ and we ain't got no confirmed kills, it's gonna be your ass! You got that, Sergeant Jackson? When I call in 'Arty' it puts all of Da Nang on red alert, and I better not be wrong. Do you understand?"

Jackson swallowed hard. He had seriously miscalculated Gunner's reaction. His Halloween-style prank didn't seem so damned funny now, and even if his men had been able to let off a little steam, it sure seemed like he was in for a rough time. "Sir, yes sir" was the only response he could make.

Satisfied with that reply, Gunner pushed to his feet and strode back to his foxhole.

There was a long moment of silence in the foxhole, in which Jackson and Baroni contemplated the results of their prank. Finally, Baroni muttered, "Hey, Jack, I think we're really gonna catch some

150

shit for this."

"Yeah, well maybe so. But wasn't it fun?" Jackson bluffed with a forced grin, slapping his hand against his knee.

"Sure Jack, just like a turkey shoot," Baroni said dryly.

Morning burst over Vietnam in a haze of purple, blue, and orange sunrays. It found the Marines of First Squad scouring the cratered hillside in search of the bodies from the invisible enemy attack of the night before.

Stepping close to Doc Weathers, Carrigan remarked, "You know, Doc, I ain't even found so much as a blood trail, much less a body. In fact, I didn't even see any gooks last night. I was just firing because everyone else was. Did you actually see any gooks, Doc?"

Weathers shook his head. "Nope, sure didn't. I kept my eyes peeled all night, too. Kinda baffling, isn't it?"

"Baffling? What's that mean?"

"Nothing, Carrigan, nothing."

Jackson and Baroni promised one another not to tell the other squad members about their bad joke, mainly because of the repercussions that might fall on them if they knew. It had turned out to be a really bad idea.

Jackson just hoped he'd get a trial before his probable execution and had decided glumly that Gunner might not want to be that kind. After all, if he'd been made to look like a fool, Gunner wouldn't be in too

151

damn good of a mood. Nor would he be prone to listening to the lame explanations that he'd been bored and had wanted to liven up the night. And now here he was, pretending to look for enemy bodies that didn't exist while Gunner waited and got madder by the moment. Jackson took a swipe at the brown grass with the point of his rifle. The situation sure didn't look good. . . .

"Jackson!" Gunner's voice floated out over the compound as he searched for the sergeant.

"Sir, yes sir. Down here," came the resigned reply.

Gunner arrived at the bottom of the newly landscaped hillside in a cloud of dust, brushed himself off, and snarled at Jackson, "Well, have you found any dead NVA, Jackson?"

It didn't seem reasonable to pretend anymore, but one glance at Gunner's hostile expression gave Jackson all the impetus he needed to give it a last shot. "No sir. Charlie must have dragged 'em off during the night, sir. You know how sneaky those little bastards are, sir."

Gunner's expression altered to blunt disbelief. "Yeah? That's an inventive reply, Jackson. You better hope HQ buys it, 'cause I sure don't! I'll be back." With that vaguely threatening promise hanging in the air, Gunner pivoted and stalked off, leaving Jackson to contemplate his brief career as a sergeant in the U.S. Marines.

It was two days before Gunner made good on his promise. Storming back into the Marine camp, he didn't look too damn happy. He searched for and

152

found the men of First Squad lounging beneath the shade of a few scraggly trees on top of a rounded hill.

"All right, you bunch of shit-for-brains," he bellowed. "Fall in!" His glance shifted from man to man until it focused on the one man he really wanted to see. . . . "Jackson, front and center!"

Snapping to attention, Jackson and the members of Third Platoon rose to the Gunner's command.

Gunner began pacing up and down the top of the hill with his hands behind him, pausing every now and then to direct a glare at Jackson in a sort of grim punctuation.

"Well, Sergeant Jackson. You did it. It seems that the assault we endured the other night by the invisible enemy—oh, excuse me, I mean the enemy that only you seem to have seen—has earned us a new assignment. Now, the brass seems to think that if we are such gung-ho Marines we feel compelled to fire upon a nonexistent enemy and call in heavy artillery, we might do a little better in the jungle." He gave a thin, humorless smile at the concerted echo of faint groans. "That's right. We are now heading back to Chu Lai to the First CAG—Combined Action Group—where we will then be assigned to a hamlet right smack-dab in the middle of it all. We will work together with the Popular Forces in that area as a CAP—Combined Action Platoon—unit in order that we might 'win their hearts and minds,' as the brass are fond of saying. The goal is to drive out the Vietcong insurgents by going on short and long range reconnaissance missions. This, they state, will make the hamlets safe from the enemy. Does that sound like fun, Sergeant Jackson?" Gunner growled with all the

153

subdued fervor of a hurricane.

"Sir, yes sir!" Jackson managed to reply.

"Gooood. Because you probably will be walking point most of your time, seeing as how you like to fire that big weapon of yours so damned much!" He stepped close to Jackson, until his face was only an inch away from the sweating sergeant's nose, and grated through clenched teeth, "There are times when I think you believe that gun is your dick, and every time you pull the trigger you get off. . . ."

Jackson could think of no appropriate reply for this remark, so he wisely remained silent and sweating as Gunner glared at him. A full sixty seconds ticked past in tense silence before Gunner snorted in disgust, pivoted on his heel, and snapped over his shoulder, "Now saddle up!"

As Gunner disappeared in a small whirlwind of dust and anger, the men of First Squad relaxed and began to grumble among themselves in their usual "Bitch" fashion. Even Jackson, who always tried to keep a positive attitude in spite of the circumstances, found himself swearing vehemently. "Shit, a CAP unit! . . ."

The hump back to Da Nang went quickly, and it was no time until the men found themselves aboard hot, musty deuce-and-a-half trucks barreling along rutted roads back down south toward Chu Lai.

Chu Lai was a marked contrast to the compound where they'd been for the past weeks. It was a huge air and Marine base with jet runways, wooden barracks instead of sandbag bunkers, roads of asphalt instead of dirt, and even flagpoles and manicured lawns. Not bad for the Marines from the primitive jungle.

They had been in Chu Lai for two or three days before they finally received their orders. Jackson hated to share the bad news, but the men in his squad were waiting expectantly. He gave them all a hard look and took a deep breath.

"Well, boys, it looks like this. We already know First Squad is assigned to be a CAP unit in a small hamlet called Tou Lon. . . ." He waited for their groans to subside before continuing. "So let me give you the details. It's about thirty or so klicks from here. Seems that it just so happens to be right in the middle of Indian country. The reason we get to attend this dance is because the unit that was there got taken out by Charlie the other PM on what was supposed to be a routine night patrol. All of 'em except the lieutenant, that is, who's still there waitin' on us. Any more questions? I'm all for gettin' out of here." There were none, and he nodded, letting his gaze drift over the assembled men. They were tired of waiting for the worst, and now that it had come, maybe it wasn't as bad as they'd feared. Jackson managed an encouraging smile. "Well, look at it this way. . . . This place is hot," he said cheerfully. "Maybe it's cooler out there—weather-wise and action-wise!"

"I thought we were looking for action," Mudboy piped up in a disconsolate tone, and Jackson laughed.

"It was looking for action that got us this gig, Mudboy," he retorted. "You ready for more already?"

Shrugging, Mudboy muttered, "Maybe."

Jackson shook his head, wiping at the beaded ridge of sweat on his forehead with the back of one hand. Dirt smeared the handball glove he wore and he began to peel it off his hand. They had all taken to wearing them lately, kind of like a badge of recognition banding them together.

"We gonna hump it or hitch a chopper, Sarge?" Smitty asked.

"We're big time now. A slick's gonna pick us up and fly us over. We'll be leaving in a few hours, so get all your gear ready."

Blades whirred in a deafening roar, sounding like an angry locust as the UH-1 Huey began its swift descent to the helipad. The gunship escort buzzed close by. First Squad craned their necks to get a good view of their new home.

A small village of thirty or so huts could be seen a half klick to the east. To the west sprawled the Marine camp. Three rows of concertina wire marked the perimeter in a rambling spiral. Within the confines of the bristling wire squatted a canvas and plywood command hootch, rifle squad hootch, small arms ammo dump, a four-hole latrine, mortar ammo building, and a mortar pit. Home sweet home.

When the chopper finally settled in a bumping hop on the ground, the men of First Squad leaped from the craft and began to unload their supplies from the metal belly. It fell to Sergeant Jackson to search for the lieutenant, and he trotted toward the command hootch. The canvas and screen door slammed softly behind him, and he stood for a moment while his eyes slowly adjusted to the dimmer light in the hootch. Then he saw the lieutenant sitting and staring blankly at the walls of the tent.

Feeling awkward and uneasy, Jackson began, "Lieutenant Campbell?"

His head slowly turned. "Yes, uh . . . yes." His eyes seemed to struggle to focus on Jackson, and if he noticed the sergeant's confusion, he didn't bother commenting on it. His voice was thin and reedy as he asked, "Sergeant Jackson?"

"Yessir." Jackson paused and frowned. It was apparent that the lieutenant had had quite a shock. Jackson could just imagine how devastating it would be to lose all your men in one skirmish. Lines of grief still marked the man's face, lines that seemed to go soul-deep. Jackson waited. He did not intend to intrude by speaking unless addressed first.

Slowly, the lieutenant stood and greeted Jackson with a brief handshake and a "Glad you're here" that didn't sound heartfelt.

A brief silence, then, "Uh . . . listen, Sergeant. Just . . . uh . . . get you and your men squared away and settled in, and I'll talk to you a little later. Your hootch is the next one down. Just go and make yourself at home." A slight smile flashed for an instant, a forced compression of the lips into a travesty of good humor that looked more macabre than comforting, then he continued in the same monotone, "I've got some letters to write and some paperwork to do right now. I'll brief you and your men a little later." There was another brief pause, then the lieutenant asked, "Is there a medic in your squad, Ser-

157

geant Jackson?"

"Yes, sir."

"Fine. Send him over here as soon as possible. That will be all for now." The lieutenant's face turned back to the blank wall, and he continued his former study of the canvas as intently as if he were regarding an expensive painting. It was obvious that he was dismissing Jackson and maybe even the war from his mind.

Feeling as if the officer wouldn't notice if he stripped mother-naked and did a hula dance in the middle of the hootch, Jackson saluted and replied, "Yes, sir" as he headed for the door.

Stepping outside, he took a deep breath and found that he was relieved to be out in the hot, steamy air again. It smelled . . . fresher. The command hootch had been dark and oppressive, and the lieutenant had given him an eerie feeling of death and finality. Jackson wondered if Gunner knew the officer seemed to have lost it. . . .

Jackson caught up with his men and gave them the word on the living arrangements, then told Doc to visit the lieutenant. Turning to the rest of the squad, he forced a grin and said, "Let's go see our new homes, boys!"

When they entered the First Squad's new hootch, it looked as if others were still living there. The men jerked to a halt in the doorway and stared inside. There was the inescapable feeling that the previous occupants had been abruptly interrupted in their daily lives and had just stepped out for a moment, leaving behind the things people usually do. Personal effects of the ghostly squad were still intact. Pictures hung on the walls—photos of smiling freckle-faced American girls in short skirts and high hairdos—footlockers spilled over with their books, half-opened packages from home were strewn on bunks beside opened letters, an occasional helmet collected dust in a corner. The men of First Squad suddenly felt like intruders.

Taking charge, Jackson quietly ordered his men to collect the belongings in each bed space and place them in a sack. "It can be sent back to their families," he added softly. It was apparent from their expressions that the men were thinking this could be them in the future, that someone could come along and take their place and take their space and sack up their remains to ship back to The World. It was not a welcome feeling.

And it was not helped by the lieutenant's abrupt arrival moments later. He burst in through the screen door of the hootch and stood for a moment, his face ashen and blank, his eyes unfocused. Then he attempted a smile that never reached his eyes and began to speak softly to the men staring at him.

"Men, my name is Lieutenant Campbell, and I welcome you to Camp Rascal. I apologize for the delay in meeting you. I—I . . . haven't been myself for the past couple of days." Pausing to clear his throat, the officer looked away, seeming to speak to the far wall as he intoned, "I just lost twelve of the best damn Marines that I ever knew, and I don't know why. It was a routine patrol, just routine, and they've never returned from it. No bodies have been found. I have based my assumption that these men are no longer alive on reports from our so-called

PFs—Popular Force—friends that happened to be on this particular patrol and informed me of the ambush. How they managed to survive but not my men is still an unsolved mystery. I should mention that this has had an adverse affect on my view of the PFs. One thing will not be tolerated: None of my men are allowed to converse in any manner with the locals. They cannot be trusted. We're saddling up at 0500 hours to find out just what has happened." Turning blindly in Jackson's direction, the lieutenant murmured, "Sergeant, please follow me. We need to talk."

Campbell eased out the door with Jackson close on his heels. The sergeant shrugged in answer to the silent inquiry he saw in Baroni's eyes, then passed the line of racks to follow the lieutenant.

When they arrived at the command hootch, Campbell took out a creased and folded map and motioned for Jackson to come closer. Pointing with a shaking finger, the lieutenant traced the route his men had taken on their fatal patrol. For the first time since Jackson had met him, Campbell's voice held a pitch other than a monotone.

"Why, why the fuck did this happen to them?" he agonized harshly. "Hell, we've been kicking Charlie's ass wherever we found him! These men should have known better, Jackson. We have over one hundred and twenty confirmed dead VC to our credit. We know the difference between a picnic and an ambush, for Christ's sake!" Taking a deep breath to regain control, Campbell met Jackson's steady gaze. "Why on this particular night were the VC able to wipe out an entire squad? It doesn't make sense unless one

160

considers the fact that there must be an informant. My idea is that it is a PF informant. They knew the patrol route that night and it would have been so easy. . . . I've learned not to trust these people, Jackson, not even the ones on 'our side.' "

Campbell's lips curled in a sneer, and to Jackson, staring at him in the dim light of the small, naked bulb hanging over the desk, he looked half-demented. But—and the thought was chilling—maybe he was right.

"Didn't you talk to the PFs, Lieutenant, and ask them what happened?" he questioned.

Campbell gave a harsh laugh. "That's like asking the cat who killed the mice! Oh, you get answers all right, just not the right ones! It's 'Ma-deen' this and 'Ma-deen' that, until a man wants to puke. . . ."

"Ma-deen?" Jackson echoed in confusion.

"Yeah. Haven't you really listened when they say Marine? It's *Ma-deen*, with a nod of the head and a big wide smile, while the whole time they're putting a booby trap in your mess kit!"

Jackson remained silent as Campbell worked himself into a frothing tirade, his voice rising higher and higher, losing none of its West Point diction and enunciation. "I detest their singsong accents and sneering, flat little faces! Those faces hide centuries of evil behind them, age-old hatreds that have been harbored against the West since time began!" Straightening, Campbell said more calmly, "I have decided that there will be no more PFs on patrol recon. We will do it all. Do you understand this, Sergeant? Ignore any orders to win the hearts and minds of these people. From here on out, we shall do what Marines have been trained to do—slay the enemy. And we shall do it on our own terms, with whatever weapons we find best suited! Do you understand my meaning?"

Jackson nodded slowly. "Yes, Lieutenant, I think I do." And he did. He recognized in this half-mad officer some of the same feelings he'd felt, the emotions that had stirred him when he knew he should be more civilized. There was a reckless hatred combined with a burning desire for vengeance, and Jackson suddenly recalled the VC kid who had wounded Baroni; Captain Dai, the murderous ARVN officer who had ruthlessly thrown a countryman to her death from a hovering chopper in Song Cau; and the nameless VC kid who had killed Myers. Yes, it was easy enough to understand Lieutenant Campbell and easy enough to want to do what he was suggesting: kill.

Day broke, illuminating the First Squad's efforts to saddle up for a "little hike in the woods" as Jackson often referred to a search and rescue mission. Only, this search and rescue mission had a more grim purpose.

Lieutenant Campbell and Jackson were carefully going over the topic relief map as the other members of First Squad shrugged into their packs. There were muttered comments and a great deal of bitching about the fact that one or two of them had forgotten to get laid before being sent to Indian country, but other than that, First Squad was in a rather subdued mood.

Campbell led the way from the camp up into the highlands. He had a good idea of the location of the ambush, knowledge garnered from the not-so-trusty PFs.

After a rough hump into the upper central highlands, the squad finally found a blood trail in a small clearing in the saddle of the mountain. Campbell insisted on walking point from there on out, following that trail as if he were a bloodhound, his nose almost to the ground as he pushed through jungle foliage and grass thick enough to hide an entire army. Jackson wasn't far behind, but still not close enough to shield the lieutenant from what waited around a bend in the barely visible trail.

Death would have been easier than the sight that gave the Marines a shock, jolting them into stupefied inaction.

Campbell dropped to his knees with a pitiful cry and began vomiting. There they were—the remains of his squad. Twelve of his close friends and comrades, men he'd eaten with, walked with, talked with, were tied naked to the wide trunks of trees. No one face was recognizable. Several heads looked like shapeless pulps perched atop a human torso, beaten to the soft consistency of an overripe melon. The VC had sliced every man's genitals from his body and stuffed them into his mouth. On the heads still recognizable as such, the ears had been cleanly, neatly removed and probably now decorated some VC's uniform or rifle. A putrid odor emanated from the corpses, and even the insects seemed to avoid the mangled bodies of what had once been United States Marines and Lieutenant Campbell's friends.

Nervous and nauseous, Jackson gave Campbell a close look to see if he was going to make it. . . .

CHAPTER 10

For the next few days, Lieutenant Campbell wavered on the precipice between sanity and rational deterioration. He vacillated between belligerence and bouts of deep melancholia. During this time he gave no orders—for anything. He refused to see Jackson or anyone else, and he holed up in his dingy hootch. Jackson could hear him talking and knew he was raving to himself inside the tent, yet he didn't want to report Campbell. It could be the end of his military career, and the lieutenant was a "lifer," a man who hoped to rise high in the military. So Jackson waited. And he worried.

"Hey, Jack," Baroni murmured one hot afternoon when they were all sitting and waiting and watching, wondering what was going on in the command hootch. "Do you think the lieutenant is cracking up?"

Jackson waited a moment before answering, trying to think of a way to form his thoughts into words. He didn't really *know* that the officer was crazy. Jackson understood why a man would lose it for a while after seeing his friends brutalized in that gory way, but how did he explain that to Baroni . . . or anyone else?

After a few minutes of thoughtful silence, Jackson looked up at Baroni and managed a shrug and a smile. "Hell, I don't really think he's nuts, Baroni. But I do think he needs a little time to get over this. I know how I'd feel if it was you guys I found strung up like that. I mean, I'm responsible, see, and you guys look to me to keep you from gettin' killed or worse. Yeah, I wouldn't like it either."

Baroni grinned. "Would ya be pissed, Jack?"

But Jackson didn't respond like Baroni had thought he would. There was no answering grin or rude joke. Instead his brown eyes narrowed, looking like pinpoints in his broad, dark face as he growled, "I'd *kill* a lot of gooks, Baroni. . . ."

Baroni didn't say anything else. He just nodded and looked away, sensing in Jackson's intense tone and the set of his shoulders that he had been almost as affected as the lieutenant by what they'd found. All of them had been shocked and horrified, of course, but some had managed to push it to the back of their minds, to pretend, maybe, that it hadn't happened. How could a man cope otherwise?

It wasn't until a few days later, after the mangled remains of the dead Marines had been identified and put into body bags, then put aboard the choppers that would take them on the first leg of their return journey home, that Jackson recognized Campbell's slow return to sanity.

He sat in the command hootch beside the lieutenant and listened as he talked softly about his men and the times they had shared, the closeness that had drawn them into a tight-knit body of fighting men.

"You know, Jackson, it's odd," Campbell was saying reflectively, "but men in war seem to have an unusually close relationship that is seldom matched. There's a feeling of unity, of thinking alike and acting alike that bonds men into the ultimate weapon. We were like that. It took a while and didn't happen immediately, but after training together and fighting together, we knew what each other was going to do before it happened." He paused and flicked a half-embarrassed smile at Jackson. "Do you understand what I'm trying to say?"

"I sure do, Lieutenant. I feel the same way about most of the men in my squad. We work good together and don't have to worry about a man freezin' up or losin' it under fire. I know who can do what."

"Yeah, that's the way I felt about my men," Campbell said, turning his head to stare at the blank wall again. It wasn't like his previous mood of despair, however, when he would stare for hours at the drab tent walls and say nothing. This stare was different, a difference Jackson could see.

And he found out just how different it was the next day, when he was back in the command hootch listening to Lieutenant Campbell try to talk over the radio to the S-2 officer back in Chu Lai. Anger and frustration thickened the lieutenant's voice, and Jackson shook his head in amazement at the officer's uncharacteristic language and manner. It sure wasn't West Point. . . .

"I don't give a damn!" the lieutenant was yelling

into the mike. "It had to be NVA regulars! The fuckin' VC just doesn't operate like that." Campbell's hands knotted tightly around the headset, and his face was flushing a bright, angry red as he argued, "No, sir. I don't have any other proof. . . . I just need more men to beef up the night patrols and the overall security in this area, and if I don't get it . . ."

There was a brief, stunned silence, and Lieutenant Campbell lowered the telephone and looked up at Jackson. "The son of a bitch hung up on me! I can't fuckin' believe it!"

Jackson was having trouble recognizing his officer from the man he'd grown accustomed to seeing and hearing. His face held anger and determination instead of sad acceptance and grief, and his vocabulary had roughened from its usual precise articulation.

"What . . . uh . . . what did he say, Lieutenant?"

"He said I had to have positive proof of NVA movement, like a prisoner or some kind of documents. He said he couldn't approve more replacements out here until then. The dumb son of a bitch! What the hell does he want? A written letter from Ho Chi Minh himself, maybe? Or a neat set of VC guide rules saying that they're gonna infiltrate the district? Shit!"

Still reeling from this departure from Campbell's normal character, Jackson shrugged. "I don't know, Lieutenant, but I think you've got something. That ambush wasn't done by any local Vietcong. They're more the hide-and-shoot type of soldier. That looked like the work of pros who knew what they were doing and what would get to us most."

Jackson bent over the table and squinted down at

the map spread out over the surface. It looked like a maze a man might find in Oz or the Twilight Zone. The map certainly didn't look like a carefully planned strategy for winning the war. It was more of a survival map, a hit-and-run-and-take-what-you-can kind of map.

Nodding agreement with Jackson's observation about the VC, Campbell said, "Well, it looks like we're going to have to do with what we have—twelve men. Not even a full rifle squad according to the good ole U.S. Marine Corps manual."

"Since when do any good Marines go by the book, sir?" Jackson wanted to know.

A faint smile crooked his mouth as Campbell leaned back and looked up at Jackson. The black Marine sergeant was staring back at him. They seemed to have a kindred spirit, a mutual respect for each other. It was almost as if they knew what the other was thinking.

Leaning forward again, Campbell made a steeple of his hands and said, "I like the way you think, Jackson. You're not quite like I supposed at first, even though I heard from Gunner you're supposed to be the biggest—oh, what was the word he used?—*Shitbird* was the correct term, I believe, in this man's Corps along with your men. You do know that most men have to volunteer to get on a CAP unit, but I understand that your squad had it thrust upon them. Is that correct?" Campbell asked.

Jackson shrugged. "I guess you could say that. Gunner told the brass that we like to fight so much we even create our own firefights against imaginary enemy soldiers. Can you believe that?"

168

"Well, without wounding your more sensitive feelings, I must say, yes, I can," Campbell replied with a trace of amusement in his face.

For a brief instant, Jackson could see a flash of the former officer Campbell must have been before the tragedy of the ambush, and he suddenly knew that the lieutenant would make it. Life had dealt him a harsh blow, but he would weather it. And Jackson had a feeling that Campbell meant to have some "pay-back" before too long. The lieutenant's next words proved him right.

Moving his steepled fingers to rest against his chin, Campbell eyed Jackson closely for a moment, then said, "It doesn't take much imagination to realize that my men were fighting a pretty damned ruthless crowd when they were ambushed, Sergeant." Campbell paused for a brief moment before continuing, "You know, some people think CAP units are for cherries and shorttimers. Well, it's just not so. I have the inescapable feeling we are going to see more action than we ever dreamed of in this place."

"I'll bet that's partly because most of the units are closer to the larger fire bases than we are here," Jackson said.

"Probably." Campbell was quiet for a moment, then said, "You know, when this concept was originated, it based its operations on the premise that eventually security would be turned over to local South Vietnamese authorities. Our entire purpose for being here in Vietnam is supposed to be only for 'strengthening' the government."

"You mean, we're not supposed to do anything out there in the jungle?" Jackson asked in disbelief.

"We're just supposed to smile, hold hands, pass out Band-Aids and Kool-Aid or something?"

Campbell smiled. "Something like that. However, I do believe that since the NVA sent their regular divisions south across the DMZ, forcing the Third Marine Division to be taken off 'pacification' duties and deployed north, our function has changed a great deal. Orders are now coming through that require more than just providing local security for South Vietnamese hamlets to drive out the Vietcong insurgents. Now we are being subtly asked to search for VC and information leading to them. There are four CAG—Combined Action Group—headquarters. First CAG at Chu Lai, Second CAG at Da Nang, Third CAG at Phu Bai, and Fourth CAG at Quang Tri. That's a lot of CAP units out and about, Sergeant Jackson, a lot of men who could rack up a lot of confirmed body counts. I don't think HQ intends to ask too many questions if we turn in a good score sheet."

Jackson grinned. "No, sir, I don't think they will. It would be kinda like cutting off your nose to spite your face."

"That's for certain. Do you have any good mortar men in your squad?"

"Yes, sir. Delisi and Gagliano, the Stud Brothers as we call them," Jackson replied with a wide grin.

"Good. We need two good men to operate those 81mm mortars." Campbell leaned forward. "Listen, here's what we are going to do for the next few days: You and your men will learn the area; you will know it as well as you know the backs of your hands. It is imperative that you do so. Since we can't get any

170

more backup, we are forced to go out in four or five man fire teams. At least two patrols will flank each other in case one of them gets into trouble. We will begin tonight."

Campbell spread out the map and traced dotted lines and heavy black lines with his finger, plotting the patrol routes and showing them to Jackson.

At 0100 hours that night, Jackson and the other men in his squad were awake in their hootch, blacking out their faces and cleaning and checking their weapons. Lieutenant Campbell slid into the hootch and looked around at them. "You men ready?" he asked, his gaze sliding back to Jackson.

"Yes, sir. I think you should take Crawford, Mudders, and Smitty with your team. I'll take Carrigan, Baroni, and the Bug with me. That leaves Gagliano and Delisi to handle the 81mm mortars back here, since they were trained for it. Doc can monitor the radio. Sanchez can handle the rest." This last sentence Jackson said with a hard look at Sanchez. The Mexican just shrugged

"Sounds good," Campbell said. "You got your PRC-6, Jackson?"

"Yes, sir." Jackson patted the big hand-held radio at his side with one hand.

"Don't use it unless you absolutely have to. There's no way of confirming if the VC or NVA have 'ears' close by. If you do have to talk, use the codes we discussed earlier. Do you understand that?"

"Yes, sir" was still Jackson's only reply. He knew the lieutenant was nervous and apprehensive, but he also knew what he was doing. This might be new territory for him and his men, but it was an old war as far as he was concerned. There were few rules that could be applied, and only one rule that seemed to hold fast irregardless of the terrain: kill or be killed.

Jackson had become adept at hiding his own nervous reaction, but that didn't mean he wasn't having doubts about his longevity. A man would have to be a fool not to think about things like that, especially in this kind of mission when the squad was basically on its own. There would be no Gunner to call on for 'Arty,' no back-up units waiting just beyond a hill or thicket. This was guerrilla warfare, plain and simple. Hide and wait and watch, and maybe—just maybe— you might get the first lick in before the VC knew you were there and blasted you into eternity.

A full moon hung low in the eastern sky, a bright silver circle occasionally masked by a drift of shifting clouds. This was good and bad. On the one hand, the clouds were good while moving across open land because a man or squad was more difficult to spot in the dark. On the other hand, however, when a man reached his desired ambush spot and was well hidden, the moon could illuminate any enemy activity and lend the element of surprise to those waiting. A fair-enough deal when it could be arranged, Jackson figured.

They humped through the tall grasses and thick underbrush, batting at insects and trying to be as quiet as possible. All preparations had been made with secrecy in mind. Dogtags were tied to shoelaces and smeared with boot polish, and their faces had been darkened to keep them from reflecting moonlight and alerting the enemy.

"Not," Jackson had said with a grin, "that *I* needed too much polish on my face! Just enough to get the shine off will do for me."

"Naw, Sarge," Smitty had agreed. "You're black enough as it is! I think you're just making us smear this gunk on our faces 'cause you're lonesome for your soul brothers!"

"You guys are my soul brothers," Jackson had replied, and there had been no argument with that. It was the truth and every man knew it. There was no line between race or religion out in the bush. There was simply "us" and "them." They were all Marines and all fighting together for survival. Maybe in some squads or platoons there were racial slurs, whether against black, Mexican, Italian, or otherwise, but in First Squad, Third Platoon, a man was liked or disliked because of his personality and that was all. And it wasn't a bad feeling to have.

When the two fire teams got a good hundred meters on the outskirts of the camp, they split from each other. Jackson and his three men headed in a northwest direction, while Lieutenant Campbell and his team headed in a southwest column, filing silently through the night.

Their rendezvous, if all went as planned, was to set up ambush sights on either side of the saddle of the mountain where the other Marines had been taken just days earlier.

It was slow moving for Jackson and his team. Every nerve in his body was strained and tense as he walked point and listened to night sounds that might have sounded friendly any other time. Now they only

173

seemed ominous and dangerous. Jackson moved cautiously through the brush, gently pushing aside the towering, sharp edges of elephant grass. His one handball glove offered little protection. Flexing his fingers, Jackson reflected on the inanities of the Marine Corps, and how the tiniest want could escalate into a necessity before the order filtered through the system and was filled. Gloves were essential in the bush, yet his squad had received handball gloves. Some of the equipment—if it worked at all—didn't work that well, and yet to send it back would be to do without. If it wasn't for the packages from home, he would have no writing paper or pens. A small thing, yes, but necessary nonetheless. Those letters to The World were sometimes all that held him together. The time he spent with pen and paper briefly transported him out of Vietnam and back to a world that was sane and orderly, where the biggest danger was a mugger or a speeding truck, not a murderous ambush and enemies filled with hatred.

Jackson pushed on, trudging through rice paddies that rose knee-high with filthy water and tickling green shoots. His boots sloshed through the water with soggy squelches that sounded overloud in the dense quiet, and he was glad the moon was still playing hide and seek with those clouds. Jungle foliage rose sharply to the left and the right, and they were tunneling into the thick trees with each forward step they took. Jackson could almost smell death in the air. It hung like vines roping down in front of his face, waiting just ahead, lurking like the invisible Cheshire cat in a tree or behind a hump. He shuddered lightly and hoped none of his men noticed.

Maybe his imagination was working overtime and nothing waited ahead. Maybe.

Boots crunched small twigs and dried leaves underfoot, and a musty fog permeated the silence. It hung in gauzy drifts that couldn't be seen in the dark, and now it was so quiet he could hear the men breathing behind him. Fog did that. It shrouded the surroundings so that everything sounded louder, and Jackson hated it. He swallowed hard and kept pushing forward, pausing every three or four meters to check from side to side and occasionally his rear. They were slowly making time—a klick an hour—but he still had this feeling of impending doom hanging over him. It had to be the jungle that gave him that feeling, that made him feel as if he would be ambushed before he could set up his own death trap for the VC.

When they finally got to their destination on top of the small knoll overlooking the saddle to the south, Jackson heaved a sigh of relief. All his premonitions had been wrong, maybe. He and Bug took first watch, while Carrigan and Baroni slumped under a tree to cop a few Z's.

Now that they were settled into position, Jackson could hear all kinds of sounds. The night he had thought so quiet and still held a variety of noises. Monkey chatter mingled with the sleepy chirp of exotic birds, and the occasional slow swing of a tree branch or vine made a soft, rustling nose that set teeth on edge and made the hair on the back of their necks prickle. Jackson had never considered the fact that the sound of a gentle breeze in the trees could be so noisy. Crouched down beneath the shelter of some kind of thick bush that he couldn't identify, Jackson waited.

It wasn't foggy in the higher spot they'd chosen, and the shadows were sharper. Two hours passed, two hours of watching every movement in the dark shadows unbroken by moonlight. It was beginning to take a toll on Jackson's night vision. He was seeing things that weren't there. Jackson discovered that if he stared at one particular bush or tree stump too long, it became a moving enemy. He shifted his gaze from spot to spot, pausing for only a moment or two at a time, realizing that if he continued staring in one direction too long he would imagine action where there was none. To give a false alert could be fatal.

The Vietnam night had its own rules, its own laws, and Jackson was now beginning to get a Master's degree in the fine art of night movements.

He sat stiff and still for what seemed like an eternity and must have descended into some sort of mental daze. Before Jackson realized what was going on, Baroni was nudging him in the side and whispering urgently, "Jack, wake up! It's got Carrigan!"

Snapping wide-awake, Jackson gave a shake of his head and whipped around to look at Baroni. "What—what are you talkin' about, man?" His voice came out in a low growl.

Baroni's hand clamped down on his arm, and he gave a warning shake of his head to indicate silence, mouthing, "I don't know, but it's the biggest fuckin' thing I've ever seen!" His whisper grated into the air and he scooted closer in a kind of duck-waddle as he added, "Huge!"

"Speak up, Baroni," Jackson said. "If the VCs

have got Carrigan, they sure as hell know we're here!"

"But—but it's not VC! A bear or lion, maybe. I don't know, but it picked Carrigan up in its mouth and is dragging him down the hill over here." Baroni gave a violent shake of his head as he jabbed his arm in the direction he wanted Jackson to see.

Jackson reacted quickly, poking the still-sleeping Bug with one hand as he snapped out an order.

"Bug! Gimme that infrared you got! Quick!" Jackson grabbed Bug's pack and began to rummage through it.

Startled from his sleep and half dazed, Bug mumbled, "Here it is." He pulled up the small infrared telescope from a leather necklace under his shirt.

To run blindly through the jungle after Carrigan and whoever—or whatever—had him would be courting death. He had to find out what direction and what had him. It was already dark in the jungle with the press of the trees overhead, and the vague splinters of moonlight that had been able to filter through had been obscured by clouds a few hours before, making visibility nil by now. Without the aid of the night scope Bug carried, it would have been nearly impossible to see. Jackson positioned it and squinted through the instrument, scanning the terrain in a slow sweep.

Success.

There in the vivid eye of the scope, Jackson made out the image of an enormous creature. It strolled along slowly and gracefully, slightly swinging from side to side with its burden draping from huge jaws and dragging along the ground.

"Shit!" Jackson exploded. "The damn thing acts like it just picked up dinner from the local meat market!" He yanked the scope down and fumbled for his rifle.

"What is it?" Baroni was demanding frantically. "What is it?"

"A tiger!" Jackson growled as he found his fifty-caliber and lunged to his feet. He followed through the brush as quietly as he could, not wanting to warn the huge beast or scare it into taking off with Carrigan. And how in the hell had that animal *lifted* Carrigan? The huge Montana coal miner had to weigh two hundred and fifty pounds, yet the tiger was carrying him as daintily as a picnic lunch!

Jackson inched down the other side of the hill where the cat was casually dragging Carrigan. He hoped that Carrigan was still alive. It didn't seem possible, not with the blood-slick stones he stepped over on the trail, but he had to hope. And how to get Carrigan back without alerting every VC in the area? That was a problem, too.

Lifting his fifty-caliber, he made his choice. Another quick glance through the infrared, and he sliced off a round to the rear of the animal, hoping to startle it into dropping Carrigan and fleeing into the jungle. It worked like a charm.

As Carrigan dropped to the ground like a stone, Jackson again ripped off another round, and this time the leaping tiger was the one dropping to the ground. It fell from midair, landing in a crumpled heap of bloody fur and white fangs.

Rising from his crouched position, Jackson stretched to his full height and took a deep, steadying breath. It had all happened so quickly, and there had been so little time to decide, to react. For a moment he just stood there, not running forward to see about Carrigan or the tiger, just trying to assimilate what had happened.

Then his radio crackled, bringing him back to earth with a thud.

"Big Bad Wolf! Big Bad Wolf! Come in, this is Papa Bear. What's the trouble? Do we have Victor Charlie? Come in, come in, Big Bad," the lieutenant's radio spurted into the cool, now-quiet Vietnamese night. It brought a quick return to reality for Jackson. Shaking uncontrollably with reaction, he returned the transmission.

He fumbled in the darkness with the recessed control knob of the radio, flicking it from Off through Stnby and Trns/Bcn to Trans/Vce. His thumb pressed the receiver, and he cleared his throat to speak.

"Negative, Papa Bear. Abort, Papa Bear. No Victor Charlie. Repeat. *No Victor Charlie.* Just a little visit from a—a pet from the wicked witch of the north. Do you understand? Over," Jackson said in a rapid blur, trying to recall which fairy tale code he was supposed to be using. Mother Goose or the Wizard of Oz? Hell, he couldn't remember right now! He tried to continue the conversation, "Meet you back at Oz or Kansas or . . . ahhh . . . Never-Never Land. We'll circle the wagons at the OK Corral. Do you understand, Papa Bear?"

The radio crackled affirmative, but it didn't sound very convincing, and he could hear the disgust in the static voice filtering through. Too bad. He'd momentarily lost it, but given a few minutes, he might be able to make up for it.

Jackson sprinted toward Carrigan with a feeling of dread. Bug and Baroni were hot on his heels as he reached the huge limp form lying on the ground. To Jackson's utter amazement, Carrigan was alive and talking when they got to him, cursing the tiger and the Marines almost in the same breath.

"Hey, Carrigan!" Bug said, kneeling beside his fallen comrade. "You okay?"

"Hell, no! I'm bleeding like a stuck pig!" the Marine shot back in a wheeze. "I feel like I've been through a meat grinder, but I don't think I'm dyin'. . . ."

Blood soaked Carrigan's torn jungle utilities as Jackson examined him, and he shook his head in amazement. "I can't believe you're still alive! Man, there's fang marks in you as big as a machete!"

Carrigan managed a weak grin. "Are my guts still inside or outside?"

"Inside," Jackson assured him. "But I don't know how."

"I'm tough," Carrigan said with another wheezing breath. "And I learned something in Montana: Play dead when you've got to. I figured that tiger had to think kinda like a grizzly does, so I played possum. The more I squirmed the harder he clamped down, so I did what came natcherly. . . ."

"Don't talk anymore right now," Jackson said quickly when Carrigan began to cough. He could see the slick shine of blood oozing between the Marine's fingers as he held his side and realized that he could bleed to death before they got him to a medic.

"Carrigan, can you walk?" Jackson asked.

"Yeah, I think so."

"Well, come on. We gotta get outa here quick. We just blew any chance we had at surprise, and every VC in the general neighborhood is gonna be down on our ass in a few minutes."

Baroni and Bug were kneeling beside the prone body of the tiger, a huge animal stretching well over seven feet from nose tip to tail. Jackson shouldered the huge Montana coal miner and lifted him so that his feet were dragging the ground, and as they passed the tiger and Marines, Carrigan muttered, "Hey, Sarge, looks like you shot him in the balls. . . ."

Sidestepping the tiger, Jackson slated one quick glance down. "Yeah, yeah," he muttered, "I've felt that ways myself a few times."

Bug and Baroni caught up with Jackson and the wounded Carrigan, gathering up the gear they'd left behind as they quickly vacated the area. No point in sticking around and waiting for the inevitable. The VC could be a lot worse than a tiger.

Jackson's heart almost stopped beating from fright as they rounded a turn in the path and caught a glimpse of uniformed soldiers just ahead. Then, realizing it was the second team, his breathing began to return to normal and he regained the use of his muscles. For one brief instant, he had thought it was death waiting ahead.

"Jackson!" Campbell said in a low voice, striding briskly forward. "What the hell happened?"

"Carrigan here almost got eaten by a fuckin' tiger," Jackson panted as he walked closer to the other men. "Somebody give me a hand with all this gear." He tossed Smitty and Crawdad the extra pack and Carrigan's M-14.

Fortunately, the hump back to the camp went without incident. When they arrived, Doc immediately examined Carrigan's wounds. "God, what the hell got a hold on you? A damn tiger or something?" Doc Weathers demanded as he peeled off the coal miner's shirt and began to clean the puncture wounds.

"You got it, Doc." Carrigan rippled with pain as he tried to grin.

After a brief start of surprise, Doc nodded. He immediately grabbed up his bag and delved into the contents, coming up with a syringe and small glass bottle. "Here, let me give you something for the pain," Doc said as he filled the hypodermic with a liberal dose of morphine.

It didn't take long for Carrigan to feel the effects of the painkiller, and he began to relax while Doc cleaned his wounds and bound him as best he could. "I don't think I can do much more than that for now," Doc quietly told Jackson. "I've called in a medevac, and they'll get him back to the hospital at Chu Lai as soon as possible."

"Is he gonna make it, Doc?" Jackson asked with a frown.

Opening one eye, Carrigan looked up at Jackson and Doc Weathers. His face split in a hazy grin as he muttered, "I ain't gonna let no lil' bite take me outa this war when I'm having so much fun, Jack. . . ."

Sergeant Jackson and Doc Weathers exchanged

grave looks over Carrigan's chewed body and said at
the same time, "Sure, Carrigan!"

CHAPTER 11

A couple of months rolled past, and the tiger incident faded in the face of more pressing problems. The men of Camp Rascal grew closer with each night patrol they survived. They began to feel invincible. There were more than seven confirmed dead VC for the new unit under their belts, but so far no *real evidence* of NVA regulars in the area. The lieutenant had asked numerous times for more men from HQ, but to no avail.

That decision still held. Jackson strolled casually into the command hootch as the lieutenant was breaking connection with the captain on the radio. He perched on the edge of the desk and folded his arms across his chest, knowing the answer before he asked the question.

"Well, what's the word, Lieutenant? We gonna get those extra men we need?"

Campbell wiped his face with his hands and shook his head as he said wearily, "The captain said he couldn't send us any because right now most of the Marines are being sent up north to the DMZ for battalion operations. But he said he would do what he could as soon as possible."

"Yeah, it's pretty hairy up there. I tell ya, Lieutenant, I'd rather be here any day than dancing with Mr. Charles up there! I like the freedom of the jungle."

Campbell looked up at him. "That's right," he said, suddenly recalling what he'd heard about Jackson and the men of the First Squad. "You and the Bitches did a little dance at Operation Hastings, right?"

"Yeah. It's a different game. I mean, death was random in a big battle. Mortars fell where they wanted to, with no regard to rank or reason. Half the time you would swear it was even our own artillery that was blowing away our men. At least in the jungle down here, you can pick and choose your shots. A little more one-on-one-type deal, if ya know what I mean."

"Yes, I know." Campbell leaned back and regarded Jackson thoughtfully. The sergeant seemed to have adapted well to the jungle warfare and was growing more deadly with each passing day. If Command wanted something done, Campbell was inclined to send Jackson and his men out to do it. They'd get the job done swiftly and efficiently. "Yes, I believe you may be right, Jackson," he said slowly. "Jungle warfare has its advantages."

The night's patrol went smoothly, without incident. The men returned to the camp just as the sun was beating a hot path over the eastern horizon. Light glinted from the metal sides of a slick that was buzzing down to the helipad as the fire teams trooped through the wire surrounding the camp.

Weary from his night of humping and waiting, Jackson squinted at the slick. It couldn't be. But it sure did look like it. . . . No, he told himself, it couldn't be!

Smitty echoed Jackson's thoughts, blurting, "Man, it can't be! What's he doing back here?"

Grinning like a clown as he tumbled from the chopper and onto the helipad, Carrigan gave a one-handed wave. At his side bounded the huge form of what looked from a distance like a wolf. Jackson and Smitty sprinted to the edge of the helipad and greeted Carrigan with hearty hugs and handshakes. They regarded his canine friend with less enthusiasm.

"How the hell are ya, big man?" Jackson asked with a grin bisecting his broad face from ear to ear.

Smitty chimed in with his annoying Groucho accent, "Yeah, what's happening, big Tom? What's the matter? Cat got your tongue?"

"Everything's great, man! Just great. I only had to get about forty-nine stitches, see?" Carrigan lifted up the edges of his shirt and displayed a neat row of stitches as if they were a coveted trophy.

"What a coincidence! The same number as your IQ," Smitty joked.

Delisi elbowed his way close, glancing from Carrigan to the huge dog that sat on its haunches with its tongue lolling from between open jaws. "Shut up, Smitty," he said, his eyes resting on the dog. "Give Carrigan a chance to tell us about all those sweet little nurses' hearts he busted back in Chu Lai. Come on, did ya get any?"

"Is that all you think about, Delisi?" Jackson turned around to ask, and the short Italian grinned and nodded.

"Yep. Sure is."

"Yeah," Gagliano said. "Girls 101 was the only subject Delisi took back in high school. I think he flunked out, though. . . ."

Carrigan gazed at the assembled members of his squad and grinned even more widely. "Well, boys, I didn't break no hearts, just a few cherries, but they gave me a Purple Heart for injuries received in action." Carrigan shrugged. "Yeah, they said it was bad enough a wound to be sent back stateside, but I missed you bitches. I had to come back."

"Likely story!" Bug snorted rudely. "More than likely, you hung onto their coattails and begged to go home!"

"Or got drunk and signed up to come back here," Smitty put in. "Like I've always said," he added, "this numbskull don't have any brains."

"Hey! What's with the pooch here?" Jackson asked, his attention captured by the patiently waiting animal at Carrigan's side.

"I dunno. Some dudes had the bright idea of assigning me to a dog. I had to go through more training than the dog did. . . ."

Carrigan was interrupted by shouts of laughter from his squad, and he gave them all the benefit of his middle finger and a good-natured grin. "What kinda training, Carrigan?" Jackson asked when he stopped laughing. "How to piss on a fire hydrant or something?"

"No, how to smell out shitbirds like you guys!" Carrigan shot back. "This is a *special* dog, for *special* people. That's why I've got him and none of you do!'"

"Yeah, yeah, yeah," Mudders hooted. "What in the hell does he do?"

"Funny you should use that particular phrase, Mudboy, 'cause this dog's familiar with hell.'" Carrigan paused, let the pause develop to just the right second, then said, "His name is Devil."

Looking at him, Jackson could well believe it. "Well, what *does* he do, Carrigan?" he asked.

Carrigan shrugged. "Seems that he's some kind of LURP dog. The guy said he was specially trained down in Bien Hoa for trackin' gooks and sniffing out booby traps."

"Why the bad name?" Jackson asked.

"Devil fit him. You'll see why." Carrigan patted the meaty German shepherd under the chin and received a wet tongue along his hand in return.

"He looks like a devil," Crawdad said. "Look at his eyes. They're redder than hell-far!" His Mississippi accent was in full bloom, and the men laughed.

The slick was still blowing up dust when the lieutenant joined them, greeting Carrigan and looking askance at the dog. "What's this we have here? A new addition to the unit?"

"Seems HQ couldn't send us any more men, so they gave us man's best friend, Lieutenant—a LURP dog," Jackson said.

"Better than nothing," Campbell replied.

Devil trotted docilely beside his new squad as they walked Carrigan back to their hootch and caught up on all that had gone on since his unexpected vacation. The rest of the day was spent in sorting through the resupply left by the slick that had brought in Carrigan, reading mail, and opening packages from home.

Smitty took this time to show Carrigan something that he thought might interest his friend. They walked over behind the command hootch where Doc had a table set up and was working on something. Metal containers filled with different types of chemicals and such were strewn across the table's surface.

Smitty rounded the corner first and said, "Finished yet, Doc?"

"Yeah, come on back," Doc said with a wide grin.

Carrigan could hardly believe his eyes. There on the table was the beast that had almost ended his life.

"Yeah, Doc here is an old hand at the fine art of taxidermy. Learned it from his ole man up in the mountains of northern Idaho. We all thought you might like the hide as a souvenir from your little tour here 'in-country' in this fine Republic of South Vietnam." Smitty rocked back on his heels and smiled, waiting for Carrigan's reaction.

"He's seven and a half feet long, not counting the tail," Doc said. "We are talking trophy size, to say the least. Here ya go." Doc then grabbed the hide and head of the huge beast and handed it to Carrigan.

"I can't believe it! Thanks, guys. We got to get a picture of this for the folks back home," Carrigan said as he stared at the hide of the enormous beast. "They won't believe it!"

"Great idea! I'll round up everybody for the picture!" Smitty was off like a bolt of lightning, yelling for someone to go look for a camera and telling them to meet in front of the CP.

"Come on, Bitches! Give some big cheeses, only if it pleases. We might even make the cover of *Stars and*

Stripes!" Smitty was cajoling as he tried to marshal the squad into some sort of line and get them to look happy.

The men of Camp Rascal were all smiles and thumbs-up when the flash from the old Polaroid camera made them blink even in the broad daylight of the hot Vietnamese sun.

After the picture was preserved for posterity, the tiger hide and head was mounted just below the makeshift wooden sign above the Command hootch's door. It read: "Camp Rascal."

CHAPTER 12

Mudders stormed into the rifle squad's hootch. "Bugman, you in here?"

"Over here," Bug answered as he looked up from the book that he was reading. Entitled *The Guerrilla—And How to Fight Him*, it was a collection of excerpts from the Marine Corps Gazette. Bug was the type of guy that was a reader, not a geek-type guy or a bookworm. He had always said that "Knowledge is power, and one can never have too much power."

"What is it, Mudboy?" he asked without much interest

"You got a crate over at the mortar ammo dump. I thought it was just another box of mortars when we got the resupply yesterday, but this one has got your name marked on it. *Special Delivery* is written all over it! PFC Paul Clayton. Come and check it out," Mudders said with a gleam in his eye.

Roused by curiosity, Bug followed Mudders to the ammo dump and found a huge wooden crate standing on a pallet. He immediately reached for something to open it with. The crowbar moved in a levered motion as the top of the crate was pried open.

"Shit, the ole man came through this time," Bug said with a wide grin.

"What is it?" Mudders asked, frowning in confusion.

Bug grabbed the instruction manual that was sealed in plastic and lying on top of the crate's contents. It read: "MINI-SID Seismic Intrusion Device, Department of the Army." At the bottom it read in small letters: "Central Intelligence Agency, 1966."

"Just something that's gonna save our asses around here, that's all," Bug returned in elation as he tore into the contents of the crate. "Go get Sarge," he added.

Bug was like a kid in a candy store as he read the manual with an avid expression. It wasn't until he'd reached the end that he noticed a handwritten letter stuck in the back. It was from his father.

"Dear Son," it read. "I know it must be tough for you over there in Vietnam. You know I could have pulled strings to get you out. I didn't. Your mother still holds that against me. But you've got to learn for yourself what the hell is going on over there. The next best thing I could do was equip you with all the latest technology that I have at my disposal. I know you'll do just fine if you have the right tools. I've also enclosed a couple of the latest briefs on electronic surveillance. Also enclosed are a couple of editions of *Popular Mechanics*. Love, Dad. P.S. If you need anything—I mean anything!—just contact Lieutenant Danny Sutherland in the supply depot at Chu Lai. He's my friend. And by the way, I won the election. Don't forget to write your mother."

Bug laughed to himself as he finished the letter.

Shaking his head as he refolded it and put it back into the envelope, he murmured, "Damn, Pop! You're quite a guy!"

Jackson pushed open the doors and strolled into the room, looking around with mild interest as he asked, "What ya need, Bug?"

"Come here and take a look what dear ole Dad sent me. A little care package from home," Bug said as he rummaged through the crate and unwrapped one of the devices.

"What the hell ya got here?" Stepping closer, Jackson peered curiously at the huge wooden crate.

Grinning with pleasure, Bug held up a cylindrical device. "They're called SIDs—seismic intrusion devices—and they're great. You can hear and detect any mechanized traffic for up to three hundred meters, and foot traffic up to one hundred and fifty meters. No more guessing where Charlie will be patrolling from now on, Sarge," Bug said with a wide grin curling his lips.

Impressed, Jackson stepped closer. "How many you got there?" he asked.

"About a dozen or so . . . hey!" Stopping, Bug lifted up another bulky package from inside the crate. "Shit, four extra receivers, spare batteries, and microphones, too! The ole man has really outdone himself this time." Bug gazed at the equipment, fondling it with sheer delight.

Jackson looked at Bug with a new respect. He'd always known he was mechanically inclined and loved to tinker with any kind of electronic device, but this beat everything! Bug rose several notches in his estimation as he began to explain the intricacies of the

193

electrical workings of the device, few of which Jackson understood. Hell, a man would have to be a college professor to understand some of what he was saying! Shaking his head, Jackson had the thought that this guy ought to be a fuckin' general or at least go into politics. With a shrewd brain like his, he'd be a sure thing.

"Just listen to this!" Bug exclaimed as he thumbed through a manual, pausing every few pages to scan them. " 'When the MINI-SID senses a valid seismic disturbance, a 6-volt, 15-millisecond MINI-SID detect signal is sent to the AAU.' That's an Audio Add-on Unit," he looked up to explain before continuing. " 'If three MINI-SID detect signals are received during a 29-second period, a 300-millisecond timing pulse is generated. During this 300-millisecond time interval, the background noise sensed by the microphone is sampled to establish a level of voltage in an automatic gain control (agc) circuit. The level of agc established controls the gain of the audio amplifier, which amplifies the output of the microphone. The output of the audio amplifier, 0.3 to 1.0 volt rms, is sent to MINI-SID for transmission. The duration of the audio sent to MINI-SID is 15 seconds, which starts at the end of the 300-millisecond time interval. If the three MINI-SID detect signals are not received during the 29-second period, the AAU resets itself. When the AAU is. . . .' "

"Okay, okay, Bug," Jackson interrupted hastily before he could go on. "I get the idea."

Bug gave him a beatific smile. "Ain't this great?"

"Yeah, it's great. Come on, Bug, let's go show the LT," Jackson said as he grabbed him by the arm and pulled him away from his new toys.

Bug grudgingly obliged, and it wasn't long before Lieutenant Campbell was sharing Jackson's enthusiasm for Bug's brains. The rest of the day and well into the night found Lieutenant Campbell, Sergeant Jackson, and PFC Paul "Bug" Clayton studying the maps, reading the instruction manuals, and plotting the possible locations to set the devices.

They'd been working for a while when Campbell asked idly, "Bug, about your father. In what capacity did he work for the CIA?"

"Ah, hell, Lieutenant, he did a lot of covert operations in Germany and the South Pacific during World War II, as well as the Korean conflict. As far as exactly what he did, I'm not quite sure. He was always gone. I never saw him except on holidays and such. He retired a couple of years ago. But he still goes out of town for extended periods of time. We still don't know exactly what he does. Pretty much a reserved-type guy."

"Well, he must have some real pull with the higher-ups who really count in order to get equipment like this sent to you." Campbell eyed the equipment.

"Bug, you got it down on how to read the receiver's signals? I mean, as far as the distance goes from the device to the sound?" Jackson looked up and asked.

Bug nodded. "I think so, but I would like to give it a test run right around here to make sure."

Rising to his feet, Campbell stretched to ease tensed muscles. They'd been sitting for a while, bent over the equipment and instruction manuals. "You've got it. What do you want us to do?" he asked.

"Well, why don't we set one about a hundred meters

from the perimeter here, with just one person walking as quiet as possible toward it. When I get a reading, then we will know the exact range of the device. Then we can have one man walk a circle around it in a fifty-meter radius so I can differentiate the readings," Bug said as he continued perusing the manual.

Jackson clapped his hands together. "Let's do it!"

The testing was successful, and Bug had worked out the electronic glitches of the device. The next move was to test it on Charlie.

The patrol went out the next morning to set a SID in a prime area some five klicks from the camp. It was an area that the lieutenant had studied on maps and with reports, and which he thought was a possible area for a tunnel complex. Daylight recon was not new to the Marines, but it sure seemed like a long time since they had done it. They were more accustomed to the night shadows that hid them but also hid the VC. The squad considered it almost a breeze. Carrigan was determined to test the "Devil Dog," so they brought him along to see what he could do.

It wasn't long before the Devil got his due. It was Carrigan's turn to walk point, and he had Devil at his side. The brush was thick and the wild animal trail so overgrown that he had to slash a wider path with his machete. Sweat rolled down his face, and several times Carrigan had to stop and wipe it from his eyes with his sleeve. After such a brief pause he started to push forward again, lifting his machete high to bring it across a tangle of vines looping in front of the trail.

Devil began to growl fiercely, his hackles rising as

he took a few stiff-legged steps forward to block Carrigan. A chill rippled up the Marine's spine and he froze in place, not knowing what the animal could smell out there in the brush. VC? Another tiger, maybe? Standing stiff and still, Carrigan whispered, "What is it, Devil? What is it, boy?"

"What's the problem, Carrigan?" Jackson asked, pushing forward to check it out.

"I don't know. The Devil is going crazy! Something is wrong, and I don't know what," Carrigan answered, shaking his head.

"Let him go. We'll see what happens."

As if understanding Jackson's order, Devil bounded off in a series of leaps, heading down the trail a good five meters before he stopped and began pawing at the ground. His black nose roved the area as if he were a grazing cow, sniffing and snorting, pausing, then snuffling along the ground again. It was obvious to the trailing Marines that Devil had found something.

Carrigan was right behind the dog when Jackson yelled for him to stop. "Big man, stop. It might be a booby trap!"

Jerking to a halt, Carrigan and the men behind him stood stock-still. The Marines waited, sweating it out as time ticked past. When nothing else happened, no VC swarming or Bouncing Betty exploding, they began to breathe easier. Then they moved cautiously forward, approaching the excited dog with furtive, wary movements. Jackson was right. It was a booby trap! Devil was pawing frantically at a small hole in the ground.

Kneeling down beside the dog, Jackson pushed aside a pile of damp, rotting leaves to reveal a hidden

197

pit. The leaves and grass on top formed a flimsy covering that hid punji sticks as sharp as needles, lining the sides and bottom to stick into an unwary Marine's foot. The VC usually smeared the pointed sticks with excrement so that infection would go deep into a man's foot, and only the swiftest medical treatment could avert the poisoning of the injured Marine's system.

Crouching beside Jackson, Bug nudged him in the ribs. "You know what that means, don't ya, Sarge?" His mouth tightened as Bug added, "We might be near or on top of a tunnel!"

The rest of the afternoon was spent searching for an entrance to the suspected tunnel. It went undetected. Even the Devil couldn't uncover a hole or an entrance. Weary and disgusted, they decided to plant the seismic device in the immediate area of the punji hole.

There had to be a tunnel nearby, they reasoned. Why else would there be a booby trap in the immediate area? It wasn't a regular Marine travel route, but rather a path well off the usual tracks. The VC were, in all probability, Jackson figured, trying to protect something. It was his bet it was something very important.

Pleased at this opportunity to use his new toys, Bug went to work. Using his entrenching tool, he dug down one and a half feet, then carefully bured the MINI-SID. Pulling the camouflaged antenna to its full height, he stretched the ten-foot microphone cord in a directional position and planted the spikes of the microphone into a tree. He then transplanted fresh brush around it to keep it from being too obvious to the wary VC. The entire operation took about half an hour.

Pleased at the results, the Marines marched on. The rest of the day was spent patrolling and planting more devices in the hills. It was around sunset when the seven Marines turned onto a switchback of the small trail and a stream bed came into full view. They stopped, crouching down when they saw the khaki-clad figures of three NVA soldiers sitting by the bank. Two black-pajamaed figures were in the process of stripping down to take a bath.

Jackson shot a grim smile at Baroni, whose eyes were narrowed on the enemy. "What'dya say, Baroni? Looks like the NVA and the VC are working together on this one. Do we take 'em?"

"You bet" was the savage reply, and there as the muted clink of rifles being slung up to a firing position. By this time, two of the VC were already soaping up in the stream, laughing and splashing one another with geysers of water. Perfect targets.

It was Carrigan who opened up first, half rising and holding his M-14 at waist level as he sprayed the VC with a hail of bullets, firing so rapidly it was almost as if it were a single blast. As he crouched there shooting, he inadvertently released Devil's choker chain, freeing the dog to run into the bush. Cursing softly under his breath, Carrigan couldn't take the time to call him back or go after him. The dog was on his own.

Meanwhile, the rest of the squad flanked hard on the downstream side, opening up with their automatic weapons and giving Charlie hell.

Carrigan's first magazine of ammo took down the NVAs on shore like a row of dominoes, while Jackson, Baroni, and Bug's rifle fire tore into the water, boiling the other two alive in a froth of bubbles and bullets. It took only sixty seconds to waste them, with no return fire.

The only fire left was in the eyes of the Devil as the dog emerged from the bushes on the opposite side of the stream from the Marines and charged the fallen NVA with furious growls and static electricity that lifted his hackles. Sharp teeth ripped at the throats of one of the fallen NVA, and he gave a fierce shake of his head, slinging blood and gobbets of flesh like crazy.

"Damn! Look at that!" Jackson said, awed by the ferocity.

"Yeah," Carrigan muttered, sliding down the muddy banks with his rifle held over his head. "The sight of a slant-eye drives him nuts, don't it?" It wasn't until Carrigan reached the dog and managed to grab the trailing leash that Devil reluctantly released the frayed ends of the NVA's jugular vein. Shrugging, Carrigan gave the panting dog a pat on his head and said, "Good boy!" Devil gave him a slack-jawed grin, his bloody tongue lolling from his mouth. It was an eerie sight.

Jackson was splashing into the shallow waters of the stream in a futile effort to catch the bodies of the other two VC, but it was too late. They swirled along in the swift-moving currents of the stream, spread-eagled and staring at nothing, black-rimmed bullet holes seeping blood as they slowly cartwheeled downstream.

"Don't worry about getting them, Bug!" Jackson yelled as he grabbed at one of them and missed. "Let's just do what we have to and get the hell out of here!"

He clambered back up onto the slick sides of the banks and sloshed to where Carrigan and the others were rifling the pockets of the dead Khaki-clad NVA.

"Mudboy," he said, panting and out of breath from his efforts, go upstream about fifty meters and stand watch. Crawdad, you go fifty meters downstream and keep an eye out. We could have company soon. Move it. . . ."

Jackson was already turning and reaching for the radio to report back to Camp Rascal. He made contact and gave his report, having to speak loudly to be heard over the growling and snarling of Devil, who seemed to be upset over something.

The amount of energy that Carrigan was using to hold back the Devil was incredible. "Sarge, I gotta do something with this dog. He's going nuts!" Carrigan said as Jackson finished his report and stuck the headphone back into the pack.

Jackson put the field phone away and studied the raging German shepherd closely. There was something odd in the way the dog kept it up, surging against his leash like he'd gone mad. "We'll take care of him," Jackson assured Carrigan.

Pulling out his K-bar, Jackson strolled over to the spot where one of the NVA lay. Sunlight glittered along the sharp blade as he flicked it past the corpse's head. Rocking back on his heels, Jackson held up an ear that he'd neatly sliced away from the skull. Then he tossed it to the dog, muttering, "That ought to calm him down."

Nimbly catching the ear in his gaping jaws, Devil lay down with it between his huge paws and began chewing it like it was a Milkbone. Faintly bemused, Carrigan just stared at the animal for a moment, obviously rethinking his close proximity to a dog that demanded ears for treats.

"Damn! This dog is the devil himself!" Carrigan eyed the dog greedily smacking and chomping down on the severed ear with all the enjoyment of a baby with candy.

Jackson grinned. "Yeah, I'm just glad he's on our side and don't like dark meat!" he said as he began to go through the enemy documents found on the bodies.

It only took a few moments to realize they had been pretty lucky. "Oh, ye-e-es!" Jackson crowed as he eyed the bodies of the dead NVA. "This ought to prove to the S-2 guys that we ain't just fighting the locals around here. Maybe now we can get more support. Come on, let's get these bodies back to Rascal!"

When they reached the banks, they saw that Crawdad had managed to fish out one of the VC bodies from the stream. He had dragged him up onto the banks and was looking rather proud of himself for his efforts. He was dripping wet and breathing hard, but successful.

Flicking a glance at the naked body of the VC, Jackson suggested, "Let's take him along, too. You know how the brass loves body count. And bring along his pajamas. . . ."

The men made it back to the CAP with their NVA trophies intact. They displayed them in the middle of the compound and Jackson went to fetch the lieutenant. It was a welcome sight to Lieutenant Campbell when he stood looking down at the NVA bodies. He'd been right. His hunch was correct, and since it was, maybe now the brass would give him the men needed to do a proper job of freeing the South Vietnamese villagers.

"Well done, Sergeant Jackson, men of First

Squad," he approved as he stared at the bodies.

But when Campbell's gaze drifted to the water-soaked body of the VC owner of the black pajamas, his expression grew ugly. Fists clenching at his sides, Campbell grated, "I knew it! You son of a bitch!" Losing control, the lieutenant drew back his foot and kicked the dead VC in the head. It rolled to the side, the sightless eyes still staring into eternity. "What the—"

"What? What?" Jackson asked, leaping forward in alarm.

"What?" Campbell yelled back. His face was white with fury, his lips drawn back over his teeth in a feral snarl.

"Yeah," Jackson said. "What?"

"What?" You ask me *what*?"

Confused, and not certain if Campbell had lost it again, Jackson answered, "Yeah, what?"

Campbell seemed to calm down slightly. Regaining control with an obvious effort, he was panting slightly as he replied, "That's one of those damned PFs. One of the ones that were on the ambush the night my men were killed!"

Jackson was silent. He could almost see the hatred emanating from Campbell as he glared down at the dead PF.

Then Campbell was saying calmly, "I intend to string him up in the square in the middle of the village. We shall make an example of him for all the village to see. It should be an object lesson to any who aspire to the same end."

Jackson immediately protested the decision, but not on the grounds that it would be inhumane. "No, we can't do that, Lieutenant. It would let everyone in the village know that we're on to them. Don't let them know anything. Our knowledge is our power!" Jackson found himself quoting the Bug's favorite line.

"I don't care, Sergeant Jackson. We *want* them to know what in the hell is going on here!" Campbell once more nudged the dead VC with a kick of his foot, then spat on the body with contempt. It was his final decision.

CHAPTER 13

Rotar blades whirred noisily as the Hueys flopped down on the Camp Rascal helipad, seeming to just hover as they disgorged their human cargo. Weary Marines tumbled from the open side doors, fourteen new faces regarding the Combined Action Platoon of Camp Rascal. Ducking the whirling blades, the new men surged forward to wait in a line as they recognized an officer approaching.

It was blazing hot, with the sun high above and beating down on the compound with a vengeance. Jackson and Campbell were waiting for the new men and left the shade of the hootch to meet them when the chopper finally touched down. A tree line soared beyond the camp in a curved arc, cupping the compound in a protective clearing, and the branches swayed from the strong currents stirred by the metal birds. Other than that, there was no wind at all, just hot, searing sun.

Sergeant Jackson and Lieutenant Campbell strode

forward and eyed the ragged line of new replacements with relief. Jackson's narrowed gaze flicked over them quickly, assessing and estimating the worth of these new men. He took notice of the deep creases and furrows in the men's faces, and he was satisfied. Those were lines that only a lot of action "in-country" could mark on a young man. Nodding his approval, Jackson remarked in an aside to Campbell, "I'm glad to see that HQ didn't send us a bunch of cherries."

Grinning, Campbell nodded his agreement. "Yeah, these boys look like they've seen some action."

One of the men separated from the others and walked forward with a loose, easy stride. His dusty camouflage helmet bobbed to one side, and his youthful face held no hint of a smile or a welcome. Cold gray eyes regarded the officers as he paused in front of them and asked carelessly, "You Lieutenant Campbell?"

It wasn't exactly military protocol, no salute or proper greeting, but Campbell let it pass. "Yes, I am. Are you Sergeant Pearcy?"

Pearcy's gaze slid from Jackson to Campbell. "Yes, sir."

"I'm glad you're here." Campbell held out his hand to the new member of the CAP and said, "This is Sergeant Jackson with me."

Seeming rather startled by this polite greeting and introduction, Pearcy paused for only an instant before he took the outstretched hand Campbell offered. After giving it a quick pump, Pearcy then took the hand Jackson held out to him. His quick gaze seemed to assess and classify in a matter of seconds, and Jackson had the inescapable feeling that Pearcy had spent a lot of his days prowling in the jungle, where a man had to live by instinct alone.

"Mind if I dismiss my men?" Pearcy asked in his abrupt manner. "They're pretty tired."

"Certainly," Campbell replied, and Pearcy swiveled around and gave the order to dismiss. The men spread out in ten different directions at once, each seeming to know where to go and what to do.

"Looks like you guys have seen a little action before," Jackson observed after a moment.

Pearcy nodded. "Yeah, been up by the 17th parallel, with battalion operations. To tell ya the truth, I'm glad to be here."

"Well, welcome to Camp Rascal. It's not much, but it beats the hell out of dodging mortars," Campbell said, then added, "It looks as if you and your men could use some food and a cleanup. Sergeant Jackson will get you acclimated and show you around. I have some business I must attend to in the village, but I'll meet with you both later in my hootch, gentlemen." Giving a nod of his head, Campbell pivoted to walk away.

"Before you go, Lieutenant," Pearcy said quickly, "I think there are some other people you might want to meet."

Pausing, Campbell turned back around to ask, "Who's that?"

Pearcy pointed over his shoulder. "The two ROKs over there. Somebody ordered them up from HQ. Good guys as much as I can tell, and they speak perfect English, too," Pearcy added.

Squinting against the sunlight, Campbell said, "Bring them over here. You're right. I'd like to meet them. I've heard nothing but good things about ROKs. They're supposed to be among the bravest and fightingest men in the world's armed forces." Campbell looked at Jackson and arched his brows in a curious sort of way as Pearcy pivoted abruptly and strode toward two men looking up at the tiger head mounted over the doorway of the command post hootch.

When Pearcy paused beside the two men, Jackson narrowed his gaze on the Republic of Korea soldiers. He was surprised by their appearance. Though short, they were stouter than any other Asian persons he had ever seen, with taut, muscular builds and broad shoulders. They also had healthy color in their faces unlike the Vietnamese, who looked undernourished and anemic from lack of a proper diet.

Pearcy and the two ROKs conversed rapidly for a few minutes, then the two men strode forward in a brisk military walk to greet the lieutenant.

The older-looking Korean gave a quick, respectful bow to Lieutenant Campbell and said in a soft voice, "Hello, my name is Sergeant Lee Bock Song, and this is Corporal Kim Il Sun, Army of the Republic of Korea, Tiger Unit." Sergeant Lee gave a snappy American salute, which Campbell returned.

Noting the tiger emblem on the RKO's shirtsleeve, Jackson said, "Oh, that's the reason the two of you were gawking at the tiger over there." Grinning, he gave a mock bow in return to the Koreans, and they did the same. "It's proper etiquette, Lieutenant!" Jackson whispered loudly at the bemused officer, and Campbell flashed him a wry glance as he imitated the Asian salute.

"Yes, that is a very big tiger. It is the mascot for our branch of service to our country," Sergeant Lee said as he straightened, puffing out his chest in pride.

Feeling rather foolish for bowing and hoping no one had seen him, Campbell asked, "Tell me, Sergeant Lee, why exactly are you here? Headquarters failed to notify me of your impending arrival." Shrugging when Jackson gave him a pained look, Campbell tried to remind himself not to look a gift horse in the mouth as he waited for the answer.

"We are assigned to your Combined Action Platoon to better acquaint you and your brave Marines, along with the Popular Forces of the village of Tou Lon, with the martial arts of Tae Kwon Do" was the bland reply, followed by, "And we are also to aid in what language skills we know to further the winning of their hearts and minds over to the freedom of which our free countries are so well accustomed." A big smile followed this accented reply, and Sergeant Lee gave another short bow.

Campbell seemed momentarily taken aback, but he managed to rally after a moment. "Well, Sergeant, you can dispose of any notion of winning the hearts and minds of this village. It would be like beating a dead horse, if you understand what I mean. It's of no use. May I see your orders, please?" Lieutenant Campbell asked politely when the Korean officer gave him a confused stare.

"Yes, I have them here." Sergeant Lee dug into his shirt pocket and removed his papers. They were done in triplicate. Excess of paperwork, Campbell had been heard to say, was a ruse devised by military personnel who had no desire to actually go to war and preferred remaining in safer quarters that were surrounded by paperwork and not the enemy.

As the Korean handed the papers to the lieutenant, Jackson pushed his helmet to the back of his head and observed, "Yeah, the locals around here are about as worthless as tits on a boar-hog."

The Korean turned a blank look toward Jackson, obviously not understanding the comparison for a moment. Moved to explain, Jackson opened his mouth just as the explanation presented itself to Sergeant Lee. Lee broke into loud, raucous laughter that sounded like the screeching of truck brakes, startling Jackson.

"Ah, I see! I see! Very clever, Sergeant Jackson!" Lee approved with a wide smile.

While Lieutenant Campbell perused the papers of the new members of CAP Rascal, Jackson took the opportunity to ask a few questions about the art of Tae Kwon Do.

"Do you concentrate more on the upper or lower body development in Tae Kwon Do?" Jackson asked, hazarding a guess as to proper terminology. He knew little about the history or technique used in warfare by the ROKs but did know that it was easy to get a man to talk about what interested him.

"I would be honored to show such a fine black American marine the finer techniques of my art," Sergeant Lee said in his singsong English accent.

Responding in kind—polite and as precise as he could make it—Jackson said, "I would be more than honored for you and Corporal Kim to teach me and the men in my squad your superior knowledge of martial arts."

It would come in handy, like the words he had begun to silently recite to himself. Lying in his bunk at night, Jackson had thought of a lot of things, one of them being that he should have a slogan to help him get through the days and nights on patrol. It never hurt, and sometimes it helped a lot to have something to hold onto; even if it was like Mudders and his crazy affinity for souped-up cars that kept a man going, it was something. Some of the men in First Squad had families to go home to, wives and kids waiting on them, or just a sweetheart. The World seemed so far away and was beginning to hold an aura of unreality for Jackson. How long had he been here, anyway? It seemed like years, when it had only been nine months. Certainly not long enough to forget what hot dogs smelled like, or hamburgers grilling, or the musky smell of a woman after a long night of loving. No, he had to have his own creed to go by, to survive by, and he'd chosen the one about knowledge being power. One can never have too much power. It was true, and he intended to find out everything he could and survive this goddammed politicians' war he'd been embroiled in. It still made him mad that he was the one over here busting ass and getting shot at while home newspaper headlines screamed about draft dodgers and protesters, and good men bought a one-way ticket out in a body bag with their dogtags tied to their big toe. Yeah, it was a hell of a war, and he was in it up to his ass, just like the rest of First Squad. His men counted. They were real. The rest of the world could go to hell.

When Lieutenant Campbell called Jackson into his hootch a while later, he informed him that the ROKs' credentials had been checked out with HQ and they were to be advisory consultants and teachers to the Marines in the Vietnamese language as well as martial arts. Jackson made a sour face.

"I know enough gook-speak, Lieutenant! Knife—*kai zowa*, tooth—*zing*, captain—*da wi*, clock—*damn ho*, hurry up—*di di*, come out—*lai day*, surrender—*choi hoi*, Marine—*madeen numba one* . . ."

"All right, all right, Sergeant Jackson, you've made your elusive point. You may not need to speak Vietnamese fluently, but it is vital that you understand the language. It could save your life one day."

Jackson patted the weapon belt slung around his waist and said smugly, "This will come closer to saving it than anything, Lieutenant." A razor-sharp machete hung from the green webbing, and a .45 was tucked neatly into the side holster. Three other knives and a small-caliber pistol decorated the rest of the belt, making it droop heavily around his hips. Campbell's eyebrows rose.

"Perhaps, but orders are orders." Campbell gave an irritated shake of his head. "You've been over here for a while, haven't you, Jackson?"

"Yessir."

"You may need R&R some time soon."

Jackson grinned. "Suits the hell out of me! Tokyo?"

It was Campbell's turn to make a sour face. "I've had reports on your antics in Tokyo, Sergeant Jackson."

"Maybe Saigon, then. They've got stereo systems real cheap there, I've heard, and girls wearing slinky *ao dais* instead of those damned shapeless

212

pajamas. . . ."

"Enough, Jackson!" Campbell barked. "Let's get back to the issue at hand, if you please."

Shrugging, Jackson complied. The lieutenant could get pretty touchy at times, and this seemed to be one of them. He leaned forward, listening as Campbell told him that the ROKs would be going out on patrol with them at times and outlined the correct procedure for these missions.

The men of First Squad quickly discovered that they were no match for the agile Koreans. It didn't take long, and it didn't take but a few times for them to learn.

Grinning, Carrigan had taken the diminutive Korean corporal, Kim, up on his challenge to fight. He had circled him a few times on the mat laid out on the ground and had even managed to lunge at him before all hell broke loose.

"Shit, I didn't know the little fucker had so much kick to him!" Carrigan mourned after the Korean corporal lashed out with a foot and knocked the huge Montana coal miner to the ground. He sat on the mat nursing his bruised jaw.

The others were crowded around, more than a little awed that not only had Corporal Kim beaten the huge, mountainous Carrigan, but he had done it in under five seconds.

"Hell, I didn't think a little ole kick from a slant—I mean, smaller man," Crawdad corrected himself hastily, "could knock down a much bigger man that quick!"

"Karate was designed for the weaker and the smaller in stature, honorable PFC Carrigan. Think what a large American marine could do with such a disciplined control in hand-to-hand combat." Sergeant Lee reached down to help Carrigan up from an undignified heap on the mat, smiling.

"Yeah," Carrigan muttered, his face flushing a bright red as he accepted the Korean's hand.

"So sorry to embarrass you," Lee said, much to the Marine's chagrin. It was bad enough to *be* embarrassed, but did he have to broadcast it? Lee tried to smooth over his partner's triumph over the Marine, saying, "You must try to keep a low stance. You are too big a target for a little man such as myself or Corporal Kim," Lee added, and Carrigan just muttered an agreement.

Sanchez, lurking on the fringes of the squad, commented something like, "Yeah, I'd like to see the little fucker dodge just one of the rounds from my M-14 here."

"Shut up and lissen up!" Jackson growled, shaking his head at Sanchez. He hated the man's sneering attitude and the way he would avoid any kind of manual labor. If there was work to be done, it was a safe bet that Sanchez would be nowhere close by. And now he hung back and just watched while everyone else tried to learn. What a weasel, Jackson thought to himself.

Sergeant Robert L. "Bad Black" Jackson took instruction a lot more seriously. He wanted to soak up every tidbit of information he could, listening closely and watching the lightning-quick Koreans as he practiced the seventeen different deadly hand punches and a host of foot kicks they were taught.

Jackson was obsessed with learning every bit of information or instruction that could help him in the fight to stay alive and leave this godforsaken land called Vietnam.

On the nights he and the "bitches" didn't have patrol, Jackson could be found in his bunk studying maps and plotting routes through the jungle. There were plenty of times he and Bug stayed up after hours and mapped quadrants of the MINI-SIDs that they had planted or replanted. And if they didn't do that, they were in the command hootch listening to the SID's AAU (Audio Add-on Unit) receiver for daytime movement. Jackson was becoming a student of sorts, a student of survival courses and post-graduate courses in killing.

PFC Paul "Bug" Clayton supplied the necessary technical manuals to Jackson. He had reams of them. Manuals for the Mini Seismic Intrusion Device were his newest ones, but he also had field manuals with titles such as FM 5-31 BOOBY TRAPS, or TM 31-200-1 UNCONVENTIONAL WARFARE DEVICES AND TECHNIQUES, a manual Jackson found most helpful as it had references with chapters listing Incendiary Systems, Explosives, Small Arms, and a host of others. His personal favorite was the fire fudge igniter, made of a solution of granulated sugar (1 part) and potassium chlorate (2 parts) in hot water (1 part). It resembled white sugar fudge when cooled to room temperature and solidified, but was excellent for igniting incendiaries. Of course, there were the more common ones such as exploding cigars and cigarettes, but those weren't even unusual anymore after the new James Bond movies came out. He'd seen *Goldfinger* before leaving Memphis and could remember being impressed at the time. He wasn't so impressed now.

Jackson absorbed knowledge like a giant sponge, soaking it up and filing it away in different sections of his brain, knowing he might need it at any time. Any of it could come in handy, and any of it might just save his life or the lives of his men.

With each passing day, he was becoming more and more convinced that he would make it out. All he had to do was listen, learn, and stay awake. It shouldn't be too hard for a man to do if he applied himself. After all, he had things to do when he got back to The World, things he should have done a long time before. His wife—or ex-wife—would have to do some explaining of her own, maybe. Or maybe he would ignore the hell out of her and pretend she didn't exist. He could go home a hero, maybe, with a parade down Main or Front Street, with folks waving American flags and hailing him as one of the heroes of this lousy war. . . . Jackson had to laugh at his own daydreams sometimes.

And he laughed at himself. Why bother with any of it? Why not just take out as many VC as he could before they took him out? That would be more like it, more to the point of this whole damned war, wouldn't it? And sometimes he wondered why he was playing their game for them, why it was him and First Squad who had to duck bullets and wallow in mud or broiling sun while fat politicians sat in air-conditioned hootches and issued orders right and left. Well, to hell with the politicians and their air-conditioned asses. He intended to fight this war any damned way he could, any way he liked. If they didn't like it, let 'em come out to the jungle and tell him about it.

CHAPTER 14

Night patrols grew more successful with each successive use of the Seismic Intrusion Device, letting them trace their patrol routes with less danger. The new knowledge of the area's hidden traps kept them from stumbling unawares through the dark.

The SIDs came in real handy one particular night when First Squad waited just off a rambling jungle trail. No VC had been spotted in the area, but Bug kept picking up evidence of night movement on the sensitive equipment. The squad ranged on both sides of the trail near the SID and waited. It was nearing 0400 hours—past time for their return to Camp Rascal—when Jackson gave the signal to give it up.

"Not yet, Jack!" Bug whispered. "The equipment senses something out there."

"Man, you've been sayin' that all night, and the only thing I've seen is a lot of monkey shit." Jackson slanted him a disgusted look. "I know this SID stuff is your baby, Bug, but don't you think you're going overboard on it? I mean, it don't tell us exactly where they *ain't*, if you get my drift."

Bug gave him an exasperated look and said, "They thought Edison was crazy, too. . . ."

"Oh, for Chrissake!" Jackson muttered. "A quarter hour more, man, and that's all!"

Crouching in the damp and trying to surreptitiously ease his aching, cramped leg muscles, Jackson contemplated stepping further back into the bushes and relieving himself. He was tired. His eyes were scratchy from lack of sleep and he wanted to get back to camp. It was the third night in a row that he'd not had any sleep, and he was going to hit his rack and not wake up for ten hours. He was about to fall asleep in position.

Jackson reached out and put a hand on Bug's shoulder, intending to lean forward and tell him that he was going to step into the bushes. As he started to lean forward, a movement caught his eye along the trail. Being so tired, he wasn't certain he'd seen it. He closed his eyes, then opened them again. Nothing, then another flicker outlined against the lighter fog that was drifting up from the floor of the jungle.

"Bug . . ."

"Jack . . ."

Both spoke at the same time. Sudden quiet, and Bug's equipment was going nuts.

"Okay," Jackson said after a moment. "I'll give the signal when they get right past us."

"The beeps are constant, Jack! There's a lot of movement goin' down! And I ain't talkin' about tigers, man. This is something *big* moving the ground!"

Jackson wanted to let out a long whistle when he saw what the something was. It had to be an entire battalion, and they were moving down the trail only a few yards from where First Squad crouched in the bushes.

Swallowing hard, Jackson immediately forgot about any sort of action. Secrecy and stealth were the imperative actions on this particular patrol, and if the Bitches could keep from being detected, they just might make it home to Camp Rascal in one piece.

Every man on the squad apparently thought the same thing, because there were no precipitate actions. No one attempted a shot or moved a muscle or even drew in a deep breath. More than likely, they all held their breaths until the entire battalion had passed. Then they waited an extra quarter hour to be certain they were gone. It wasn't until they were safely back in Camp Rascal that Jackson acknowledged how handy the SID had been.

"We might have attacked that first squad and not known about the rear if it hadn't been for those damned beeps," Jackson said to Bug.

Pleased, Bug said, "See? This ain't a bad little toy, Jack!"

"Nope," Jackson agreed. "It sure isn't."

The assistance of the Devil dog's nose was also invaluable, and he took up where the SID left off.

Pearcy and his men, including the ROKs, ranged in opposite directions. Between the teams, they were getting the job done. The body count was rising, with confirmed kills growing higher in number. HQ was pleased, Campbell was pleased, and Pearcy was pleased. Only Jackson wanted more.

* * *

In the weeks that passed, First Squad found themselves going deeper and deeper into Indian country. It wasn't at all unusual for the patrols to be out humping the boonies for three weeks at a time with no resupply. Resupply was too often the slowing down of a chopper overhead and a drop.

Sometimes the chopper would be met by enemy snipers and would pause for only an average of three seconds, if that long. The load would be let loose to fall near the specified LZ. Often as not, the supplies would be gone by the time the patrol could get to them, carried away by farmers or VC. It left them with little to eat. They lived on what they could find to eat or buy from the scattered villages they humped through. Once they bought litchi fruit, called "eyes of the dragon" by the Vietnamese because of its similarity to a huge eye. Pupillike dark seed and surrounding white flesh inspired the name, but to Jackson it sounded ominous.

"Hell, I don't want to eat that!" he said in disgust, tossing it back to Baroni.

"Do you want grapefruit then, Sarge?"

Glancing up at Baroni's hopeful expression, Jackson relaxed slightly. "Yeah, Baroni. Give me some grapefruit."

He peeled it back, watching the sullen faces of the villagers and feeling like they were watching and waiting. Waiting for what? For him to choke on it? For sniper fire to blast from the trees surrounding the isolated village?

Jackson gave a quick motion of his hand, ending the negotiations between Smitty and one of the high-pitched, cackling-voiced old woman he was haggling

221

with over a scrawny chicken.

"Leave it, Smitty!" he barked, surprising all of them. "Let's get the hell out of Dodge. . . ."

"But a *chicken*, Sarge," Smitty protested in a pleading voice, and Jackson shook his head.

"I've got a feeling, Smitty."

The Marine immediately ceased his bargaining and joined Jackson and the others grouped at the village gate. He'd learned not to question Jackson's "feelings." It could be fatal, for the sergeant seemed to sense VC as easily as the big German shepherd that traveled with them. All the men were learning to rely on their instincts and gut feelings, on the subtle differences in the terrain around them or even a different feel to the night air.

As it turned out, Jackson wasn't too far wrong in his feeling this time, either. A few klicks down a thin jungle trail, which meandered like a blind cat through the overgrown bushes and trees, they came upon an innocuous-looking old man with a pointed straw hat and shapeless pajamas. He was leading a tired cow, staring down at the ground and ignoring the patrol just ahead of him as he plodded toward them. Walking point, Jackson gave a hand motion for the men behind him to stop.

"Ask him where he's goin', Baroni," Jackson instructed.

Baroni rattled off the query to the old man, who swung his head from side to side and shrugged his shoulders. His reply was a sharp staccato of sound that seemed much too loud for the lush quiet of the jungle.

Turning back to Jackson, Baroni said, "He says

he's going back to his hootch, Sarge."

Sweeping a glance at the dense jungle foliage, Jackson frowned, feeling the warning prickle on the back of his neck again. It was just like the one he'd gotten in the nameless little village a few klicks back, a feeling that someone was watching and waiting.

"Where's his hootch?"

Baroni turned back to the old man, who by now had advanced to only a few steps away. But when he asked the question, the old man broke into a run, diving headfirst into the bushes at the side of the trail and quickly disappearing. The Marines opened fire, spraying the spot where he'd gone with a hail of M-14 bullets.

"Hey," Carrigan said in some surprise when the echo of their fire faded, "he left behind his cow. Ain't that kinda unusual?"

"Hit the ground!" Jackson yelled then, and dove into the bushes just like the old man had done. A shattering explosion erupted, and metal fragments and cow flew all over the place. Showers of blood and raw meat rained down on the Marines, and Sanchez got hit in the leg with a hot metal splinter.

"Damn," Baroni muttered to Jackson, spitting out mouthfuls of dirt and leaves and taking a mental assessment to see if he'd been hurt, "I never heard of anybody wiring a cow to explode!"

Jackson pushed back his helmet, looked at Baroni, and laughed. "You've got a steak hanging over your helmet," he explained when Baroni just looked at him. "And I guess the VC figured we might search that little bastard but wouldn't think about the cow until it was too late."

"Yeah, well we didn't even have time to do much of anything," Baroni replied. He tugged at the long strip of raw meat draped over his metal helmet and held the bloody piece in his hand, looking at it. "Hey, Sarge . . ."

"Yeah?"

"You in the mood for steak tonight?"

"Beats the hell out of Smitty's skinny chicken!" Jackson shot back.

First Squad was being followed. The VC must have been shadowing them for a while, hanging back, watching their movements without being seen. Small traps sprung up everywhere they walked, and if it hadn't been for Devil a few times, men would have been hurt. Doc had removed the metal frag from Sanchez's leg, and he walked with a limp but he walked. Punji pits yawned beneath unwary feet, and trip wires were strung across even the remote trails that were little more than a faint path hacked through thick foliage. First Squad was definitely on the "hit list" of the VC, it seemed. The villagers were terrified by them when they entered and would refuse to leave their huts unless ordered to do so.

It was frustrating. Here were the people they were supposed to protect and befriend, and they couldn't coax them out of their huts to give them any helpful information that might keep them from being killed.

"What the hell!" Jackson growled when they stood in the middle of a deserted village and saw the evidence of hasty departure.

"They're scared, Sarge," Baroni offered.

224

"I know that. But don't they know they've got a better chance of winning this war with us on their side than them damn commies?"

"I don't think they consider that," Bug put in with a thoughtful frown. "They just consider the fact that their farmlands are being destroyed and the way of life they would pursue in peacetime has been banished. I don't think these poor folks know *who* is on their side, Sarge!"

"You may be right," Jackson conceded, "but they could at least be smart enough to figure out that we don't treat them like the VC do."

Sweat streamed down from under helmets, and the air was so thick and oppressive that it was hard to breathe. It was dusk, and swarms of insects drifted past in hazy gray clouds. Jackson batted impatiently at the worrisome bugs and gave the order to reconnoiter and resupply.

Grinning, he added, "We might as well go ahead and help ourselves to what they would have willingly given us if they'd been here!"

Sneering, Sanchez said, "Kinda like the VC, huh, Sergeant? I thought we didn't treat them like those gooks do!"

Snapping around in a quick motion, Jackson's fist lashed out and caught Sanchez just under the chin, jerking his head back and sending him sprawling to the ground. He lay gasping, off balance because of his gear and heavy pack, floundering like a landed fish and just as furious.

"What'd you say, Sanchez?" Jackson demanded, stepping closer. " 'Cause if you're disobeying orders, I might just have to thump ya."

Sanchez glared but shook his head, indicating that he had nothing else to say.

"Good. I must've not heard you right, then," Jackson said, and turned his back on the Marine. "I'd hate to think one of my men might argue with me."

"No fear of that," Smitty said with a Groucho waggle of his bushy eyebrows. He subsided when Jackson shot him a quelling glance.

The reconnoiter and resupply from cooking pots and market baskets was quickly completed, and the men of First Squad moved on into the jungle twilight.

Recon: The definitive explanation of this term as applied to most squads was a patrol sent out for an indefinite period of time to seek out and discover any useful information as to the movement of troops or the location of enemy outposts. Secrecy was the main objective, so that the unit's mission would not be discernible to the VC. That was the definitive explanation for most squads. But not First Squad.

Their explanation was more like search and destroy. HQ tactfully referred to it as Reconnaissance, but they knew what was implied behind that catch-all word. The enemy was to be sought out and eliminated wherever they could find him. Plain and simple, find and kill. Acquired information was helpful; body count was required.

And Jackson was finding it easier and easier to kill without a single qualm. It wasn't just a job anymore; it was an obsession. Hatred for the VC was forming into an implacable wall that barred any mercy.

The squad humped through a small village tucked

into the shadow of a mountain on their way back to camp one day, and they found to their surprise that it was friendly. The people came out to greet them and offer food and information, a novelty to the tired and frustrated Marines.

Most of First Squad was young, with the average age being twenty. These were men with kid brothers and sisters, some even with children of their own, albeit only babies. And the Vietnamese children had an exotic beauty and shy charm that appealed to men far from home and lonely for their families. When the children grouped around the Marines to look up at them with huge liquid eyes full of curiosity, the men took the time to play with them. They tried talking to them, but got mostly giggles in return because of their unskilled command of the Vietnamese language.

Smitty passed out candy bars, and Gagliano and Delisi—being Italian they both came from large, happy families—gave the kids piggy-back rides. For a while, the Marines were able to forget their mission and pretend they were out on a Sunday afternoon walk and playing in the park.

Jackson, who had no special love for the people who seemed to him devious and deceitful, softened slightly, sat under a tree, and let his men relax for a while. There were times he could almost like these people, and this was one of them.

"Hey, Sarge!" Crawdad said, indicating a little girl of about ten years old. "This kid has an infected cut. Okay if we treat it?" He pulled forward a thin girl with long dark hair and huge eyes. She had a pretty face that she hid in Crawdad's shirtfront. He coaxed her into turning around so that Jackson could see the long, ugly scratch on her arm. "She cut it on some wire, Sarge. It's pretty badly infected. Think we should treat it?"

"Did you get mamasan's permission?" Jackson asked.

"Yeah, she said it was okay. I think she's scared the kid might lose her arm."

Jackson thought about it a minute, looking at the little girl as she clung to Crawdad. The child seemed terrified, staring at the black Marine with wide eyes and a quivering bottom lip. He was obviously the first black man she had ever seen.

Shrugging, Jackson said, "Yeah, let Doc take a look at it."

Doc Weathers took special pains with the shy little girl, who seemed more frightened than reassured by his calm manner and large black kit filled with shiny metal instruments. He carefully washed the cut, cleaned it out with antiseptic, and gave her a tetanus shot. To ease the sting of the needle, he gave the child an entire package of chewing gum, two candy bars, and a package of Kool-Aid. Then he covered the cut with a Band-Aid strip.

That impressed her the most. She held out her arm and gazed at the flesh-colored adhesive bandage with delight, babbling in Vietnamese to the other children crowded around. The girl's mother seemed equally delighted, and finally Baroni told Weathers that it wasn't anything medical he had done, but the sign that she was to be kept safe that had made them so happy.

"What sign?" Weathers asked in confusion.

"The Band-Aid. They think it's special magic, you

know, something to keep away evil spirits."

"Man, you're kidding!" Weathers sighed and said, "And I thought I just had a great bedside manner."

"Oh, you do, Doc, you do," Baroni assured him with a wide grin. "But you usually need a good dose of penicillin after your bedside visits, I hear!"

Baroni was referring to one of Weather's visits to a "boom-boom room," or whorehouse. It had been quite a while before, but the experience had left Weathers with some temporary reminders of his brief sexual encounter. The men in First Squad had not let him forget it for very long.

Now Weathers aimed a playful punch at Baroni, and the men began to tussle on the ground. The villagers gathered to watch, laughing and crowing in their singsong voices. It could have been a Sunday afternoon anywhere if not for the heavy weapons the Marines carried.

First Squad was sorry to have to pull out of the village and for the first time felt as if maybe they were making some headway with the people.

After two days' rest in camp, First Squad was sent out on another patrol. They took the same trail they'd recently used back, intending to set some SIDs near the village where they'd enjoyed a lazy afternoon.

As they neared the village, Jackson noted that it was quiet, not as bustling as it had been two days before. He slowed down, sensing that something was wrong. No one came out to greet them, not even the children. Instead, they all remained in their huts or even ran when they saw them.

"Sarge? What's wrong?" Baroni whispered uneasily. He was looking from right to left as if expecting to see armed VC burst out of the trees.

"I dunno, Baroni. You're the language expert. Let's ask."

But the Marines didn't have to ask. It was apparent as soon as they rounded a bend in the trail and saw the village square. There was a well in the center of the square, and off to one side was the wooden hut of the village elder, an impressive building for an important leader. The VC had been there, all right, and they had left in their wake a grim warning to the villagers not to be friendly with the Marines.

"Oh, dear God!" Baroni moaned, and Jackson could feel his heart drop to his boot toes.

Spread-eagled against the side of the hut was the little girl that Doc Weathers had treated for an infected cut. The VC had impaled her to the wall with a wooden stake driven through her small body just above her pubic bone. She hung there, upside down her long dark hair trailing in the dust and blood that had congealed below her tiny corpse.

Baroni was barely able to talk, and it was left to Bug to piece together the story of what had happened from the reluctant villagers. The VC had come through not long after the Marines had left and, seeing the bandage on the child, had known that the villagers had been friendly to the Marine patrol. They had hung the child there as a warning, with the promise to return if the villagers didn't heed it. It had taken agonizing hours for the girl to die, and her mother had been forced to watch, forbidden to try and take her down by threats of retribution upon the entire village. Now the villagers—and especially the mother—considered the Marines as deadly.

Doc Weathers, with tears dripping down his face, went to take down the girl's body, but Jackson stopped him.

"No, Doc. Forget it."

Weathers rounded on him furiously. "Forget it! What the hell do you mean, *forget it!*"

Jackson's voice was cold as he said, "If you take that girl's body down, the VC are liable to make good on their threat. And besides," he added more softly, "she's past hurtin' now, Doc."

Seeing the sense in what Jackson said, Weathers nodded. "I guess you're right, Sarge. Let's get out of here. I don't think I can stand staying around when I know that I—I was responsible for that little girl's horrible death."

Jackson put a hand on his shoulder. "Hey, you're no more responsible for her dyin' than Chrysler's responsible for car wrecks. I mean, you were here, Doc, and you did what you had to do. The VC are the ones who killed her, and if you really want to help, help kill VC."

The day after finding the dead child, First Squad went on another search and destroy mission. They ranged a lot farther from Camp Rascal this time, heading south parallel to the highway east of Tou Lon. The road ran south to the Mang Buk airstrip.

High in the mountains southwest of Tou Lon, the squad came across four black-pajamaed VC who immediately opened up on the Marines. The firefight was hot and brief, then the VC retreated into hiding. A typical approach for the Vietcong. Hit and run. This time Jackson decided to go after them. Feelings were running high in the squad, and it was time for a little payback. There had been no casualties on either side, and he intended to change that in their favor.

Using Devil to track them, the Marines traced the VC all the way down to a spot not far from Dak Ket. It wasn't a short hump, and it took them several days. Feelings ran high against the VC, feelings of hatred and frustration, and it kept them going.

They stumbled across another small hamlet hidden in the overhang of a mountain, only this one was not friendly. It consisted of ten or eleven leaning huts.

A small rickety fence circled the perimeter of the village, obviously not to keep anyone out but to hold in their chickens and piglets. The Marines stayed on the outskirts of the hamlet and hid in the tall grass and thick bushes, watching for over two hours to see if there would be any sign of the enemy. There was no movement at all except the chickens scratching for feed and lean pigs rooting in the dirt. The villagers didn't even glance in their direction but kept on with their daily tasks. An old mamasan squatted by a smoking fire, cooking something in a large pot outside one of the hootches.

Finally, Jackson gave the signal. He moved from his hidden position in the jungle to scout out the village, taking Carrigan and the Devil with him. Leaving the rest of the squad to flank the village on the north and to the south, he told them to stay out of sight. Jackson and Carrigan moved forward slowly, half expecting the VC to open up again. Quiet. Nothing moved but the wind and smoke. Feeling a little bit better, Jackson and Carrigan inched toward the gate of the village.

As Jackson moved to lift the latch of the village gate

with the barrel of his M-14, Devil went berserk. The dog began snarling and barking, practically foaming at the mouth as he snapped at Jackson. When Jackson didn't halt quickly enough, the dog grabbed his pants leg with his teeth and gave a sharp tug, tearing the material.

"Dammit, dog!" Jackson said, shaking his leg. "What's the matter with him, Carrigan? He's actin' crazy!" The dog was braced against moving, his forefeet dug into the ground and his teeth firmly latched in the material of Jackson's pants leg. It wasn't that common for a dog to mess with any man other than his handler, and Jackson began to wonder if the animal had been bitten by a bamboo viper or something that might have caused this lunatic reaction.

"Hold it, Jack!" Carrigan said quietly. "I see something." He took a cautious step forward, then sucked in a deep breath as he spotted the potato masher grenade fastened to the other side of the gate hinge. Still not releasing his breath, Carrigan said tightly, "It's a booby trap!" and took a quick step back.

Sweat popped out on his brow as Jackson stood there trying to catch his breath. He followed Carrigan's example and did a quick two-step backward, wiping away the beads of cold sweat from his brow with his dirty handball glove.

"That was close, man, way too close!"

"If Devil hadn't barked, you might not have . . ."

Carrigan's remark was interrupted with a rapid burst of AK-47 and M-14 fire from the tree line beyond the village. Jackson and Carrigan threw themselves to the ground, lifting their heads to see two VC at the south of the village fall from a tree and into the brush. The two Marines retreated to the tree line some fifty meters back, and found that Gagliano and Delisi had taken out the VC. Bug and Baroni were skirting their flank, stopping just on the inside of the tree line.

Stretching out to a firing position, Jackson took aim at the village gate and let go with a ten-round burst. It hit his intended target perfectly.

The grenade attached to the gate exploded in an earsplitting blast that ripped a ten-foot hole in the fence. The villagers cowered in their huts or a convenient ditch, while the animals squawked, squealed, and grunted in a terrified frenzy. Satisfied that at least one booby trap had been detonated successfully, Jackson then motioned for the rest of the squad to move in.

As he and Carrigan and the Devil loped back toward the ragged entrance now skirting the village, pigs ran past them in pink and brown streaks. Several swine and fowl lay dead and bloody on the ground, but only one owner seemed inclined to protest. He was jabbering shrilly, with tears and mud mingling on his face. Jackson ignored him. None of the villagers had bothered to warn him about the rigged gate, had they? Well, he certainly wasn't about to feel any responsibility for a few dead pigs and chickens. Let the VC console the damned gook!

"We're gonna search every hut and every hole in the ground—and let Devil do the sniffing," Jackson ordered.

Carrigan gave an affirmative reply and began taking the Devil through the line of hootches. The huge dog bounded forward eagerly, and the silent, watching villagers moved swiftly out of the way.

Jackson turned around, his gaze flicking over the straw mats and huts. No one was talking or trying to argue with the Marines. They just watched. Besides the old man, the only other sound was of a baby crying. It was too damned quiet to suit Jackson.

"Come on, Bugman. We're gonna find out what the hell is going on around here!" Jackson said over his shoulder. He was already striding forward, pointing and telling the rest of the squad to search the hootches.

Stalking down the dusty main avenue of the tiny village, Jackson saw an old woman hunched over a cooking pot and ignoring everything. That was a bit too much for him. Didn't she care if they blew up her whole goddammed village and kin? Apparently not, and he thought that was a bit strange. The Asians were inscrutable, yes, but how could anyone ignore a potato masher grenade and an entire squad of angry Marines? Not bloody likely!

He stopped in front of her hut. "Bug, ask her how many Vee Cee are in the area."

Anxious to show off his hard work in the Vietnamese tongue, Bug stepped forward and squatted down beside the old woman. He talked to her in what sounded to Jackson like fluent Vietnamese, but she kept shaking her head as if she didn't understand.

"Tell her to talk or we'll find a way to make it easier for her," Jackson suggested, lifting his rifle in a threatening manner.

That seemed to work better. The old woman began to jabber in a high-pitched tone that sounded like an air siren, apparently listing her grievances against the Marines instead of giving out information, because

Bug kept trying to explain that they hadn't meant to kill her pigs. Jackson was losing patience. The old crone had the black, betel-nut-stained teeth so common to the people over there. He'd heard that if a girl reached twenty and didn't have black teeth, she wasn't considered a good marriage prospect for a young man. But that didn't matter now. This woman's personal habits could include fucking dogs for all he cared. He wanted to know about the VC.

"Ask her again, Bug," he said, pulling back the rifle and letting the sunlight glint off the long bluish barrel.

Bug complied. "She said there's not any VC at all, Sarge."

Jackson exploded. "Who the fuck does she think she's kidding? I guess that old man rigged up the grenade? Well, fine, 'cause if these villagers are responsible for that trap, they can be considered VC! Tell her that, Bug."

Bug did, and the old woman began to rattle hysterically again. Bug was having trouble understanding her, and he kept telling her to slow down. At last he said, "She admits that there's VC in the area, but not here."

"We know that! Ask her how many, and if she can't come up with a good answer, tell her this village is gonna be 'Zippo city' in about two minutes."

Though weeping and wailing, the old woman still had the same answer for Bug. Jackson could feel his face getting flushed with anger, and he decided to see if she could understand that.

Turning to the woman himself, Jackson took his lighter from his top pocket and lit it just under the

236

small grass roof of the hootch. He asked quietly, "Mamasan, how many Vee Cee?"

"No Vee Cee! No Vee Cee!"

The straw roof began to smolder, and the sharp smell curled into the air. "Okay, mamasan, I'm gonna ask you once more. How many Vee Cee?"

Crawdad and Mudboy gave a yell, distracting Jackson, and he turned around, snapping his lighter shut and sticking it back into his shirt pocket. They were carrying something between them—a wooden crate.

"Look what we found, Sarge!" Mudboy said, panting with the effort of carrying the heavy crate. He let it drop to the ground so the sergeant could see the handmade potato masher grenades, AK-47 ammo, and C-rations. "It was in a spider hole underneath a reed mat," Mudboy said, pointing to a hut.

"No Vee Cee! You bitch!" Jackson growled, whipping around and Jap-slapping the old crone to the ground with his clenched fist.

Screaming even louder now and holding her jaw, she shrieked, "No Vee Cee!" Her head bobbed on her shoulders, and her wrinkled face sagged in blurred folds as she glared up at Jackson.

Getting the same wrong answer twice in a row was all he needed to light his fire and the dried grass of the hootch's roof.

Within seconds, the hootch's roof was ablaze in spite of the mamasan's futile efforts to beat it out with her bare hands. Ignoring her, Jackson told the others to then round up all the people and take them outside the rickety fence.

Smitty and Delisi had dragged the crate away and were laying out the C rations on the ground. "Looka

237

here!" Delisi said, holding up a tin can, "Peaches! We haven't had peaches in months, and the VC manage to get them."

"These are probably the same guys who've been getting our drops," Smitty said, sorting through the cans.

The tin cans were sorted and distributed, and Jackson stood looking down at the leftover tins of ham and lima beans. Something clicked in his mind, and he turned to Bug.

"Bug, you got any C-4 plastic?" he asked as he bent down and lifted one of the unwanted cans of ham and beans. He juggled it from one hand to the other, his mouth pursed in a thoughtful frown as he waited for an answer.

Bug grinned. "No, but I think I can rig this grenade to do the trick, if I'm reading you right." Kneeling beside Jackson, Bug worked quickly to wire the grenade to the interior of the crate so that it would detonate upon the lid being lifted. "There," he said when he was finished. "All set for Charlie's dinner."

"Yeah. Well, let's leave Charlie a little appetizer for his dinner this evening," Jackson muttered, squinting as he watched the flames from the hootch grow higher and higher, meshing into the hot Vietnamese sun. He turned around.

"Stud brothers—Gagliano! Delisi! Get those VC bodies over here. We're gonna show mamasan what a Vietcong looks like." A tight grin curled across his baked black face as he regarded the stubborn old lady.

Mudders and Crawford dragged one of the VC back, while Gagliano and Delisi lifted the other from the brush. They began stripping the bodies of weap-

238

ons and clothes, then they tied them to a tree on the outskirts of the village.

Pulling out his bayonet, Jackson ripped open the dead VCs' bullet-torn abdomens as casually as he might have gutted a fish.

"Maybe if we tie you to this Vee Cee for a while, you'll recognize another one if you happen to see him," Jackson said primly. A red-hot fury had enveloped him, and all he could see at that moment was a ten-year-old Vietnamese girl spread-eagled on a wall. Other images superimposed themselves on his mind in a whirring flash, images of good men and friends exploding into bits of flesh so tiny nothing could be found to send home in a body bag: Kennard's bayonet-slashed belly; Myers crouching down beside a young boy and getting a knife in his chest for his sympathy; twelve good men tied to tree trunks with their genitals stuffed in their mouths.

"These are Vee Cee, mamasan!" Jackson grated. "Think you might know another one if he comes calling?"

"No Vee Cee, no Vee Cee!" the old mamasan kept saying.

"No Vee Cee? Take another look, you lyin' little gook!" With that, Jackson grabbed the back of her head and shoved it into the bowels of the dead VC.

"I think she might want to talk now," Jackson said when the old woman collapsed onto the ground, retching and weeping. He released her, stood up, and wiped his bloody hands on his pants, then looked at the quiet Marines who were watching him with wary expressions. It occurred to Jackson that they were looking at him just like they had looked at Lieutenant

Campbell when he had lost it.

"What the hell is wrong with you guys?" he demanded harshly. "Get a damned grip! This is war, not a fuckin' walk in the woods! If there were two VC here, then that means that there could be twenty ahead of or behind us."

Carrigan shifted uneasily from one foot to the other, then asked, "Uh, Sarge? Are we going to leave her like that?" He indicated the old woman with a jerk of his thumb.

"I ought to," Jackson shot back, then had an idea. He knew of a perfect warning for the VC. Most American soldiers in Vietnam had taken to leaving an ace of spades pulled from a deck of cards on the bodies of their kills. He'd leave something a little more definite, just to thumb his nose at the VC and show them that he wasn't afraid of them, that he didn't give a damn if they knew just *who* had gutted some of their men. In fact, he wanted them to know. . . .

"Crawdad, you still got that wanted poster you drew?"

Crawford blinked, then said, "Oh, that? No, you took it."

"Well, draw me another one, Crawdad. And make it real good. Make it look as much like me as you can. And fill us all in."

Catching his drift, Crawford went through his pack and found some paper and a pen. It didn't take him long to sketch an inkblot with a helmet, ten stick figures, and the words "Bad Black and the Bitches."

"Perfect," Jackson pronounced, and the men of First Squad nodded agreement.

They just watched as Jackson took the piece of

240

paper and tacked it to the tree trunk above the dead VC that were hanging there like overripe fruit. It was his signature, his warning, and an announcement of vengeance.

Turning to the old woman who was sitting on the ground and gagging, he said to Baroni, "Tell her that we'll be back, Baroni."

None of the Marines said much as they shouldered their packs and turned back along the trail, leaving behind a destroyed hootch, frightened peasants, and two dead VC. All in all, it hadn't been a bad day.

CHAPTER 15

Sergeant Jackson slashed at tree limbs and over-hanging branches with a vengeance on the hump back to Camp Rascal, his mood as black as his skin. None of the men even attempted to speak to him but let him go his way without comment.

Baroni and Bug exchanged worried glances, giving one another a high sign to indicate that they were concerned, but remained silent. First Squad endured the mumbled curses and occasional snarl with forti-tude. It was obvious that, though all of them could use a rest, Sergeant Jackson needed it most. The weight of command could hang heavy on a man.

Camp Rascal was reached in subdued, tense si-lence. It was only when the after-action reports were filled out that Lieutenant Campbell learned of the events and the poster naming First Squad as the cul-prits. He sat back in his chair for a moment, thumb-ing his bottom lip and staring at the wall in thoughtful silence. Then he sent for Baroni and Clayton.

Bug and Baroni knew what the lieutenant wanted even before he asked, and they hastened to assure the

242

officer that Sergeant Jackson hadn't gone over the hill.

"No, sir!" Baroni said. "I think he's sane, if that's what you mean. He's just stressed, like all of us, Lieutenant. He didn't do anything wrong, maybe just a little unorthodox by military terms."

Campbell stared at Baroni and Bug for a moment, his hands folded into a steeple and grazing his chin. Then he nodded and said, "I think Sergeant Jackson needs the R&R that's due him . . . before he really loses it. I also think that you need to be with him, Baroni, Clayton. You three men are pretty tight, aren't you?" Without waiting for an answer, Campbell continued, "How do you men like the idea of going to Japan for seven days? I thought you might. . . . I can get the paperwork put through pretty quickly, and you men can inform Sergeant Jackson of his impending R&R."

"Fucking A!" Baroni was saying. "Don't worry, Lieutenant, we'll take good care of Jack. Why, we won't let him do anything but rest and relax—in typical Marine fashion, of course." He was grinning widely as he added, "We'll be drunker than three skunks for that whole week, sir! And it'll do us good, real good!"

Bug, worried as always about details, asked, "Will we be going to Chu Lai first to fly out?"

"Any particular reason for needing an answer to that?" Campbell wanted to know.

Grinning, Bug shrugged and said, "Yessir. My father's friend is at the supply depot in Chu Lai. He's got a lot more supplies I might need in the near future—with your permission, of course, Lieutenant."

243

The lieutenant nodded, well-acquainted with Bug's savvy about electronics. "Yeah, I can route you guys through there if you want. Now, why don't you men find Jackson and I'll inform him of the correct procedures to be followed."

"I know where he is," Baroni volunteered. "Mail call was an hour ago."

"Yeah, he's back at the hootch reading his mail," Bug said.

Swinging open the squeaking door of the hootch, Bug stuck his head in the opening and said, "Hey! Is it safe to come in?"

Jackson barely glanced up from the letter he was reading. His face was furrowed in a frown, and his big hands were clenched into tight fists around the fragile edges of the ink-scrawled paper.

It didn't take a psychic to figure out that the letter wasn't a good one. Bug sidled into the hootch, wondering if it was a good time, then deciding that any-time was a good time to tell a man he had a week of R&R. He chose to start out slow, feeling out Jackson's mood before he delivered this good news, however.

"What's the matter, Sarge?" Bug asked.

This time Jackson looked up. "It's my older brother, Raymond. He got wounded up around the DMZ." Pausing to suck in a deep breath, Jackson turned his gaze toward the tent walls. He reminded Bug of the daze Campbell had been in a few months earlier, and it gave him an eerie feeling that he tried to shake off.

"Hell, Jack. I didn't even know you had a brother.

Is he a grunt, too?"

When Jackson's head snapped up to stare at him, Bug took a cautious step back until he saw the sergeant's shoulders relax. Giving another sigh, Jackson shook his head again. He spoke in a monotone, just like a man in shock, and Bug knew something bad must be wrong.

"Yeah, he's regular Army," Jackson answered like a zombie.

"How bad is he hurt?"

Another shrug of his shoulders, and the letter was carefully folded and stuffed back into the envelope. "I don't know," he said after a moment. "Mom just said he's at an Army hospital in Japan. Dammit! I hope he ain't no fuckin' vegetable or something like that. . . . You don't understand, Bug. Raymond's the best damn songwriter and guitarist I've ever heard sing or play. If he couldn't do that—if he couldn't play anymore—I don't think he'd want to go on. Music's his life, see."

Bug did his best to try and soothe Jackson's worries. "Don't worry, Jack. Listen, the Army's got the best statistics so far as medical survival. The medevac helicopters are really making a name for themselves in Vietnam. I mean, as far as recorded history goes, Vietnam has taken fewer body counts than any war we've fought so far. They also have the highest ratio of the wounded being recovered."

The conversation lagged, and Jackson said nothing for a few minutes. Bug shifted from one foot to another, and when the silence dragged too long, he said, "So, your brother's a musician, huh? Has he written any songs that have been on the radio or anything? Is he any good?"

A smile flickered. "Good? He's the best. That little sucker can write a tune on a streetlight! I ain't never seen nothin' like it, Bug. One of these days the corner of College and McLemore Streets is gonna bless the day they ever heard my brother strum a guitar. There aren't many like my brother."

Bug laughed. "What the hell is so special about College and McLemore Streets, man?"

"Special! Why, don't you know anything about music, Bugman? Hadn't you ever heard of Stax Records? Shee-it! Stax Records is famous for The Memphis Sound! And if my brother comes outa this, Stax will be famous for Raymond Jackson. He's the best fuckin' songwriter that ever . . ." Jackson stopped to take a deep breath, then finished, "I hope he's all right."

"Yeah, so do I, Jack. Look, don't sit and worry about it like this, man. The lieutenant has a little surprise for ya."

Jackson groaned. "Oh, no! Not another one of those three-week patrols, I hope!"

"No, no, Jack! A real surprise. I mean a nice one," Bug amended when Jackson began shaking his head again. "Listen up. . . ." Jabbing his finger at Jackson, Bug punctuated each of his words with his forefinger as he said slowly, "We . . . are . . . gonna . . . go . . . see . . . him . . . right . . . now. . . ."

Jackson sagged back against his rack and gazed at Bug suspiciously. "What do you mean, Bugman?"

Bug sat down on the rack opposite Jackson's and arched his eyebrows in a decent imitation of Smitty doing Groucho Marx. "It's kinda a mystery, see. Ya need to go and see the lieutenant, see. He'll tell ya the good news."

"You do a lousy Groucho, Bug. You sound more like James Cagney," Jackson commented as he rose from his bunk and strode toward the screen door of the hootch. "A *drunk* Cagney, at that!"

"Oh yeah?" was Bug's parting shot. "Well, you ain't no John Wayne yourself!"

Japan. Paper houses, *nobis*, *tabis*, kimono-clad women with soft black hair and softer giggles. Perfumed faces and bodies that smelled sweet instead of sweaty. The first stop for the three Marines—a geisha house.

Three full hours of soaking in the warm water of the Japanese bathhouse slowly relaxed the grimy, muscle-sore men. Giggling young women plied bars of scented soap and hot, fluffy towels, and Jackson just knew he'd died and gone to heaven. He'd forgotten what civilization could be like, what a bath in warm water, with soap and clean towels and even shampoo, could feel like. The best shower he'd gotten back in Indian Country was in a rainstorm or under a cold waterfall, while others stood watch so a man wouldn't get his head blown off while he soaped up and rinsed off. Hell, this was living. This was what made life worth living, he amended silently, stretching out and closing his eyes as the Japanese girl soaped his arms, shoulders, back, and lower.

Then things got really interesting. He was told to get out of the water and lie atop a mat on the floor while she dried him off. No wonder the Japanese men frequented these houses, Jackson thought hazily as the girl anointed his aching body with some kind of oil and massaged it in. He could feel the aches and pains ease away from him, leaving him floating in a kind of netherworld of physical relaxation. Even the slight sting of the oil in the cuts made by elephant grass, jungle rot, mosquito bites, felt good. It felt good just to be *alive* and know he was alive. No mortars were in danger of dropping on his head for a week. No dodging of bullets or ducking booby traps would be required. Nothing would be required for the next seven days except that he stay alive enough to ship back to his squad. And that suited the hell out of Sergeant Robert L. Jackson.

A big smile of satisfaction curved his mouth as he lay on that rice mat and felt the soothing medicine of soft hands working over his body. Eight months of "humping-the-boonies" dirt had been slowly dissolved into the magic of the Japanese bathhouse. And the smiling girl was giving him something else to think about with her skilled hands. It was an interesting proposition, and he didn't need much prompting. He might as well take it while he could, while he was in civilization. There was nothing left to remind him of 'Nam, nothing except quickly fading memories. And those would be left behind for now.

"Well, Jack," Baroni said in such a lugubrious tone that Jackson had to laugh. The Italian rifleman was wrapped in a kimono and drinking saki, his legs folded under him as he regarded his sergeant with a beatific smile. "Well, Jack," he continued slowly,

"I'm just about ready to hit the town. How 'bout you?"

Jackson gave a contented sigh, nodded, and glanced over at Clayton. The three Marines were in a common room now, having eaten a light meal served by the women. "Suits the hell out of me. How about you, Bug?"

"No arguments here." He lifted the paper-thin cup of saki, the potent Japanese liquor, and made a toast. "To a six-pointer night, men!"

"Six-pointer?" Jackson echoed.

"Yeah. Wine, women, song—and more wine, women, song."

After their laughter died down, Jackson said in a more sober tone, "I've got something to do first."

"See your brother?" Bug guessed, and Jackson nodded.

"Yeah. Now that I've got the ground-in dirt off me, I think I need to find him. We were real tight as kids, see, and I want to see how he is."

"Sure, Jack. If he's in an Army hospital in Osaka, we'll find him."

But that wasn't as easy as it sounded. Finding the Army hospital was easy, but finding an enlisted man by the name of Raymond Jackson wasn't.

Sergeant Jackson's attitude could have had something to do with his lack of success. He stalked through the front door of the field base hospital like a storm, loudly demanding his brother's location from the front desk clerk. He was met with a cold stare and the information that he didn't know anything about one Raymond Jackson.

"The hell you say!" Jackson flashed angrily. His

mouth was set in a straight line and his fists were clenched. It didn't look so good for a Marine officer to be shouting at an Army enlisted, and Bug did his best to placate Jackson.

"Jack, are you sure he's in this hospital?"

Jackson whirled on him. "Is there another Army hospital in Osaka?"

"No . . ."

"Then, this should be it! I know he's here, and this dumb motherfucker's playing some kind of game. . . . What'sa matter, don't you like Marines?" Jackson demanded of the clerk, whirling back around and glaring at him.

The clerk looked back down at the papers in front of him and ignored Jackson. Others standing around began to stare, and Bug tugged at Jackson's sleeve. "Come on, man. Let's not get into trouble before we have a chance to get into real trouble. . . ."

Jackson jerked away. "I know he's here, Bug. I got a letter from my mother, and she says he's here. This guy's just too damned lazy to look for him."

The clerk finally looked up. His face was indifferent and his tone faintly sarcastic as he intoned, "I'm sorry, Sergeant. I have no record of him being here. Maybe he's in Tokyo. At Camp Soma?"

"And since when did they start spelling Tokyo O—S—A—K—A, you dumb fuck!" Jackson shot back. Baroni was tugging at his sleeve, and he impatiently shook him loose. One glance at the men's faces, though, and Jackson realized that he was not going to get what he wanted by acting like a guy just out of the jungle. He tried again, softening his voice and taking a deep breath. "Look, I came a long way and this is the only time I got that I can see him. If I don't find him this week, I won't get to see him at all. He's hurt, and I want to find my brother. Maybe you can understand that?"

"No, I can't say that I do" was the cool reply, and that did it. Jackson lost his last tentative hold on his temper. Without stopping to think about it, he drew back and slammed his fist into the clerk's face, knocking him away from the desk and back against the far wall. The skinny clerk gave a slight "woof!" and slowly slid down the wall, his head tilted at an odd angle and his eyes glazed.

"I think," Bug said judiciously, "that the guy you just coldcocked was telling the truth. Your brother's not here, Sergeant. But the MPs may soon be. I think it's time to leave."

"I second that motion," Baroni said less calmly. He grabbed Jackson's arm and gave him a push away from the desk, and was surprised when he followed as docilely as a tame lamb.

"Bitch, bitch, bitch," Jackson commented as they hurried down the sidewalk.

"We need to get a drink and calm your ass down," Bug said to Jackson as he put out a hand to stop Baroni. They were in front of a Japanese bar, with bright lights edging the windows and signs painted with clumsy English lettering underneath the henscratches that passed for words in the Japanese language. "See? A bar. This ought to help us all out," Bug said as he guided them through the doors and into the dimly lit bar.

251

Though none of them could speak a word of Japanese, it didn't matter. The crafty, commercial Japanese—ever ready to cash in on sound American dollars—catered to the young servicemen on leave from Vietnam. Everything was Westernized. The menus were written in English, the waiters or waitresses spoke reasonable English, the drinks were given English names.

Since World War II had ended, American troops had been stationed in the occupied country in one form or another. At first it was a genuine occupation, with servicemen stationed at various bases throughout Japan—Tokyo, Tachikawa, Osaka, and other cities. Families had joined the servicemen, and for a time, the service had provided each officer's family with a Japanese servant. This was not to humiliate the people; it had a twofold purpose. The Japanese were taught American customs and language, and the Americans were familiarized with Japanese customs. It was an education of sorts for both sides, and both benefited in unexpected ways.

It had continued until 1960, when Japan signed a security treaty with the United States. It provided for cooperation between the two countries in matters of defense and economics, and also for the maintenance of all the United States military bases. Although the treaty received strong opposition from Japanese Socialists, the bulk of the people liked American GIs . . . and the money brought in by the Americans.

The memory of their last visit to Japan had faded, and the three Marines were now loose on the town of Osaka. The fiasco of Tokyo was a distant, dim recollection at best, and even if remembered, it would not have mattered. They had just spent eight long months in jungle warfare, hot firefights, ducking mortars, and seeing their friends die. A little trouble with the military could only be a welcome diversion.

Potent whiskey was washed down with more whiskey, and it didn't take long for the three Marines to have the feeling of omnipotence at their beck and call. They were alive after incredible odds, after skulking in the jungle and fighting off squads of VC bent on their destruction. Hell, they were damn near invincible!

Baroni, leaning squint-eyed against Jackson, hiccoughed and suggested, "Let's buy the—the whole bar a round of drinks, Jack! Whatdya say?"

Jackson regarded him with drunken compassion. "Sounds great, Baroni. We're good guys. Helluva nice guys, ain't we? Bartender! A round of drinks for every man here, and woman, too! . . ."

The pleased bartender began pouring drinks right and left, while Baroni, Jackson, and Bug looked on with wide smiles, accepting thanks with nods of their heads and benevolent expressions. They felt magnanimous. Weren't they great guys?

"Hey," Bug said after a few minutes, leaning one elbow on the bar's edge as he tried to focus on Jackson, "how are we gonna pay for all this? I don't think I got that much money with me."

"Pay for it?" Jackson echoed. "Why should we pay for it? We're over there fighting a war, and they expect us to come in here and pay for their drinks? Well, of all the hard-assed things I've ever seen, these motherfuckers are the most!"

Conveniently forgetting that it was their suggestion, the three indignant Marines stood up from their bar stools and pushed their way through the crowd to the door. No one noticed or attempted to stop them, and after leaving and sauntering down the sidewalk, the three began to laugh. It was a pretty good joke.

"Can you see the look on that guy's face when he finds out we're gone?" Baroni gasped between spasms of laughter.

"Yeah, but it won't be nothin' compared to the look on the face of that fat owner!"

This further amused them, and they were still laughing when they stepped into the next bar. It was to begin a ritual that would last the entire day. They would order drinks for everyone in the house, then duck out the back if they couldn't just walk out. It became a contest to see how many they could get away with, and the more bars they came to, the drunker they got. Only one barkeeper gave chase, but he was quickly lost within the space of a few blocks.

"Shall we?" Jackson asked when he could catch his breath, indicating the next bar with a wave of one arm.

"By all means," Baroni said with mock seriousness.

When they entered the dimly lit bar, stepping in from the bright sunshine glittering on the concrete streets and sidewalks, it took a few moments for their eyes to adjust. Jackson felt his way forward, bumping into a few chairs and tables in the process.

"You guys Marines?" a deep voice inquired from the direction of the bar, and Jackson's head swiveled toward the sound. It was a large American, and he was staring at them.

"Yeah. You wanna make something of it?" Jackson demanded defensively.

He shook his head. "No, I just think you boys deserve a drink on me. You see, I'm a Marine of sorts, too. A merchant marine, and you guys have saved my ship more than once down in the South China Sea."

Jackson relaxed and decided that the guy must be all right. After all, any man who wanted to buy *them* a drink couldn't be all bad!

The three highly intoxicated Marines shouted their orders at the bartender, and when the drinks arrived, they listened solemnly as the older merchant marine toasted them and the Marine Corps. That called for another round.

"I'll drink to that!" Jackson said as he killed the last of his boilermaker.

"Me too!" Baroni chimed in.

Bug took a little longer to answer because he was still trying to down the first drink.

While Bug and Baroni stood talking to the older merchant marine, Jackson let his gaze wander. It stopped, focused, and lingered on one of the most unusual-looking young women he had ever seen. She was sitting across the room, her legs crossed and her slit skirt riding high on her thighs, but that wasn't what grabbed his attention. Jackson gave a shake of his head, but the vision was still there. He nudged Bug and muttered, "Hey, Bug! Am I seein' things or what?"

Bug looked at him. "Whatdya mean, Jack?"

"That girl four or five tables away. Her hair's blond, but her eyes are slanted. Is she Japanese or am I crazy?"

"Probably both," Bug quipped. He didn't want to tell Jackson that he was having trouble seeing that far.

Four or five tables away could have been four or five miles away at this point in time and alcohol consumption.

"Naw, really, Bug! Am I seein' things?"

Bug started to answer, then froze. His eyesight was still good enough to recognize trouble when it walked in the door, and two Military Policemen had just entered the bar.

"Shit, Jack! Look!"

"That's what I've been doin', Bug," Jackson complained. "But you won't tell me if I'm seein' what I'm seein'. . . ."

"Not that! Over there."

Bug turned Jackson to stare in the direction of the door. "Holy shit," Jackson muttered.

"Trouble?" the friendly merchant marine leaned forward to ask as the two MPs began asking questions about three Marines who had been frequenting bars up and down the street.

There wasn't time to answer before the MPs got close, but the wily stranger figured it out for himself. He sat back, sipping at his drink and waiting as the MPs approached.

One of them stuck out his jaw, raked Jackson, Bug, and Baroni with a cold stare, and said, "You Marines fit the description of the men who've been causing a lot of trouble today. I think you men had better come with us."

"Excuse me," the merchant marine stopped them. "You gentlemen must be mistaken. These men have been here with me all day. They can't be who you want."

Hesitating, then checking their notepads again, the

MPs looked the three up and down one more time. It was obvious that they didn't agree with the merchant marine, but it was also obvious that they didn't think it was worth pursuing. The notebook flapped shut, and the MPs pivoted and left.

Jackson laughed until his sides ached, then laughed some more. Things weren't going too bad on his first day of R&R, in spite of not being able to find his brother. Maybe he should give the blond Japanese girl a try while his luck was still with him.

Straightening his shirt, Jackson swaggered over to her table and gave her his best smile. "Hi, gorgeous. You look like you could use some company."

For an instant he thought she was going to freeze him out, but as she looked him over she began to smile, her dark almond-shaped eyes flickering over him with interest.

"Hello, Marine. I always like handsome company," she said in a soft singsong voice that sounded like it came from a wet dream. Jackson slid into the chair beside her.

It was the best week he could ever remember having. He spent almost all of it inside, in her tiny apartment above the bar and in her wide, comfortable bed.

Jackson delighted in the feel of Tsugi's soft, peachy skin and the sweet, scented smell of her. Her pale hair was silky to the touch, framing her heart-shaped face in a kind of oval that brushed against her shoulders. She was small and compact, with firm thighs, a flat stomach, and small pointed breasts that seemed to beckon for his hand. And she knew more positions than he'd ever known existed, making him feel like a contortionist at times, or a human pretzel. But he didn't have a single complaint, except that the time was too short and R&R was over too quick and Tsugi had to stay in Osaka and he had to go back to 'Nam. He still hadn't been able to locate Raymond, but maybe he'd already been released. Jackson hoped that was it. Other than that, things were great.

And maybe he'd get back to Osaka sometime and look her up again. She had promised to send him a real tree at Christmas, and he had that to look forward to, as well as the thought of his next R&R.

Jackson clung to that thought as he boarded the shiny metal bird that would wing them back to the war.

CHAPTER 16

"Damn, it stings like hell!" Jackson muttered as he stood with spraddled legs, trying to urinate in the bushes.

"You shake it more than twice and you're playin' with it, Jack!" Baroni teased. He was sitting not far away and cleaning his weapon, every now and then glancing in Jackson's direction.

Jackson didn't feel like listening to any teasing. He was hurting. "Where's the Doc? My johnson feels like it's gonna fall off." Wincing, Jackson gazed down with dismay, recognizing the thick yellow discharge. "Shit!"

"What'sa matter, Jack?" Baroni asked innocently.

"The damn bitch gave me the clap," Jackson observed as he stared sadly down.

Baroni gave a hoot of laughter. "Doc, get over here and bring the penicillin," he called out. "Jack's gonna need it."

"Why don't you just find a fuckin' microphone and make sure everybody knows about it?" Jackson shot at him.

But Baroni was enjoying himself too much to be quiet. His grin was all over his face, and his dark eyes were narrowed with amusement as he gave another burst of laughter and said, "Ahh, Sarge, you knew better. A Japanese girl with blond hair? Man, you shoulda seen that one coming a mile off! And hey," he added, "you never did say if it was blond where it counts! . . ." Baroni ducked to avoid the tree limb Jackson flung at him in exasperation.

"Add injury to insult, Baroni!"

"Man, you said that thing was *tight*. Now I know why. It was swollen with infection, Jack!"

"Shut up, spaghetti breath! I oughta thump—" Jackson began in a mock growl, but the Doc and Gagliano moved into earshot.

Delighted with his audience, Baroni twisted the verbal knife a little more. "Hey, I'm just mentioning it! I mean, me and Bug didn't see you hardly the whole week we were in Osaka. And all we heard was about the different positions and how she was one hell of a woman in bed!" Baroni said.

Surrendering to the inevitable, Jackson was given little choice but to go along with Baroni. "Yeah, it was fun while it lasted, Baroni. Too bad you couldn't even pay some chick to give you any . . . oh, did I say something wrong? Well, I just hope Tsugi remembers the Christmas tree."

"Too bad she didn't remember her penicillin," Baroni shot back, and Jackson gave in.

"All right, all right," he said as he paid the dues for his rest and recreation in a subdued moan.

"Yeah, but she already gave you your biggest present!" Baroni continued, then tried to sing the verses to "I'll Be Home for Christmas," changing the lyrics to "I Got the Clap for Christmas."

"Shut up, Baroni. Don't make me laugh. It hurts when I laugh. You fuckin' wop," Jackson added in a mocking tone that no one took seriously. It was common enough to pay tribute to a man's heritage in a backhanded sort of way, and none ever took offense when it was said in that context. None in First Squad took offense at the other's attempts at humor, even a humor that would have been mistaken in The World. It wasn't the same out there, where a man's skin color couldn't save him from being shot. Often, what saved a man from being shot was his buddy, and it didn't matter what color his buddy's skin happened to be.

"If you two are through trading insults for a while," Doc Weathers said, flipping open his medical kit, "I'll do what I can for your little problem, Jackson."

"Hell, it ain't no *little* problem, Doc!" Jackson protested, which immediately earned him more teasing from his men. Things like "He don't think of it as little" or "It's a little dick with a big problem" or even "Haven't you ever heard that all blacks have overgrown ones?" filled the air for a few minutes before subsiding.

Laughing, Doc said he was glad they had a new target now, instead of him. He'd heard enough about his own dose of clap. Then he gave Jackson a sizable dose of penicillin and told him to refrain from sex for two weeks. Jackson gave him a withering stare and said he'd try, then gave the order to his men to "Saddle up!"

"Como on, Bitches, let's get the fuck outa here. We're gonna be at the Rascal before Christmas. I don't care how many VCs are between here and home!" Jackson said as he hoisted his pack.

He had never been anywhere but in Memphis, Tennessee on Christmas, where there was always a chance of snow. The weather in Vietnam didn't seem at all like winter, but the spirit was one of optimism for Jackson as well as the men. It was damp and rainy, and they shivered in the bone-deep chill at times as they hovered over a fire built with cans of fuel instead of a Yule log. It was at this time of year they all felt the homesickness that accompanies the yuletide season.

The long hump back to camp passed with only one casualty—Jackson's sex life. The rest in Osaka had done the angry sergeant good, and he had an altered attitude about life. He seemed to relish the little things now. Maybe it was because he knew he had never been promised tomorrow and had decided to just make it day to day.

His new philosophy was simple: Take out Charlie where Charlie was, and enjoy the rest with a free and joyful spirit. But December 24, 1966 would linger in his memory for a long time.

It was on that day that a veneral-diseased blond Japanese prostitute sent the lonely Marines of CAPs Rascal the scrawny scrub brush pine tree that only remotely resembled an American Christmas tree. It would have been a poor sight to the average American who celebrated the holiday with a lot of glitz and glamour, but to the homesick Marines it was a bright reminder that another world, a more sane world, a more loving world, existed. The skimpy branches held more than a few needles and ornaments, they held a promise.

Christmas Eve that year of 1966 found the Marines of Camp Rascal huddled in the confines of their hootch and reminiscing about home, family, and friends. The humble tree was being solemnly decorated with makeshift tinsel and grenades for ornaments. Each man took a turn at decorating, relating tales of favorite Christmases past and dreams of when they returned to them.

Some gifts were exchanged, creative gifts, like Crawdad giving Mudboy his last two cans of C-rats peaches and a half-carton of Winstons. Carrigan opened his package from home and found the best damn Montana huckleberry jam ever tasted. He generously shared it with the squad. The Bug showed Jackson the gift he had for him— a new infrared scope that he had mounted on Jackson's fifty-caliber. The Stud brothers, Gagliano and Delisi, even exchanged gifts—phone numbers of different chicks that they had known in different ports.

Sitting back that night, Jackson, for the first time since he had left The World, took a good look at the men he had lived with and fought with. Sanity told him they were little more than teenagers. Reality forced him to see the difference between normal American teenagers and these. These hardened, battle-honed teenagers were trained killers. They had the beardless faces of American youth, but their wide, ingenuous eyes were masked with a steely expression of ruthlessness at times, and it was a jarring discordance with what should be. It was unnerving if a man wasn't expecting it, and Jackson could understand

263

why men new to 'Nam were nonplussed when first confronted with a young face and old eyes.

Eyes. Eyes told all. All of them, including the Mexican shitbird Sanchez, had developed the thousand-meter stare. It was a look that only men who've grown up too hard and too fast develop in just a couple of months "in-country." It was a look that gazed past the ordinary and into the murky depths of things normally not confronted in a saner world. They all had it; they had all earned it.

Jackson viewed his men as a father would his young at Christmas. These guys were his only family, the only ones who knew where he was at and where he was coming from.

And on Christmas Eve, Jackson broke all the rules and took a chance at being corny. He stood and said, "Hey, it's Christmas, and where I come from, we sing on the Lord's birthday." With a crusty, off-key voice, Jackson began singing the first verse of "Silent Night."

Much to everyone's surprise, all the Marines joined in together. And just as remarkable—they all sang on key. It was a heart-choking moment for all of them, the voices rising and fading, cracking and growing stronger as each man dealt with his own private thoughts on that holy night. To Sergeant Robert L. Jackson, lost in his memories of home and family, the tiny flickering candle perched atop that leaning scrub pine Christmas tree conjured up the spirit of what Christmas really meant—a promising light in the darkness of the world.

CHAPTER 17

Christmas was over. It was the beginning of a new year in more ways than one. Pearcy and his team ranged farther north, toward the Laotian border, and Jackson and his squad were counting ears farther south.

Counting VC ears had become a major pastime for First Squad, and usually finicky Lieutenant Campbell didn't say a word. He managed to look the other way. It wasn't unusual to see a man with ears strung on a nylon cord and hanging around his neck, but normally those were men who had been out too long. Now First Squad had a man with an affinity for ears—Sanchez. It was the only thing Jackson had found to like about the Mexican in a long time.

The men had found that the best way to save the ears slashed from the enemy was to put them inside the small plastic C-rat fork and spoon containers. It kept them from stinking until they were well "seasoned" and made them easier to string on a cord. The ROKs had the most reason to save the ears, as they were being paid a bounty for each VC ear they brought in. Their government paid them extra for these proof of kills, so Sanchez began turning over his strings to the ROKs.

The days had begun to drift into a routine of sorts, with one mission after another melding together. One day First Squad would be high in the mountains, setting up an ambush for the VCs hiding in the rocks and in the bunkers. The next week would find them down in the valley, ducking bullets from AKs and hiding in banana groves.

The banana groves weren't bad places to be when they weren't riddled with bullets, and First Squad didn't mind scouting them out. There were always ways to bring down the fruit and enjoy something that didn't come out of a C-rat can. The overlapping leaves that formed the trunk of the fragile trees made climbing them impossible, and Smitty was elected to bring down a stalk of bananas one wet afternoon.

"Go on, Smitty!" Jackson said. "You can do it, man."

"Yeah, if he don't bring down a whole herd of elephants on our heads," Crawford grumbled. When they all looked at him, he gave a shrug. "I heard the VC are using elephants to carry pack loads of rice and stuff up in the mountains."

"Like Hannibal crossing the Alps!" Bug said with a laugh.

Jackson stretched out underneath a tree and let the rain beat down while he opened up his C-rats with the P-38 opener thoughtfully provided by the Marine Corps. "You guys do what you want. I'm gonna eat while there's time—before the elephants get here."

"Funny guys," Smitty grumbled. He lifted his M-

14 and took aim. The peace of the day was shattered with the loud clatter, and a minute later the stalk of bananas lay on the ground at their feet. Smitty was grinning from ear to ear and bragging about his skill as a big game hunter.

"They're green," Jackson said. "And why didn't you just cut down the tree instead of shooting it down and letting every fuckin' VC in the area know where we are?"

"Hey, I'm doin' the best I can, man," Smitty complained, waggling his eyebrows. "Kids today!" he added in his best Groucho voice. "Can't never please 'em!"

Rain spattered down on their slickers as the men huddled in a circle and ate C-rats warmed with heat tabs. The smaller banana trees provided shelter of a sort, with the big oval leaves acting as umbrellas.

As designated RTO for the day, Smitty had the PRC-6 on his side. He happily placed it on the ground beside him and began peeling green bananas while the rest of the Bitches watched. No one else seemed inclined to risk a bellyache, but Smitty was said to have a cast-iron stomach.

"See any sign?" Jackson asked Bug after a few minutes, and Bug shook his head.

"No. The SIDs haven't turned up any VC in this area. I think maybe we need to hump over to that saddle back up on the ridge and take a look-see."

Jackson agreed, and the squad saddled up and moved out. It was raining harder up near the ridge, and vision was poor. Overhead in the trees monkeys squabbled, and it was so quiet they could hear the chatter of birds and their own footsteps in the leaves

267

and undergrowth. Devil was with them, and Carrigan had him on his leash as he walked beside Jackson.

"Hey, Sarge," Carrigan said after an hour or two of humping without seeing anything, "did you ever stop to wonder how the VC hide so quick? I mean, we've had kills and not been able to find the bodies. Those little fuckers drag 'em away too quick."

"Yeah, they've got hidey-holes all over the damn place," Jackson said.

"More than that," Carrigan said. "They've got these damn tunnels, like up at the DMZ on Operation Hastings. Hey, did I ever tell you we were right about those tunnels?"

"What do you mean?"

"Those noises we heard. The damn VC had a hospital in some of those tunnels, Sarge, I swear!"

"Go on, man! A *hospital*?"

"Yeah, it's true. I heard it when I was at Chu Lai getting my tiger bites sewn up. Some guy was in the hospital who was a tunnel rat down around Cu Chi in the Iron Triangle. He told me they sent him up around Hastings, and not far from there they found an entire, North Vietnamese hospital underground. Beds, tables, doctors, the whole nine yards, Jack."

Shaking his head, Jackson said, "Man, I knew those tunnels were something else, but how did we miss a whole NVA hospital?"

"Hell, from what he told me, those tunnels have been dug in this ground for centuries. These people are good at hiding from the enemy, Jack, which explains why we can't find bodies when we hit 'em. There's probably a hole nearby and they just toss 'em in it to keep our body count low."

"Great. Well, I ain't no tunnel rat."

"Count me out," Carrigan agreed. "I have trouble with aboveground, man."

"Yeah, but—"

A shout from Mudders, who was walking point, drew Jackson's attention and his head snapped up to listen.

"Sounds like he's in trouble!" Baroni said, and the squad was pushing through the wooded trail to find Mudders. Jackson and Carrigan reached Mudders first. Devil-dog was dancing madly on the end of his leash, growling and snarling and barking like an enraged wolf. Carrigan was having a tough time holding him as the squad stared in amazement.

It was Mudders, all right, and he was up to his ass in orangutan. Or what looked to the squad like an orangutan. Campbell told them later that orangutans hadn't been seen that far north in a hundred years, but whatever it was, it was a damned big primate and it was beating the hell out of poor Mudders.

"Let the Devil go," Jackson said after a second of amazed silence. He was grinning and couldn't hold back his laughter as Mudders struggled with the hairy primate. The big creature was sitting on Mudders's back and pounding the hell out of him, jumping up and down, screeching and bellowing in rage, tearing clumps of Mudders's hair out by the roots while the poor guy tried to protect his head. His boonie hat lay not far away, and his M-14 had been knocked from his hand and was lying in a pile of dead leaves. Rain beat down as the gibbering primate clawed and bit at Mudders's head and churned up a mess of mud and leaves.

When Carrigan released the German shepherd and it bounded forward, the creature stretched to its full height and bellowed a challenge at the dog. It was about four feet tall, with a leathery face and hairy body, long arms and big hands. It beat its chest with its fists, and its yellowed fangs showed through thick lips curled back. Devil-dog didn't hesitate, and the primate apparently decided that the dog wasn't as easy a target as the Marine. It leaped from Mudders's back and ran in a sort of lope, knuckles almost dragging the ground as it hit the trees.

Baroni lifted his rifle to shoot and blasted away at the animal. It dropped to the ground and lay there. Jackson looked up into the trees. "Look, Baroni. There's another one with it," he said, pointing. Another primate of almost the same size waited on a branch in the trees, bouncing around and screaming, and Baroni shot it, too.

Jackson walked over to Mudders and poked him. "Hey, Mudboy, what're you doin' down there?"

Mudders rolled over, spitting leaves and mud from his mouth. He had claw marks on his face and blood dripped from scratches and a split lip, but other than that he was unhurt.

"Why the hell didn't you shoot that damn gorilla instead of standing around?" Mudders demanded as he sat up.

Jackson reached down and removed a huge leaf from Mudders's hair. "We thought you were making boom-boom with it," he replied with a grin, and the squad hooted with laughter.

"Naw, I was too late for that." Mudders shook his head. "That's what he was doin' with his mate. That's why he jumped me, I guess. Thought I wanted his girlfriend. . . ."

"What?"

Looking kind of sheepish now, Mudders nodded. "Yeah, I was lookin' around, see, and came into this clearing. Well, I saw those two monkeys on the ground gettin' it on, and I just kinda stood there and watched for a minute, you know. It was funny-lookin'."

"A monkey Peeping Tom!" Smitty burst out. "Hell, you're sick, man."

Mudders was getting mad. "Look, I didn't know at first what they were doing! Then by the time I figured it out, the big bastard almost beat the hell out of me. Jumped me before I knew what it was gonna do, and my field hat went one way and my rifle the other."

"Great Marine *you* are!" Baroni scoffed.

Mudders was definitely mad now. He shot Baroni the bird and asked if he wanted to see how great he was.

Baroni was grinning. "Naw, I wouldn't fight a man who fucks monkeys. . . ."

Mudders took a swing at him and Baroni ducked, dancing around and taunting Mudders, laughing at him while the furious Marine charged again and again. Finally, Jackson put a halt to the fun.

"Okay, enough. Let's go. Get your rifle, 'Tang,' and come on. . . ."

"Tang!" Mudders shouted. "Shit!"

Mudders took a lot of kidding for a while, and though he got mad about it at times, he was pretty good-natured. He even began bragging about having wrestled a huge hairy ape and eating monkey meat. The squad skinned and cooked the animals and, after a lot of discussion, decided the meat didn't taste too bad.

In the following weeks, First Squad began to have the feeling that they were being trailed. It wasn't the first time Jackson had felt that way, but it hadn't been as noticeable until lately. Every patrol they humped came up with an ambush waiting on them, and some near misses. They had to go to ground or risk being killed or captured. It seemed like the VC knew whichever route they intended to take and would be waiting. Only blind leaping luck had saved their skins so far.

Frustrated and furious, First Squad had doubled their efforts to track and kill the VC. But even a score of seventeen kills didn't eliminate the problem. The area boiled with VC just waiting on First Squad. Not even Pearcy and his ROKs encountered as many of the enemy near Laos. It all seemed to center on the Bitches. The squad would arrive at a spot and find evidence of VC activity; sometimes the fire would still be smoking and the ashes hot. Or there would be C-rat cans rigged up to blow apart when they came on them, or trip wires tied to tree branches hanging in their path. Once they came across a sweep of claymores curving out in a daisy-chain. The Bitches grew cautious to the point of paranoia.

"I think we need to move to a new area," Jackson told the lieutenant one evening after another near miss on patrol. "This one's too damned hot!"

"That's not too unusual in this sort of guerrilla warfare, Sergeant," Campbell began, but Jackson shook his head.

"No, it's more than that, Lieutenant. I think it may be the Dac Cong. Man, I can *feel* somebody watchin' us. It's like they're waitin' on us, know we're comin', and are ready."

Campbell just stared at him for a minute, then said, "Maybe you should take them out, then."

Jackson stared back at him. "How do I go about doin' that?" he asked after a minute.

Leaning forward, Campbell smiled. "I used to like playing cowboys and Indians when I was a kid, Sergeant. It was a great game, with the Indians hiding in the bushes and waiting to ambush the good guys, and the good guys waiting in the bushes to ambush the Indians. . . ."

"Which are we, Lieutenant?" Jackson interrupted. "The good guys or the Indians?"

"Patience, Sergeant, patience. I'm getting to that. It's not always so cut-and-dried. And it depends on which side you stand as to whether you're a good guy or a bad guy."

Shifting impatiently, Jackson waited while Campbell got to the elusive point, thinking that he wasn't going to like this conversation at all. He wasn't too far wrong. Campbell finally leaned forward and looked him in the eye, his tone growing serious and oddly stilted.

"I want ten men to go into the mountains near Dak Ket, Sergeant. Orders from Command state that you are to return to the unnamed village where you encountered the VC soldiers and left them on the gate as a warning. Reports have it that the village is now 'hot.' It's a free strike zone. Your mission is to find VC, draw out enemy fire, and determine their position and

273

rank. Then eliminate them. You were right when you said that there is someone watching you and your men. There is." Campbell paused to let that sink in, then continued, "I have received information that indicates First Squad has, shall we say, incurred the dislike of a certain high official in the NVA. This official has not yet revealed his identity, but we believe that he was present in the field the day you and your men saw action near Dak Ket. I believe you and the Bitches stumbled onto a lot more than you bargained for in that little skirmish."

"Dak Ket? You mean, this is because of the VC we gutted?"

"Yes and no. They were not just VC. They were NVA regulars that you happened to stumble onto on their main stopover on this finger of the Ho Chi Minh Trail. But yes, near Dak Ket is the unnamed hamlet where you left a poster. That sketch has obviously enraged someone, Jackson, and unless you and First Squad want to end up as POWs or worse, you'd better find out who's behind this. The rumor is they want more than just your scalps."

A shiver raced down Jackson's spine as he recalled all he'd heard about VC atrocities and tortures perpetrated on unfortunate Americans. Death was one thing, torture was another.

"So . . . uh . . . what do we do out there, Lieutenant? Sit around and wait? Or do we have specific orders? If we're sent out to bait the trap, can we spring it any way we want to?"

"Act on your instincts, Jackson."

That almost satisfied Jackson. "What about air support or mortars?"

"You can't count on that. You will have to more or less be a . . . ahhh . . . free agent of the U.S. Marine Corps. This is mainly because you will probably be too far in-country to do any good with the radio transmission unless you can get to a high enough spot on a ridge to transmit the PRC-25. Remember the codes. I'll be monitoring it if you can get through. Oh, and you are to deviate widely from the more commonly traveled roads and trails, setting a course that seems to wander aimlessly, with no particular purpose in mind. This will take much longer and be rougher but, in the long run, safer. Have you got all this, Sergeant Jackson?"

"No, not exactly. Are you telling me I'll have no support whatsoever on this patrol? Gee thanks, Lieutenant," Jackson said. He wasn't quite certain that the lieutenant wasn't just kidding him, but Campbell's serious expression never wavered and he slowly began to realize that it was no joke. They were going to be strictly on their own.

"No air or artillery support," Campbell reiterated. "No B-52's. No Cobras. You're on your own. If you are lucky, we can manage to drop a resupply at predestined areas, but that doesn't mean it will be there when you get there. You're unofficially 'Force Recon' in this area. Do you understand?" the lieutenant asked again.

Jackson nodded. He understood too well. While part of his brain warned him that he was getting into a serious situation, another part was exhilarated at the sense of danger and reliance on his own survival skills. This should be a good test. His men were battle-honed and ready. And there was also the "Bug" to rely on as far as technical assistance and surveillance support. Yeah, they could handle it!

"Jackson," Campbell said, and the sergeant looked up at the lieutenant. Campbell seemed to be struggling to say something—or maybe it was *not* to say something—because he had to clear his throat a couple of times as he seemed to search for the right words. "Jackson," he repeated, "I want you to know that my thoughts and prayers will be with you every step of the way."

Nothing else was said for a moment, and Jackson had the inescapable feeling that there was a lot more behind this mission than Campbell was telling him. Or was allowed to tell him. He met the lieutenant's steady gaze for a brief span of time, then nodded once.

"Sure, Lieutenant. I know that."

Standing, Lieutenant Campbell stuck out his hand and Jackson took it. "Good luck, Jack."

"Thanks, Lieutenant."

The squad stayed in camp for two days, oiling and reoiling their weapons, packing provisions and rigging up some of Bug's special effects explosives. Sergeant Jackson toiled ceaselessly at plotting an "aimless" course on the relief map he would be using. It would take a week of hard travel through mountainous terrain as well as jungle growth to get there. Any NVA watching should be confused as to their ultimate destination.

This was going to be a special mission, Jackson told the Bitches, a fact-finding mission to flush out VC from the village near Dak Ket. And in the process, maybe they'd discover if and who was trailing them.

"I'm thinkin' that after that last raid on 'No Name' village, we've made some pretty good enemies in the NVA and with the VC. The old mamasan wasn't too happy the last time I saw her, and I'm thinkin' that maybe an uncle or nephew or brother's behind all this."

"Yeah, Sarge, but to follow us up in the mountains and then down in the valleys, too? Come on, do you think any of the VC or NVA have that much time or pull?" Smitty asked.

"Maybe not one of them, but what if we pissed off her nephew and he's kin to Ho Chi Minh or something?" Bug reasoned. "It's possible."

"But not likely," Crawdad said.

"Maybe not, but I don't know what else to think. There ain't no other reason why all these VC would be taking the trouble to trail us," Jackson said.

"If they're following us so hot and heavy, why haven't they been able to kill us off by now?" Carrigan asked. "They've had plenty of time and opportunity."

"We've been pretty damned lucky, that's why," Bug pointed out, and no one argued. It made more sense than anything else that had been said, and it didn't really matter anyway.

"But no radio contact?" Carrigan asked. "Is this search and destroy mission that important, Sarge? I mean, is this just to satisfy us, or to satisfy the brass?"

No one had an answer to that, and the squad was left with just as many unanswered questions as before. It didn't make sense that the VC would have a vendetta for just one squad, but it also didn't make sense that their movements were being traced otherwise. Whatever, it had been two weeks of it and Jackson was tired of waiting for the other shoe to fall. He was rather glad to be forcing their hand.

"We leave at 0300 hours," he told them, and the men of First Squad nodded. Only Doc Weathers was missing, gone to Tokyo on R&R, leaving them without a medic. Campbell had ordered Smitty to carry the medical supplies on the long-range patrol mission.

None of them got much sleep that night. All were tense and unable to relax. Going out on patrol always held a certain element of danger, but to go out and actually act as bait for the VC, with the specific purpose of having them fire and reveal themselves, was a bit more nerve-racking than the hide and shoot sort of stuff they'd been used to doing. They were setting themselves up as bait, and not a man of them didn't have his doubts about if he'd be back.

It was pitch dark when they slipped out of Camp Rascal and into the brush. They were heavily armed with knives, pistols, machetes, and well-loaded packs. Reverting to former procedure, Jackson carried the fifty-caliber receiver and Baroni had the rest. That was their only "big gun." The rest would be strictly primitive—knives, bayonets, and their wits.

Rain fell in bone-chilling sheets, filling their lungs with water instead of air, and the men trudged in silence through the thick jungle. Even with the foliage woven in a tight arch overhead, rain managed to penetrate and make them miserable and wishing for the heat again.

Every step was a struggle. Mountainsides were cut by a series of flooded streams raging past, the banks slippery with dank, rotting vegetation that crumbled beneath a man's boot. Carrigan walked point. He moved cautiously down a steep decline, a vague shadow not too far ahead of the rest of the squad. Then he suddenly disappeared from sight, dropping away as if the ground had swallowed him.

Catching up, the others could see the weak ground had broken away from him and he'd tumbled down the rest of that slope head over heels. A broad tree had stopped his rapid, silent descent in a jarring assault, and Carrigan was trying to catch his breath when they got there.

"You hurt?" Jackson asked in a soft, terse voice.

Carrigan shook his head. "Naw. Just my ankle, and it'll do."

"We'll clean your gear while you check it out."

He wasn't hurt, just bruised, and his boot had a long rip in the leather side. They cleaned as much of his gear as they could see in the dark, then moved on.

Heavy backpacks overfilled with extra ammo and supplies constantly slid atop their shoulders as they stumbled through the muck and mud churned up by the rain. As it grew light, they felt safe enough to converse in loud shouts that could barely be heard over the pounding of the rain overhead. The noise didn't bother the men; it was the silence of the jungle that got to them and made them jumpy.

When the rain finally stopped, it was as if someone had cut off the valve. It just quit with no warning, and they were suddenly aware of a variety of noises around them. The men exchanged wary glances with one another and began to walk more quietly. Jungle silence was eerie, with only the monkeys and birds overhead and soft rustlings in the brush around them.

"I'd settle for a good firefight right now," Baroni muttered to Jackson. "Even Puffy would sound pretty good."

"Don't you like peace and quiet, Baroni?"

"Yeah, but this is too damn peaceful!"

"I wouldn't mind seein' a Phantom or two up there," Carrigan said in a wistful tone, tilting back his head to stare up at the sky barely visible through the thick leaves overhead. Not watching where he was going, he stumbled slightly. Jackson leaped forward in a reflex action.

"Keep your eyes on where you're goin', Carrigan, or you may end up flying with your own set of wings!" Jackson snapped at him, giving the huge Montana boy a rough shove to the left.

When Carrigan looked down, he saw the discolored sand to the right of his feet and gulped. By now, most of the squad had learned to recognize a punji pit by the discolored sand used to disguise it. The top layer was of sand, the next leaves, the next a flimsy mat that would give way and send a man crashing into a pit that might only be two feet deep or might be a tiger pit with stakes at the bottom. It never mattered that much which it was. Both were deadly.

Jackson poked at the sand with his rifle muzzle and it gave way, revealing a pit about two feet deep. Sharpened punji sticks reared up. They were set about a hand span apart so as not to miss.

"Thanks, Sarge," Carrigan said, sucking in a deep breath.

"That's two near misses in one day, Carrigan. We're not starting out so good. I'd like to finish this mission with the squad intact, so watch your step."

Smarting from Jackson's sharp tone, Carrigan nodded while the rest of the squad remained silent. This wasn't the usual patrol and they all knew it. They shifted from one foot to the next, heads swiveling constantly as they watched the trees around them.

"I feel like fish bait," Smitty muttered, "just waitin' on a shark to grab me."

Jackson heard him. "Yeah, and you smell like it, too!" he shot back.

"Naw, Sarge, that's his last girlfriend," Crawdad argued, and tension eased as the squad laughed.

Jackson had a schedule of sorts planned, and he stepped up the pace, pushing the squad. He intended to get back to "No Name" village and set up an ambush. "No Name" village was where it had all started, and that's where he intended to end it.

The squad forded shallow streams and swollen ones, splashing into them sometimes waist-high, rifles lifted over their heads as they waded through. Close to the end of the first day they had to ford the Nam Nim River in one place, but when they got there it was flowing over its banks in a rushing torrent.

"Shit," Jackson said, hunkering down to stare at the river.

"Can't we go around it?" Baroni asked.

"Yeah, and lose half a day."

"Are we on that tight a schedule?"

"It's not the time that counts, it's how much quicker we can get to Dak Ket before whoever it is that's watching and tryin' to figure out what the hell

281

we're doin'. Once they know where we're headed, they've got time to set up an ambush for us. See?"

Baroni nodded. "Yeah."

Jackson stood up. "Link hands. We'll cross like the women and kids do."

Carrigan slanted a dubious glance at the muddy rushing waters that foamed past. "In that?"

"Just hold hands with your loved one, Carrigan. We'll get you across," Jackson said.

"We'll be exposed to any VC who happens by," Bug said, and Jackson nodded.

"Yeah. So who wants to stay behind and stand watch while the rest of us cross?"

No one said a word. The gear was strapped to a fallen log they pulled out of the mud and floated across by holding onto straps wound around the circumference. They had to wade across in water that slid past their chins, heads held high and one hand holding the log, the other holding the belt of the man in front. Jackson walked point, and he helped Baroni and Carrigan pull the others. The current surged around them with greedy fingers, but they all made it to the other side.

They were all exhausted and, after lying on the muddy banks for a few minutes of recuperation, found shelter underneath a rocky crag. They rested for several hours while the rain beat down and chill seeped into their bones. No fire was lit. Green wood would smoke and give them away to the VC or mercenaries who roamed the jungle and counted coup on any American unlucky enough to get caught. They sat and shivered and ate C-rations, burying the cans afterward.

"Ain't this the life?" Delisi observed.

"Yeah. And to think I could be snug and warm somewhere in the Hanoi Hilton or something," Gagliano said gloomily, shivering in his poncho.

"If our plan doesn't work, you may have a reservation waiting for you," Jackson said, and no one said anything else for a while.

After three hours rest, they started out again, moving through the dark jungle and listening to every sound. At least the rain had finally stopped, and now there was just a hazy warmth permeating the air. Secrecy was still the order, and the men filtered as quietly as possible through the trees, trying to blend with the shadows. Their faces were blackened and nothing else glittered in the dark.

The ammo supply was still good, as they had found nothing to shoot at and nothing had found them. Uniforms and boots were soggy. Muscles were tense, and every little sound set teeth on edge.

"What's that?" Baroni whispered, putting out a hand to stop the others. "I heard something."

No one said a word. They stood there, eyes straining in the dark as they tried to see. Vague rustlings and snapping of twigs filtered through, and Baroni whirled around on the path as a shadow suddenly loomed ahead. There was a sibilant hiss, then a thud and a muffled cry before the figure pitched forward.

"VC," Jackson pronounced him, moving forward and looking down at the corpse. "Who got him?"

Bug stepped up and pulled his K-bar from the man's chest, wiped it on his trousers, and slid it back

283

into its sheath.

"Not bad, Bug," Jackson said. "Get his rifle and ammo. We may need it before this is over with."

The AK-47 was slung over Bug's shoulder and the ammo belts lifted. "I wonder if he was alone."

"Not likely" was the soft answer, and the team moved forward again.

Now they had even more confidence in their reactions and felt a little more sure of themselves. The first encounter had been easy. The VC hadn't known they were there and hadn't had time to offer any resistance. It wouldn't be that way very many times, however. Ten men in the jungle was as noticeable as a herd of elephants in a roller rink, and they knew it.

Vegetation grew so thick they had to hack their way through in a few spots and finally decided to chance taking a more well-used trail to make more time.

"I'd rather take my chances with the VC than hack at this shit," Gagliano muttered, and Jackson agreed.

They hit the trail a few hundred yards to the south, then bore southwest. It curved around a hogback, then dropped over a ridge, finally breaking out of dense brush onto a shallow plain of scrub grass and trees. Farms dotted the little valley, and in the rising sun the team could see huts scattered more thickly on the upper slopes where the soil was better.

Delisi walked point about a hundred yards ahead of the others. From the rear he looked like a Vietnamese dressed up as a Marine because he was so short and skinny, and Jackson nudged Baroni.

"He struts like a Vietnamese fighting cock, don't he, Baroni?"

Baroni grinned. "Yeah, Delisi's cocky, all right!"

284

A burst of rifle fire snarled just ahead, and Jackson whipped around just in time to see Delisi let off a long burst of automatic fire as he broke cover from a stand of trees. Somehow Delisi had managed to walk right into the middle of a patrol of tribal mercenaries. They were fanned out in a line in the chest-high grass beyond the trees and seemed just as surprised as Delisi.

The squad quickly formed a V behind Delisi as the short Italian swapped rifle fire with the mercenaries. Several of the enemy had flung themselves to the grass and were firing from that position.

"They're close together, Sarge," Baroni said. "See? Four or five of 'em are bunched up tight."

"Yeah, five men drawn in so tight means that there's a large patrol or unit somewhere close by," Jackson shot back. "Shit!"

"We're in it pretty deep, huh, Sarge?"

"Yeah. Come on, Bitches. Let's rock and roll!"

The two ends of the mercenary patrol had been separated by Delisi's fire and now fanned out to tighten a noose around the Marines. It looked like there were close to twenty of them, split into three different teams. Delisi's first blast of fire had killed at least one man and wounded another. Single shots puffed up from the tall grass as the Marines charged forward.

Withering blasts from ten rifles parted the grass and mercenaries. The Bitches ran over the men trapped right in front of them, killing the five, then flanked left to catch those still out in the open. Four more mercenaries died in a rolling blast as the Marines bulldozed through. The rest clammed away with their AKs as the Bitches ran like hell to get out of range. A bullet whizzed past Jackson's cheek like an angry bee, and they kept running.

The firing faded as the Bitches gained more distance. They kept advancing at a quick clip, never halting but moving on, not changing direction until they reached the bottom fringe of a steep green slope. Then Jackson abruptly switched direction, altering their course from north to northeast, taking them back to a point parallel with where they had emerged from the jungle. Working their way to the higher slopes, the Bitches began to feel like Army boots as they marched, marched, marched, traveling in a parallel line.

The air was moist and hot, clogging their throats and noses with each steamy breath. They walked single file in places, trodding through trees and along the sloping edge of a broad field before dropping back to the road below. It wound around the mountain in a gentle curve that reminded Jackson of an apple being peeled, white and shiny and curling down. They zigzagged in case their firefight had spawned any "watchers," going from the wider road to a mountain trail that curved just above in a parallel run.

The Bitches swung back to the mountain trail just before it rose sharply and cut a turn to the right. Trees shadowed the trail, providing decent cover from the side, and they proceeded at a fast clip.

About ten yards from the turn in the trail, a small convoy of military vehicles rounded the curve and roared down the straightaway at the stunned Marines.

CHAPTER 18

Khaki-clad men bounced inside the open jeeps, laughing and talking and not noticing the Marines in the road at first.

"NVA!" Jackson snarled as the Bitches broke for the trees.

The thick jungle growth had muffled the engine noise until the vehicles had rounded the turn and bore down on them. As the Marines scattered, the drunken NVA inside the jeeps noticed them at last. Jackson and Baroni broke to the left; the rest of the squad broke to the right.

It was apparent that there was a great deal of indecision inside those jeeps, because none of the armed NVA lifted a rifle for the split seconds it took Jackson and Baroni to gain cover. The lead driver then apparently decided to run down the men still left in the road and veered his muddy green jeep in their direction.

Automatic fire began to chatter belatedly as the NVA opened up, and bullets whined past to smack into rock and trees and send hot splinters flying through the air. Smitty waited coolly until the lead jeep drew abreast of him, then let fly with his M-14. The front windshield of the jeep shattered and glass flew. The grinning driver and his passenger were dead before the broken glass could clear the jeep, and the vehicle lurched sharply to the right, hit a rock, then skidded from the road and down the wooden slope. It came to rest against a broad tree and exploded into a towering gray funnel of smoke and flames.

The second car screeched to a quick halt, causing the third car to crash into the rear, sending passengers tumbling everywhere. The third vehicle then bounced away, across the road, and ended in a shallow ditch on the other side.

"There's five to a jeep!" someone yelled, and men began scrambling.

For the first time, First Squad was working as a team without direction. No one asked or needed to ask what to do next. They acted independently, but for the good of all.

"*Lai day*, you bastards!" Jackson was shouting, pointing his M-14 and spraying the second jeep with fire. *"Lai day!"* None of the NVA seemed to want to come out but returned his fire as best they could. Jackson was on one knee beside the road, his eyes stinging from the smoke of burning rubber tires and gunpowder but still keeping up a general sweep while leaving one eye on his men.

One man was still alive in the wrecked jeep, and he ducked for cover behind the vehicle.

"I'll get him!" Baroni shouted. He loped from behind a tree as Jackson put down some heavy cover fire. The lone NVA cowering behind the jeep never saw

Baroni until it was too late. Waiting until he was ten feet away, Baroni hit the target at a run, firing from the hip just like the old Saturday night movie cowboy.

As if in slow motion, the NVA turned, his face and head disintegrating in a foamy shower of blood and flesh. It simply disappeared from his shoulders in a curious geyser. His body sagged, and oddly enough his hands still gripped the rear tire attached to the bumper, letting go slowly as the headless corpse slid to the ground.

Bitches in front, Bitches behind, Bitches at the side. They were everywhere, firing and ducking and taking out the ten NVA as if each man had been assigned a particular enemy to dispose of. Clockwork and precision seemed to be the order of the day, and for men who had seen no action in a couple of weeks, it was damn good. Or so Jackson said when the air had cleared and the dust settled.

"You Bitches don't do too bad!" he added in a sort of anti-climactic statement. Bodies were sprawled on the road as if carelessly flung there, and the men were methodically stripping them of weapons, ammo, and papers.

"Looky here, looky here!" Delisi said, holding up a pack of papers.

"Important?" Jackson asked, taking them.

"They list luncheon dates for the next week, Sarge!"

Jackson grinned. "They just might, Delisi! Shall we attend the next social with them?"

"Aren't they written in gook?" Bug asked curiously, sliding over to take a look.

"And code?" Carrigan added.

"Definitely gook and probably code," Jackson confirmed.

"Then how in the hell do you know what they say?"

"I don't," Delisi defended himself. "It's just a joke, man." He rattled the sheaf of papers. "But it stands to reason that these things may be important, and if they are, we should destroy them. We can't take a chance on getting captured and them falling back into enemy hands."

The papers were burned, the Marines watching until every last scrap was soot and ashes. The fire from the jeep raged high, towering black clouds rising into the air and drifting on the wind currents. It was a dead giveaway.

"What about secrecy?" Baroni wanted to know.

Turning, Jackson looked at him for a full minute. "You don't think somebody's going to suspect we're in the area now, Baroni? I mean, this is our second firefight of the day here!"

"Not to mention the dead gook in the woods," Mudders reminded.

"Not to mention the dead gook in the woods . . ."
Baroni shrugged. "Yeah. I guess you're right. But we ain't nowhere near Dak Ket and we've already blown our cover."

"Then they'll be waitin' on us, and maybe that's the best way after all," Jackson said softly. He indicated the dead NVA with a sweep of one arm. "We don't seem to work too bad together, Baroni."

After a moment of silence, Baroni grinned. "No, Sarge, we sure don't!"

Jackson looked back at the devastation in the road as they humped it out of there, and he knew that they would make it as a team. There was a big difference now, a change that had come since their search and destroy patrols out of Camp Rascal, and he didn't know how it had happened. Maybe it was because they knew they were on their own miles from help. Or maybe it was because they all felt as if they had something to prove now. Whatever it was, it was working.

They continued south through the mountains. A jagged range of peaks loomed ahead, reaching four thousand feet in the air. As the Bitches moved along an eastern slope the jungle thinned, straggling out to grass and bushes and an occasional copse of woods. There was never a level surface but always an incline or descent, so it seemed as if they were constantly stretching to walk. They covered fifteen to twenty miles a day in those mountains, walking rugged terrain with a few short breaks in between. The pace was grueling even for a seasoned soldier.

Jackson led them up a slope that was so steep it seemed to go backward, and by the time they reached the crest their muscles were screaming for a rest. Huffing and puffing for breath, they rested at last on a level ledge and stared out over the scene below.

The back of the incline descended gradually. Below, a peaceful valley was nestled between ragged ridges, and farms sprouted up out of the green slopes like weeds.

"Looks like the Tennessee hills," Jackson said, and Baroni laughed.

"Complete with pigs, Jack?"

291

"Complete with pigs."

"I think I smell some," Gagliano put in, and pointed to a clearing not far away. About two hundred yards down the slope was a bamboo hut quilted in by garden plots and fences. Chickens scratched, a few goats were tethered under a tree, and some pigs rooted happily in the dirt. Domestic tranquility beckoned.

"I don't know about you guys," Delisi said dreamily, "but I'm ready for a home-cooked meal."

"Do you mean like fried chicken?"

"Or roast pork," Delisi said. "Veal scallopini, lasagna, and—"

"Collard greens!" Mudders interrupted.

Baroni and Delisi made faces, while Jackson grinned. "Let's not waste any more time," the sergeant suggested, and they rose from the hard rock and scrabbled down the slope toward the tiny farm.

They waited in the trees, watching the farm for a sign of activity. Two hours passed and no one moved. Either the farm was deserted—which didn't explain the livestock left behind—or the peasant owners were off somewhere working in rice paddies. Jackson gave the order to move in, and they rose from hiding and proceeded stealthily forward. No one offered a sign of protest as they scavenged up a decent meal.

"I know one thing," Gagliano mumbled around a mouthful of rice and boiled chicken a short time later, "I never remembered that it took so long to get to Dak Ket the last time."

Jackson looked up at him. "It didn't, Gag. We're not taking the road this time."

"As long as our 'element of surprise' is gone, why bother?" Gagliano wanted to know, and Jackson couldn't answer. There didn't seem to be a rational answer other than that the brass wanted to see just how good they were and how many VC they could kill. In the past days of travel, he had come to the conclusion that it wasn't just his desire to find out who had been following them that was spurring him on. It was an irrational need to prove himself and the Bitches to Campbell and Gunner and anyone else who had ever wondered how that squad of misfits had kept from getting killed. He had a goal, but somehow it had become muddied in the process of getting there.

"Sarge?" Gagliano prompted, and Jackson shrugged.

"Why do you want to know? Aren't you having a good time, Gag?"

Grinning, Gagliano pushed another mouthful of rice and chicken into his mouth. "Yeah. The best."

"Then shut up and enjoy yourself."

An hour later they were on their way, with fresh vegetables and even a few carefully wrapped eggs stuffed into their packs. The brief rest and hot food had done them a world of good. The Bitches felt refreshed and ready to tackle anything, even more mercenaries.

The tribal mercenaries who inhabited the mountains were tough to predict. They weren't drilled and trained the way the NVA or even the VC were. There was no method to their fighting, just primitive instinct and reaction, and these they used to great advantage. Without knowledge of tactical warfare, those mercenaries were dangerous. They fought for whoever paid the most, and they fought with any weapon they could get, whether it was American, Chinese, or Russian.

At the worst, they had been known to use pitchfork and spear. It didn't matter. And because they were fighting for gain, it made them more vicious. There would be no interrogation of prisoners, just a fight to the death. Those savage warriors would fight for money or revenge, and the Bitches had "wasted" a lot of them in that first firefight. Jackson kept a close watch as they moved deeper into the jungle.

Rain started again, and the Bitches wrapped themselves up in their slicks and kept humping. The rain gave the air a different smell and feel. It wasn't the hard, driving rain of earlier in the day and it didn't obscure their vision; it just left them wet and miserable. Mud sucked at boots and splattered on uniforms, squishing as they trudged up gummy slopes and slid down slimy hills.

"We should be near Saigon by now," Carrigan muttered unhappily at one point, and the others laughed.

"Don't be a pussy, Carrigan!" Delisi said. He was walking beside the huge Montana boy and looked like an ant next to the mountain. Carrigan just looked down from his considerable height and shook his head.

"You beat all I've ever seen, Delisi. Are you so loud because you're so little or so little because you're loud?"

"Hell, I was born mean! I used to be six foot two, but it took a whole battalion of Marines to get me this size."

"Wonder why it is that I believe that?" Carrigan asked.

"Beats me!" Delisi shot back with a grin.

"Lissen up!" Jackson said in a hiss, and the

294

Bitches paused to listen. There was a faint rumble just ahead and a low-pitched murmur like voices. No one had to tell them to take cover when they saw Smitty, who was walking point, hit the ground.

After about five minutes, Smitty crawled backward until he reached the squad.

"NVA scout patrol," Smitty mouthed, and Jackson nodded.

"How many?"

"Six. They don't know we're here, 'cause they're walkin' too fast and careless."

Another nod from Jackson, then, "How far apart?"

"Spread out single file maybe a hundred yards . . ."

"No fire," Jackson ordered softly. "There's bound to be a much larger unit behind a scouting party of six men. We have got to take 'em quiet, or we could chance gettin' caught between a split faction."

"One on one?"

"Yeah. Leave a rear guard in those trees just behind us." There was the soft metallic clink of machetes and knives being drawn, and Jackson gave a nod of satisfaction. "Smitty, Bug, Carrigan, Baroni, and Sanchez come with me. Crawdad, Mudboy, and the Stud brothers stay in the trees and cover."

"I have a feelin' we're gonna wish Doc was here with us instead of banging chicks in Tokyo," Baroni muttered.

Jackson didn't answer. His gut was tight, his nerves sharp and taut. There wasn't enough time to stop and rationalize what they were doing; there was only time to survive. They could be any random squad out on a search and destroy mission until someone put together their route and figured out where they were headed. It would take the right someone to do it, the someone who was behind the brick walls they'd been hitting.

"Okay, Baroni," Jackson said, lifting his machete. "You and Sanchez and Bug go about two hundred yards up and wait for them to pass, then take the last three in file. Smitty, Carrigan, and me will hit the first three. Wait for us to make the first move."

"Roger," Baroni said, and moved out.

Jackson lay in tall grass and waited, not bothering to take off his pack. It might lend extra weight and not bog him down, and he didn't plan on having to run too fast or too far if things went right. He crouched behind a tree and motioned for the others to do the same, counting on the element of surprise to slow the NVA scouts' reactions. Sometimes it worked; sometimes it didn't.

Smitty had been right. The NVA were careless. They ranged through the knee-high grass in a ragged file, not looking left or right, just walking like they were on a Sunday school outing. Their rifles were slung carelessly, with barrels pointing downward. Beyond them Jackson could see the tall grasses quiver, and he knew that Baroni, Sanchez, and Bug must be in position.

Jackson tensed and poised to lurch up, his machete in his hand to slash the lead man's throat, when he heard a rifle pop. His head whipped around to see Sanchez standing up in the tall grass. Dammit! The stupid bastard had stood and taken fire before Jackson could take out the lead men!

Pandemonium erupted.

The NVA scouts shouted at one another as they tried to figure out how many of the enemy were around

296

them, firing indiscriminately. Jackson rose from the grass and the man he had targeted saw him. The NVA took off through the grass like a gazelle. He leaped and bounded over the terrain in several huge jumps before Jackson caught up with him, one hand snaring the back of the man's shirt and swinging him around.

This was hand-to-hand combat, face-to-face and only inches from the enemy. It was frightening and exhilarating at the same time. Jackson's foot swept the snared NVA's legs and sent him to his knees before he could bring his AK-47 up and fire. Straddling him immediately, Jackson slashed down with his machete. The NVA managed to deflect the blow with his rifle, and there was a clang as the blade bounced off the barrel. It quivered in his fist, and Jackson tried to steady it, bringing it back toward the NVA in a chopping motion again. The NVA grabbed his wrist with both hands and tried to force the blade away. Jackson had his weight and leverage on his side as he bore down with the machete, and the NVA was swiftly losing the struggle.

The man's face convulsed painfully, and he choked out several syllables that Jackson had trouble understanding at first. Then it dawned on him what the NVA was saying.

"Bad Black . . . Bad Black . . ."

Jackson hesitated, staring down at the man for a long moment. *Bad Black?* How in hell did he know what the men in his squad called him? Then it hit him—the poster Crawdad had drawn and tacked to a tree above the dead NVA. Jackson leaned harder on the machete, bearing down.

Finally, the point pierced the skin in the NVA's

throat and severed the jugular. Cutting a man's throat was never the clean business it appeared on television or in the movies. A man with his throat cut dies in a fountain of blood and loud, choking noises, and the NVA did now. Jackson was suddenly reminded of helping his grandfather kill pigs one autumn. That had been a much cleaner business, with his grandfather sticking the sharp knife in the side of the neck and jerking out the front, severing the pulsing vein in a clean stroke. There had been no horrible gargling sounds, not even a squeal, because it had been done quickly and efficiently. This was butchery, but the smell was the same.

It was over quick, and Jackson pushed off the body and looked around to see what was happening. He had gotten his man and hoped the others had done the same. Sounds of fighting reached his ears, and he leapfrogged over the tufts of grass and ruts to find the Bitches. He was careless. A man leaped at him from the grass almost at his feet, slamming his rifle against Jackson's head and knocking him to the ground to lie in a dazed heap.

"Dammit!" Jackson thought hazily. "Stupid, stupid, stupid!"

Jackson felt for his machete, but it had been slung a few feet away, out of reach. He struggled to rise but his pack was too heavy as he lay there on his back like an overturned turtle. He stared up through a fog of NVA blood, his own blood, and the blur of his vision, and saw the NVA grinning as he lifted his rifle butt to smash it into his face.

Is this the last thing I'm gonna see? Jackson thought, and he closed his eyes to shut out the sight.

Then he heard a grunt. He opened his eyes in time to see Baroni swing his machete again. The first blow had severed the NVA arm that held the rifle; the second removed his head as cleanly as a tree limb. Jackson took Baroni's offered hand to get up.

"Havin' trouble, Jack?"

Not bothering to answer, Jackson just gripped his hand for an instant longer, then let go. It was enough. Baroni understood the silent thanks.

"Is all that your blood, Jack?" Baroni asked then, but there was no time to answer. A burst of rifle fire snarled behind them, and they dropped to the ground. Silence then.

"Sound out," Jackson said when it had been quiet for a few minutes, and the Bitches counted off. They were all alive, at least. Jackson looked over at Sanchez, but the Mexican couldn't meet his gaze. He knew he'd almost killed them all. After another few minutes, they slowly rose to count the dead and assess the damage to the squad. Final count: Bitches 6, NVA 0.

"Not bad!" Baroni said admiringly, and Jackson agreed.

"Yeah, Baroni, but we need to get the hell out of Dodge instead of stand here and congratulate ourselves. The rest of the NVA unit had to hear all our noise. I don't want to be standing here when they come boiling over that hill!"

It was a sentiment shared by the entire squad, and they resupplied their ammo from NVA belts before moving on.

Night comes earlier in the jungle than it does in the fields or hills. The sun can still be shining beyond the trees, but it can't get through the thick cover overhead. The Bitches pushed on in the eerie twilight that hung in hazy shrouds, deeper and deeper in-country.

They hit the Di River where it snaked down toward Dak Ket and stopped on the banks. A highway ran parallel to the eastern banks, several miles away. It was the highway that cut south to Dak Lack a little northeast of Dak Ket, then ran down to the airbase at Mang Buk. They were on course and not too far from their goal.

Position: 15 degrees latitude by 108 degrees longitude in civilian terms. Not bad for a squad of misfits. A look back at the rugged terrain they had traversed in a week was inspiring. There had been no easy treks along the roads like the last time. This had been hard humping through mountainous, primitive country. And they were living off the land like scavengers, saving precious supplies for that time when there might be no food available.

After a quick scan of the map he carried, Jackson took their bearings. "Head west," Jackson decided. "That patrol whose scouts we took out may be using the main road. Let's skirt around a while."

A wood and dirt footbridge spanned a narrow strip of the river not too far west, and the jungle trail took a Y right past the bank. They approached cautiously and decided to wade through and not chance any booby traps.

"I can leave 'em something to remember us by, though," Bug offered, and Jackson took him up on it.

"Do it, Bug."

"Just like home!" Bug crowed, and he rigged up a trip wire across one end of the footbridge. He strung it across and attached it to a grenade at each end that would pull the pin when the wire was tripped. The wire was camouflaged by dirt and grass, and the job was done.

"Think they'll see that?" Carrigan asked, eyeing the wire and displaced grass.

Bug was busily digging in his pack. "Might, Carrigan. I think I'll give 'em something else to do if they see this one."

Using a pressure release device, he rigged up another trap and used a scattering of stones to camouflage it at the opposite end of the bridge. Whoever crossed the bridge better do so in daylight and with their eyes open. If one wire didn't get them, the other would.

"Let's go!" Jackson urged, and they struck out across the shallow water below the bridge, moving carefully to the steep bank opposite. They spread out along the edge of the trail that forked to the right about ten feet above the embankment. It wasn't much more than a wide dirt track wandering through the jungle in a seemingly aimless direction. Baroni was point man. After a short wait Jackson waved him across, and he leaped up and ran in a sort of half crouch.

When Baroni disappeared over the lip of the road and down into a gully choked with underbrush, Jackson motioned to Sanchez to go. As Sanchez stood up there was a shout in Vietnamese, then a rifle chattered loudly.

"That's Baroni!" Jackson said as Sanchez took cover and there was the distinctive pop of AK-47's answering his fire

"Let's go get him," Sanchez said as he started to get back up and go over the hill. Jackson stopped him. "No. Not now."

Sanchez stared at the black Marine. "What? You ain't gonna go get him, man? You just gonna let him get hit? That's a lot of lead they're throwin' over there, and—"

"Can it, Sanchez!"

Furious at his sergeant, Sanchez looked to the others for agreement, but none said anything. They looked away and stared across the shadowed ridge as if they could see Baroni. Night was pressing down fast and it was getting harder and harder to see.

"Chit, man," Sanchez muttered. "And I thought Baroni was your friend."

Jackson's mouth tightened and creases bracketed his lips as he glared at Sanchez, but he didn't say anything. He could hear Baroni throwing lead back at the NVA, using semiautomatic fire in erratic bursts. Jackson's mind was clicking fast as he tried to consider every possibility. Apparently the NVA had tracked them for hours since that firefight with the advance scouts. It was more than likely that they had passed within yards of one another in the dark jungle and not even known it. The large unit of NVA must have split to search both sides of the river for them, and now Baroni had stumbled into a hornet's nest waiting just across the ridge. Sanchez was too stupid to understand why Jackson wanted to wait.

It became immediately apparent when the other NVAs emerged from the thick fringe of trees about thirty meters to the left of the hidden Marines. Sanchez slanted Jackson a chagrined glance and shrugged

302

his shoulders as if to say, "How was I to know?" *The dumb-fuck*, Jackson thought.

The NVAs obviously thought all the action was on the other side of the ridge, and they hit the road above the Bitches lying in the grass on the bank. They made a perfect silhouette against the setting sun as they trotted across the wide road toward the gully. Jackson lifted a hand and waited until they were in the center, then gave the signal.

Nine Bitches blasted away at the dozen NVA caught in the road. Three of them were lifted several feet off the ground by the concerted firepower of M-14's, their bodies hacked by hot bullets. One of them disintegrated in a foamy shower of blood and bone and bits of flesh, his head just disappearing as if erased. Two of the NVA were shoved down by their own buddies and trampled in the mad rush to get to cover, four of them died trying to get to the brush and trees at the side, and three made it over, albeit in pretty bad shape. Blood formed huge puddles in the middle of the road.

By now, the NVA unit must have thought they were cut off and surrounded by a much larger patrol than just ten angry men. Jackson decided to move it out and attack before they figured out what was really happening.

He jumped up and headed for the spot where the three surviving NVA had gone to ground, and the others scattered out behind him in a fan shape. No one fired. They waited. Jackson was loping down the middle of the road as if he had all day, his automatic weapon held at any easy position to fire. The survivors reacted just as he had hoped.

They stood up and clambered onto the road to see if

they could determine the direction of the withering fire they had encountered, and saw Sergeant Robert L. "Bad Black" Jackson sprinting toward them with a wide grin on his dark face. It must have been disconcerting to the wounded NVA, to say the least, but they didn't have much time to worry about it. Jackson's automatic fire blew them off the road in less than five seconds.

Unfortunately, he didn't stop running soon enough. He kept going down the road and over the ridge into the gully, trying to reach Baroni, and found himself right in the middle of a hornet's nest of NVA. To his surprise Sanchez was right behind him, and the Marines and NVA all began wildly firing at the same time, bullets bouncing off trees and sky. Some of the NVA hit their own men and quickly realized that automatic fire was hampering their effectiveness.

Sanchez and Jackson looked at each other, then Jackson shrugged and shouted, *"Chieu hoi, chieu hoi!"* at the stunned NVA soldiers. The NVA must have thought the muddy black Marine sergeant was crazy, hollering "Surrender, surrender!" when he was in a gully and surrounded by the enemy.

Laughing like he was insane, Jackson shouted again, "Bitches!"

It was like the mating call of a wild moose, and Bitches poured into the gully like hot lava from a volcano. Quarters were too close to fire without risk of hitting their own men, and it was now hand to hand. Time spun in a whirl of lunge, thrust, and rip. The Bitches fought with a ferocity none had realized they possessed, using teeth, claws, knife, machetes, or gun.

When the NVA managed to disengage and run,

Jackson heard a long rattle of automatic fire follow them. Baroni was still pinned down somewhere in the bushes just ahead, and Jackson figured that it had to be him. He brought up his M-14 just as Baroni flushed two more NVA out of the bushes. They ran straight at Jackson, and he let fly with a round, dropping them.

Then it grew quiet. The only sounds were of fading voices as the NVA retreated and of harsh breathing as the Bitches watched and listened. There was the distant snap of tree limbs and crashing feet on the jungle floor, and Sanchez made as if to go after them.

"No," Jackson said to him, breaking the sudden quiet. "Let them go, Sanchez. We can't get 'em all, and there may be more out there waiting."

Sanchez nodded, wiping blood and sweat from his eyes with his filthy shirtsleeve. "All right by me, man. I'm kinda tired of smellin' these stinkin' gooks right now."

Shaking his head, Jackson said wearily, "Count off!"

Amazingly, not one of them had been killed or sustained serious injury. Carrigan had a deep cut on his right arm. Jackson was bleeding profusely from the side where a bayonet had sliced him and he had a head cut, but nothing that would stop him. Baroni, stepping up and regarding his buddies with a grin, didn't have a single scratch on him. He stood there and looked at the bedraggled, bloodied bunch of men and shook his head.

"You guys are a damned mess!" he said.

"Look what I found, Sarge."

Jackson turned his aching head to stare at Baroni. He was holding up an M-79. An *American* M-79. The single-shot 40mm grenade launcher gleamed in the firelight of their camp in the rocks.

"Where the hell did you find that, Boney?"

"Some of our playmates left it behind. Wonder where they got it?"

"I can just imagine," Jackson said. His head throbbed and his side ached. Smitty had dispensed medicines from the kit right and left, but he had taken nothing to dull the pain. If he took the edge off his pain, he might also take the edge off his mental faculties and ability to react. That could mean death.

"It's 2200 hours, Sarge," a voice reminded, dragging Jackson back from the fog of pain where he'd wandered.

"Yeah. Get some shut-eye. We need to *di di* outa here in a couple of hours."

A low laugh thrummed through the soft night air, and Jackson turned to look at Sanchez. The Mexican was grinning at him, his teeth white in the glow of the firelight.

"What'cha laughin' 'bout, Sanchez?" Bug asked lazily.

"You shoulda seen our sergeant in that gully back there today, man! There we're standin', with NVA all around us and lookin' at us like we was their next meal, and he says to 'em *'Chieu hoi, chieu hoi!'* Can you believe that chit, man? Neither could them damned NVA!"

Even Jackson had to laugh at his own temerity, and Baroni turned to look at him. "That was a little audacious of you, Sarge," Baroni said.

"Audacious? Hell, it was downright dumb!" Gagliano said in a loud voice.

Shrugging, Jackson said, "Well, I thought they might want to surrender before we took 'em out."

Chuckles met that remark, and then silence fell. Rest was badly needed, and with an NVA unit roaming somewhere close by, they weren't likely to get it. Sleep had to be grabbed in snatches, with fifty-percent watch. Gagliano, Jackson, Baroni, Sanchez, and Bug were watching, while Delisi, Crawford, Mudders, Carrigan, and Smitty slept.

0100 hours, and the Bitches were on the move. They filed silently, like ghosts, through the thick trees. Rain fell in a soft, rhythmic pattern, wetting faces and hunched shoulders, making the Marines generally miserable. Rain again. Shit. What a country.

"Hell, Sarge," Baroni grumbled, "not even the VC are out in this soup!"

"Then we ought to make good time," Jackson shot back.

There was no quick answer for that, and Baroni just sighed and shrugged. They humped until the sun filtered through a hazy gray mist over the eastern edge of the mountains, barely visible through the thick tree line that broke only occasionally. Dak Ket lay in a small valley below, at the edge of foothills that rose gradually into the mountains. They were almost there.

CHAPTER 19

Dak Lack lay on the main road to Mang Buk, on the banks of the Ngh. Dak Ket squatted several klicks to the west, through mountainous jungle, and the Bitches' target village lay between. They approached cautiously, deviating from the trail and not knowing if an ambush was waiting on them as they hacked through the jungle toward the village only six klicks away.

There was.

Jackson, crouching in the thick cover of bushes, froze when he felt a twig fall from the trees overhead and land on his neck. His eyes darted to the right and the left where the rest of the Bitches were fanned out, then shifted up to look in the trees.

Somehow, the Bitches had managed to come to rest under snipers without being seen. It could be because they had been moving slowly, looking for booby traps, trip wires, and the like. Whatever it was, they had managed to get right under the snipers and were now trapped. Unless Jackson could get a good look and see how many were sitting up in the trees, he had no way of knowing if they could take them. There could be one or two, or ten of them, greatly increasing the odds against survival.

Cutting his eyes to Baroni on his left, Jackson mouthed the word *snipers* and Baroni nodded. He'd seen them, too. The Bitches squatted in virtual suspension of movement as they waited for Jackson's signal on what to do. Each man understood the odds and would follow his lead.

Apparently, the snipers had expected the Bitches to come down the main trail, because they were arranged in the trees so that they had a clear view of the track running through the jungle, but were exposed to the men below. Cautiously settling back on his heels, Jackson could see five men, all armed with scopes and sniping rifles, sitting in several different trees about thirty feet up. Great odds if they hadn't been thirty feet up and directly overhead, so that even the smallest movement below would be detected and the Bitches would be blown away before they could take aim.

Jackson's mind whirled for a full minute as he explored the options. Diverting their attention seemed to be the best avenue to travel, and he slowly, as if in a time-frame click of movement by movement, withdrew a grenade from the clip. Even that tiny action seemed too loud, and sweat poured from his brow down his face. Jackson could hear the beads of sweat drop from his chin to his shirt, and he realized he was holding his breath when his lungs began to ache from lack of fresh oxygen.

Baroni was watching him, and Jackson slowly

drew back his arm. Baroni understood. The Italian was braced and ready when Jackson pulled the pin and let fly with the grenade, lobbing it through the trees to land in a spot several meters distant.

The explosion started the snipers firing in that direction. Jackson rolled onto his back and aimed his M-14 into the trees, firing and shouting at the same time. The rest of the Bitches opened up. A sniper fell like a dead squirrel and dropped into the bushes a few feet away. A bullet smacked into Jackson's pack, tearing through the heavy canvas and supplies then flesh before exiting out the front of his shoulder. Not pausing in his roll and fire routine, Jackson brought down another sniper with a *brrrrp* from his rifle. He could hear someone behind him give a hoarse shout of pain, and he knew one of the Bitches had been hit. There wasn't time to stop and check, no time for anything but firing.

A grenade blasted somewhere close by, and Jackson's head rang as dirt and shrapnel showered down on him. He knew he was hit but, oddly enough, felt no pain. That would come later. Now his adrenaline was pumping, and his brain refused to recognize the fact he had been hit as he kicked out and fired into the trees again. Blood fell on him and he didn't know from where until he looked up and saw the man draped over a thick tree limb. Half his face had been blown away and blood dripped down like rain, spattering over Jackson. He moved, still firing into the trees. It took a minute before he realized there was no return fire, and he gave the signal to halt. Jackson counted six bodies, one man more than he'd seen in the trees. They were NVA regulars, clad in the khaki uniforms common to their army.

They'd gotten them all. Now it was time for reaction, for fear to flood in and take over, even if it wasn't admitted aloud. The Bitches exchanged glances and congratulations as they completed the job of cleanup, taking ammo and food packs. Three of them had been hit, none critically. Crawford had taken shrapnel in his legs and side, and was chewed up pretty bad by the metal fragments. He was still functional but would be in pain and stiff from his injuries for a while. Jackson had taken a hit in his shoulder, but the bullet had gone through in a shallow trough, just taking skin and stinging like hell. Sanchez had taken another hit, this one in his upper arm. Smitty was digging out the bullet and giving him penicillin, but Sanchez refused the morphine.

"Chit, man. It's just a little scratch," he said with a weak grin.

Jackson had the thought that before this was all over, he may even decide Sanchez wasn't too damned bad. The Mexican had a way about him that made him unlikable, but in combat he carried his load. And that was the main thing.

"Well?" Baroni said into the silence that descended. "What'cha think, Sarge?"

Jackson's head rotated painfully. He stared at Baroni. "About what?"

"About blondes, brunettes, redheads—snipers and VC! Hell, I don't know, Jack. Our odds of getting out of here, maybe."

Shrugging, Jackson said, "We'll make it. We've

got a job to do, remember."

More silence, and each man labored with his own thoughts and fears. They'd covered a good distance in a reasonable length of time, and their goal lay so close yet still so distant in terms of practicality. Obviously, someone was waiting on them. A chance meeting with NVA, VC, or tribal mercenaries was one thing, but this had been a planned, concerted effort to stop somebody, and the somebody had to be the Bitches. Who else did they expect along this back road? Even Dak Ket wasn't exactly a main village along the usual route of travel, and the nameless little hamlet that was their goal was even less likely a place to set up an ambush. Why? There was only one answer to that question, and that was that someone knew they were coming.

Wincing against the pain in his shoulder, Jackson finally gave the signal to move out. There was no point in resting too long and letting muscles and wounds stiffen.

"Okay, Bitches. These men were obviously an advance unit, which means somebody is coming up behind us. Time isn't on our side, but Somebody up there must be, 'cause we shoulda gotten blown away just now. They had the advantage, but luck or fate or whatever you wanna call it stepped in. Let's not press it. Be careful. No firing unless we have to. When we get to the village, spread out and watch, just watch. Don't go in until we know the odds."

"You expect them to be there waiting on us?" Baroni asked.

"I expect them to be *every*where waiting on us,"

312

Jackson shot back. "And you better do the same. That way we won't be surprised."

No one said anything for a full thirty seconds, then Jackson hoisted his heavy pack over his throbbing shoulder. "No questions? Let's hump."

The Bitches hugged the west wall of a sharply rising ravine as Jackson led the squad down a dried-up streambed. The sheer rise of the sides protected them from being seen by the enemy walking a track parallel to the ravine, but it also kept them committed to the same trail for the next ten miles. The streambed meandered through the jungle in a snaking course, east, west, and elbowing north before cutting south again.

Jackson's plan was to stay with this dried-up bed until it reached a fork near the highway, then hump the lower slopes of the ranges running parallel to the highway to the west, keeping the valley between the squad and the Mang Buk highway. According to Jackson's timetable and plotting, the Bitches were supposed to pass a hamlet prior to reaching their ultimate destination before morning the next day.

They left the streambed at the last hamlet before Dak Lack. The plan was to skirt it by night, but as they were a couple of hours ahead of schedule, they waited in the tree-lined banks opposite the sleepy village. It was no more than a few leaning hovels perched on the edge of the dried-up bed, but it seemed to see quite a bit of traffic.

While the Bitches waited, two NVA patrols passed

by in double-file formation. Both patrols marched westward, in the same direction First Squad had to travel. Jackson and Baroni exchanged significant glances but didn't speak. They were tired and apprehensive, and not prone to conversation for a while. It had been hard work humping this far, and their scratches, cuts, and wounds were aching and worrisome. Beyond the hamlet waited another two hours of marching for First Squad, across open ground with no cover. It had to be accomplished at night. Dark couldn't fall fast enough.

Jackson watched the last patrol's march through the hamlet with his field glasses. It progressed smoothly, with the officer in charge yelling out orders in a high-pitched, irritating whine. He didn't seem to have control over his squad and they didn't seem to respect him very much, not an unusual occurrence with a young man who was little more than a peasant given rank. Some of the older NVA officers had a more quiet discipline that garnered respect without the bravado and shouting this officer employed. Maybe that would be a fact in First Squad's favor if forced to fight these soldiers in the near future.

Night fell in lingering black shrouds, slowly blanketing the area. Jackson still waited until he was certain it would be safe. It was almost midnight when he gave the signal for the first two-man team to cross the wide streambed to the opposite side. Delisi and Gagliano moved out, running in a half crouch down the sides, across the flat bottom, and up the opposite side in less than two minutes. Twenty minutes passed before Mudders and Crawford followed in the same running crouch, then another twenty went by before Smitty and Carrigan, another twenty before Bug and Sanchez, and Jackson and Baroni waited until last. In all, it took an hour for the ten men to cross a hundred meters of ground, a little larger than a football field. Jackson's compulsive need for cover could only keep them safe for a while. It was inevitable they would run into trouble sooner or later.

When Jackson and Baroni scrabbled up the bank and joined the others, they discovered the body of a lone peasant lying in a blood-soaked puddle.

"What the hell?" Jackson began, and Sanchez shrugged.

It didn't matter. Without another word, the peasant was stripped of his garments and valuables. Hopefully, the villagers would think bandits had done it.

The Bitches moved on through the fringes of the river forest until it gradually thinned to steep slopes of grass and rocks. Still humping, they reached the foothills, then turned to follow the slopes southwest.

Rugged terrain stretched in front of them, but they traversed it without incident. They had to climb sharp grades upward until the foothills finally tabled out into a flatter level. Trees grew more thickly here, but the bush thinned at ground level. There were times that the trees ended and nothing but open ground was between the squad and any chance patrol.

Then they reached the last obstacle before their destination—three miles of thick jungle. Jackson decided to make camp and rest before pushing on to the last leg of their mission.

They set up camp in a copse of trees and rocks thrusting up from the ground. The hump-backed boulders and grayish slabs lay in a weird tumble like fallen playing cards, looking completely out of place in the thick trees. Jackson snuggled up to one of the granite rocks and lit a cigarette.

"Hey, Jack," Baroni said, coming to crouch down beside him, "what do you want to do with the gook clothes?"

He was pointing to the peasant outfit they had removed from the hapless farmer killed a short time earlier.

Jackson shrugged and said, "Keep 'em. We may need 'em for something."

"Hell, the only one they'll fit is Delisi!" Baroni said with a tired laugh. He sat down beside Jackson and accepted the offer of a cigarette. Smoking was a luxury none of the men had allowed themselves since beginning this mission. It would be too easy to spot them at night, too easy to smell the smoke during the day. But now, up in the shelter of the rocky overhang, Jackson relieved some of his tension. It was the best cigarette either man had ever tasted.

"Tomorrow's the day," Baroni said after a while, and Jackson nodded.

"Yeah. Sure is."

Silence stretched, then, "I wonder if Mudboy and Crawdad still love C-rats as much as they used to."

Jackson grinned. "I doubt it. I heard Mudboy tell him that he could have his pound cake and peaches

316

and stick it where the sun don't shine, and Crawdad answered that it already tasted bad enough."

Both weary Marines laughed softly, then grew quiet. The next day's events were hanging over their head, and they knew they needed to rest up for the stress ahead.

"Jack?"

He turned to look at the dim outline of Baroni's face in what was left of the moonlight. "Yeah?"

"Whatever happens, I want you to know you've been the best damned sergeant I've ever had."

Jackson couldn't say anything for a moment, then he said in as light a tone as possible, "Hey, man! Don't talk like we ain't gonna make it! If I'm the best damned sergeant you've ever had, don't you think I can get us through this shit?"

Baroni grinned. "I said you were good. I didn't say you were fucking Superman, Jack!"

"Yeah, well, just 'cause there ain't no phone booths around here, don't be too damn sure of that, Baroni!"

The last few hours of the night passed in an easy, companionable silence.

They were still a few klicks from "No Name" village when they stumbled on a jungle clearing teeming with NVA. It was the only trail leading into the clearing, and as they began to back out, they heard the sound of approaching soldiers. Giving hand signals like crazy, Jackson motioned for them all to squat down in the bushes and wait.

The squad fanned out and waited, sitting as still as possible as three uniformed NVA passed within a foot of them along the trail. Sweat rolled down Jackson's face in rivulets, and he could feel wet patches under his arms. This was not a good place to be, he thought.

"How many down there?" Baroni asked softly.

Jackson's field glasses slipped against his sweat-slick face as he peered through them, then replied, "About twenty to twenty-five. Too damned many."

"What do we do? Go around?"

Pointing to the left where the jungle grew so thick it would take chain saws to get through, then sweeping his arm to the right where the mountain rose abruptly in a steep incline, Jackson asked, "How?"

"We just wait for them to move then?"

Their conversation was being carried on mostly by mouthing the syllables. The decibel level was almost at zero. It wouldn't do to be overheard chatting chummily in the bushes.

Stumped for what to do next, Jackson figured they had no other choice than to wait.

"You got any other ideas?" he mouthed to Baroni.

Baroni shrugged and mouthed back, "Gimme a minute."

It was Bug and Delisi who came up with the most daring thing they had yet tried. Withdrawing as cautiously as possible to several meters away, Bug hastily rigged up a trip wire to a tree felled by winds. It lay across the path leading to the clearing, not blocking it but making it necessary to push the branches aside. Jackson and Baroni kept a lookout

318

as he was doing his work, and time ticked in an eternity of seconds before Bug was back in the bushes beside them.

Jackson slid a glance at Delisi and gave a dubious shake of his head. "This ain't gonna work," he mouthed.

Bug gave a quick nod of his head and a thumbs-up sign. "It's got to."

The element of surprise again. If it worked, great. If it didn't, First Squad would cease to exist. Jackson fretted over the use of just luck as a weapon. It could never be counted on, and he hated being forced into this kind of position. It could go either way. Their lives didn't depend on skill or training, but on the luck of the draw.

But in the end, it was luck that saved First Squad.

After hours of waiting, the NVA finally ended their apparent conference, and most of the unit began the march back down the trail, leaving only four men in the clearing. Jackson and Baroni gave the signal, and each man gripped his weapon and held it at ready. Grenades were pulled off belt clips, and K-bars and bayonets were freed for use.

The first five men in the passing NVA unit somehow missed the trip wire strung from tree to ground, and Bug shook his head in disbelief. Sweat dripped from the end of his nose and he swallowed hard, lifting his eyebrows and shrugging his shoulders when Jackson looked at him and scowled. Bug's blond hair was plastered close to his skull from the sweat of strain.

Then it hit. The next soldier's foot caught the trip

wire and strung the C-4 explosives Bug had rigged. It rippled back along the ground wire he'd laid and set off the three grenades in a kind of daisy chain, taking out six of the NVA at one time.

The force of the explosion vibrated along the ground and sent showers of metal, rock, and tree down on the Bitches, but none lethal. They were just far enough away.

Four of First Squad boiled out of the trees and into the clearing to take out those soldiers left behind, while the other six took advantage of the momentary surprise to take out the eleven men left standing in the trail. Surging forward, Jackson, Baroni, Sanchez, and Bug caught the brunt of the NVA's recovery. The soldiers swung around and began firing their AK-47's with that hollow pop-pop-pop. Bullets flew like rain, and Bug felt several tugs at his backpack and knew he'd been hit. Only luck and several pounds of C-rats kept the bullets from penetrating the bulky pack.

He fired at close range, and an NVA exploded right in front of him in a crimson burst of blood and gore. Turning in an efficient motion, Bug slashed upward with his K-bar and slid it into the neck of a soldier trying to fire his weapon. He didn't have time to be clean and neat, but hacked at the man clumsily. With the noise of the M-14's and AK-47's clattering all around him, Bug could barely hear the harsh gurgling sounds the NVA made as he dropped to his knees in a sort of slow-motion.

Jackson was ducking the onslaught of bullets an NVA was throwing at him, coming up on one knee and firing from the hip, his weapon jumping in his hands almost of its own accord. He saw the NVA going down right and left, and could hardly believe their blind luck. They were doing it! It was working, and against all odds. . . .

Leaping over the fallen body, Jackson kept his finger on the trigger, squeezing off rounds and feeling invincible. Hell, maybe he *was* Superman after all.

Then it was over, and only the faint echo of the shots hung in the air, along with the smell of death and blood. Sanchez calmly bayoneted a wounded NVA, finishing him off where he lay.

Panting, breathing so hard his rib cage ached, Jackson said, "Let's get rid of the evidence."

"Like they won't know what's happened here?" Bug said.

"They'll know something happened, but they won't know to who or how for a little while. Anything to slow 'em down, Bug, anything to slow 'em down."

"No Name" village sprawled before them like a repeat of a bad dream. It was almost dark now, and they could see the pinprick of cooking fires at intervals. No one said anything, but there was the concerted rumble of empty stomachs as the scent of boiled rice and chicken drifted to them on the stiff breeze.

Spreading out in a crescent, the Bitches crouched and waited and watched. Waiting and watching was becoming commonplace. Some of the men had even learned the little trick of detaching their mind from what was happening yet retaining the ability to note any unusual movement. That helped take their minds off the discomfort of remaining in one position too long, not even moving to swat at an insect. They just watched. And waited.

Every little movement in the village was noted. Things seemed to be normal. The villagers did not seem to be in a hurry and the livestock was penned in the cages and being fed as would be normal at this time of day. Several water buffalo lowed softly, sounding like the plaintive moans of wounded, and Jackson saw Carrigan's quick shiver. He smiled to himself. All their nerves were strained to the breaking point. Even action was preferable to waiting, but wait they must. It would be suicide to walk into a village that was armed to the teeth and waiting. It had to be determined safe.

"Just how safe is a 'safe' village, Sarge?" Baroni asked through clenched teeth. "How do we know they won't welcome us, then stab us in the back? And what do we expect to find here, anyway? Ho Chi Minh himself? Why all the shit about getting back here?"

Jackson didn't answer for a minute. Then he said slowly "I think there's more to this than appears, Baroni. And I think Campbell knows it. He says he got his orders from higher up, and I don't think Command really gives a damn if we go a couple of weeks without seeing VC or if we think there are VC trailing our movements. We're just one small squad

322

in a big fish pond, if you get my meaning. We're expendable. But somebody's been making a nuisance of himself and has the brass pissed off. Even if we end up wasted on this mission, he'll show his hand. I think that's what the brass wants—to know who's fuckin' 'em over."

Baroni didn't say anything, and Smitty and Bug, on either side of Jackson and Baroni, didn't offer any comment. The others were spread too far out to hear the conversation.

"So, you're saying that it doesn't really matter if we complete the mission," Smitty said quietly. "What matters is that we draw fire and reaction from the enemy."

"That's what I'm saying."

"Well, shit!" Bug exclaimed. "I feel like a damned sitting duck on one of those rotating firing ranges! We pass by, they take a shot, hit or miss, win the prize or lose. . . . Shit!"

Jackson shrugged. "Look at it this way: We *do* have a personal interest in finding out who's behind our sudden popularity with the NVA."

That seemed to make sense, and they agreed with Jackson that the best way to find out was this way.

"I just don't like bein' *used* man," Smitty said.

"Yeah. They should have told us," Bug agreed.

Just looking at them, Jackson said, "Why?"

"Well—well, because they just should have, man! It's not right to send a squad out knowing they don't have a good chance to make it back and not even tell 'em about it!"

"Hell, Smitty! Every time we go out we've got a

good chance of not making it back!" Jackson said in disgust. "Don't you remember Myers? Grover?"

Subdued by the reminder, Smitty nodded.

"Yeah, well, let's do what we have to do and not worry about what the brass is doin'. We'll just take care of our end of it."

CHAPTER 20

Sitting outside the village perimeter, Jackson noticed the stucco building at the north for the first time. He didn't remember it being there before, but it had obviously been built in the past century when the French had occupied Vietnam. French influence was evident in the leaning structure. The walls were crumbling, and the windows had blackened soot around them as if the building had been fired. By who? he wondered idly. NVA? VC? American troops? Not that it mattered. These people caught in the cross fire of war didn't much care who had killed their children or burned their temples. It all came out the same in the end. The civilians were the losers. And the statues inside the crumbling temple had probably been removed long ago to preserve them, anyway, so now it was a wasted building. Just a silent, grim reminder of the war that raged in Vietnam.

Jackson shifted position in the bushes, his gaze moving slowly from left to right and back again. The village was still peaceful, looking like any primitive collection of huts. Except that it wasn't. His sixth sense again, telling him that the Bitches weren't alone.

On his right, Baroni shifted impatiently. "So when do we move, Jack?"

"Not yet."

Baroni nodded. He wasn't in any great hurry to walk into a trap now that they were here.

"Baroni!" Jackson nudged him with an elbow. "Look." He pointed toward the lopsided stucco temple. An old man was tottering along, carrying a straw basket. "What do you think he's doing?"

Shrugging, Baroni said, "I dunno. Carrying an offering to his god or something? Don't they leave rice and fish to their ancestors or Buddha or somebody?"

Jackson was scratching the stubble on his chin and frowning. "Yeah, but it don't look like there's anything in that temple, does it?"

"Does that make any difference?" I mean, a church is a church, isn't it?"

"Sometimes. It's also a place of refuge, if you get what I mean."

Baroni got it. He nodded slowly. "Yeah. You're thinkin' that maybe there's something inside that temple?"

"No, someone."

"Like NVA or VC?"

"Right."

They sat and watched while the old man entered

the broken entrance of the temple and disappeared. He didn't reappear for several minutes, and the basket was gone when he emerged into the deepening twilight. Shoulders hunched, he trotted back down the dirt path to the village and ducked into one of the hootches. Jackson's gaze flicked to the shell of the burned hootch belonging to the stubborn old mamasan who had defied his questioning, and he wondered briefly if she had regretted not talking. Not that it mattered. She had harbored VC. That was enough to condemn her in Jackson's book.

Insects began to buzz in loud squadrons, worrying the hidden men in the bushes. They itched to slap at the nagging pests and swear loudly, but had to resist. The Bitches weren't in the best of shape. The long trek through hazardous terrain had taken its toll in physical and psychological wear and tear. They were all on the edge and teetering. Anything could set them off, and Jackson knew that the strain of waiting was wearing on the men. Even Bug was fretting, twisting the stock of his M-14 back and forth in his hands like it was a dishrag. His yellow handball glove looked like a bright banner in the gloom, and Jackson motioned for the men to remove them. Just that flash of dingy yellow could give them away to any enemy watchers.

The handball gloves were peeled away and stuffed into pockets or backpacks. Jackson returned his attention to the village settling in. Night was just beyond the mountain fringe, hovering with great dark wings that would hide covert actions. It crept slowly over the ragged peaks until finally reaching the foothills and valley edge, blanketing the unnamed village and waiting intruders.

"Do we go in?" Baroni whispered.

Jackson desperately wanted to storm in and get it over with. They needed a resupply badly. There had been no sign of the promised drops, but he hadn't really expected any. Campbell had made it clear they were on their own. He wasn't even certain that slicks would come in to pick them up when this was over. *If* any of them were in any condition to radio for slicks, he reminded himself silently. His gaze flicked to his men. They were depending on him, and he couldn't make up his mind what to do. He looked back at the quiet village and rejected his earlier plan. It would be too risky now. They were tired and their reflexes might be too slow. He didn't want to be responsible for a single death, and with the injuries they had incurred in the past week, he wasn't certain how responsive the Bitches would be to an almost certain savage onslaught.

"Let's go in!" Baroni grated softly. He looked like his nerves were jumping, and his weapon quivered in his hands as if it had a life of its own. All the men were jumpy, and Sanchez had the look of a wildman. His field hat was pushed to the back of his head and his eyes were wild and white, his lips pulled back over his teeth so that he reminded Jackson of a piranha.

"Shit!" Jackson muttered. "I'm in charge, and I ain't leadin' no suicide mission."

"We came all this way," Baroni reminded. He licked his lips, and Jackson understood that they all felt the same way. Nine pairs of eyes swerved in his direction.

The Bitches waited for his signal to move out. He looked at them. They expected him to send them in and were waiting for it. They wanted to go, wanted to fight, and he suddenly understood that he couldn't back down now. It would be demoralizing and would possibly endanger their return to Camp Rascal. They had to complete their mission as planned. He gave a nod of his head.

It was obvious to him that enemy forces were in that village, even if unseen. The thing was—where? The squad wasn't large enough to split its attack on two separate ends. It needed to be concentrated in the area where it would do the most good, and Jackson had a hunch that the temple would be a good place to start.

Normally, the Vietnamese had a strict code of behavior regarding their religion. They seemed to adhere to a form of ancestor worship as well as Buddhism, but this particular stucco temple had all the earmarks of a French-inspired church. Graves and Buddhist shrines were sacred to the Vietnamese, but a Catholic temple would garner no special feelings of reverence.

Jerking his arm, Jackson motioned Sanchez and Mudders toward the left of the burned-out shrine, then signaled for Crawford and Carrigan to flank from the right. He extended his hands to indicate spreading out, then nodded to Bug and Baroni to go with him. Delisi and Gagliano would cover them from the bushes.

"Still got that M-79?" Jackson mouthed, and it was tossed to Baroni. The sergeant turned to look at Delisi. "This is it. Our mission will be complete after we make final contact here. Use the radio if you have to. You know the codes."

Delisi nodded and grinned. "Right, Sarge," he whispered back.

Weapons were checked one last time to hopefully prevent jamming, as the M-14's were prone to doing. In a hot firefight many a soldier had lost his life because of the jamming of his weapon.

Jackson hefted a confiscated AK-47 under one arm and his M-14 under the other. He draped belts of ammo across his shoulders in an X, so that he looked like a Mexican bandit, then grinned at Sanchez. Sanchez grinned back, understanding the reason for Jackson's amusement. They all looked like Mexican bandits or wildmen or both. None of them had shaved or bathed in a week, and they were covered with blood and bandages as well as mud. Dograges were wound around most of their foreheads to keep sweat out of their eyes so as not to obscure their vision for even a moment. It could be fatal otherwise. Jackson had the thought that if any Americans could see them, they would probably be shot on sight as mercenaries. Only later would it be discovered that they were on the right side. Or were they? Whatever, First Squad was ready to fight.

Tensing, Jackson took one last look at the village before giving the "go" signal. Women and children had been wandering about freely, so he felt sure that whoever was in that village had their complete confidence and vice versa. A tight knot formed in Jackson's throat as he thought of the villagers' duplicity. He gave the signal to move, adding the final command, "No quarter."

They fanned out as planned, Sanchez and Mudders to the south, Crawford and Carrigan to the north, Jackson, Baroni, and Bug taking the middle.

There was no loud hoopla and fanfare like in the movies, but a calm, orderly advance that bordered on stealth. Delisi and Gagliano set up the fifty-caliber and readied plenty of ammo as the Bitches flitted through the trees and brush.

Jackson was walking point, with Bug and Baroni in a V behind him, slipping silently up the trail toward the village. They were approximately fifty yards from the nearest hootch when they bumped head-on into two startled peasant men.

With a rifle slung under each arm and his fingers stuck into the trigger guards, caressing the slender triggers that could so easily take them out, Jackson must have presented a terrifying spectacle to the two stunned men. It would have been much better for them if they had dropped to their knees or at least made some friendly overture. But they didn't and they died.

When one of them pivoted and tried to run, opening his mouth to scream out a warning, a K-bar hilt suddenly sprouted from between his shoulder blades. He sank slowly to the ground and the other man realized he would meet the same quiet fate.

Falling to his knees, he babbled in Vietnamese, and Bug looked up at Jackson.

"What's he sayin', man?" Jackson asked tersely.

"I dunno, Sarge. Sounds like he's saying something about a leader."

"Whose leader? Is he VC? NVA? Ask him."

Bug shook his head and turned back to the man. He asked him the questions, but the man was shaking so hard and had tears rolling down his face and choking him, so that he couldn't answer. All that could be understood was the wailing lament "No die, no die" over and over again.

"Tell him we won't kill him. He won't die if he tells us what we want to know," Jackson began, but the villager apparently felt that he couldn't trust the Marine. He lunged for the pistol Bug was carrying, and suddenly a knife protruded from his throat. This newest threat had quickly, silently been eliminated.

Jackson turned his head to look at Baroni, who shrugged and grinned, then reached for his knife.

As the men were ordinary peasants and not soldiers, it was obvious that the entire village must be peopled by hostiles. There wasn't a single qualm about wasting the two men. Their bodies were dragged off the beaten track and into the bush, then hidden with a thatch of limbs and branches. Not that secrecy would be necessary in a very short space of time. Unless their hand was somehow forced, the Bitches would wait for Jackson's signal fire to begin their assault.

A burning desire to avenge all the wrongs he'd seen since hitting Vietnam consumed Jackson, and his mouth tightened with determination. These were the kind of people who wired their own toddlers to booby traps and sent them into a crowd of GIs or Marines. The village represented the Vietcong, the mercenaries, and even the deceitful members of the Army of the Republic of Vietnam. And there were times when Jackson thought he hated the ARVNs and the villagers like these the most. At least with the VC and the tribal mercenaries, a man knew where he stood. They had chosen sides and made a statement. It was the right thing to do; even if he didn't agree with the side they had chosen, he could agree with their right to make a choice. But it was the others who made him want to just grind them down until there was nothing left, the smiling, blank faces who said "Ma-deen numba one, Ma-deen numba one" the whole time they were slipping a grenade in your pocket. Yeah, those were the ones he really wanted to get. And now was his chance.

Jackson, Baroni, and Bug ran hunched over, their weapons clanging softly against their bodies. One of the hootches was a large, square straw-thatched structure and stood almost in the center of the village. It seemed to have the most activity, and they steered in that direction, going from shadow to shadow. Laughter trickled from one of the small windows formed by just an opening in the bamboo and straw.

A strong current of exhilaration raced through Jackson, making his nerves tingle. This would be the first enemy action they had initiated solely on their own, not because they had to do so. It was exulting, dangerous, and crazy, and he loved it.

Allowing Baroni time to circle the hootch with the M-79, Jackson and Bug waited. Sweat trickled down taut faces and into their eyes, and Jackson was glad for the dograg he had wound around his head to hold it back. He checked the straw huts in a sort of crawling crouch, determining that most of the occupants were villagers and not soldiers. There was no telltale thump of boots instead of padding of bare feet on straw mats, no clink of weapons instead of pots or pans. Everything seemed in order, which meant that the hostiles must be bivouacked elsewhere. They had to be drawn out.

Sinking back into position with his AK-47 under one arm and his M-14 under the other, Jackson waited. It was left to Baroni to signal the start of the assault with the M-79.

The first blast was briefly preceded by the empty whomp of the grenade launcher, then the thud and rattle of the hit, followed by a shattering explosion inside the large hootch. And then all hell broke loose.

The flimsy bamboo and straw structure collapsed like a house of cards, and wild screams shrilled into the night. Jackson's M-14 chattered and the AK pop-pop-popped.

People poured out of buildings pureed by the force of grenades exploding inside straw houses, and what damage the M-79 didn't do, the Bitches did with their automatic weapons. It's amazing what kind of destruction mere bullets can wreak on structures built to withstand monsoons and high winds.

A few peasants had snatched up weapons on their way out of huts not instantly demolished, and they were attempting to fire at the Bitches. Grenades were hurled through the air in graceful arcs, sending bodies spattering in every direction and successfully stemming much of the resistance.

Through the haze of smoke and fire, Jackson could see Mudders and Sanchez torch a hut and shoot the occupants. Many of the villagers were shot down as they tried to leave the huts, and grenades were then tossed into the empty buildings.

All this had happened in split seconds of time, one event following another so swiftly that it took only fifteen or twenty seconds from the first whomp of the M-79 to the exodus of villagers from their burning huts. But in that space of time, the men hidden in the abandoned temple at the north fringe of the village had time to emerge with weapons blazing. Crawford and Carrigan were waiting as the NVA spilled from the stucco ruins and into the village.

More grenades blasted, and the pop-pop-pop of AK-47's was everywhere. It was a firefight with trained soldiers as well as untrained villagers, and the Bitches were "rockin'-n-rollin' " with smooth, efficient movements. Automatic fire racketed through the night in spitting flames of orange and yellow. Khaki-clad men scurried in orderly confusion, the dark shadows hiding the Bitches so that they fired at anything that moved. Women and children screamed, cut down by men they had sheltered and cared for in the temple ruins. It was mayhem and madness.

Jackson paused in the light afforded by a burning hut and glanced around for his men. He could see Mudders and Sanchez through the smoky gloom. Sanchez looked crazy, as if he were on some bad drugs, firing from the hip at any movement in the dark, his M-14 rattling furiously in his hands.

That image was imprinted vividly on Jackson's mind, the tall Mexican with his cammo-streaked face and arms full of death, shouting hate and defiance at the fleeing enemy until he was cut down in a hail of return fire. It was a scene straight out of a nightmare.

The whole world looked like his vision of hell, Jackson thought then, glancing around him. Flames rose into the dark sky and people were screaming shrilly, while burst after burst of automatic fire chattered in a deadly symphony. It was total chaos. Smoke stung his eyes and nose and burned his throat, and he could smell the sickly sweet stench of burning flesh. Sparks drifted through the air to land on his bare arms and he didn't even notice until the hair was burned away, and Jackson wasn't sure he cared. Campbell had been right. The brass had been right. This village was "hot."

Those men were NVA, hidden in the temple by these people and given aid, while the villagers calmly denied any knowledge of VC. Well, old mamasan had been right, Jackson figured. She hadn't lent aid to VC, just the whole fuckin' North Vietnamese Army.

Furious at the deception and wondering just how many Americans had died because he hadn't realized this village was harboring and helping the NVA, Jackson stormed across the flame-lit square toward the stucco temple. Both his guns jumped in

337

his hands, and he screamed at the top of his lungs as he advanced.

He felt instead of saw Baroni and Bug behind him, covering him, and knew that Delisi and Gagliano would cover their end of it. In spite of superior odds, the element of surprise had finally worked in their favor the way it was meant to do. They had attacked a fortified village and were overrunning it. That would look good on the Bitches' records and maybe give them a little credence with the brass.

Scores of bodies lay on the ground, and Jackson ran and leaped them without pause. As he neared the shelled ruin of the temple, he saw a man detach himself from his unit and make a break for the jungle behind the village. A man ran in back of the deserter, apparently acting as guard. Jackson moved on instinct. He swerved direction and ran after them, his AK taking out the rear guard man. This action served to halt the fleeing soldier in his tracks.

Harsh, ragged breaths escaped Jackson in painful breaks as he approached the man standing in the shadows with his hands raised above his head. But it wasn't until the burst of another grenade lit up the night sky that he recognized him: Captain Ngo Dai of the Army of the Republic of Vietnam.

CHAPTER 21

Several seconds ticked past as Jackson stood in stunned silence. Whatever—or whoever—he had expected, somehow the ARVN Captain Ngo Dai had not come to mind. Maybe he should have. There was intelligence that not all the members of the ARVN forces were loyal to the Americans, and Jackson had certainly never trusted the bastard from their first meeting. But to find Ngo Dai in league with the enemy and in obvious cahoots with NVA forces was still a bitter pill to swallow.

Without pausing to think about it, his first reaction was a swing of his rifle stock to catch the stocky captain under the chin and send him reeling backward.

"Captain Ngo Dai!" Jackson spat. "I should have figured you would be low enough for this shit!" Breathing heavily, he stood over the prone officer with both gun barrels pointing down at him. "Give me an excuse to blow you away, mother-fucker, please!"

Trying to regain his composure, the ARVN officer just wiped the blood from his mouth in a slow, careful gesture. A crafty smile curled his bleeding lips as he gazed up at the murderous face of the black Marine standing over him.

"If you will just allow me to stand, Sergeant 'Bad Black,' I will explain to you my mission."

"Explain from down there, you son of a bitch!"

"Very well." Clearing his throat and carefully rising to a sitting position, the captain put his arms around his knees. "I was assigned to do undercover work with the NVA, and you have blown my cover, Sergeant. It will not go well with you when your superiors discover what you have done. They will be most displeased at your inadvisable actions. . . ."

"You're speaking much better English, I notice!" Jackson snarled. "I wonder if your inability to *understand* English has improved!"

The captain's icy stare never wavered. And his supercilious smile made Jackson's index fingers itch to squeeze on the triggers and blow him to hell.

"I see that your temper has not improved, Sergeant. I imagine that a year or two in the stockade will teach you patience, however. Perhaps you should learn the Asian trick of holding your emotions in—"

Jackson's rifle stock snapped up again, catching the captain on the other side of his jaw and sending Ngo Dai sprawling back in the dirt. Flames illuminated the flash of hatred in his slanted eyes as he slowly turned over to look up at the furious Ma-

340

rine. Leaning slightly, he spit out a tooth. He lay half on his side, glaring up at Jackson.

"You were talking patience?" Jackson asked. "Let's see what the brass have to say when I take you back as a POW, Captain! I have a feeling your story won't exactly jibe with what they have to say about—"

"Look out!"

Baroni's warning came an instant too late. Dai's hidden hand snapped up to fire a .45, and the bullet spun Jackson around. He barely heard Baroni's racketing M-14 take out the traitorous ARVN officer. His legs had crumpled beneath him and he was firing aimlessly in the air, his reflexes sending messages to his index fingers to fire his weapons. Dimly, as if from a great distance, Jackson could hear Baroni's "Hey, Sarge! Watch it!" But then everything went black, and Jackson felt himself sinking faster and faster into a whirling vortex of spinning lights and inky darkness.

Slowly regaining consciousness, Jackson became aware of a loud whirring that sounded remarkably like chopper blades above him. It couldn't be, of course, because he was dead. That bastard had shot him, and he hadn't even gotten to finish him. God, he hated that . . .

But then he felt a jerk and his body began to radiate pain throughout all the nerve endings, and

341

Jackson knew he was alive. He hadn't died after all. Or this was hell. It almost didn't matter. Music was coming from somewhere, but it sure didn't sound like harps and trumpets. He frowned.

Something warm and wet fell on his face, and Jackson tried to blink it away.

"Hey! Hey! Medic, medic!" a familiar voice screamed above him, and Jackson opened his eyes to say testily, "Stop all that damned shoutin', Baroni!"

"He's alive, Bug, he's alive!" Baroni was yelling and laughing at the same time." Unashamed tears streamed down his face as he hovered over Jackson like a mother hen with its only egg. Or at least, that's the analogy offered by an unknown man perched in the open cargo doors of the slick lifting them out. He punctuated that comment with a devastating burst of fire.

Blinking, Jackson painfully turned his head to look at the vague shadow of the door gunner. "What the hell happened back there, man?" he asked Baroni.

"Don't worry about it now, Jack. Delisi radioed out and called up the medevac to get you out of—"

"Did everybody make it?"

"Sure, Jack," Baroni said a little too hurriedly. "It all came off all right."

"Yeah, Jack," Bug agreed quickly. "The rest are on the other slick."

Unwilling to argue and too weak at the moment,

342

Jackson gave a nod of his head. He could feel a thick wad of bandages wrapped around his skull and knew the ARVN officer's bullet must have hit something. He managed a grin.

"Good thing he aimed at my head. My skull's kinda thick. If he'd of aimed somewhere else . . ."

"Can't you get that chatterbox to pipe down?" the door gunner asked cheerfully. He glanced over at Jackson and grinned widely. "Man, you ain't done nothin' but talk since you climbed aboard this slick, and my favorite song is playin' on the radio. . . ."

That explained the music. This crazy door gunner had his own elite stereo system hooked up in the medevac, and he was happily blasting away with his machine gun and singing along to the lyrics.

"Bannister, man, you're not wrapped too tight," Bug said calmly.

Wild Bill Bannister grinned again, not at all offended. "I know. Too many drugs, man. All us former deejays gotta do something to unwind."

"But do you have to play that song so loud?" Bug asked.

But Bannister wasn't listening anymore. He was shouting out the chopper door. "All right! This is for all you Vee Cee down there. Listen close, Charlie!" *Brrrrrp!* went the M-60, then Wild Bill was shouting again. "Here's a tune by Junior Walker and the All Stars, you little yellow bastards! It's called 'Shotgun'!' "

Listening closely over the whirr of the chopper, Jackson could barely make out the words to a popular song he'd heard many times on the radio.

"Shotgun! Shoot 'em 'fore they run now! Shotgun!" the stereo system was blaring, and Jackson began laughing.

This was the craziest war he'd ever seen, but then he hadn't seen too damned many. He was still laughing when he lost consciousness again.

"Come on, man! Admit it! We got the shaft!" Baroni was saying angrily. He perched on the edge of Sergeant Robert Jackson's hospital bed, his face a tight knot of anger and frustration.

"Well, shit, Baroni. What'd you expect?" Jackson asked mildly.

"I didn't expect Campbell to shaft us, man!"

Peering from under the white swathe of bandages laced around his head, Jackson managed a smile. Not that he felt like smiling, but what the hell. Never expect anything and you never got disappointed, he'd heard.

"Look, Baroni, Campbell didn't shaft us. It was higher up than that and you know it. Campbell was up and up. He knew what was going down, and he tried to tell us without breaking security."

Baroni subsided, and Bug moved closer. "He's right, Baroni. This was not a sanctioned mission, like the man said. If word was to get out to the ARVNs that one of their own had successfully managed to go so high up with his deceit, then it would be demoralizing to the rest of the ARVNs. And like we were told—it just might give others the same idea."

"But to be told our mission would be an embarrassment if it was known!" Baroni burst out. "Man, that's cold! It won't even be on our service records!"

"And you won't get a medal to impress the chicks, right, Baroni?" Jackson teased, though he didn't feel much like teasing. Maybe it would hit him later, when the morphine he'd been given for the bullet crease on his scalp wore off, but now he didn't really care that First Squad was getting the unofficial shaft. They were all getting leave, weren't they? Devil dog had been given to another squad. Carrigan, Mudders, Crawford, Weathers, Delisi, Gagliano, and Smitty were already in Tokyo. And hell, his tour was up in five more days. He was an official short-timer and didn't give a rat's ass what the Marine Corps did now.

"They shipped Sanchez's body back to the States today," Bug said suddenly, and there was a moment of quiet.

"Maybe I wronged that Mexican," Jackson said after a moment. "He was a good man to have in combat. Too bad he had to buy it."

"Yeah," Bug said. "He may have had some

faults, but he was no coward. Man, he took out a bunch of them before he died. You would have been proud of him, Sarge. He died still fighting."

More silence while the three men paid solemn tribute to the memory of a member of First Squad. Then Jackson said, "He probably saved my life back there. I'll never forget that."

"Me either," Bug agreed. "It's a damn shame his family won't know that."

"Shit," Baroni said after a few minutes, "I hate to think nobody noticed that we were even here, or that we didn't make a damn bit of difference."

"Ah, but there's where you're wrong, Boney," Bug said cheerfully. "I have proof that we made a difference. We made a *big* difference!"

Even Jackson perked up when he saw the large sheet of rice paper that Bug pulled out of his pocket and very carefully unfolded and spread out on the blanket. It was a Vietcong poster, and Bug had found hundreds of them in the temple where they had flushed out the NVA and the notorious Captain Ngo Dai. They were being distributed throughout the countryside, in every large and small village and hamlet.

Smoothing out the wrinkles, Bug cleared his throat and translated aloud: "WANTED DEAD OR ALIVE—BAD BLACK AND THE BITCHES, FOR CRIMES AGAINST THE PEOPLE OF VIETNAM."

Ten figures were roughly drawn on the paper,

one of them a dark inkblot with a helmet.

Jackson grinned, even though it made his head ache. "No kiddin', man!"

"No kidding, Jack. And not only that, but there's a reward for our asses."

That brightened Jackson even more. "A reward? How much?"

"A hundred thousand piastres a head."

"A hundred thousand piastres! Shit, how much is that?"

"Seeing as how a P, or piastre, is worth roughly less than a penny, I'd say about"—Bug calculated rapidly in his head and finished—"ten thousand American dollars apiece."

"Shee-it!" Jackson and Baroni said together.

Then Sergeant Robert L. Jackson began laughing. He banged on the green blanket across his knees with one fist and laughed long and hard.

"Do you know how much ten Bitches are worth, man?" he finally asked. Without waiting for an answer, he said, *"One million piastres!"* Then he added, "Not bad for a bunch of Bitches dancin' with Charlie!"

AFTERWORD

Robert L. Jackson returned home to Memphis, Tennessee and went to Stax Studios to join his brother Raymond, who had been wounded at the DMZ and honorably discharged from the Army. But before Jackson did, he served three more tours in the Marine Corps.

The accolades awarded to Robert Jackson as an engineer/producer since returning to civilian life are numerous. Some of the famous recording artists he has worked with over the years include:

Isaac Hayes
The Bar-Kays (one platinum, 8 gold albums)
Shirley Caesar
Eddie Floyd
Albert King
B.B. King
Rufus Thomas
Carla Thomas
Emotions
William Bell

Anita Ward (one gold album, 4 platinum singles)
Staple Singers
Oris Mays
Little Milton
Stevie Wonder
Davy Jones
Denise LaSalle
Shirley Brown (gold album, platinum single)
Brenda Eager
Ebony Webb
Quick
Chocolate Milk
Joe Simon
Frederick Knight

He was nominated for a Grammy and won a Dove Award as a chief engineer when working with Shirley Caesar.

THE TOP NAMES IN HARD-HITTING ACTION:
MACK BOLAN, DON PENDLETON,
AND PINNACLE BOOKS!